Toby inched closer. "I mean … fference if I'd told you how I … ou?"

"How did you fee…

She didn't know. … guard. That kiss… it was diffe… d taken Toby by surprise. "I l… always had. Maybe that's why … teased and challenged her.

Jane stared past him at the mountains. "I liked you too."

"But you said—"

"That kiss terrified me. And I was so embarrassed when everyone saw us kissing." Jane turned her face back to his. "I didn't want to like you. I'm not sure I want to like you now. It's not safe." An honest doubt lingered in Jane's eyes. He could see it there holding her back.

"I understand. But my feelings for you are real." That's all he knew. His feelings for Jane ran deeper than his doubts. Toby brought his hand to her jaw and guided her lips to his. Jane's chest rose with a sharp intake of breath, and he knew she felt it too—the same desire pouring through him.

Jane swung her leg over his hips, and he shifted to his back, guiding her to lie over his body. Their lips found a rhythm, moving together, opening so he could explore the wet heat of her mouth with his tongue.

Jane raised her head, her eyes closed, her breathing ragged, and Toby took the chance to kiss his way down her neck, lingering just below her ear.

"I definitely want to like you now," she gasped.

PRAISE FOR SARA RICHARDSON

"Sara [Richardson] brings real feelings to every scene she writes."

—Carolyn Brown, *New York Times* bestselling author

A COWBOY FOR CHRISTMAS

"Tight plotting and a sweet surprise ending make for a delightful Christmas treat. Readers will be sad to see the series end."

—*Publishers Weekly*

COLORADO COWBOY

"Readers who love tear-jerking small-town romances with minimal sex scenes and maximum emotional intimacy will quickly devour this charming installment."

—*Publishers Weekly*

RENEGADE COWBOY

"Top Pick! An amazing story about finding a second chance to be with the one that you love."

—*Harlequin Junkie*

"A beautifully honest and heartwarming tale about forgiveness and growing up that will win the hearts of fans and newcomers alike."

—*RT Book Reviews*

HOMETOWN COWBOY

"Filled with humor, heart, and love, this page-turner is one wild ride."

—Jennifer Ryan, *New York Times* bestselling author

NO BETTER MAN

"Charming, witty, and fun. There's no better read. I enjoyed every word!"

—Debbie Macomber, #1 *New York Times* bestselling author

First Kiss with a Cowboy

Also by Sara Richardson

Heart of the Rockies Series

No Better Man
Something Like Love
One Christmas Wish (novella)
More Than a Feeling
Rocky Mountain Wedding (novella)

Rocky Mountain Riders Series

Hometown Cowboy
Comeback Cowboy
Renegade Cowboy
Rocky Mountain Cowboy (novella)
True-Blue Cowboy
Rocky Mountain Cowboy Christmas (novella)
Colorado Cowboy
A Cowboy for Christmas

First Kiss with a Cowboy

A SILVERADO LAKE NOVEL

SARA RICHARDSON

FOREVER
New York Boston

This book is a work of fiction. Names, characters, places, and incidents are the product of the author's imagination or are used fictitiously. Any resemblance to actual events, locales, or persons, living or dead, is coincidental.

Cover design and illustration by Daniela Medina

Forever
Hachette Book Group
1290 Avenue of the Americas, New York, NY 10104
read-forever.com
twitter.com/readforeverpub

First mass market edition: May 2020

Forever is an imprint of Grand Central Publishing. The Forever name and logo are trademarks of Hachette Book Group, Inc.

ISBNs: 978-1-5387-1715-8 (mass market), 978-1-5387-1714-1 (ebook)

Printed in the United States of America

OPM

10 9 8 7 6 5 4 3 2 1

In loving memory of Grandma VanMeter

Chapter One

Jane Harding paused in front of the fine-dining restaurant with a name she couldn't even pronounce.

The sleek, dark windows, old-world brick façade, and the line of Mercedes and Teslas lined up in front of the valet stand only proved this restaurant was far above her pay grade as an adjunct professor at Cal Poly. Her agent had summoned her here for dinner, which meant she was about to get either really great news—like her editor loved the new book she'd turned in, or extremely terrible news—like her editor had hated it and Jane's agent wanted to soften the blow with good wine.

Jane's heart made a sudden leap for her throat. Admittedly, she'd struggled to put two sentences together in her second attempt at a novel. The first novel? No problem. But there had also been no pressure—she hadn't had an agent or editor yet. She'd simply written for herself, and then had sent the manuscript off never expecting it would get published, let alone become a bestseller. After the success, her publisher had been so excited and asked that another manuscript be delivered within six months so they could keep the momentum going.

The problem was, Jane seemed to have lost her momentum and, in its place, lived a lingering fear that she was simply a one-hit wonder.

Glancing down, she straightened her blue silk blouse and smoothed the black slacks she'd spent a small fortune on so she could dress the part of the successful writer. Whatever her agent said tonight, Jane had to make this writing career work. Her contract teaching literature at the university was up as of last week, and after her trip home to Colorado in a few weeks, she had no job to come back to.

"Confidence," she murmured, as though saying it would somehow help her build it. All she had to do was march in there and act like a real writer, like she knew exactly what she was doing, like she belonged in this world of fancy restaurants and Teslas and Mercedes.

Whirling, Jane made a move for the doors, but one of the parking attendants bumped into her and knocked her purse off her shoulder. It fell to the ground with a thud, everything spilling out onto the sidewalk—her wallet, wadded tissues and receipts, tampons, and part of an old apple she'd eaten between classes yesterday and had forgotten to throw away.

"Oh no!"

The attendant hurried off without so much as a sorry while Jane squatted to collect her things. What was that? Oh geez. Her face flamed as she picked up the tattered condom wrapper that one of her students must've slipped in her purse as a joke because it definitely wasn't hers. So much for looking sophisticated. All around her, people hustled into the restaurant averting their eyes as though they couldn't see her predicament.

Ducking her head, she managed to shove everything back into her purse and scrambled to her feet again before practically diving into the restaurant to escape the stares and whispers from people waiting in the valet line.

The restaurant's interior put out a dim, calming vibe, but her heart continued to race, and her cheeks pulsed with embarrassment. Hopefully no one in here had seen the spectacle through those dark windows. She rushed to the hostess station doing her best to look detached and annoyed rather than humiliated.

"I'm here to meet Caroline Benning," she said as briskly as her very successful agent would have.

"Of course." The young woman picked up two menus. "Ms. Benning called and said she was running a few minutes late, but she would like you to be seated." She led Jane past a gigantic fish tank with all varieties of tropical fish swimming around and into the intimate dining room.

At seven o'clock it seemed nearly every table was full—a few couples who looked like they were celebrating something, a few tables of what looked to be businesspeople continuing their workday over appetizers and wine. She could really use a glass of wine right now…

"This will be your table." The hostess gestured to a table for two in the corner. "Ms. Benning has already ordered a bottle for wine you," she said, pulling out Jane's chair. "It will be here momentarily."

"Oh. Great." Jane sat. A whole bottle of wine for just her? Yeah, this definitely wasn't going to be good news.

"Your waiter will be right with you." The hostess handed her a leather-bound menu and then regally walked in the opposite direction. Jane took a second to look it over, but still found it difficult to focus. Between the nerves and the lingering embarrassment from the scene on the sidewalk, she couldn't quite decide what she wanted to eat. She set down the menu in front of her and let her eyes wander.

An older couple sat nearby, and they appeared to be fighting. The man had a scowl on his face while the woman leaned halfway over the table and said something, her jaw rigid and her eyes narrowed.

Hmmm. Maybe he'd had an affair. Or it was possible his wife had made the reservations here and he'd forgotten it was their anniversary.

The woman caught her eavesdropping, so she moved her gaze to the table of nicely dressed businessmen she'd walked past earlier, and one of them was staring directly at her.

She quickly looked down. She must be mistaken. She couldn't remember the last time a man had stared at her like that. Well, there was Alex from the math department, but he didn't count. Jane peeked up again, and yes, the man was definitely still staring. He smiled a little when their eyes met, and Jane's cheeks filled with an entirely different type of heat.

Smile back. She thought she did, but was it too big? Not big enough? She didn't know, but the man said something to his friends and stood up. Oh wow. He was walking over to her. This is exactly the kind of meet-cute she'd write about in her romance novels! A man spots a woman from across the room—okay, from a few tables over—and then, overtaken by this instant chemistry between them, he makes his way over. Except that had never happened to her.

"Hi there."

He was so handsome. Tall with chestnut-colored hair and a squarish jaw. Jane peered up into eyes the same color as the ocean outside. *Speak!* she reminded herself. "Hi." Geez. Why'd she have to be so shy? Why couldn't she come up with something witty to say? If she were sitting behind her computer she could, that was for sure.

"I'm not sure how to say this…" The man leaned in closer. He even smelled good.

It's okay, Jane silently coaxed. Just say it. Maybe he wanted to tell her he felt this strange connection to her when he'd looked at her. Maybe he was going to ask her out. Lord knew it had been a while since she'd been on a date…

"You have a huge rip in the back of your pants."

Jane blinked up at him. "Excuse me?"

"Your pants," he murmured discreetly. "There's a huge rip in the seam. I figured you didn't know. I probably wouldn't have noticed but your underwear is…pretty colorful."

Oh, sweet Jesus. She'd worn her bright red underwear with the silver polka dots! Her lucky underwear—the pair she'd been wearing the day she'd signed the contract with her publisher. Obviously, her luck was running out. Her scalp suddenly burned. It must've happened when she'd crouched down outside. How the heck did a two-hundred-dollar pair of pants rip right up the seam?

"I figured you should know," the man said awkwardly. "I mean, I would want to."

"Right. Yes." Jane swallowed a fireball of humiliation. "Thank you for the information."

"You're welcome." He smiled at her. "I hope you have a good night."

"Uh-huh. You too." A good night? Seriously? She was

not going to have a good night. In fact, things could only get worse from here. This is why she rarely went out. These kinds of things always seemed to happen to her. It was almost as bad as *that night*—the one time she'd let her guard down and it was still the most embarrassing moment of her life. Jane started to gather her purse. She should leave before her agent got there. She could bolt out of the restaurant and never show her face here ag—

"Sorry I'm so late." Caroline appeared seemingly out of thin air. The blunt cut of her red hair seemed to fit her curt personality. The woman was always so efficient and direct. Even her wardrobe exuded a certain sharpness. Jane imagined she had a whole closet of black dresses at home and a second closet just for her scarves.

"The wine isn't even here yet?" Caroline barked. "Are you kidding me?" She slid into her chair across the table in a huff. "I suppose we won't get our dinner for another two hours either."

Two hours? Jane glanced over at the man who'd informed her about the underwear situation. He seemed to have completely forgotten all about her and was chatting with a woman who'd come over to their table. Ugh. Of course. That woman probably didn't understand needing lucky underwear at all. Jane refocused on Caroline. She needed this night to be over. "Actually. I'm not going to be able to stay for dinner. I'm...um...not feeling well." It wasn't a lie. Her stomach churned and a headache had started to pound in her temples. That's what being the center of attention always did to her. It made her want to hide. She needed a nice hot bath and some ice cream for dinner.

Caroline's frown indicated she had no sympathy for Jane's health concerns. "But we have important things to discuss, my dear. Timely, important things that simply can't wait." Her glossy red lips pursed together.

And there it was. The bad news her intuition had told her to expect. She might as well get this over with, split pants or not. "They don't like it, do they? They don't like the book?" Of course her editor hadn't liked it. Jane didn't even like it.

"They *hate* it," Caroline clarified. "*I* hated it. What the hell happened, Jane?" Her agent's resonant voice carried. "This book is light-years behind your last one."

"I don't know," Jane half whispered, doing her best to keep the conversation between the two of them. "I guess I have writer's block or something."

"Well you need to get over it." Caroline paused when a server approached.

"One bottle of Chateau Margaux Pavillon Rouge." The man made a grand presentation out of opening the bottle and pouring a taste into the wineglass before handing it to Caroline.

Her agent sniffed at the rim of the glass, her nose wrinkled, and then she swirled the glass before taking a microscopic sip. "I hate it." Caroline handed the glass back to the server. "Bring me the Caymus Special Selection Cabernet Sauvignon instead. And bring us a free cheese plate for waiting so long," she called to his retreating back.

Normally the rude tone would've made Jane cringe but given what she'd been through in the last hour she was all out of cringes.

"The only thing they liked in the whole book was your hero," Caroline said getting back to business. "Keep him and scrap everything else."

"The hero? Are you sure?" The hero was actually the one thing she wouldn't mind completely scrapping.

"What's not to love?" Caroline demanded. "The hero is every woman's dream—rugged, sexy, confident."

Or a total show-off. Jane would never admit it in a million years, but she'd based the hero on Toby Garrett. And it was true, he was every woman's fantasy. She'd gone to high school with the cowboy, and he wasn't only charming and good-looking. He was also crazy smart, a straight-A student, and a star athlete. Oh, and he happened to be the one who'd tempted her to let her guard down *that night*.

She hadn't intended to write a hero based on Toby, but between the looming deadline and the writer's block, she'd suddenly found herself looking up old yearbook photos of him and Googling his stats out on the rodeo circuit. She'd rather not explore why.

Not that she had to worry about anyone finding out. Her writing career was a secret—protected by a pseudonym. Not even her mom or her best friend, Beth, knew about it.

When she'd first started writing, it had simply been a way for her to escape, to take the edge off the hours she spent by herself after she'd finished college and grad school and no longer had a rigorous schedule to keep her so busy. She'd filled her world with friends...only they weren't real.

On a whim, she'd submitted the manuscript to a contest and she'd ended up with a publishing contract. She signed it on one condition—she would never have to reveal her true identity. Knowing no one else would ever learn she was the one behind those words had given her a courage she'd never had. It ensured no one would ever see more of her than she wanted them to.

"The hero stays." Caroline's glare dared Jane to argue. "You have six weeks to turn in a new book or I'm afraid they won't offer you another contract."

Jane choked on a sip of water. "Six weeks?" There was no way. She hadn't been able to write a solid story in six months, let alone six weeks. "I'm leaving to spend three weeks at my mom's ranch in Colorado. My best friend is getting married. We're going to be so busy with all the events—"

Caroline's smile looked more terrifying than friendly. "Well it sounds like that might be the perfect opportunity for you to find some inspiration."

Chapter Two

Toby Garrett sat at his mother's breakfast table finishing off a plate of fried eggs and potatoes and enough bacon to hike up his cholesterol.

"It's so wonderful to have you home." His mother piled another helping of potatoes onto his plate, but he had no intention of eating them. He had a diet to stick to. Okay, so it wasn't an official diet, but he couldn't start eating himself into a coma at every meal or he'd never be able to get back out on the circuit in time to qualify for nationals.

In the silence, his mother raised her eyebrows slightly as though waiting for the obligatory response.

"It's nice to be home," Toby said pouring himself another cup of coffee. It wasn't. He wasn't supposed to be home. He was supposed to be climbing on the back of a bull this weekend in Oklahoma, but at only three months post-op from rotator cuff surgery, he wouldn't be doing that again for a long time. If ever.

The doctor's warning was on constant replay in his head these days. *Some people never regain full strength…*

He wasn't some people. He was a bull rider, damn it. A good one too. And this injury-enforced time-out was making him crazy.

"What have you got planned today?" his mother asked, sitting across from him.

"Oh, well let's see…" He pretended to mentally sort through the many options he had. "Actually, nothing. Because you refuse to let me lift a finger around here." He'd offered to repaint fences and muck out the stables and tear down that old shed his dad had been promising to demolish for years, but his mother wouldn't hear of it. She'd prefer he sit around all day while she cooked and cleaned for him.

"You know what the doctor said." His mother had perfected the don't-you-dare-argue-with-me stare. "You can't risk reinjuring that shoulder."

Yeah and in the meantime, he was losing his mind. He'd never been one to sit still. His mom had told him once he'd started crawling, he'd left her in his dust, and she'd been chasing him ever since.

"Dad is driving down to Denver today." His mother buttered a piece of toast. "You should go with him."

"Actually, I promised Ethan I'd head over to the café. He and Beth have some wedding stuff they want to talk about." As if they needed his help with any of those details. But it was better than making small talk with his father on a two-hour drive down the mountain. The ability to keep conversation light, and entertaining, was a skill he'd inherited from both his parents. But being home again was reminding him of all the things they didn't talk about, of how they tiptoed around the lingering pain left behind by his brother's death, and the silence between them had become deafening.

"I can't believe the wedding is coming up so fast," his mother chatted. "Those two make such a cute couple." She went on about Ethan and Beth, and how amazing it was that they'd been together so long, but Toby wasn't listening.

What would happen if he asked his mother to put out the pictures of Tanner they'd packed away when they'd moved here the year after his brother died? Or he could ask his father if he remembered that summer they'd taken the Disney cruise…their last vacation as a family. But they didn't do that. They didn't confront things that made them uncomfortable. They simply skirted around the past like it was just another piece of furniture in the house.

And everyone wondered how he'd become such a good performer inside the arena.

"Before you go, why don't you bring down your laundry?" his mom asked sweetly.

Toby caught her in a deadpan stare. "I'm capable of doing my own laundry." Hell, he'd been doing his own laundry since he'd moved out and he'd only ever ruined one pair of socks.

"You need to take it easy," his mother reminded him for the thousandth time since she'd coddled him in his hospital bed after the surgery. "Besides that, you don't know how to work our washing machine. It's finicky."

"Right." Toby shot her a grin meant to call her out. "The *washing machine* is finicky. Okay. Sure."

"Hey." His mom tossed a napkin in his direction, but she smiled too. "I have certain ways of doing things, that's all. Forgive me if I have nightmares about the red socks mixing with the delicate whites."

"It's no big deal." Toby waved her off. "I do it all the time." What he didn't do all the time? Discuss laundry over breakfast. It was a crying shame that this is what his life had been reduced to.

Grabbing one more piece of bacon, he pushed away from the table. "Gotta head out. Promised Ethan I'd be there by eight." To be honest, Ethan hadn't even requested his presence at the café today, but Toby couldn't sit here with a whole day of nothing looming in front of him. Being back home made him too antsy. It gave him too much time to think. He had to get out. He had to do *something*.

"Don't forget to bring your laundry down," his mother called, but he was already halfway to the front door.

"I'll do my own laundry later," he yelled back, jogging the rest of the way before she could counter.

Not convinced she wouldn't chase him right out to his truck, Toby loped across the yard and jumped into the driver's seat, giving the engine a good rev before he peeled out. It felt good to drive away—from the house, from the sadness his mother was always trying to compensate for. Even though it was still cold, Toby rolled down the windows and let the brisk wind hit his face. The only thing he remotely liked about being home was seeing those mountains again.

The peaks rolled past the windows, still looking soft and blue in the early morning light. Somehow, over the years, those mountains had grounded him, they'd shaped him. Maybe it was the mountains that had made him reckless and wild. For so long they'd fed his hunger for adventure. Funny, the very place that had bred that in him now made him feel trapped.

Toby rolled through town. Not much had changed in Silverado Lake since he'd moved here as a brokenhearted kid. The square brick buildings still lined Main Street with shout-outs to the town's mining heritage—wooden boardwalks instead of sidewalks, saloon doors on the antique shop. Then there was the library. Toby slowed the truck to admire what his anonymous donation had bought the town. It still had an old west feel to it with the stone façade and columns, but it was also the grandest building in the entire town—as a library should be.

He might not have been free to acknowledge his lost twin brother at home, but the last time he'd come to visit he'd realized he could honor his brother's memory another way. The library was raising funds for a renovation and he'd donated money anonymously, so his family would never know, but the plaque on the outside of the refurbished library read IN MEMORY OF TANNER.

Tanner had loved to read. And when he'd gotten too sick to focus on the words, Toby had read to him. The only thing his brother wanted in life was to be a cowboy, and they knew he never would be—not with his condition. So, Toby had made weekly trips to the library in their old town to check out every book he could on cowboys. Toby had known he couldn't save Tanner, so as he would read, he would change the characters' names and make his brother the hero of every story. When he couldn't get to the library, he'd make up his own stories to tell him—stories about two brothers who took on the wild west.

Driving past the library, he shook off the memories. Maybe his parents had it right. Maybe it was better not to think about it or talk about it. *We have to move on*—that's what they'd always said. So, he'd force himself to move on yet again.

Ethan and Beth's café sat on the outskirts of the main

drag, one of the more modern-looking establishments in town. They'd whitewashed the exterior bricks and added black shutters like you might see at a café in Paris. Not that Toby had ever been to Paris.

Diesel trucks and four-wheel-drive SUVs packed the parking lot at the Surefire Café. Toby squeezed his truck into a spot near the doors. It wasn't T-Mobile Arena, but at least there was a crowd here, and the people in town loved a good bull-riding story. Toby was always happy to oblige. Once a storyteller, always a storyteller.

He sauntered through the doors already knowing that Chester, Jimmy, Bruce, and Matthew would be seated right inside the doors lamenting over the shoddy newspaper coverage of the town's most recent scandal—the anonymous "vandals" who had put a bright pink tutu on the town's bronze statue of miner George Jackson. The retirees had spent every Saturday morning in that same booth since Beth's uncle had bought the diner twenty years ago.

"Tobster, what's up?" Bruce dropped the newspaper and raised his hand for a high five as soon as Toby stepped inside.

"How's it goin', man?" Chester quickly started to clear the end of the table. "Pull up a chair, have a seat."

"Don't mind if I do." Toby found an empty chair at a nearby table and dragged it over, straddling it.

"How's the shoulder?" Matthew eyed Toby's left shoulder as though trying to assess the injury. "Sure looked like a nasty one."

"It's good." Toby shrugged to prove he could still move it. Never mind the achy stiffness. That would go away in time. "It's practically all healed up." Maybe if he said it enough, that would eventually be true.

"Woweee, I watched that clip." Jimmy shook his head.

"The way that bull tossed you? I thought you were a goner."

"It darn near stepped right on you," Chester added.

"I held on over eight seconds though," Toby reminded them, lest they forget it had also been one of the best rides of the event. Before his shoulder had snapped. "I thought I had him." Toby felt it again—that rush of adrenaline deep in the center of his chest. "I was almost ready to jump off, but then the bull spun into that one-eighty."

"Damn, but what a fight you put up, boy." Jimmy raised his coffee mug. "I've watched every ride. You wanna know something? You're one of the toughest SOBs I've ever seen out there."

He wouldn't lie and say it didn't hurt like hell sometimes. But riding made him feel closer to his brother. It was one way he could keep Tanner's memory alive, if only for himself. "Well, it means a lot to have my hometown behind me."

Matthew slid over an empty mug and the coffee carafe. "So, what're you doin' these days? How're you keepin' yourself busy?"

"I'm not." Toby poured a full mug of the rich black coffee. His mom made it too watered down for his taste. "Unfortunately. Doc hasn't given me clearance yet." He eyed the gentlemen sitting around him. In fact, this could be the best crowd to talk to about his current predicament. "I'm looking for something to keep me busy. Got any ideas?"

"I heard Mara Harding is looking for help out at the ranch," Chester said. "It even comes with a place to live as far as I understand it. There's a caretaker cabin right on the lake."

Mara Harding. He remembered her. Remembered her daughter Jane too. How could he forget? "Is that so?"

Working at the ranch could be interesting. At least it would get him outside.

"She's sitting right over there." Jimmy pointed to a booth on the other side of the room. "Maybe you should talk to her."

Toby studied the woman. He'd always admired Mara Harding. After losing her husband, the woman had taken the family's dude ranch and turned it into a successful destination wedding venue. "You know, I think I will talk to Mara." Toby pushed himself up to a standing position, temporarily forgetting about his bum shoulder. "Thanks for the chat, gentlemen."

"You bet." Chester raised his coffee mug. "You tell her she'd better hire you or she'll have us to answer to."

Toby couldn't help but grin as he walked away. Knowing what he knew about Mara, she wouldn't hire him unless she wanted to, gang of retirees doing their best to persuade her or not.

Mara watched him approach but he couldn't read the expression on her face. "Hi there." Toby smiled as he pulled out the chair across from her and sat. The woman looked remarkably the same as she had when he'd been in high school. Her hair had grayed around her temples, but other than that, Mara's face still had that regal porcelain skin set off by wise brown eyes.

"Well, Toby Garrett." A reserved smile held a fair amount of distance between them. "I heard you were home. Your mama's delighted, torn up shoulder or not."

"She sure is." His mother probably hoped he'd never be able to climb back onto a bull. If she had her way, she'd keep him at home. Hence his reason for sitting here. He might as well get down to it. "Hey, I heard you're looking for some help around the ranch."

"I am." She lifted her coffee mug and held it in both hands as though her skin was chilled. "My maintenance man took off to be a traveling musician." Exasperation laced her voice, but her expression didn't change. "I guess that's what you get when you hire a guy who lives in his van."

Toby had to laugh. "Some people were meant to be rolling stones." Until they got sidelined with an injury and stuck in their hometown again, that was. "But it's your lucky day because I happen to be looking for a job."

Mara chuckled. "*You're* looking for a maintenance job?" She set down the mug and leveled him with a skeptical glare. "Something tells me you don't need a job."

He might not need the money, but he couldn't sit still anymore. "Oh, trust me. I need a job. I need to stay busy while I'm here. And it wouldn't hurt to have my own place either," he added, allowing his eyes to plead with her.

Mara's chin tipped up with both amusement and understanding. "It's always hard coming back home, isn't it?"

"Hard" wasn't quite the right word. Frustrating. Maddening. Claustrophobic. "You have no idea."

Mara folded her hands on the table as she gave him a thoughtful look. "What about your shoulder? Your mother will have my head if you hurt yourself again."

"My shoulder is fine." He did the arm raises his PT had shown him and even managed to conceal the wince. "It's almost completely healed. And anything I don't feel like I can do, I'll definitely ask for help. I swear."

The amusement playing on the woman's lips only proved she didn't believe a word he said. She had his number. Her son Wes was just like Toby, only Wes was the badass who lured the bull away from riders after they got thrown in the arena. "You're sure you want to work at the ranch?"

"I'm sure." He needed the physical activity, the distance from his own family. "It'll be on a temporary basis, of course. Come August, I'm out of here." And he wouldn't be looking back. "But at least that'll give you time to find a good quality employee for the long term."

Mara nodded and seemed to mull it over. She took her time, that was for sure. For a minute, Toby thought she might say no.

"All right then." She gave a helpless shrug. "At least hiring you will save me the background check. When do you want to start?"

"Today." Toby stood before she could change her mind. "I'll head over after I have coffee with Ethan." And he'd be bringing all his stuff with him. His mother wouldn't like it one bit, but he'd promise to visit.

"Great." Mara pulled out her phone and started typing. "I'll text Louise right now. She can have the housekeeping staff get your cabin ready."

"You won't regret this." Toby flashed her the grin that never failed him.

"I know I won't." Mara picked up her coffee mug again. "If there's one thing I know about you, Toby Garrett, it's that you're a real hard worker."

"Just wait." He'd been sitting around so long he probably had enough pent-up energy to finish a week's worth of work that very afternoon.

After bidding Mara a thankful goodbye, he headed to the coffee counter where his friend Ethan was working alongside Beth. Those two had been together forever. Even in high school, they were just one of those couples that worked. Though they owned the café, not a day went by that they weren't behind the counter in some capacity—today it appeared they were short a barista.

"Morning," Ethan called over the hiss of the espresso machine.

"Morning." Toby slid onto a stool where he could talk to them both. "Beth, you're looking lovely today."

"Uh-huh." She didn't look up from the artwork she was fashioning into the foam on a latte. "Don't worry. I'll have your Americano up momentarily."

"Thank you," he said with a grin. He hated Ethan's Americanos.

"So, what were you and Mara Harding talking about?" Beth slid the latte she'd been working on down the counter to a waiting customer.

"She gave me a job." Thank God. "And a cabin to go with it."

"A job?" Beth stopped working. "And what'd you mean a cabin? You're going to *stay* at the Silverado Lake Ranch?"

"I think it's a great idea." Ethan stepped out from behind the espresso machine. "I can only spend so much time taking you fishing."

Exactly. Beth should be glad Toby would be occupied so he didn't take up so much of Ethan's time. "Why shouldn't I work at the ranch?"

Beth's hands went straight to her hips.

Uh-oh.

"Um...what about everything that happened between you and Jane senior year?" She leaned over the counter. "Don't you think living at the ranch will be awkward?"

Hell no, he hadn't forgotten about kissing Jane. He hadn't forgotten about her walking away from him afterward either. But what did that have to do with anything? "Jane doesn't live at the ranch anymore." As far as he'd heard, she only made it home once or twice a year.

Beth looked at him like she wanted to smack him upside the head. “Well she’s coming into town later this week, seeing as how she is the maid of honor in our wedding and everything.”

Wait a minute. “Jane Harding is the maid of honor?” That spark inside of him ignited again. All through high school he and Jane had competed for every academic title. He’d been hell-bent on baiting her into arguments and competitions, but it wasn’t until he’d kissed her that night that he realized why. The second his lips had touched hers, the chemistry humming between them had exploded and he realized he’d always been attracted to her.

Beth’s expression turned even darker. “Have you read any of the emails I’ve sent regarding details for the most important day of my life?”

“I’m not a big email guy.” Especially when all his colleagues were using email to keep him up to date on everything he was missing out on the circuit. He’d likely be avoiding email until August.

“Yes, Jane is the maid of honor,” Beth grumbled. “And you’re the best man, in case you didn’t know that either.” The woman pointed her stirring spoon at him. “And I swear to God, Toby, you’d better behave yourself.”

“I always behave myself.” He reassured Beth with a wink. It had been years since he’d seen Jane Harding, but suddenly this wedding sounded a lot more interesting.

Chapter Three

Jane coasted into the city limits of Silverado Lake, Colorado, on fumes, her economy rental car protesting with a shudder as she veered into the lone filling station's empty lot. She eyed the old-school gas pump from her driver-side window. You still couldn't pay outside like you could at every other gas station in America. Obviously, nothing had changed around here.

With a huff, Jane dragged herself out of the driver's seat and popped open the gas cap on her rental. While the unleaded flowed into the tank, the vintage pump click, click, clicked with the uptick of each cent. While she waited, Jane glanced out at the mountains. Drifts of snow still crusted the granite crags at the tops of the peaks, tapering off to meet the stunted pines at the tree line. It was a beautiful view but coming home reminded her how much she missed her father. Yes, the mountains made a stunning backdrop, but they were treacherous too.

Not wanting to think about the accident that took

her father, she leaned against the car with a defeated sigh. This would take at least fifteen minutes. But then again, everything moved slower in Silverado Lake—time, people, the economy. The only thing that moved fast was the latest gossip.

Yes sir, news of a scandal traveled at the speed of light in Silverado Lake. She remembered all too well. For the most part she'd avoided being the target of everyone's gossip, until *that night*. The memory rekindled, bringing with it a full-body flush. It was funny how embarrassing moments seared themselves into both the brain and the heart. She remembered every detail about that New Year's Eve party her mother had at the ranch so she could help Jane "come out of her shell."

Except Jane hadn't wanted to come out of her shell so while all her peers played games and partied in the great room, Jane snuck off into the office across the hall to read. That's where Toby had found her, and, of course, had baited her into an argument about archetypes in *The Lord of the Rings*—the book she'd happened to pull off the shelf. It had gotten heated, as usual, and they'd gotten in each other's faces. Then Toby changed everything by kissing her.

She still didn't know how she'd gotten caught up in the kiss, how it had managed to reach deeply inside of her, bringing her so far outside of reality that she hadn't heard the voices or the footsteps before half of Toby's football team plowed through the door. The guys had made such a scene that everyone else had crowded into the office too, and there was Jane, practically sitting in Toby's lap, their arms still tangled together. The next day at school Toby had made a big spectacle in the hallway—asking Aubrey to the winter dance while Jane looked on as though he wanted to make a point.

Yeah, she definitely should've stayed in her shell.

She'd be willing to bet her first edition of *To Kill a Mockingbird* that at least someone in town would bring it up just like they did every time she came home for a visit. That was the other thing about embarrassing moments—no one else seemed to forget them either.

The loud click of the pump snapped her back to the present. To what mattered. *That night* had happened years ago. She might have been slightly socially awkward back then, but she was a different person now. She'd worked as a professor at one of the most prestigious universities in the country and she'd had a book published, thank you very much. Not that she wanted to mention the book inside Merle's General Store and Filling Station. Everyone in the RV park on the other side of the lake would know by noon.

Smiling past the sting of old memories, Jane returned the nozzle to the gas pump and hurried across the parking lot so she could pay Merle. And Patti, no doubt—the husband and wife duo who owned the station made sure to be there every day so they wouldn't miss out on any of the gossip.

Arming herself with a convincing smile and positive vibes, she trucked through the doors.

"Well, I'll be!"

She hadn't even stepped fully inside before Patti darted around the counter where the ancient cash register sat. She must've seen Jane coming.

"I wondered who was driving that foreign-made car! Calamity Jane Harding, that's who!"

The nickname brought on a wince.

"C'mere stranger!" The woman flapped her arms and then brought them around Jane in one of her smothering hugs. Patti Norman might've stood all of four foot six, but she had enough strength to suffocate a grizzly bear.

"By God, I can't believe it." Merle skirted the counter and came to join his wife. He wasn't much taller. They'd always reminded her of those miniature statues you found on the top of a wedding cake. "Look at you, kid. It's been ages since you've been home for a visit."

It hadn't been *that* long. She'd been in town last Thanksgiving, but she never stayed more than a few days, and she kept a low profile.

"What've you been up to anyway?" Patti asked, ushering her to the counter. The woman eased herself onto a stool and sat gingerly, as though her back hurt. "Your mom hardly says a word about you!"

The revelation wasn't all that surprising, but it still nicked her heart. Her mother had never seemed to get her. Not the way her father had. Instead of letting her be, Mara had always tried to change Jane, buying her different clothes, prodding her to invite friends over, to be more popular. It had almost seemed like Jane had embarrassed her mother.

That was ancient history though. Things were different now that she'd grown up. Coming home didn't mean she had to revert back to the shy girl she'd been in high school. She recalibrated her smile. "I completed my doctoral program in literature last year and I just finished a contract as an adjunct professor at Cal Poly." Of course, she also had that side gig writing sweeping historical western romance novels, but no one could ever know about that. Especially not Patti. Good gravy, that woman would have a million questions for her, and she'd likely be offended by the sex scenes.

"A professor?" Patti gave Jane a good long look up and

down, as if she didn't quite believe her. "Well isn't that something?" She gave her head a slight shake. "It's so good to see you again. I wasn't sure if you'd make it home for the big wedding."

"I wouldn't have missed it for anything." Besides that, this little time-out at home would hopefully help her find the inspiration she needed to write a brilliant story. Surely being around a wedding—a couple in love—would give her some ideas.

"Cal Poly . . ." Merle reached over to straighten a row of pork rinds on the shelf next to them. "Never heard of it."

"It's in California," she explained, hoping they wouldn't ask too many more questions. As of now, the university didn't have a spot for her to teach in the fall, and she had a book to write if she wanted to continue supporting herself. Anxiety squeezed at her throat. "It was good to see you both, but I'd better get going. According to Beth we have a lot to do." She and her friend couldn't be more opposite. Beth loved the thrill of waiting until the last minute to do pretty much everything, while Jane was a planner. She didn't like to leave anything up to chance.

"Sounds like that wedding is going to be the event of the summer." Patti stood and rang up Jane's total at the register. "It's a good thing Toby is working at the ranch getting everything all spruced up."

"Toby?" As in Toby Garrett? He'd come home too? Panic swelled beneath her ribs. "What ranch? Where's he working?" Jane handed over her credit card. Had he come back for the wedding? She couldn't imagine him leaving the circuit for anything, even with Ethan being one of his best friends. Toby had never been one to walk away from any spotlight.

Patti ran Jane's card, but the machine was ancient.

Please wait.

"He's working out there at your family's ranch," Merle said. "Didn't your mama tell you?"

Jane's lungs grasped for breath, but she ended up gulping back a throatful of shock. "Of course, she told me," she managed to say without sputtering. "I forgot, that's all." She shot a desperate glance at the credit card machine.

Please wait.

"Toby's always been a good kid," Merle said. "He's been a lot of help out there at the ranch since he's been back. I just ran into him at the hardware store not twenty minutes ago. He had a whole list of things he needed. Sounds like he's doing your family's old place a bunch of good. You won't find a more trustworthy employee."

Trustworthy? Oh, no. She'd learned the hard way she couldn't trust Toby.

"You know..." Jane leaned into the counter in a conspiratorial pose, but really her knees had started to buckle. "I'm not clear on why, exactly, Toby came back." Why on earth was he working at the ranch? And worse yet, why was this news having a physical effect on her?

"Why, he got injured," Patti said importantly. "Something with his shoulder, I think. Had to have surgery and everything. He hasn't said much about it to anyone in town since he's been back, but rumor has it he's been seeing specialists in Denver."

"I coulda told him that would happen," Merle insisted. "He was such a smart kid and he threw it all away to be a bull rider." The man gave her a glance. "Wasn't he valedictorian back when you were in school?"

"We were co-valedictorians, actually." Toby never let her have any title to herself. He'd even petitioned to be her copresident of the literary society, saying it wasn't fair that they'd never had a male president. They'd competed for everything in high school and it seemed like she could never beat him no matter what she did.

"Co-valedictorians? Well doesn't that beat all?" Patti whapped her husband's shoulder. "Looks like you'll be buddying up again."

"I'm not sure what you mean." Jane stared hard at the credit card reader, trying to make it think faster.

Please wait.

"Surely you must've heard that Toby is Ethan Rockford's best man! From the sound of things, those two have kept in touch all these years."

Jane stared at her across the counter. Beth had never mentioned Toby was going to be the best man. She'd probably been worried Jane would've refused to come...

"From what I hear, Toby is still single." Patti nudged Jane's shoulder with hers. "I don't see a ring on your finger yet. You two would make an awfully cute couple, if you ask me. Maybe that little kiss back in high school was only the beginning."

Little kiss? There had been nothing little about that kiss. She'd learned her lesson when it came to Toby Garrett. "Are you sure he's working at the ranch?" Why would he want a job at her family's ranch? And why in the world would her mother have hired him?

"Oh, I'm sure honey. I heard he moved into one of the cabins a few days ago."

Please wait.

The green words on the credit card machine blurred together. Jane was done waiting. "Here." She dug into her purse and threw two twenties on the counter and snatched her credit card back. "I'll see you both soon, I'm sure," she called, heading for the door.

"Wait!" Patti scrambled to follow her. "What about the transaction? And you need change!"

"Keep it." If Toby was at the hardware store, now would be the perfect time to head to the ranch so she could talk to her mom about unhiring him before he got back.

Chapter Four

"We need to replace the gate." Toby gave the metal barrier a swift kick, but it still stuck. Not surprisingly, the hardware store hadn't had anything he needed to fix it. He'd put in an order, but they'd be waiting a few days. "Hinges are rusted out. One of these times we're gonna close it and not be able to open it again." Besides that, it was the first thing people saw when they drove up to the Silverado Lake Ranch, and it didn't exactly scream luxury destination, but he was working on that. Mara had done a heck of a job maintaining what she had, but the ranch had weathered over the past few years. Since moving in, he'd re-sided half of the outbuildings and repainted every peeling wall. And he still had energy to burn.

If his most recent appointment with Dr. Petrie was any indication, he had time to do a lot more work. "We should have something custom built and add a big sign. Something that makes a statement." He could round up a couple of big logs, maybe even add some stone…

"I guess you're right." Mara worried her lips. She wasn't your typical ranch boss, being that she only stood about five feet tall and never left the house without a fresh coat of lipstick, but she'd surprised everyone after her husband had passed away twelve years ago by keeping the ranch afloat. She'd even managed to attract some high-end clientele for weddings. But one of the brides who'd come confessed to him she'd been tempted to turn around and bail on the place when she'd driven up in her luxury SUV and saw the old rusted gate. The pictures on the website highlighted the more modern amenities like the main lodge and the small chapel for indoor wedding ceremonies, but you had to get past the gate to see them.

"It's definitely time to spring for a new gate." The older woman chuckled at her pun. "You can price it out and let me know the damage?"

"Sure." He'd only been working on the ranch less than a week, but already Mara had come to rely on him for making the maintenance and facility decisions. It was almost like she'd forgotten he would be a temporary fixture around here. The second his shoulder healed and he got clearance from the docs, he'd be headed back out to the circuit to make up for lost time. Still, while he was here, he'd do his best to upgrade as much as the budget allowed so she'd be in good shape for a few years at least. "I'll do some research and get back to you. If I do most of the labor myself, we can keep the costs down." And he could keep being too busy to notice how out of shape he was getting while he sat on the sidelines of his life.

"You're the best!" Mara declared. "I don't know how I lucked out getting you to work here, but I'm sure glad I did."

"It worked out for me too." Better than he could've hoped for. It had been good to have his own space again, though he had made sure to head back to his parents' house for dinner the other night.

Mara looked down at the ground and kicked some gravel with her boot. "Since we're talking about the gate, I suppose it's also time to address this driveway—"

A car engine hummed behind them. Turning, Toby moved off to the side so the sedan could get past. "Wonder who that is."

"That would be my long-lost daughter." Mara's eyes followed the car as it drove past the aspen trees. "Finally coming home to stay for more than a few days."

"Jane?" Toby squinted at the car but shadows from the trees blocked out the windows, piquing his curiosity. "She doesn't come home very often, huh?"

"She's only come home for a few holidays." Mara started walking down the drive, following the car's path. "I'm grateful Beth decided to get married this summer. That means I don't have to wait until Thanksgiving to spend some time with my daughter."

"Should be a fun wedding." He thought about Beth's warning for him to behave. As Ethan's fiancée Beth probably knew too much about Toby's personal life—and his lack of committed relationships. But she likely had nothing to worry about with Jane. The woman had never liked him. Sure, there'd been that one hot kiss their senior year, but afterward, Jane had made it pretty clear she didn't want anything to do with him.

Which shouldn't have surprised him. She'd never seemed to like him much. Most of their interactions back then had revolved around bickering. He obviously irritated her, and she drove him crazy. But at the New Year's Eve party things had been different. Mara had hosted the event at the ranch, and everyone was having a blast. Everyone except for Jane, that was. Toby hadn't even noticed she'd been missing, but on his way back to the great room from the kitchen he'd spotted her lying on a couch in the office reading *The Lord of the Rings*.

She'd looked more carefree than he'd ever seen her that night, her slippers on, her long dark hair spread around her. To this day, Toby was still a Tolkien fan. Not that he would've admitted it to anyone else, especially back in high school, but Jane understood. They must've sat there on that couch for an hour arguing about what Gollum symbolized. Jane had been so intense, so passionate, and the next thing he knew, he was kissing her. The bigger shock? She'd kissed him back. The force of it had almost knocked him over. He'd kissed plenty of girls, but not with that much fire raging between them.

Before kissing her, he hadn't thought Jane was capable of fire. Competitive? Sure. Intense? Definitely. But he'd never seen her show passion for anything besides books and studying. That kiss had been full of passion though. They'd been so into each other, neither one of them had noticed his buddies walk in until the razzing started. It had taken all of two seconds for Jane to bolt out of that room. He'd followed her, finally caught her at the end of the hallway. He told her he liked her. He would've kissed her again, but Jane held him off. He remembered her exact words. *Well, I don't like you. It was a stupid kiss. It didn't mean anything.*

The kiss had obviously repulsed her, so the next day he did what any self-respecting eighteen-year-old kid would do—he made a very public winter dance proposal to Aubrey, a cheerleader he'd dated on and off, making sure

Jane saw the whole thing go down. He'd left Jane alone like she wanted, but he hadn't stopped noticing her.

Now, anticipation swirled through him at the prospect of seeing her again. Toby followed Mara and watched Jane get out of the car. The sun captured her at the right angle to show her coppery highlights. She'd let it grow longer, that's the first thing he noticed. It went down past her shoulders to her mid-back. She still wore glasses, but her face had changed. Her cheeks had filled out and seemed to have more color. She'd always been petite, but a fitted sweater showcased curves he hadn't appreciated all those years ago.

Jane didn't look in his direction, but she greeted Mara with a hug. "It's good to see you, Mom."

Toby didn't move to catch her attention. He didn't move at all. He stood stock-still transported back to that night on the couch, their arms tangled around each other, their lips exploring. He still couldn't understand how the kiss had hit him so hard when it didn't seem to affect her at all.

"Everything looks the same." Jane gazed at the lodge farther down the hill.

Great, she was still avoiding him eight years later.

"God, the lake looks gorgeous," she went on, fully turning away.

Toby couldn't see her face, but a wistfulness breathed through her tone.

"Everything's not the same at all!" Mara waved Toby over. "It looks even better since Toby started working here. It's probably been years since you've seen each other."

"It's definitely been a long time." Jane's gaze skimmed right over him.

She didn't remember him fondly, that was for damn sure. He tried to warm her up with a smile. "Good to see you again."

Instead of acknowledging the words, she went around the back of the car and popped the trunk.

"Toby has been very helpful with everything around here," Mara gushed. "He's a whiz with a hammer and nails."

"Hmm." Jane struggled to lift out a large suitcase and a carry-on bag.

Toby inched closer. "I can take those for you." The main house was a long haul and that thing looked heavy.

"No thanks. I can handle my own baggage." The rosy flush on Jane's cheeks deepened. "I mean, I don't need help. I'm fully capable of carrying bags to my cabin."

Her cabin? She wasn't staying at the main house with her mother? And why did she assume he thought she wasn't capable? Jane had been one of the most capable girls he'd ever known.

"Goodness, Jane. Let the man help." Mara nudged Toby toward the suitcase. "It'll give you two a chance to catch up."

Ha. She didn't want to catch up with him.

Jane's shoulders seemed to stiffen. "That's okay. Really. I've got it." She shouldered the strap of her laptop bag, lifted the carry-on in her opposite hand, and started to drag the suitcase toward the path that led to the cabins, but the wheels kept getting caught on rocks. Muttering to herself, Jane staggered forward, tripping as she yanked the suitcase over the gravel.

Toby shared a look with Mara. He couldn't just stand there and watch.

"Why don't I take the bags for you?" He followed Jane at a distance, letting her make the choice. She'd made it pretty clear she didn't want to be alone with him, but she hadn't said anything about her mother. "Then you and your mom can catch up."

Jane paused and turned to him. Some elusive emotion flashed in her eyes before she steeled them again. Surprise maybe? "If you really don't mind. Mom and I have a lot of catching up to do." Jane set down the carry-on and laptop bag, let go of the suitcase, and stepped aside.

"Don't mind at all." Toby slung the strap of the laptop bag onto his good shoulder and picked up the carry-on on that same side, leaving his left hand to drag the suitcase.

"She's in cabin four," Mara called over, amusement flashing in her eyes.

"You can just leave everything on the porch," Jane instructed. "I won't be long."

"Will do." He started out in the direction of the cabins.

Mara walked over and slipped her arm around her daughter. "Come on. I'll show you the new reception hall." Her mother started to pull her away.

"Wait," Jane called after him. "Be careful with that one." She pointed to the laptop bag. "My laptop is in there."

"I can handle it," Toby assured her. "Trust me."

A sharp raise of her eyebrows told him it would be a cold day in hell before she trusted him. And yet she had trusted him once.

Jane glanced back, her eyes meeting his, spiking his curiosity.

That night so long ago was the one time in all the years he'd known her that Jane had seemed to let down her guard.

And he couldn't help but wonder what it would take for her to do it again.

Chapter Five

Jane couldn't help but look over her shoulder again. She'd like to know how Toby had gotten back from the hardware store so fast. So much for talking her mother out of hiring him. All her mom had done when Jane had gotten out of the car was gush about what a great job he was doing.

Forcing herself to look straight ahead, she walked faster. She hadn't been prepared to see Toby standing there when she'd driven up. During her high school years, she'd assumed, or hoped, the adrenaline rushes Toby had given her had more to do with the thrill of competition than it did with the cowboy himself, but the hard pound of her heart and the perspiration itching on her palms as she and her mother walked toward the house obliterated that theory.

The truth was Toby Garrett had always been...what, exactly? Not classically handsome—he was too rugged for that description. Wild and a little bit dangerous maybe. Intense. Yes, that definitely fit. His dusky blue eyes seemed to flash with whatever emotion he happened to be feeling at the time.

She'd seen those eyes fill with irritation when she would correct him in class. She'd seen them flash with humor on more than one occasion when he'd teased her about getting anything less than 100 percent on a test.

The way Toby's eyes had flashed a few minutes ago had looked an awful lot like intrigue. Or maybe she was imagining things. What she wasn't imagining was the feeling coursing through her own body. It had been at least ten minutes since she'd driven up and seen Toby standing there with her mother, yet her heart still beat as hard as if she'd run all the way from town.

Anger. That's what this had to be. After all, she'd never gotten to give him a piece of her mind after he'd snubbed her in front of the whole school. It was all anyone could talk about for at least a month. How Toby had kissed her one night and then asked Aubrey to their winter formal the next day like Jane had simply been another notch in his belt.

Sure, she'd told him it was only a stupid kiss. Of course she'd said that! She knew what Toby had been like, how he was all about having a good time but never really caring about the girls he was with. And then he'd gone and proved her right. That was what had her so flustered. The drumming of her heart had little to do with infatuation and everything to do with unexpressed anger.

"Watch out!" Her mother yanked on her shoulder and steered her away from walking straight into a fence post. "Are you okay?" she turned Jane's face to hers. "Have you even heard a word I've said about the upgrades Toby has already made to the ranch?"

Jane stopped walking and looked around. Her gaze

settled on the lodge sitting on the lake's shore. Simply seeing it filled her with such longing for her father. He'd designed the log building and had helped with the construction. The lodge still had that grand appeal, but it was true the ranch had aged. In her brief visits home over the last few years, she'd noticed the cracks in the logs, the dents in the siding on the cabins. It had to be so much for her mother to manage. She deserved to have more support. But still…did Toby have to be the one helping? "Why didn't you mention hiring him? I could have prepared myself for all the high school flashbacks."

Her mom grimaced. "I'm sorry, honey. I should've mentioned it when you called to say you were on your way. I've just been so busy preparing for the season." Her mom's eyes looked weary. "I needed help and he needed a job. Besides," she put her arm around Jane and pulled her closer, "you're not that shy high school girl anymore. Toby doesn't know what he missed out on."

"I'm definitely not the same girl." And she wouldn't fall for the same act twice. "I was just surprised that he would want to work here." He probably could've had his pick of jobs in Silverado Lake with how popular he'd always been.

"I was too, but I think he wanted to keep busy while he's in town. And he's working pretty cheap." Her mom glanced behind them as though making sure Toby had disappeared. "You want my opinion, he still feels bad about how he acted after the New Year's Eve party. The poor man's obviously grown up a lot since then. You both have."

The poor man. It was all Jane could do not to roll her eyes all the way back into her head. The poor man who'd always had girls falling at his feet. The poor man who happened to be crazy smart and smoldering hot. The poor man who was the perfect model for a hero in a romance novel. That secret was definitely going with her to her grave.

"From what I've seen he's a completely different person now," her mom went on, gently elbowing Jane in the side. "He's always been a good-looking guy, but that boy really turns heads these days."

"I guess." Jane was too honest for her own good. Besides, if she attempted to lie and claim Toby was not good-looking, her mom would see right through her.

Never mind his magnetic eyes, that sandy brown hair of his had grown longer, fringing the tips of his ears. He didn't have to do a thing to his hair, of course. It simply had that sexy disheveled thing going on. But it was his smile that was most dangerous. That smile came on easily and suddenly, pulling whoever witnessed it into a sort of conspiratorial fantasy. Toby's smile held something that made people want to know his secret.

"Hello?" Her mother waved a hand in front of her face. "Did you hear me? I asked how things were going with the professor."

"Oh." Jane refocused, suddenly regretting ever mentioning her colleague from the math department. "We weren't a match." She'd been on a few dates with Hudson, but he'd gone on and on about the probabilities of them getting married someday and she finally had to tell him he had a zero percent chance of that happening.

And anyway, why did she need a real man—with all his flaws—when she got to make up the perfect man in her books? Not that she could tell her mom that. A whole new set of worries came flooding back in. The looming book deadline was creeping ever closer and despite spending hours at the computer before she'd left California, she'd come up with nothing.

Jane tried to let the whole Toby thing go with a sigh. Really, her mom was free to hire whomever she wanted. Mara was right. It had been years. The past shouldn't matter anymore. She had bigger things to focus on. "Sorry." She rubbed her forehead. "I have a huge headache. I should go lay down." Or write a chapter. Two chapters maybe? "Let's finish the tour after dinner." She didn't wait for an answer before trotting away.

"But you haven't seen the new reception hall yet!" her mother called.

"Tonight," she promised. "I think the drive wore me out." The flight, the drive, the reunions.

Jane hurried down the path that led to the cabins dotting the shoreline of the lake. She'd almost forgotten how beautiful this place was. That crystal-blue, glacier-fed lake against the backdrop of those carved mountain peaks demanded to be admired. It was the kind of setting she wrote about—wild and unfathomable. She'd almost forgotten how vibrant the colors were—the blue in the sky, the green on the mountainsides.

"Janie! Oh my heavens, you're home!" Louise practically jogged down the path to meet her. "Your mama told me you'd arrived, so I had to chase you down before you got too far." The woman had been a part of their family since Jane was eight years old. She'd be nearing sixty now, but you'd never know it with Louise's spirited energy. She'd always been able to do pretty much anything—cook, bake, and her standards for keeping things clean were unparalleled. She still didn't look a day over forty with her lovely blond hair and bright welcoming smile.

Jane hugged the woman tightly. "It's so good to see you."

"You too, girlie." She held Jane at arm's length and seemed to make an appraisal. "You look thin. Have you been eating the cookies I sent?"

"Every single one of them." Jane couldn't find cookies as good as Louise's anywhere in California. "But I really miss your homemade lasagna and your broccoli cheese soup. Oh! And that amazing steak you marinate for three days."

Louise laughed. "Well, there'll be plenty of time for all that, won't there? When your mom told me you were staying so long, I almost couldn't believe it."

"It'll give us plenty of time to catch up." Jane looked out at the mountains again, realizing how much she'd missed this place. How much she'd missed her mom, Louise, the lake.

"Hi there, ladies."

Jane spun around. Toby had somehow snuck up on them from the parking lot.

"Don't worry. Your bags are all safe and sound on your porch." He held out a key. "Only dropped your carry-on once."

Taking the key from his hand, Jane forced a laugh. He'd better be joking. "As long as it was only once." Why did her voice sound so high and weird? There went her heart again too. Bumbling around in her chest. Good God. You'd think she'd never talked to a hot cowboy before.

"Well, I have a dinner to prepare so I'll leave you two alone." Louise winked at her, though Jane wasn't sure why.

"Do you need help?" Jane started after her friend. "I can come with you."

"No." Louise all but pushed her back toward Toby. "I'm sure you kids have a lot to catch up on. Come by and see me tomorrow." She hurried away, not giving Jane an opportunity to argue.

"I'm headed over to the café," Toby said, clearly not picking up on her discomfort. "You want to come with me?"

"I'm sorry, what?" He wanted her to go to the café with him? Like they were best friends or something? "Why would I want to go to the café with you?" She could give him the benefit of the doubt and assume he'd grown up some. She could even be distantly grateful that he'd been such a help to her mom, who looked more tired than usual. But that didn't mean they had to be friends.

"We're supposed to meet Beth and Ethan for lunch," Toby said. "Didn't they tell you?"

Beth hadn't told her much about anything having to do with the wedding. Originally, Jane had written it off as her friend's love for spontaneity, but now it had all started to make sense. "She said something about getting together but I never got the details." Important details like the fact that Toby was going to be the best man.

"Sounds like they want us to help them plan a wedding shower." Toby didn't seem to find it difficult to stare into her eyes. As a matter of principle Jane refused to look away from him even though she wanted to.

"I need to settle in." More accurately, she needed to escape. She'd built a quiet life for herself. This visit home was already more drama than she typically endured in an entire month. "Can you tell her I'll catch up with her later?"

"But you're the maid of honor." Toby's smirk lit her fuse. "Isn't planning stuff part of your job?"

"I'm sure you can manage without me." What experience did she have planning wedding events anyway? Though she couldn't deny she did have a way with details. She suspected that's why Beth had requested she come home three weeks before the actual wedding.

"You know..." Toby looked thoughtful. "You're probably right. I do have some good ideas for a party."

"Great." Jane slipped past him. "Let me know what you guys come up with and I'll help out however I can."

"I'm thinking we all go to that new brewery on Main Street. Get a keg. Have a cornhole tournament. We can order some chicken wings too."

Chicken wings and cornhole for a wedding shower? Jane stopped and turned back to him. She couldn't walk away from that. "It's a shower for the bride and the groom. Not a bachelor party."

With a coy grin still lighting his eyes, Toby shrugged as if to say, *What's the difference?*

Oh, this man. He knew she could never walk away from a fight. "Beth hates beer. And cornhole, for that matter."

"You have a better idea?" Toby asked too innocently.

"As a matter of fact, yes. I have a better idea." She walked back to face off with him like they'd done so often in high school. "Something elegant and classy for starters."

Amusement sparked in Toby's eyes. "I'll drive." He pulled keys out of his pocket.

"For the love of God, there should be wine. And flowers. Definitely music." She marched past him, leading the way back to the parking lot.

"Wine and flowers sound fine to me, as long as I get to wear my jeans." Toby's long stride carried him a few steps in front of her. Those sinful jeans, fitted and tattered, displaying one of the cowboy's best attributes.

Eyes straight ahead, she reminded herself.

As long as she didn't look at Toby's butt in those jeans, she'd get through this just fine.

Chapter Six

Here, let me get that for you." Toby sprinted over before Jane could reach the passenger's side door handle on the same Dodge Ram truck he'd driven in high school. At one time it had been a sleek navy blue, but the paint had faded and the dings and dents in the body made it look like the truck had been well used.

A flashback hit the second she climbed into the passenger seat. She'd almost forgotten that she'd ridden in Toby's truck once back in high school. It hadn't been long after her father had passed away...a month maybe. Toby had seen her try and fail to start her dad's old Jeep in the school parking lot about ten times. When she couldn't get it to turn over, she'd rested her head on the steering wheel and started to sob for what felt like the millionth time since his funeral.

She hadn't known anyone had been watching her, but Toby had simply opened the door and reached in to take her hand, helping her out and then leading her to his truck.

It still smelled the same as it had then—like grass and campfire and summer. They hadn't talked the whole ride to her house. She had tried so hard to pull herself together, silently gagging back tears, inhaling deep, painful breaths and holding them so no more sobs would slip out.

When Toby had pulled up in front of her house at the ranch, he'd looked over at her with sad eyes. "I'm really sorry," he'd said quietly. "I know it doesn't seem like it, but things will get better. It takes a while. More than a while. But things get better." She'd wanted to ask how he knew, but then he'd shocked her by laying his hand on her arm. Even though she'd known him since he'd moved to town in the third grade, Toby had never touched her before. It hadn't been a romantic gesture—more of a show of solidarity, but the touch had made her body tingle with anticipation. It had been the first emotion other than grief she'd felt since the worst day of her life. That was when her silent, secret crush had officially started.

And it had ended the day he'd stood in that hall gloating when he'd asked Aubrey to the winter formal, she reminded herself. After he'd kissed her that night, she'd had to protect herself from him. He'd been a player back then, and from the way he was acting now not much had changed. So there'd be no tingling. Not when it came to Toby. Maybe he'd done one nice thing for her back in high school, but there were plenty of other things he'd done that weren't so nice. She'd focus on those instead. "You have the same truck," she said when he scooted in next to her.

"Yeah. It runs great." He started the engine and backed out of the parking space while he clicked in his seatbelt.

"I would've thought you'd bought a new one by now." Especially with the notoriety he'd gained in the rodeo world. Not that she'd followed his career that closely. She'd seen something about prizes he'd won when he'd gotten a lot of congratulations from mutual acquaintances on Instagram.

"Nah." He kept his eyes focused on the road, carefully navigating the rutted driveway. "No reason to buy a new truck. I can't seem to part with this one. Maybe because it was my first car. I saved up and bought it myself."

"I thought your parents bought it for you." She hadn't meant to sound so surprised, but she'd assumed his parents had given it to him as a gift. They were one of the wealthier families in town, and they liked people to know it.

"Why would you think that?" He turned to look at her, amusement playing on his lips. He had to know why. His dad was a doctor who commuted to Denver. They owned one of the largest acreages in town and threw their money around every chance they got.

She decided to be diplomatic. "Your parents could've afforded to buy you a truck."

"Believe it or not my parents didn't make everything easy for me." He turned his eyes back to the road. "We weren't the perfect family by a long stretch." Before she could ask him what that meant, he flicked on the radio to a country station.

"So, do you like living in California?" he asked, turning onto the highway that led to town.

The quick change of subject caught her off guard. "I guess. I mean, the ocean's nice." She didn't like the crowds or the cost of everything. "I liked teaching there." She couldn't claim to have much of a life outside the university and her own imagination. Really, she could live anywhere as long as she could teach and spend her free time writing.

"You're a professor now, huh?" Toby pulled the truck to a stop at the one stoplight in town. A family crossed the street in front of them, waving. Toby waved back, flashing a smile. The man obviously still knew how to turn on the charm.

Jane tried to focus. "Uh. Well, I was an adjunct, but the university doesn't have a spot for me in the fall so they didn't renew my contract."

"Still. That's pretty impressive." He eased the truck forward through the intersection going five miles under the twenty-mile-per-hour speed limit. "Not all that surprising though. I always knew you'd be a big deal."

Jane had to snap her mouth shut so her jaw didn't hit the floor. "You did?" Toby Garrett always thought *she* would be a big deal? She almost laughed. Yeah, right. He couldn't charm her that easily. "Whatever."

"No, seriously," he said, his grin fading. "Back in high school, you were...different."

Different. It was the same word her mom had always used to describe her. Her mother had been so sure something was wrong with her. She'd worried that Jane was too withdrawn. The opposite of everything her mom had been at Jane's age. She'd even asked the doctor about it once. *Jane seems...different than most of her peers.* The doctor had told her mother that everyone had different personalities and there was nothing wrong with that, but that didn't dissuade her mother from obsessively reading parenting articles and encouraging Jane to be more social.

Toby braked at a stop sign and looked over at her. "I meant that as a compliment in case that wasn't clear." His eyes held her gaze.

It definitely hadn't been clear because Toby didn't

compliment her. He'd teased her, but he'd never complimented her. They'd bickered back and forth in more than one classroom debate, but that had been the extent of their interactions. Jane didn't even know what to say.

"You were different because you were so much smarter than everyone else. And you didn't seem to get into all the drama and the stupid superficial things most of the girls cared about. That's a good thing."

Suddenly the vents felt like they were pouring out heat. "You were smart too." And attractive. And charming. He'd pretty much had it all. Still did, apparently.

"I was never as smart as you. I only pretended to be." Toby slid that heart-stopping grin her way. And her heart did. It stopped. She pinched the palm of her hand to get it going again. This was classic Toby. Flirting, saying whatever he had to in order to win people over. That happened to be his strength. Never mind they had this whole history he obviously wasn't about to bring up. She wasn't about to fall under his spell again. "Well I'm glad you can finally admit it." She shot him her own smirk. "You were definitely never as smart as me." Liar. He was every bit as smart as her, but she'd never let him know she thought so.

Toby laughed. "I still beat you on our AP history final."

She was about to remind him it had only been by a half percentage point, but they drove past the library and she gasped. "What happened?" The old square brick building had been replaced with a much larger structure. "I just went to the library when I was here over Thanksgiving last year!" And now it was gone?

"They rebuilt it this spring." Toby slowed the truck as they rolled past. "What do you think?"

"It's beautiful." The stone and columns and arched

windows made it look like a palace. The sight made her smile. They'd taken one of her favorite places and made it even better. She'd spent so much time in the library—finding a quiet corner to cozy up with a book. Especially after her father had passed away. The librarian had finally added a beanbag chair to her favorite spot. "That must've cost them a fortune." It was easily the nicest building on Main Street now.

"Some anonymous donor funded it." He seemed to admire the entrance as they drove past.

"That had to have cost hundreds of thousands of dollars." Back when she was in school, no one had cared much about the library. It had been quiet and deserted—a true escape.

Toby simply shrugged. "Maybe. At any rate, it's a heck of a lot better than it was when we were in school. Remember how many times they had to evacuate because the electricity used to short out?"

The memory made her smile. "At least once a week it seemed."

"Well they're not going to have to worry about that anytime soon," he said, and she couldn't help noticing the smile playing across his face. As a writer she'd made sure to build her people observation skills, and she thought she detected a hint of pride lurking behind that smile.

"So, no one knows who donated the money?"

"Nope." He kept his eyes steady on the road. "It's a mystery."

Uh-huh. She'd always been good at solving mysteries, and her instincts told her Toby had had something to do with the transformation. "Hard to keep anything a mystery in this town," she commented, still watching him. His eyes always gave him away. How did he not know that by now?

"Ethan and Beth gave the café a face-lift too."

If that wasn't an intentional change of subject, she didn't know what was, but she let it go. She shouldn't care one way or another if Toby had been involved in rebuilding the library. His involvement definitely shouldn't create the warm stirring sensation she suddenly felt low in her belly.

The cowboy pulled the truck in front of the small storefront café that anchored one side of Main Street.

"Wow." The library definitely wasn't the only thing that had changed. She climbed out of his truck admiring the work Ethan and Beth had put into the café over the last several months.

"A lot of things have changed in Silverado Lake since we were kids."

"People have changed too," Toby said as he held open the café's door.

The words made her pause. Had he changed? She wasn't convinced.

Jane stepped inside the restaurant and Beth darted out from behind the long counter. "Janie! Oh my God!" Her friend flew across the room. "You're here!"

"You bet I'm here. You're getting married." She returned her friend's hug.

"You let your hair grow longer." Beth pulled back to inspect her. "It looks absolutely gorgeous!"

"And you got yours cut." She admired her friend's cropped stylish black hair, which was held back with a colorful scarf. "I love what you've done with this place."

Jane looked around. They'd taken the old rundown café Beth's uncle had owned and made it look more like a bistro with sleek concrete floors and local artisan crafts hung on the light gray walls. She'd heard about it in Beth's emails, but it was another thing to see all of their hard work.

"Toby came in for a weekend to help Ethan do the renovations last February." Her friend gave Toby a grateful look. "It saved us a ton of money."

"It was nothing." Deflecting the praise, the man sauntered away and slid onto the bench of an empty booth near the windows.

Jane watched him go. So, he was improving things at the ranch, likely donated money to completely rebuild the library, *and* he'd helped Ethan build Beth's dream café. It seemed Toby really would be lining up for sainthood soon.

"Are things okay with you two?" Beth whispered, looking as concerned as the rest of the locals in the café. "I should've warned you that you'd have to spend time with Toby, but I didn't want to freak you out before you got here."

"Things are fine." How many times would she have to say that over the next month? She would make sure things were fine. She was a grown woman now. She could handle Toby. "That whole kiss fiasco feels like it happened a hundred years ago." Okay, maybe not a hundred, but being back in Silverado Lake was going to require some serious exaggeration. "You don't need to worry about me. I'm here to help *you*."

"Thank God for that." Her friend led her to the booth Toby had chosen. Jane hesitated before sliding in next to him. No big deal. Their shoulders were touching but it was *no big deal*.

"Thank you both so much for coming." Beth slumped over the table as though she was ready to fall asleep.

"Things have been crazy with opening the café, and I haven't had much time to solidify the details for all the fun parties and events I promised my family."

"Like I said, I'm here to help." Jane sat at an awkward angle so her shoulder would stop brushing Toby's. "Anything I can do to make this all less stressful for you, let me know." She had two objectives in Silverado Lake—help her friend have the best wedding ever and write her damn book.

Beth signaled to the waitress. "A round of coffee, please!" The young girl nodded and hurried away. "Okay," her friend said as though getting down to business. "The first thing I need is for you two to figure out what we should do at the wedding shower I promised my grandmother we'd have."

Ethan approached with a tray of coffees and set them down before he slid in next to Beth. They really did make the cutest couple. Beth with her sassy black hair and colorful scarf, Ethan with his friendly face and cropped dark hair that matched his thick eyelashes. His flannel and skinny jeans even seemed to complement Beth's adorable red maxi dress.

"What did I miss?" Ethan asked, threading an arm around his future wife.

"I was just telling them about the wedding shower," Beth grumbled.

"Ah yes. Grandma's party." He pointed at Toby across the table. "Everything had better be perfect for Grandma B."

Over the years, Jane had heard plenty of stories about Grandma B. Bernadette came from Southern money and she never let anyone forget it. According to Beth, nothing had ever been good enough for the woman. Growing up,

Beth had only had to endure her presence once a year when her parents dragged her to Georgia for a visit, but she'd still managed to try to run her granddaughter's life from a distance.

"Not to worry. We've got this under control." Toby nudged Jane. "Right?"

"Sure." She did her best to remain as casual as Toby, even with the anxiety rising. If she moved any farther away from him, she'd fall right onto the floor. "When were you thinking you wanted to have the party?"

Beth's mouth pulled into an apologetic frown. "Grandma gets in tomorrow and she's expecting it to be tomorrow night. I didn't even want to have a wedding shower, but she insisted we do something for the family and friends who are traveling all the way out here early. I promised her we'd do something right after she got here but I haven't even had time to think about it."

"No problem," Toby said at the same time Jane said, "*Tomorrow* night?"

"I know it's last minute. It's just been crazy around here." Her friend picked up her coffee mug and took a long sip like it had the power to save her. "You know how I am when I'm stressed. I can't seem to get anything done."

Ethan rubbed his hand up and down Beth's arm. "Not like you didn't have anything else to worry about." He leaned in and kissed her cheek tenderly. "Don't worry about it, babe. Toby and Jane can handle this. They've always been resourceful. They'll figure it out."

"Uh—" Before Jane could offer practical insight on what it took to pull a party together, Toby cut her off. "We can figure it out. We'll do it at the ranch in the old barn no one uses anymore."

"Um, what?" He wanted to hold a classy wedding shower

in the old barn? Jane was thinking something elegant with flowers and wine. Had he already forgotten about their conversation earlier?

"I'm sure the local Italian restaurant can cater it," he went on before Jane could speak up.

"That sounds perfect." Beth lurched over the table to hug Jane. "I knew you could pull it off!"

"We haven't pulled anything off yet—"

"Beth!" The young waitress who'd taken their coffee order came running over. "There's an emergency in the kitchen!"

Before she could say more, both Beth and Ethan were on their feet. "We'll be back," her friend called as the two of them jogged away.

"How can you look so calm right now?" Jane asked Toby. "We have one day to plan a huge party. What about decor? Music?" They'd have to gather the supplies they could find locally, not to mention make guest lists and invitations. "And the old barn? Seriously?" That's where her mother had always stored the ATVs and maintenance equipment.

"It's rustic, but it's a stunning building." Toby sipped his coffee donning a thoughtful expression. "Your mother emptied it out a few months ago and I've been cleaning it up. It won't take much more to get it in shape."

Jane almost laughed. Typical Toby. He never hesitated to take on a project or challenge, but he didn't exactly think through the details either.

"We'll work together. It'll be great."

That playful smile of his would not convince her so easily. "But—"

"Sorry." Beth rushed over. "One of our line cooks got burned. I have to step in and cook while Ethan takes him to the clinic."

"It's fine. We've got this," Toby assured her.

"Okay. Thank you." She started to walk away. "My parents gave me a credit card for all the wedding expenses. I'll bring it over to the ranch later tonight. I'm so excited about the shower!"

"Me too!" Jane forced out a smile. They had no choice but to do a barn party. She highly doubted they'd be able to find another venue on such short notice. "Don't worry about a thing! Leave it all to us." She tried to crush the sudden anxiety with another gulp of coffee. The way Toby kept looking at her, the way he acted like they were part of some unstoppable team was freaking her out. Just how much time would she and Toby have to spend together over the next month?

The cowboy turned to face her, lifting his mug to his lips. He had very kissable lips if memory served. Soft and firm at the same time and delicious.

Good God, quit analyzing the man's lips. This wasn't one of her romance novels. She took another sip of her coffee.

"So how would you feel about a mechanical bull at the party?" Toby asked.

She almost spit out her drink. "A mechanical bull. At a wedding shower?"

"Yeah. I know a guy." Toby set down his mug. "Instead of Italian food, maybe we should go with barbecue. I could get it for a pretty good price."

"Barbecue and a mechanical bull." She squinted at him.

"What?" Her lack of enthusiasm seemed to confuse him. "I think everyone would love some entertainment."

Jane propped her chin on her fist going for an amused glare. "Let me guess. You'll be the entertainment? Big bad bull rider taking on the mechanical bull?" Toby had never exactly minded being the center of everyone's attention.

"You can have a turn too." There was that smirk again. The one that teased and baited.

"I won't be taking a turn because there isn't going to be a mechanical bull at my best friend's wedding shower." That was as bad as cornhole and wings. "I can ask Louise to design a tapas menu. Maybe her staff would have time to cook for us. And I can pick up some different wines from the vineyard so we can do a tasting party."

Toby glared back at her, his smirk gaining momentum. "I have a proposition."

Somehow, he made that sound naughty enough that she squirmed.

"How about we divide and conquer?" The devious raise of his eyebrows hooked her. "You handle the food and wine and I'll handle the entertainment."

Divide and conquer. That sounded much better than arguing with him about every little detail.

Jane raised her coffee mug to her lips as though taking her time with the decision. Toby watched her, smirk still in place.

"Fine," she said. "You have a deal. Just make sure the entertainment is something Beth will enjoy."

"Of course." Toby's smirk turned into a full-fledged grin. "In case you've forgotten, entertainment is one of my specialties."

Chapter Sev

Toby lined up the nail and pounded it into the siding, ignoring the pinch in his shoulder. The doc said it would pull like that for a while. The surgeon had tried to repair the tendon as well as he could, but it would still take some time to heal. Waiting was something Toby had never been good at.

He stepped back to inspect the job he'd done. Shoulder injury or not, he could side a building with the best of them. The boathouse was the last facility on the entire ranch that needed a face-lift. An old, shedlike structure, it housed the many kayaks, canoes, and paddleboards they kept around for the guests to use.

He knew it wasn't the most important building at the ranch, but it still made an impression…just like the gate. Especially down here on the beach. You could stand in the sand and take in the picturesque view of the mountain peaks reflected in the turquoise-blue, glacial-fed waters of Silverado Lake, the pointed pines lining the other side of line. Maybe, if you were lucky, you'd spot one gles that made this area their home. *And* you in the view of the dilapidated boathouse ding and chipped paint. Now at least it He'd chosen forest-green siding so it he surroundings, and so you'd hardly re enjoying a day on the lake.

night make this place look like a s older brother Wes strode down to d greeted him with a handshake.

l. Look who came home." Toby could s eyes. As far as he'd heard Wes had a busier schedule than he did these days. That was what happened when you were as good at your job as Wes. The guy was the most important person in the arena. People thought you had to be crazy to climb onto the back of a bucking bull, but in Toby's humble opinion you had to be even crazier to provoke that bucking bull into chasing you down.

Toby tossed his hammer back into his toolbox. "First Jane, now you." The Hardings were having a genuine family reunion. "How'd you manage to break away from the excitement?"

"I found myself with a two-week lull, so here I am." The man lifted his cowboy hat off his head and wiped away sweat. "I couldn't let my little sister have all the glory. Mom's been after me to visit."

"It's good to see you." Not quite as good as it had been to see Jane, but he couldn't tell her brother that. He couldn't tell Wes how something in his chest shifted when he looked at the woman, how he'd been thinking about her since their conversation at the café earlier this afternoon…

"It's good to see you too. I was worried about you. Heard about your wipeout." Wes eyed him as though looking for evidence of the injury. "It was a bad tear, huh?"

The doctors had called it "catastrophic" at first. Before the surgery, they'd warned he might never fully recover. But thanks to his father, he'd been seeing the best orthopedic specialist in Denver. Of course, that also meant more lectures about his career since Toby's doctor was a friend of his father's, but he'd take it. He decided not to tell Wes any of that. "It was rough, but they think the surgery was successful." He wouldn't know for sure until he had another MRI in a few weeks. "I'm doing all my rehab stuff." He was trying not to overdo the strain on his shoulder, but he couldn't sit still either. Unfortunately, he was running out of buildings to side.

"So, you think you'll be back out there this season?" Wes asked. "Maybe we'll run into each other. After the next two weeks I'm booked out through the fall."

Jealousy riffled through him. He'd give anything to be back out there in two weeks. "I'm hoping I'll be back by August." The doctors had refused to give him a specific timetable for when he could expect to be back on a bull, but he was aiming for the end of summer.

"Nice." Wes slipped his hat back onto his head. "After my break, I'm headed up to Montana for a couple of events." The man continued talking about the specifics, but Toby had stopped listening. Jane was walking along the lodge's extensive deck with her mother. He thought about the spark that had lit in her eyes when he'd offered his suggestions for the shower earlier. He'd forgotten how much he liked provoking her—seeing her face come alive, watching her rise to a challenge.

Jane looked up now and her eyes seemed to meet his,

even across the distance. He could only grin. She'd totally caught him checking her out. Mara noticed him too, and obviously she noticed Wes.

"There's my boy!" The woman came running down the hill to the beach with her arms outstretched. Jane trailed along behind her.

"When did you get here?" Mara demanded, pulling her son in for a hug.

"Just now." He stepped back. "Saw Toby here working his ass off and thought I'd come give him a hand."

Wes hadn't offered to give him a hand, but Toby didn't say so.

"Of course you did." The woman beamed. "You're always so helpful."

"Hey, sis." Wes moved past his mother and gave his sister a hug. It occurred to Toby that the two of them didn't look much alike. Wes took after their mother while Jane took after their father. Or at least, that's what he seemed to remember about Jane's dad. He couldn't remember what her oldest brother August looked like, and from what he'd heard around town, he wouldn't be seeing him back at the ranch anytime soon.

"I didn't hear you were coming home." Jane wore a genuine look of happiness at the sight of her brother.

"All Mom could talk about was you coming home." Wes smirked. "Couldn't be outdone by my sis. Besides, I haven't seen you in forever. Had to see for myself that you were actually stepping foot in Silverado Lake for more than a few days."

"She's happy to be back, right, Jane?" Mara elbowed her.

"It's good to be home. It looks beautiful." She directed the compliment to Toby. "The improvements you've worked on around here really make a difference."

Was she saying that for the benefit of her mom? At the moment Jane's face was a mask of detachment. "Glad to hear you think so." The compliment affected him more than it probably should've, but he couldn't remember Jane ever offering him one before.

"I love what you're doing with the boathouse." Mara admired his work. "Make sure you keep track of all your overtime hours."

"Will do." He wouldn't, but with Mara it was best to keep up appearances. She was always trying to offer him more money, but truthfully, he didn't want it, didn't need it. She'd worked hard over the years and he had no intention of cutting into her profits.

"Two of my kids home together at last." The woman threw one arm around Wes and one around Jane. "Now if we could get August to come home too..."

"I wouldn't count on that." Wes rolled his eyes. From the way people in town talked, it sounded like August had become some big-shot wine executive out in Napa Valley and wanted little to do with his family's modest ranch.

"Well, at least you two are here." She squeezed Jane and Wes once more before letting them go. "I have to meet with a prospective bride this evening, but we'll all enjoy breakfast together tomorrow morning. How does that sound?"

"As long as Louise makes her quiche, I'm in," Wes said.

"I can probably do breakfast." Jane hesitated. "I'll have to see in the morning."

Toby studied her. What could she possibly be so busy with that she couldn't eat breakfast with her mom and brother? Or maybe it was Toby she was avoiding. The entire staff usually hung out in the dining room to load up on Louise's mouthwatering concoctions before heading outside to work. Jane knew he'd be there, and maybe that's why she didn't want to come. It was just as well since he was supposed to be on his best behavior, but still…

"Okay, I'm off!" Mara walked away. "You'll join us for breakfast in the morning too Toby." It wasn't a question.

"Wouldn't miss it," he called, trying to gauge Jane's reaction. How the woman managed to stay so straight-faced all the time was beyond him. He didn't have that gift. Anyone who looked at him right this second could probably see he was taking her indifference as a challenge.

With a wave, Mara disappeared into the lodge, leaving him standing with Wes and Jane.

"So, this is fun, huh?" Wes looked back and forth between them before settling his amused gaze on Toby. "After what you did to my sister in high school, I thought she'd never talk to you again, but here we are."

After what *he* did? "Ummm…"

"It wasn't a big deal." Jane's face turned stony. "It was a long time ago."

Toby watched her face carefully. Had her cheeks flushed? "It was a long time ago. But I'd say it was also kind of a big deal." Although, according to Jane back then, it had been a stupid kiss.

"When she called to tell me you asked Aubrey to the dance instead of her, I almost flew home from college to beat you up," Wes informed him.

Toby couldn't respond. He was stuck on why Jane would tell Wes he'd asked Aubrey to the dance *instead* of her. He turned to Jane. "You said you didn't like me." Right to his face, in front of all his friends. But she'd wanted to go to the dance with him?

"You're right. I didn't like you." Her unwavering glare suggested she didn't like him much at the moment either.

Jane turned to her brother. "I don't remember calling to tell you anything." The look on her face told a different story though. It was a change in her expression before she masked it—a twist of her mouth, almost like a wince. And then it was gone as quickly as it had come.

Wes obviously remembered a phone call though. And there must've been a reason she'd called her brother. She must've been upset. Toby angled his face to Jane's, looking directly into her eyes. "I would've asked you. If I'd thought you would've said yes." Instead of risking it, he'd tried to save his reputation.

A stunned expression parted her lips. How could she be surprised? He'd told her that night he liked her.

Wes gave his sister a questioning look, then slung an arm around her. "Well, anyway, I'm glad to see you guys worked it out. The three of us should hang out tonight."

Jane sidestepped him and avoided Toby's gaze. "I don't have time to hang out tonight."

Not with Toby anyway. The ice in her tone made that abundantly clear.

"Why not?" Her brother didn't seem to pick up on the tension crackling between them.

She crossed her arms, her shoulders tightening. "I have a lot of work to do."

"Aren't you a teacher?" Her brother obviously wasn't about to let her off the hook. "It's summer. You have plenty of free time."

Toby cleared a laugh out of his throat. How would she argue that?

"Yeah, well...professors still have a lot to do in the summer." Jane paused as though she had to think. "There's... you know...a lot. Plans and research and going over the curriculum."

Toby didn't buy it. She'd told him that her contract wasn't being renewed in the fall. "But how often are you going to be able to hang out with you brother and an old high school friend?"

Right. Friend. Jane did not want to be his friend based on the look she gave him. He could take a hint. He almost bailed her out by finding an excuse of his own, but before he could, Wes continued his argument. "Come on, sis. I haven't seen you since I flew out to Cali two years ago."

Jane shrugged. "I'm busy." She shifted her gaze to Toby. "You'd better be busy too, seeing as how we have a party to plan."

"Forget the party for a few hours. You were always busy," her brother countered. "Hiding in your room and doing homework or reading. It's time to live a little." He looked at Toby. "Right?"

"It's true. Being a workaholic isn't good for your health." He should know. Look where all of his overtraining and extreme competing had gotten him. "Besides, that new brewery I was telling you about is a pretty cool place."

Jane's eyes dulled. "You mean the one with cornhole and wings?"

"Cornhole and wings? Sounds perfect!" Wes all but shoved his sister in the direction of the parking lot. "We'll meet you there, Tobster."

Chapter Eight

"So, what's new with you?" Wes drove down the ranch's winding driveway like the tailpipe of his truck was on fire.

She'd forgotten how much fun it was to ride with him. Jane braced her hands against the dash and tried to think of something new with her. She and Wes talked every few months, and he always had so many stories to tell about his close calls in the arena. Usually, she did a whole lot more listening than talking.

Hmmm. There had to be something new she could tell him. And yet nothing came to her. "I took on teaching that extra class last semester. Intro to literary studies." Which was a level above the classes she'd taught previously, so that was something.

"That's not new." Wes hit the brakes and turned to face her. "Come on. There's gotta be something else going on in your life. Haven't you been going out at all? Dating?"

His obvious disappointment at her lack of a social life raised her defenses. "There was a fund-raiser for the university—" She stopped herself right there. "Fine. I have no social life outside of work. I admit it." She turned to look out the window. Why was that a problem? Why did everyone else always seem to care so much about her dating habits? She was fine on her own, thank you very much.

"Seriously?" Her brother nudged her shoulder. "When's the last time you went on a date, Janie?"

"There've been a few." She hiked up her shoulders, grasping at pride. "I was seeing a colleague from the math department recently." If six months ago counted as recent.

"The math department? Yikes," her brother muttered. But at least he started to drive again.

"He was *nice*." Just...she didn't know. Boring? Truthfully no man could hold a candle to the ones she made up in her head. Of course, she hadn't really made up her last hero completely out of the blue...

"Anyway, I don't have time for dating or going out. I'm trying to build a career." She let him think she was talking about becoming a professor. The last thing she needed was for her brother to read her innermost thoughts and emotions. Besides, she'd still likely have to go back to teach. After she finished rewriting this book, she'd start looking to pick up a few classes. In the meantime, she'd saved plenty to live on for the next several months. "What about you? Who's the lucky lady of the hour?" She'd discovered turning the questions back on him usually led to a long, drawn-out response.

"Oh, you know. There've been a few." Wes had mastered the noncommittal, playing-the-field tone.

"Right. A few." Over the years, she'd enjoyed giving him a hard time too. She knew for a fact there'd been more than a few women he'd connected with out on the circuit.

"Can't settle down when you're always on the go." Her brother slowed the truck as they turned onto Main Street with its squared brick buildings and the old west signs that showed traces of the town's mining history. It was rustic and practical—not showy like the bigger resorts in Vail or Aspen. The people here liked to say the town had character, its own sort of personality embodied in the tough, hardy people who'd lived here since the town had been founded.

After driving around the corner of the bank, her brother pulled into the parking lot of a new building that was set back off the street. It had a more modern appearance with clean lines and a lot of glass. The brewery equipment was visible through the windows.

Toby was visible too. He stood outside the main doors playing the part of the alluring cowboy. He wasn't wearing his hat, but he didn't need it to look rugged and outdoorsy. His tanned skin, weathered jeans, and well-built frame worked just fine. An electrical current bolted clear to her toes before Jane could lock down her emotions. The man was a smoking hot cowboy. She was simply reacting to him like every other woman would.

"I'm real glad you came." Her brother lurched the truck into a parking spot. "You need to get out more, sis. Live life to the fullest. You never know how much time you have. You should live it up while you can."

And that was where their philosophies diverged. Their father's accident had made Jane realize how fragile life was, how easily it could be taken away. She'd begged him not to go on that kayaking trip. She always worried when he went on one of his adventure trips. But he'd gone anyway. He'd hugged her and told her not to worry and then he'd gotten into his truck and driven off.

She turned to her brother. "So, by live it up you mean risking life and limb every time you go to work?" She didn't know why she even tried anymore. They'd had this conversation so many times. Since their dad died, Wes had taken every risk he could. She suspected he had fears of his own, fears that kept him in constant motion, not that he ever wanted to talk about that.

Sure enough, her brother pulled the keys out of the ignition. "All I'm saying is you've gotta make the most out of your time here."

Jane turned to him. "I do live life to the fullest." She dreamed up whole worlds and orchestrated adventures and scandals and red-hot romantic fantasies. And she didn't have to take one risk to do any of that. "You know, maybe you should settle down some." If he could pick on her lifestyle, she could just as well pick on his.

Wes blinked at her. "Yeah, I have no idea what you're talking about." He opened the door and bailed on the conversation before she could get in another word.

For a few seconds, she watched Toby and Wes from the window. She was surprised to see Toby had changed his clothes. He wore dark jeans and a plaid short-sleeved button-down shirt. It sure looked like he'd made an effort. A distinct stirring sensation rustled through her heart and she shooed it away. He didn't dress nicer for her. Toby had always put effort into his appearance.

Outside, Toby and Wes started to laugh about something. Jane climbed out of the truck and walked over to the sidewalk to meet them.

"Ready for some cornhole and wings?" Toby asked her with a tempting raise of his eyebrows.

"Can't wait." She gave the place a scrutinizing once-over. It actually looked inviting and chic.

"We were just talking about how she needs to get out more." Wes held open the door for them, and Jane shot him a look on her way in.

"What?" Her brother rested a patronizing hand on her shoulder. "Once in a while you need to let your hair down, have a little fun. Don't you think, Tobster?"

"Definitely." The man nodded. "Luckily, fun is my specialty. I'm here to help."

"I don't need help." Especially from him.

Jane scooted past them both and stepped into the main dining area. Even she had to admit it looked like a fun place. The concrete floors were polished and shiny, the walls were covered in corrugated metal, and the space was big enough to have lawn games spread around the interior. Cornhole, of course. But also ladder ball and a giant-sized Connect 4, and bowling pins.

"Great find." Wes led the way to the bar in the center of the room.

"I don't see anyone we know here." At the café this morning, she'd vaguely recognized pretty much everyone in the room.

"That's the nice part about this place." Toby ushered her in front of him as they maneuvered around tables. "It's new. You know how a lot of the old-timers around here don't trust new places."

Oh, yes. She knew. Back in the day, most new establishments were out of business within six months.

"So far most of the customers are river rats and hikers and thrill seekers who are staying in the area. It's a great place to come and relax," Toby said, the last part dropped to a whisper only she could hear.

Right. Like she'd ever be able to relax being this close to Toby. Something about him felt so unpredictable, so hard to nail down. He was a total show-off, and yet he still drove the same truck he'd had in high school. He clearly liked to be the center of attention, but at the café earlier that morning, he'd downplayed Beth and Ethan's gratitude for helping renovate their restaurant.

"We'll take three of your best beers," Wes said to the bartender.

"Oh, not for me, thanks," Jane called politely. "I don't drink much—"

"Hair down, sis." Her brother held up three fingers to the bartender with a definitive nod.

"Fine. One beer." God knew she couldn't have more than that—especially at this altitude.

"Three *Once in a Blue Spruces*," the bartender said, sliding over their glasses. "It's one of our most popular—traditional Belgian-style spiced with bitters and sweet orange peel." Jane had no idea what any of that meant, but she took her glass and thanked the man.

"Should we get a table?" Toby scanned the restaurant.

"Actually, you two find a table." Wes had locked his gaze on a group of women playing pool in the opposite corner. "I'll join you in a few."

A few hours or minutes? Jane didn't have to ask. This was her brother after all. He'd been successfully hitting on women since seventh grade. It had always been a big joke in their family, but now she could've killed him. He'd practically begged her to come here so they could spend time together and he was already ditching her. Worse yet, he was ditching her with Toby. And beer. Lethal combination.

"How about this one?" Toby led her to a quiet table near the windows with a view of the mountains.

"Sure." Jane wished her body could take a hint from her calm tone of voice and chill the heck out. Geez, her knees had softened, and her palms had gotten clammy, and warmth seemed to be creeping up her neck.

Toby sat against the wall, leaving the chair across from him for her. She settled into it, nearly spilling her beer, and corralled a nervous smile. "This is a nice place." If she did go out on a regular basis, she might come to some low-key neighborhood joint like this. With friends like Beth. Not with a dangerous cowboy.

"I'm glad you like it." Toby took a drink of his beer and then set down his glass, his gaze intensifying. "I meant what I said earlier. I would've asked you to that winter dance if I would've thought you'd say yes."

Jane gazed across the table at him, all but shaking her head as she sipped her beer. Maybe her seventeen-year-old self would've been tempted, but he didn't need to know that. "Well, you were right. I would've said no."

Toby's head titled like he was trying to figure her out. "Wes made it sound like you were upset."

"Oh, I was upset all right." Jane propped her chin on her hand and continued staring at him, the beer bringing a surge of boldness. "I was upset that I let you add me to the lengthy list of girls you kissed." Jane sipped more beer. "But like I said, it was years ago. I'm over it." Surprisingly as she looked across the table at Toby, she realized it was true. She *was* over it. Sure, it had been a surprise to see him again, but she wasn't awkward and insecure anymore. She didn't need any validation from him.

The longer he stared at her, the more his slow smile

spread until it fully reached the corners of his eyes. "Well, if you were upset...if I hurt your feelings, I'm sorry."

Damn those eyes. So convincing. But she wasn't falling for it.

"I did kiss a lot of girls." He said it like a confession. "But only one of them stuck with me."

What a line. Jane sat back and crossed her arms, letting her body language speak for her.

"I'm serious." His eyes went all puppy dog again. "There was always something about you. You were..." He paused as though he couldn't find the right word.

What was this? Toby Garrett was struggling to flirt? Jane watched his eyes shift.

"You were special," he finally finished. "My friends gave me hell after you said you didn't like me. So, I moved on. But I should've talked to you. I knew the whole kiss thing embarrassed you and I should've made sure you were okay. I'm sorry."

Jane lifted her beer for another sip. She couldn't decide what was crazier—that Toby Garrett was sitting here apologizing to her or that she was actually starting to believe him.

"Anyway, I get why you don't like me, but I hope you'll let me make it up to you," the man finished while Jane sucked down the last sip of her beer.

Oops. Had she really drained the whole glass? "Toby..." Tingles spread up her back, settling in over her shoulders. "You don't have to make it up to me. In fact, I'd really appreciate it if we could forget the whole thing ever happened." It would be a huge plus if she could forget how his lips had felt against hers, warm and firm, and...whew, it was hot in here.

"Okay. I just wanted you to know I didn't mean to

embarrass you," Toby said. He looked at her empty glass and then back at her. "How'd you like the beer?"

"It was really good." For the life of her she couldn't remember why she rarely drank. It made reality seem much softer, lighter. It made sitting across from this man easier. "In fact, I think I'll get another one."

"I can get it for you." Before she could move, Toby pushed to his feet. She watched him walk away, her head turning to follow him. *Oh, no. No, no, no.* She swung her head back to stare straight ahead. Straight. Ahead. Rule number one: do *not* look at his butt in those jeans.

The noise around her seemed to pick up some as the place got more crowded. Toby came back with her beer and set it in front of her. "Sorry that took so long. There was a big rush."

"No problem." There were no problems. All was right in the world. A comforting warmth swirled low in her stomach bringing contentment along with it. Her brother was still over on the other side of the room, making new friends, but who cared? He'd be proud of her. She shook her hair until it fell back over her shoulders. Yes, letting her hair down. It actually felt kind of nice.

Toby sat back down across from her. He looked nice. Smelled nice too. Now that they had that awkward conversation out of the way, they could move on.

"What?" He tilted his head and glanced around as though trying to figure out what she was looking at.

She shouldn't be looking at him so closely. She shouldn't be looking at him at all. They should do less looking and less touching. They should get up and away from this table. "You know something...I've never actually played cornhole."

The confession widened his eyes. "Never? You're serious?"

"I'm serious," she whispered then lifted her glass. Somehow the beer was already half gone.

"You want to try it?" He stood as though he'd been as antsy to get up from the table as she had. "I could teach you."

"Okay." Hands pressed into the tabletop, she stood, her knees a tad wobbly. Making sure to look steadier than she felt, she started to walk away.

"Don't forget your beer." Toby brought the glass along, holding his beer in the other hand.

"Right." Jane took the glass from him and dodged tables all the way to one of the cornhole setups.

"Okay." Toby set his beer on a nearby table before grabbing a few beanbags. "Basically, you want to throw the bag and try to get it through that hole." He pointed to the wooden platform about ten feet away.

"Got it." Jane took the beanbag from him and set down her beer. For a second, she tried to judge the distance from the platform, but the slight blur in her vision made it tricky. "Hmm. Okay." She closed one eye, then the other.

"Are you trying to calculate the distance in that big brain of yours or something?" Toby teased next to her. "Sometimes it's best just to go for it. Don't overthink it."

"Right." Go for it. She wound up and chucked the beanbag at the wooden platform. Surprisingly it hit the surface and slid up, eventually falling through the hole in the middle.

"Nice shot." Toby held up his hand for a high five. She made a move to slap his hand, but her foot caught on a chair leg and sent her stumbling.

The cowboy caught her in his arms and righted her footing. Jane turned and suddenly his face came so close, those amazing lips stopping mere inches from hers. A breath sliced through her lungs and some wild instinct gave her a push. *Don't overthink it.*

"Excuse me," someone interrupted before she pressed her lips to his. Jane turned her head toward the voice.

A woman about her age stood a foot away from them. "I'm sorry to interrupt, but aren't you Toby Garrett?"

It took him a good five seconds to answer. "Uh. Yeah."

Jane backed herself out of his arms, embarrassment heating her cheeks.

"I thought that was you! We're huge rodeo fans." The woman frantically waved some of her friends over. "We were hoping we could get a picture with you. Oh! And could you sign our drink coasters?"

Toby's distracted gaze drifted back to Jane. "I'm not sure now is a good time—"

"It's a great time." Jane smiled at the group of women encircling Toby. In fact, their timing couldn't have been better.

Chapter Nine

Just one more picture!" The woman who'd introduced herself as Taven slung her arm around Toby. There'd already been so many pictures with the cell phone cameras flashing in his face, he was seeing spots. Once again, he smiled and posed.

"Here." Another woman shoved a cardboard drink coaster into his hands. "Can you sign this one for my sister? Her name's Jessica."

"Sure." Toby took the pen someone else handed him and scrawled his signature across it before handing it back. "All right, ladies. I should get back to my..." He almost said date, but that wouldn't be accurate. "Friend." At least it had seemed Jane had warmed up to him. He could've sworn she'd been considering kissing him again too, before they'd gotten swarmed.

"Thanks again," Taven called waving. "Good luck with the injury!"

"Thanks." He turned to head to the table he'd shared

with Jane, but she wasn't there. In fact...he scanned the restaurant. She didn't seem to be anywhere.

"I think I saw the woman you were with leave," one of Taven's friends called helpfully. "She went out the front door probably ten minutes ago."

Great. "Thanks."

Sidestepping the crowd, Toby hurried outside and scanned the parking lot. No sign of Jane. He jogged to the sidewalk and turned onto Main Street. Only a few people walked along the storefronts. Since the shops were already closed for the day, the streets were mostly deserted. Jane must've gone the other way. He reversed course and nearly ran into Wes as the man walked out the doors.

"I heard someone say Jane left." Her brother eyed him with amusement. "I walk away for two minutes and you lose my sister?"

"We got ambushed." Toby moved past him so he could see down the other side of the street. "But I should've refused to do the pictures." He should've ignored everyone else and focused on Jane. She'd always hated to be the center of attention. No wonder she'd walked out on him. Eight years ago and just now.

"She's around here somewhere." Wes walked alongside him. "Why'd she run off anyway?"

"I'm not exactly sure." He decided not to share his guess. "She couldn't have gotten far." She didn't have a car, so she had to be somewhere on foot.

They walked down the block, but even the residential side of town seemed quiet and empty.

"We're not gonna find her walking around." Wes pulled him back in the direction of the brewery. "Let's get in my truck. We can cover more ground."

"I guess." He squinted, searching the sidewalks across

the street, frustration boiling up. He had to talk to her. When he'd sat across the table and apologized to her, the truth of his words had hit him. Jane had stuck with him. All these years. She was special. He couldn't pinpoint the exact moment he'd met Aubrey or any other girl he'd kissed, but he clearly remembered the first moment he'd met Jane.

His family had just moved to Silverado Lake and he'd walked into a brand-new third-grade classroom, still staggering under the enormity of what he'd lost. The teacher had assigned him a seat next to Jane. He still remembered the way she'd looked at him, with a friendly curiosity. When the class started, they'd had to work a math problem together, and they must've argued for ten minutes about the best way to get the answer. Jane seemed to challenge everything he said, and it had distracted him from everything else that had been going on his life. She'd made him feel more normal than he'd felt since before his brother had died.

Toby followed Wes back to the brewery's parking lot. "She has to be here somewhere." She definitely couldn't walk all the way to the ranch. Maybe she'd gone to Beth and Ethan's place.

They climbed into Wes's truck and took a left. "Maybe she's walking back to the ranch," her brother suggested.

"That would be a long walk." Though Toby wouldn't put it past her. He'd seen how stubborn she could be. "Remember that competition we did sophomore year for charity?"

Wes started to laugh.

The school had done a weekend competition to see who could stay awake the longest, and each of the contestants had gotten sponsors. Most people had dropped out within the first twenty-four hours, but not Jane, and that had meant Toby couldn't either. He couldn't fall asleep and let her outdo him. Thirty-two hours into the competition, he couldn't stay awake anymore. He'd fallen asleep face-first in the burrito he'd been eating for dinner.

"You two were always going at it in school." Wes cruised through town on the route they would take back to the ranch, but there was no sign of Jane. "I think she always liked you if you want to know the truth."

"She said she didn't." But he was beginning to wonder.

"Of course she said she didn't." Wes shook his head as though he couldn't believe Toby didn't get it. "She changed after our dad died. We all did. But Jane... she took it the hardest. She didn't want to do anything. She was already shy, but it was like she stopped caring about putting herself out there." Wes pulled up to the stoplight and looked at him. "It's hard to understand unless you've been through it, but none of us came out unscathed."

He understood that better than Wes knew. Only instead of pulling away from everything, he'd constantly looked for distractions. "I should've treated her more carefully back then." He'd been too immature, always worried about his reputation, of what people thought of him. His girlfriends had been more of a status symbol than anything else. If he was honest that was every relationship he'd ever had. But it wasn't like that with Jane. When he'd kissed her all those years ago, it had simply been because he'd felt drawn to her. And he'd felt that way again in the bar tonight.

"It's probably a good thing you didn't date her." Wes nodded and started driving when the light turned green. "I might've had to kick your ass and then we wouldn't have been friends."

"That would've been fair." Jane was the kind of woman who deserved more, who needed more than a superficial relationship. She was smart, sure, but she also had this depth that spooked him and intrigued him at the same time.

"Let's go by Beth's." Toby turned both their attention back to the mission. It had been a good twenty minutes since Jane had run out of the brewery and they hadn't seen her on the streets.

"Roger that." Wes made an abrupt turn onto a side street and Toby gave him directions from there. When they pulled up though, the house was dark and neither Ethan nor Beth's cars were parked out front.

"Where else would she go?" Wes let the truck idle next to the curb. "I don't get why she's hiding anyway."

Hiding. Now he felt like an idiot. One thing Toby knew about Jane was that when she wanted to hide, she always found a book. "Go to the library." Better yet…"Why don't you go back and hang out with your friends at the brewery? I'll head to the library in my truck." Then he could see Jane alone, without her brother razzing her about what had happened.

"You sure? I'm happy to talk to her. She takes everything way too serious. She needs to lighten up a little."

Yeah, talk like that definitely wouldn't help. "I'm sure. The last thing your sister wants right now is to be ambushed with a lecture." Toby didn't plan to lecture her. Hell, he didn't plan to say anything. He just wanted to make sure she was okay.

"I guess you're right." Wes pulled out into the street and headed back to the brewery. "Why do you think she's at the library?"

Toby didn't think she was at the library. He *knew*. He

couldn't believe he hadn't thought of it before. "Just trust me. She practically lived there back in high school. Don't you remember?"

"Yeah. My mom used to send me over to drag her home." Wes swung the truck into a parking spot and Toby hopped out before he could cut the engine. "See you later," he called, digging for his keys. He got into his truck and drove to the library, parking out front. They were only open until eight, which gave him twenty minutes to find her. He slipped through the doors and strode to the counter. Luckily, Lucinda was working. She happened to be one of those take-no-nonsense librarians who kept a watchful eye on everyone who walked into her space.

"Toby!" She rushed around the counter to greet him. Though he'd done his best to keep his donation for the rebuild anonymous, he knew people had their suspicions. Still he'd never admit to it or everyone would find out about the loss his family refused to acknowledge. It was better to let everyone speculate. "So good to see you! What brings you by this evening?"

"I'm looking for someone." Lucinda likely wouldn't recognize Jane, being a recent transplant to Silverado Lake, so he went with a description. "Long dark hair, about the same height as you, and she was wearing jeans"—which hugged her curves nicely—"and a light blue shirt."

"Oh, I definitely saw her," the woman said with suspicion. "Didn't recognize her as anyone I know."

"She's a friend," Toby told her. More than a friend? A friend he wanted to kiss every eight years? There was really no good way to describe their relationship.

Lucinda's scowl softened. "Well I tracked her to the romance section, but then I had to help someone with the research database, so I lost her. You can start there though. She couldn't have gotten too far."

That was the same thing he'd been thinking for the last half hour. And she hadn't been too far. If only he would've realized it sooner. "Thanks, Lucinda. I'm sure I'll find her." Unless she'd somehow slipped out without being seen. He walked past the kids' section conducting a quick search in the rows of colorful picture books, then continued past reference to the back where they kept the fiction collection. There were only a few people milling around. No one he knew well. Once he reached the romance section, he moved row by row. At the very end of the last section Jane sat curled up in a chair. She had a book suspended in front of her face as though she didn't want anyone to see her. There was no disguising those legs though.

Toby headed to her, keeping quiet until he stood right in front of her. "*A Farewell to Arms*," he read from the cover. "There's some light reading for you."

Jane didn't lower the book. "Some say it's Hemingway's greatest masterpiece," she said, her voice muffled behind the pages.

Toby sat in the overstuffed chair next to her, but she shifted the book so he still couldn't see her face. "I don't know," he said thoughtfully. "I found *A Farewell to Arms* depressing."

"It's tragic," Jane corrected. "Not depressing. There's a difference." Even with the book muffling her voice, that competitive edge still came through.

"I think *Old Man and the Sea* is his greatest work." Hemingway had gotten a Pulitzer Prize to back up that argument.

Slowly, slowly, slowly, the book began to lower. "He wrote forty-seven different endings for *Farewell to Arms*."

Her eyes held a challenge. "Forty-seven. Just to get the perfect ending."

"And yet it's still a little depressing." Toby settled in. He could argue with this woman all day, watching her face color, passion brighten her eyes. Though he wasn't nearly as well read as her, he liked to try to keep up. "*Old Man and the Sea* has a better theme—a person can be destroyed but not defeated."

Jane dropped the book into her lap, her eyes zeroing in on his. "And in *A Farewell to Arms*, Hemingway explores the violent pull between two polar opposite positions—love and violence."

"Love and violence," Toby repeated. "In that book, it's hard to tell which one wins out." He studied her face and smiled. "Most people would like to think love always wins."

"And some people would argue that love is dangerous. That it hurts too much. That it always ends with loss." Shadowed emotion seemed to darken Jane's eyes.

"Those people would be right. It definitely hurts." He let her see it in him—the emotion, the understanding. "But I've heard people say if the love is deep enough, it's worth the loss." He'd tried to use his loss for good. It had driven him to ride, to accomplish things his brother never could. But like Wes had said earlier, he hadn't come out of it unscathed.

"I suppose it is," Jane murmured, studying him. "But that doesn't make it any less painful."

"No, it doesn't." Something clicked inside of him. An instinct to take away her pain, to show her a different side of love. It was a new feeling for him. What the hell was he supposed to do with it? It's not like he was qualified to show anyone a thing about love.

After a few seconds, a long sigh dropped Jane's shoulders as though she simply wanted him to leave her alone. "What're you doing here anyway?"

"Finding you," he said casually. No need to spook her. He'd keep things light. That's what he did. That's what he was good at.

"I don't want to be found." Jane started to raise the book back up, but Toby reached over and lowered it to her lap.

"Why?" He genuinely wanted to know, to understand. "Why'd you run out?"

"It wasn't my scene." Jane shrugged. "And let's be honest, there was some awkwardness between us in high school, but you don't have to apologize. You don't have to make it up to me by being all nice and flirty. I don't need that."

"I know you don't need it." She didn't need anything from him. That's not why he was here. "I wasn't saying what I thought you wanted to hear." For once he'd said what he felt. "But you don't believe me."

"Why would I?" She sat up straighter. "You've always had it all. You've always been outgoing, charming, smart, funny. Everyone has always liked you." She stopped abruptly like listing off his attributes embarrassed her. "You've never dealt with anything difficult."

That showed how little she knew about him. How little most people knew. Though she was right about one thing. "I don't know how to deal with anything difficult." He couldn't let her continue to believe his life had been all sunshine and roses. That wasn't a fair assessment. He knew something about loss too. "So I don't deal with things. I tend to ignore things." After Tanner had died, he'd tried to make everything okay. He'd tried to make his parents happy. He'd tried to fill the hole his brother had left, and he'd never stopped trying. For the first time he considered what that burden had cost him.

"Sometimes I wish I knew how to ignore things." Jane slowly raised her head again. "I've never been good at that."

"And I've never been good at apologies." He hadn't taken the opportunity to practice much. "But the one I gave you was still real." Something about Jane made him want real.

A small smile softened her expression. "It was a fine apology. Just unnecessary."

He wasn't so sure about that. If he hadn't been so obsessed with his reputation back in high school, he might've realized Jane had been hurting. He might've thought about how hard those years after her dad's death had been for her. He should've. He'd been through it himself.

The lights flickered. "The library will be closing in ten minutes," the librarian's pleasant voice warned over the loudspeaker. "Please make your way to the checkout desk."

Jane abruptly stood, looking almost as relieved as he was to escape this conversation. She walked over to the shelf in the classics section and wedged the book she'd been holding back in among the other Hemingways.

Toby stood too. "You're not going to check it out?" he asked, nodding toward *A Farewell to Arms*.

She shrugged. "I've read it four times."

"Maybe you should read *The Old Man and the Sea* again." He came to stand by her. "Or better yet, maybe you should check out something from the romance section."

"Why do you say that?" Jane's eyes went a little too wide.

"I don't know." He thought back to their earlier conversation. "Isn't a romance all about how love is risky but also worth it?" He walked to the end of the long shelf and glanced at a display of books. Looked like historical westerns judging from the mountains and the cowboys on the covers. "Take this one for example . . ." He picked one up. *Mountain Destiny* by E. J. Mattingly. "Maybe you'll find it inspiring." Toby went to hand it to Jane, but she'd frozen in place.

"We should go." She turned away from him, walking briskly toward the exit, but Lucinda stepped out from behind one of the shelves.

"Toby." She checked her watch. "I'm sorry, but I'm afraid it's time to clear out."

"We were on our way." He looked ahead to where Jane had stalled.

"That's a wonderful book." Lucinda pointed to the paperback he still held in his hands. "A real favorite around here, that's for sure."

Jane slowly crept back to them.

"I'm dying to get the author in here for one of our quarterly author visits," the librarian said. "Unfortunately, no one will reveal the writer's identity. It definitely has to be someone from Colorado though."

"What makes you say that?" Jane asked, inching closer. Toby watched her. She was acting strange. Almost afraid . . .

"Well it's obvious." Lucinda picked up another copy of the book. "You should read the descriptions of the mountains. If I didn't know better, I'd say the author was talking about our mountains right outside."

Jane's jaw dropped open, and Toby didn't miss the way her eyes shifted like they had before she'd run away from him at the bar. Something had her spooked again.

"No one knows the author, huh?" He studied the book's back cover and read the short, nondescript bio: "E. J. Mattingly is a writer, history buff, and a college professor. This is the author's first novel."

Toby looked up and caught Jane's desperate stare. Was she embarrassed because she'd read the book and didn't want anyone to know?

"I've been doing a lot of research trying to track down the author." Lucinda carefully set the book back on the display. "Think of what it would do for our little library if we were able to host the elusive E. J. Mattingly."

"It can't be that hard to find out who it is." Toby tucked the book under his arm.

"What're you doing?" A look of panic flared Jane's eyes wider.

"I'm going to check this baby out. Maybe I can help find the person who wrote it."

"That would be wonderful!" Lucinda gushed.

"You're going to read a romance novel?" Jane's expression walked the line between skepticism and dread. "You won't like it. There's no way."

"How do you know?" He flipped through some of the pages. What had her so freaked out?

"I've read it." Jane's face colored. "Trust me. It's not your kind of book."

"Not so sure about that. I've been in the mood for something different. I mean, I know it's not *A Farewell to Arms*, but the cover looks promising." And maybe if he read it, he could figure out why Jane obviously didn't want him to check it out.

Chapter Ten

Jane's fingers flew over the keyboard, barely able to keep up with the swift current of ideas that had carried her away.

After Toby had dropped her off last night, she'd sat down at her computer and hadn't moved since, minus a few trips to the bathroom and to refill her tea. After making all her phone calls to get things in order for the party, she'd opened up a new document and started a whole new draft of her novel. Her eyes were dry and her hands were cramping, but a giddiness rose through her as she watched the words spill across the computer screen.

Toby drew her in closer…

Whoa. Hold the horses. She backed up the cursor to make the critical correction. *Amos.* Amos was the hero in her story, not Toby. She shook her head. She had that same jittery sensation that had overtaken her when Toby had caught her in his arms at the brewery. She'd take the jitters, though, since they seemed to have brought her writing mojo back to her.

If only she could keep her mind from wandering. She kept replaying that moment in the brewery—she'd almost kissed him for god's sake. She'd run out so she could get herself together. And then she'd about dropped her book on the floor when he'd shown up at the library looking for her. She'd figured his fans at the brewery would've kept him occupied for hours.

A text buzzed on her phone and showed up in the top corner of her computer screen. Dang it, she should've turned it off. Only it was Beth.

SOS—need backup ASAP!!!!!!!! Grandma B is in the house!!!! See you here in 10?

Her maid of honor duties were calling. How about 30? Jane typed back. She should take a few extra minutes to shower and make herself presentable.

It took more like thirty-five minutes, but finally she pulled up in front of Beth and Ethan's house.

"Oh my God, save me." Beth bolted out the front door the second Jane parked next to the curb.

"Having fun?" Jane called through the open window.

Her friend opened the door and climbed into the car. "Why didn't we elope? Seriously, Janie. What was I thinking? So far all my grandmother has done since she got to town was talk about how inappropriate it is that Ethan and I are living together before the wedding."

"That's what grandmothers are for," Jane told her. Or so she'd heard. With her father's parents moving to France before she was born and her mother's parents passing away in a car accident when Jane was two years old, she'd never gotten to know her own grandmothers.

"I don't know how she manages to do it, but she can

judge you without saying a word." Beth let her head fall back to rest against the seat. "And she's here for a month." Wide panicked eyes found Jane's. "A. Month."

"Well, I suppose it's not too late to elope." Jane cut the engine. That wasn't an option and they both knew it. Still, they could dream for a few minutes. "We could kidnap Ethan, drive to the airport, and fly to Hawaii." Now that was Jane's idea of the perfect wedding—barefoot on the beach somewhere.

"You know we'd have to bring Toby too, right?" Beth asked.

Oh right. There was that.

Jane lifted one shoulder in a shrug. "It would be fine if Toby came." She wouldn't be as opposed to it as she would've been once.

"Really?" Beth's eyebrows shot up. "Well, someone is sure changing her tune."

"I don't hold a grudge." Especially when he happened to be feeding some serious inspiration into her writing. She'd written more compelling scenes after spending a few hours with Toby than she'd written in the last six months. She'd better not hold a grudge. She needed the ideas to keep flowing.

"Seriously, though, Jane." Beth's friend's eyes filled with tears. "We should've done a destination wedding. It would've been so much less stressful."

"Don't worry." She squeezed her friend's hand to remind her she wasn't in this wedding business alone. "Everything will be fine." In the last two months, Jane had read everything she could about being a maid of honor. She'd never been asked before. Unlike many of her female acquaintances, she didn't have a whole closet full of hideous bridesmaid dresses she'd never wear again.

In all the articles she'd read, she learned that one of her main jobs was to offer the bride emotional support and do whatever she could to lessen the stress. Since she'd made so much progress on her rewrites she had the whole day to emotionally support her friend. Besides, hanging out with Beth would distract her from wondering if Toby had read her book. He couldn't know she'd written it—she'd been too careful—but, still, what if he recognized Beau as a fictional relative of his? Okay, not so much a relative as a spitting image? What if he discovered she was getting inspiration from him now?

"I really appreciate you coming." Her friend flipped down the visor mirror and started to dab at her eyes. "Of course, my parents won't get here until next week, so they can't run interference. Their beach house in the Bahamas is getting a new roof this week and I can't do this alone."

"You're not alone," Jane reminded her. "We'll just have to keep your grandmother happy and calm until they arrive." Jane said it as though that would be the easiest task in the world.

"Okay." Her friend inhaled deeply through her nose and then exhaled as though trying to rid her body of all the tension. "We have to go back in there. If I leave her unattended too long, she'll start to snoop through my things. All hell will break loose if she finds my lingerie drawer."

Jane couldn't hold back a giggle. "I'd actually like to see that. We'll probably walk in to find a bonfire in your bedroom. She'll be burning your lacy bras and G-strings." They both climbed out of the car laughing.

"Thank goodness you're here." Her friend linked their arms together as they walked up the sidewalk. "Seriously.

I don't know how I'd get through any of this without you. I've missed you so much."

"I've missed you too." Tears gathered in her eyes, taking her by surprise. When was the last time anyone had said that to her?

"Brace yourself." Beth stepped ahead to open the door, and then gestured for her friend to go inside first. Jane walked into the entryway without batting an eye. Working at a university that was constantly trying to secure donations for the endowment, she dealt with snobby judgmental types all the time.

"She's in the living room," Beth whispered behind her, like they were entering a haunted house and about to confront the ghost.

Putting on her friendly-yet-reserved smile, Jane marched through the foyer and down the small hallway until the house opened up into the cozy living room.

Jane had pictured Grandma B as an intimidating presence, but the woman facing the extensive bookshelf in Beth's living room couldn't have stood much over four and a half feet. Her white hair was cut into a bob and styled beautifully, and it seemed everything she was wearing was cashmere. Before Jane could greet her, Bernadette snatched a book off the shelf and held it up. "*Fifty Shades of Grey*?" The woman whirled, facing her and Beth. "You've read this?"

Beth seemed to shrink, so Jane moved in closer to the woman. She might not know much about hair and dresses and what to giggle over at a girls' night out, but this she could do. "It's actually a very interesting psychological case study," Jane said, smiling pleasantly. "Hello, Ms. Wilmer. I'm Jane Harding."

"Jane taught literature at Cal Poly," Beth chimed in

from behind her. "She's very smart. And she's my best friend in the whole world."

Sneaky tears pricked the corners of Jane's eyes again. She had to admit, she'd kind of missed being someone's best friend in the whole world.

"A professor?" Beth's grandmother gave her a long, silent appraisal. "And you condone reading smut?"

"No one uses the world 'smut' to describe romance or erotic novels anymore." She spoke in her professor voice. "Not only is it a top-selling genre, it's also a gateway for female empowerment."

The woman didn't seem to know what to say to that. Jane sat on the couch and gestured for Bernadette to sit beside her. "What do you enjoy reading?"

"Mystery." The woman sat beside her, still looking bewildered but also intrigued. "The old mysteries. Mary Higgins Clark. Agatha Christie. The ones without sex or all the vulgar language," she added.

"I'm a big fan of those writers too," Jane agreed. "But I do have to say, there are so many talented mystery writers who are taking the genre in wonderful new directions. I mean, there's a lot more diversity now. And they make the stories relatable."

"Um, I think I'll go make us some tea." Beth backed out of the room and disappeared as though worried an argument was coming.

Jane wasn't worried at all. "I'm telling you, some of the greatest mysteries I've read have been written in the last ten years. These are the can't-figure-out-who-done-it, keep-you-up-all-night kind of mysteries." She could list about twenty right now.

Interest lit the woman's eyes. "I suppose I wouldn't mind taking some suggestions. Since you're a literature professor and all. My book club used to have the liveliest discussions, but I'm afraid all my reader friends have moved away."

Jane felt a twinge of sympathy for the older woman. What would it be like to have no one to share your love of books with?

The doorbell rang.

"Can you get that?" Beth called from the kitchen.

"Sure." Jane stood, smiling over her shoulder at Bernadette. "I'll write down some of my favorite authors for you. Maybe you can take some time to read while you're staying here, and we can meet to discuss the books."

Bernadette actually smiled. "That would be lovely."

The doorbell rang again. "Coming," Jane called. "I'll be right back." She walked away and swung open the front door.

Toby stood on the porch. One look at him and her tongue seemed to tie itself in knots. She would much rather discuss books with Grandma B than with Toby right now. "Oh. Um. Huh." Her thoughts raced. Had he read her book? Did he realize he was the star of the story? Her gaze fixated on his lips. Lips that had seriously tempted her last night…

"Hi." The man served up one of his eye-catching grins.

"Hey." Jane couldn't seem to get out any other words. What was that about being strong and capable again?

"We have a situation," Toby said quietly. He peered over her shoulder like he wanted to make sure Beth wasn't around.

"A *situation*." Fabulous. He knew. He'd recognized something in her book that gave her away. Had she accidentally used one of his catchphrases? Jane inhaled a deep meditative breath and closed her eyes. "What do you mean we have a situation?"

"It's probably better if I show you," he whispered, leaning closer.

Wait, was he wearing cologne? Jane inhaled. Mmmm. He smelled undeniably clean and masculine and sexy. Hey, she should remember that line and write it into her book...

"We have to go to the ranch," Toby said slowly, as though afraid he'd lost her.

"Huh?" Jane inhaled again. Was that a note of sandalwood in his scent too?

"The ranch." The beginnings of a grin danced at the corners of his lips. "There's a situation at the ranch, and I need your help."

"Oh." She tried to refocus. "You want me to go to the ranch with you?"

"Yes." Toby looked past her again. "It has to do with the party."

Ah, why wasn't she surprised? "It has to do with the party that's happening tonight? The party you promised we could deliver in a day?" she asked, letting her amusement show. It would be a little late for her to fix any situations now. She'd made a few quick phone calls to the winery, and it turned out they had the bandwidth to deliver both the wine and some tapas, so her part had been easy.

"It has to do with the party we're pulling off *together*." He said the word with a meaningful raise of his eyebrows. "But if you don't want to help me, I can always see if we can move the party to the brewery. I'd love to finish that cornhole lesson we started."

Ha. That hadn't been a lesson in cornhole as much as it had been a reminder on why she didn't drink. She definitely would not end up in Toby's arms again, inspiration or not. "I'll be right back." Jane closed the door and stepped into the living room. Beth was just bringing a tray of tea to the coffee table.

"Um, so I need to head over to the ranch," Jane announced.

"What? Now?" Her friend nearly dropped the tray, bringing it to the table with a clatter.

"Yes." She calmed her with a squeeze of her shoulder. "Only for a little while. I have to"—*save Toby's amazing butt*—"take care of a few last-minute details for the party."

"Last minute?" Bernadette frowned. "I hope nothing's wrong. I told Beth having the events at an old run-down ranch wouldn't do, but of course she didn't listen."

"The ranch is beautiful." Jane did her best not to snap. "Rustic, yes, but you won't find a more beautiful setting for a wedding or any other event. Besides," she went on, unable to stop herself. "The most important thing about a wedding is celebrating as a family. Spending time together. Wishing the bride and groom well as they start their new life together. Don't you think?"

"Well, of course," the woman said quickly.

"I'll text Beth some of those authors I was talking about earlier." Who knew, maybe reading some of her recommendations would help the woman lighten up. Jane pulled out her phone and fired off a few names. "You two can run to the library and check out some books. Maybe we can meet for coffee to discuss one on Monday."

"I'm not sure I'll have time to read much. We have so many details to attend to—" the woman started.

"I'll bet you'll find some time." With any luck, she'd spend the entire weekend with her nose in a book, so she'd leave Beth alone. "Trust me. You won't be able to put these books down."

Thank you, Beth mouthed as Jane left the room.

Jane acknowledged her with a nod. "I'll see you both soon," she called happily. Once she slipped out the door, the gumption she'd displayed in front of Beth's grandmother wilted.

Toby waited on the porch.

For once he didn't seem to be oozing confidence, and she had to admit…she liked seeing past his charming cowboy façade.

"Sorry to drag you away from Beth." Toby led the way to their cars. "I couldn't find Wes, and the maintenance staff is swamped today. I'm not sure I can handle this alone."

Good God. What were they dealing with? "Do you want to prep me?" Jane had never been one for surprises, and judging from Toby's wariness, she definitely wasn't going to like this one.

Toby opened her driver-side door for her. "I think you better see for yourself."

Chapter Eleven

Toby stopped Jane outside the door to the barn. "Hold on." He'd best prepare her for what they were about to walk into. "So, an hour ago I was finishing up the party preparations"—and by that he meant *starting* the preparations—"and I heard a weird noise."

Jane's eyebrows inched higher. "What kind of noise?"

"A squeaking sound." Damn…there went that shudder down his spine again. He could still hear the sound, like nails on a chalkboard. There was no way to sugarcoat this situation. "There're bats in there."

"Bats?" Jane lurched back a step.

"Afraid so." He wanted to lurch back too. He could handle many things—a black bear, a moose, hell, he'd even face a mountain lion. But a bat? Nothing was creepier than a flying rodent. "So, what're we going to do?"

"*We?*" Jane laughed.

"What's so funny?" This was a huge problem. They couldn't have a party in a bat-infested barn.

"You came to get me so I could rescue you." The woman seemed to find that hilarious.

If it had been anyone else ribbing him, he might've let pride take over and figured this out himself, but he couldn't get enough of Jane's smile. Even if it came at his expense, he'd take it. "I'm okay with being rescued by a pretty lady. Not a problem for me."

"Oh please." She laughed again and then gasped in a breath. "No amount of flirting is going to help you here, mister. What am I supposed to do? Run in there and karate chop them or something?" Shoulders still shaking with laughter, she started to walk away. "That's good, Toby. Thanks, I needed a laugh. But it was your idea to have the party in this barn, so I'm out."

"Hold on." He fell in step beside her. "If we don't clear the bats out, we can't have the party in there."

"*We?*" Jane turned to face him as though trying to decide if he was serious. "*We* didn't want the party in the old barn. I distinctly remember *you* thinking it was a great idea. We could've asked my mom to move around the schedule for the reception hall, but you said it would be fine in the barn."

Energy lit up her eyes, drawing his gaze to hers. Yeah, he'd definitely be fine with Jane rescuing him. "Like it or not, we're in this together." And he definitely wasn't complaining. "Think about Beth. She's counting on both of us to pull off this party without a hitch. We promised her it would be perfect."

Jane's gloating smile tightened into a scowl. She wasn't laughing now.

"We can't let this ruin the party," he went on, seeing he almost had her. "And I can't get rid of the bats alone." That was definitely a two-person job. She was the maid of honor so that automatically roped her into all wedding-related responsibilities. That's why he'd tracked her down. Well, that and he couldn't stop thinking about her after he'd dropped her off last night. And she may or may not have been the first thing on his mind when he'd woken up this morning too. They might be partners in this whole wedding business, but he'd never minded mixing business with pleasure.

Jane stared at him, and he could see the wheels in her head spinning. She was trying to think of any way out, but she wouldn't bail on him because loyalty meant something to her. Might as well add that to the list of things he liked about her.

"So, are you going to help me?" he asked again.

"Of course." Jane paced away a few steps then whirled back to him. "I know! We'll call someone. A pest person. I'm sure there's someone around here who knows exactly how to handle bats."

There was one problem with her plan though. "I called the pest control guy in town and he's in Denver for the weekend."

"Well, call another one."

Like he hadn't thought of that. "There isn't another one. I called every pest control company within three hours of Silverado Lake and none of them can make the trip before tonight."

"Okay." Jane seemed to swallow extra hard. "Well you're a big, bad bull rider. You'll have to go in there and get the bats. You'll have to capture them and then set them free outside."

While he appreciated the vote of confidence, solving this problem wouldn't be that easy. "They're up in the rafters. So, one of us is going to have to scare them down and one of us is going to have to capture them in a bag." He'd already searched YouTube for a solution—and had seen many fails in the process. "The best way to do this is by spraying them with the hose. It won't kill them, but they'll have to land on the ground, then you can throw the bag over them."

Jane visibly shuddered. "*Me?*"

He rested his hand on her shoulder, feeling her warmth beneath his fingertips. "You can totally do this." Being the gentleman that he was, he figured bagging the bats would be easier than climbing the ladder. Whoever sprayed them might get dive-bombed.

"Getting the bats in the bag is the hard job," she informed him. "You have to get close to the bats."

"Fine. You can climb the ladder and spray the water. I already got the ladder set up, so that's ready to go. Trash bags are right inside the door."

Jane's face seemed to have paled, but she nodded. "You'll owe me for this one though, Garrett."

"I'm sure I can think of a way to repay you." He flashed her his rowdiest grin. He couldn't resist. Sure, she didn't fit into his long-term plans—and he likely didn't fit into hers either, but that didn't mean they couldn't have any fun while they helped out their friends.

Jane glared back at him, but it was more playful than dangerous. "Unfortunately for you I only accept cash." Turning away from him, she plowed through the barn door like a woman on a mission.

Smiling to himself, Toby followed her into the dimly lit outbuilding. It only took a few seconds for the squeaks and squawks to start again. Cringing, he edged up against the wall and plugged in the cord for the white globe lights he'd already hung throughout the room. Jane looked above where they stood, her shoulders scrunched with what looked to be disgust. "Do they bite?" she half whispered.

He decided not to answer that. "The hose is right here. It's already on. You'll just have to pull the trigger." He handed her the nozzle and walked her to the ladder. "You don't have to climb all the way up. Probably about half-way as long as your aim is good."

She seemed to take the words as a challenge. "My aim is good. Trust me. I never miss."

"Make sure you don't, or they'll start flying around like crazy and we'll never get them down." He shuddered again thinking about the bats swooping over their heads.

Seeming to hold her breath, Jane took the hose and started to climb the ladder, slowly moving up one rung and then another.

The bats were hanging out—literally—in the corner where the roofline met the far wall. Calm for now, but he'd seen enough on YouTube to know all hell was about to break loose. "Tell me when you're going to spray, and I'll grab the bag." Even as he said it, he knew there was no way this would all go according to plan.

"How much farther should I go?" Jane hissed.

Toby looked up. That was a mistake. They might be on flying rodent patrol, but he couldn't *not* admire her ass in those jeans. What had she asked him again?

"Hello?" She turned to peer down at him and he quickly steered his gaze away from her backside. "Can you stop checking out my butt and focus on the mission please?"

Okay, so he hadn't looked away fast enough. "Don't blame me. Blame the jeans." He grinned up at her. "Let's go with two more steps up and then spray."

"Right." Jane crept up two more rungs and then lifted

the hose, aiming it in the direction of the bats. "Count of three."

Keeping one hand on the ladder, Toby reached for the trash bag with the other.

"Three, two, one." Jane pulled the trigger, shooting the water directly at the bats. They screeched and flew, swooping right at her.

The woman screamed and tried to duck but lost her balance, pitching backward. Toby dropped the bag on the ground and raised his arms just in time to catch her. They both fell to the ground with a thud, but thankfully he took the brunt of the impact.

Jane's eyes had opened wider. Somehow, she'd ended up on top of him, her lips hovering near his. He dropped his gaze to her mouth.

"Toby!" she squealed. "The bats!"

Bats? What bats? He looked to where her horrified gaze had frozen. A few feet away, the bats were flopping around on the ground, trying to fly but their soaked wings were keeping them grounded. For the moment. "You got 'em." He carefully rolled her off him and scrambled to his feet, snatching the bag on the way.

"Okay, no big deal." He eased closer to the animals. "I'm just gonna wrap you up in this bag and then I'll set you free. I swear."

Somewhere nearby Jane started to giggle. "You sound like the bat whisperer."

Even with the tension pumping through him, he laughed too. "Easy now." He started to open the bag. Damn, they looked like vermin with wings. With those sharp, pointed teeth.

Toby lunged for the bats with the open bag, covering all of them in one fell swoop. He quickly cinched the bag closed and started for the door. Halfway there though the bats must've dried off enough to start flying again. The bag jerked up and to the left. Toby pulled it back down, but those buggers weren't giving in. The bag jolted this way and that as he struggled to get it to the door.

Jane's laughter rose above the animals' creepy noises. Well at least someone was amused. When he'd finally wrangled the bag of bats close enough, he kicked open the door and stumbled into the daylight. Shit, now he had to open the bag and set the flying rodents free. He hadn't come up with a plan for the best way to do this part...

"Throw it and run," Jane suggested, still safely tucked inside the doorway.

Judging from the way the bag still jerked around, the bats weren't going to be happy once he let them out. "It's okay," he murmured, not sure if he was soothing them or himself. "On the count of three, I'm going to open the bag and get the hell out of here." Stretching the bag as far away as his arm would let him, he backed up. "One, two, three." Letting go of the bag, he dove backward and hit the grass, rolling away just as the creatures swarmed over his head.

"Go on! Get!" Jane came running at them with a broom, shooing them in the direction of the forest.

Still lying on the ground, Toby looked up at the blue sky. Jane appeared, standing over him with a smirk, her long dark hair cascading past her shoulders. "Looks like I saved the day after all." She reached out a hand to help him up, but Toby pointed over her shoulder.

"Um, they're not exactly gone." In fact, the bats were swooping their way back toward the barn.

Jane turned and shrieked, then dove to the ground next to him, crouching with her hands over her head.

"I think they're turning." Toby watched the bats make a circle before heading back into the trees. "Yeah. They're definitely gone this time." Just to be safe though he didn't move. Because of the bats, not because Jane was lying on her back next to him. Nope.

"That. Was. Hilarious." Jane turned on her side to face him. "Oh my God. Watching you try to wrestle that bag outside." The words dissolved into laughter.

"Some help you were. You laughed at me the whole time," he said, feigning hurt. In reality he loved the sound of her laugh. Hearing it—earning it—gave him a rush. Having her this close, without her shrinking back away from him made him want more.

"If it makes you feel any better, I tried not to, but it couldn't be helped." Amusement danced in her eyes. "That was definitely first-class entertainment."

"I like entertaining you." He scooted even closer to her. "I could keep going, if you want." He could find reasons to make her smile all day.

"What sort of entertainment did you have in mind?" she asked as though she could be open to considering his proposal.

"I have all kinds of things in mind." Toby took his time, focusing on the details of her face—the small dip above her upper lip, a thin scar right above her left eyebrow. He skimmed his thumb across her cheek and down her neck, brushing back her hair. "You're so beautiful."

Her eyes shied away from his. "You probably say that to all the girls."

That was true. He'd said those same words to plenty of women. But somehow it felt different saying them now. To Jane. "This time I mean it."

Chapter Twelve

Toby's lips brushed against hers, soft and light—a teasing touch that woke up parts of her that had long stayed dormant. Her heart pounded so hard it ached, and she couldn't remember the last time breathing had hurt like this. It turned out to be the best kind of pain she'd ever felt.

Her grasp on control slipping, Jane let herself fall into the kiss, into Toby, following the rhythm of his lips. She opened her mouth to him, and his tongue stroked hers while he placed a hand on her hip, hitching her body closer to his.

The feel of his strength against her electrified every nerve ending, making her tingle from the inside out. A tantalizing pressure built inside of her, settling low in her stomach. She pressed against him, forgetting about the grass and the bats and their history. Toby had learned a thing or two about kissing since high school.

"Sorry to interrupt."

Jane broke away from the kiss, away from Toby, rolling onto her back to find herself staring up at her brother. *Perfect.* Wes was going to have a field day with this.

"Can we help you?" Toby was still turned on his side facing her.

"I came to help *you.*" Her brother gazed down at them with his arms crossed and amusement flickering on his lips. "You left me a message that you had some kind of crisis?" His eyebrows peaked. "I got all worried and rushed over here, but now I can see things are under control."

Jane couldn't hold back a laugh. That image of Toby trying to drag the bag of bats out of the barn was going to stick with her for a while. "You didn't have to worry. I rescued him."

"I can see that." Her brother made a grossed-out face. "Whatever's happening here is something I couldn't have helped with."

"Definitely not," Toby agreed.

Jane sat up.

"You gonna kiss him and bolt again?" Wes asked her.

Jane huffed. If only she'd had a sister. Sisters never embarrassed each other in front of a hot cowboy.

"Yeah." Toby peered at her face as though trying to gauge his chances of keeping her there. "You gonna run out on me again?"

She rolled her eyes up to stare at the sky, seriously considering a fast sprint. Although she wasn't sure she could run right now even if she tried. Her knees had gone too soft. "Maybe in a few minutes." Even with her heart racing this way, she knew enough not to read anything into that kiss. It was sexual attraction, pure and simple. Nothing more. They were too different, and he'd all but admitted he didn't want to deal with anything real. In the moment, he made it too easy for her to forget that.

"So, what was the big crisis about?" Wes kicked some mud off his boot, nearly flinging it onto her face. "What disaster could've possibly ended with you two making out in the grass?"

Jane pushed up to her feet, not missing Toby's disappointed frown. "Toby's afraid of bats," she teased to deflect the attention away from that kiss.

Her big, tough older brother made a face. "I don't blame him. Bats are creepy."

"You provoke bulls for a living," Jane reminded Wes. And in his free time, he also regularly went skydiving or white-water rafting or heliskiing. And then there was Toby. Willingly climbing on the back of an angry bull. "In fact, both of you seem to have some kind of death wish." They had that adrenaline junkie thing in common.

"Not a death wish." Toby stood, his eyes locked on hers. "It's more of a drive to experience life."

That made no sense...

"And bulls aren't rabid." Wes searched the sky like he half expected a bat to fly at him right then.

"Well, not to worry." Jane dusted off her hands, quite proud of herself. "I took care of the bats for you both. They won't bother you boys again."

"Sweet." Her brother started to walk away. "Guess I'll see you two later tonight for the shindig then."

Toby scrambled off the ground and chased him down. "Now that you're here, I could use some help finishing the party prep."

"Finishing?" Jane called him out with a look. "I didn't see any tables or chairs set up in there." He had a lot to pull together in six hours to make this party successful.

"I have a plan."

Jane didn't doubt that one bit. "I can help," she offered. "For Beth's sake, I don't want this party to end up a total disaster."

"No, no. We made a deal." Toby prodded her away. "The barn was my idea and I'll take care of everything."

"Except for bats." It was too easy when he set her up like that.

"Maybe I didn't need your help. Maybe I just wanted to check you out in those jeans," he shot back.

Despite herself, she couldn't help smiling as she headed to her car.

* * *

Jane had never in her life obsessed about what to wear. She'd always kept her wardrobe simple. Practical. Mainly sticking to blacks and whites for work, jeans and T-shirts or yoga pants for home, she'd never put much thought into making a statement with her clothes.

Maybe that was why it was taking her an hour to get dressed for Beth's party. Currently, she sat on a pile of discarded clothes on her bed wearing only her bra and underwear, which was beginning to feel like a good option for tonight compared to everything else she'd tried on. It bugged her that she even cared. She'd spent the afternoon writing again—swept up in the story, but also in the romance. It was pure coincidence that she'd written Amos and Celeste's first-kiss scene right after kissing Toby. Also happenstance that it might very well have been one of the best scenes she'd ever written. Okay, fine. She flopped to her back on the mattress and stared up at the ceiling. She couldn't deny that Toby made her feel a little more...*inspired.* But she wouldn't let herself forget that he inspired a lot of women.

She turned back to the pile of clothes beside her. A lot of their old high school acquaintances would be attending the party tonight, and she couldn't deny that she wanted to look different than the girl she'd been in high school. She glanced at the clock for the fifteenth time in a half hour. Great. She was ten minutes late and she still hadn't decided what to wear.

From her position on the bed, she analyzed her mostly empty closet. Rather than lug two suitcases through the airport, she'd opted to pack simply, but now that had backfired. Maybe something would magically appear. A dress? A fairy godmother and some pumpkin coach drivers?

A knock at the door incited panic. Ugh. She really was late. "Hold on!" She leapt off the bed and flailed to put on her robe, tying the belt tight around her waist before she ran down the hall and opened the door.

Her mother stood out on the porch looking effortlessly lovely in a flowered sundress trimmed with lace and a pair of red cowboy boots that were scuffed in all the right places. The woman knew how to make style look easy. Somehow that gene had completely skipped Jane.

"You're not dressed yet?" Her mother checked her watch. Ever since she'd taken over running the ranch and had become a wedding coordinator, she seemed to be slightly obsessed with being on time. "We were supposed to be down there ten minutes ago."

"I know." Jane led the way back to the bedroom and plopped down onto Mount Clothes again. "I haven't been able to find anything to wear." Somehow the understated skirts and tops she'd packed for the wedding events didn't appeal to her as much as they used to. Tonight, she needed something... spicier.

"Whoa." Her mother walked into the room and surveyed the situation. "Are you actually obsessing over what to wear?"

"Maybe." The shock on her mother's face only proved this was new territory for her. There'd been a day when her mother would've loved for Jane to obsess over what to wear. She'd tried to buy her clothes, but Jane had usually opted for comfortable and practical. Much to her mother's dismay.

"I have the perfect dress for you!" Her mother clapped her hands. "You have to wear it honey. It'll look so beautiful on you!"

"Fine." She stood, resigned to her fate. At this point, Jane would've agreed to put on a muumuu and knee socks. After an hour of trying on her own clothes, she desperately needed someone to rescue her.

"I'll run over to the house and grab it." Her mother bolted out the door like she was afraid Jane would change her mind. "Stay put! I'll only be a few minutes!"

It wasn't even a few minutes before her mother tore through the door again. She must've sprinted the whole way.

"Here it is," she sputtered. "Isn't it lovely? It'll really bring out your eyes. And it'll be perfect for your figure."

Jane inspected the dress. Even she had to admit it wasn't terrible. The soft blue color was subtle yet elegant and the halter style was completely different from anything she would normally wear. It would make an impression without being over the top. Perhaps she should've listened to her mother when she tried to tell her what to wear all those years ago.

Her mother had frozen, still holding up the dress as though the anticipation was killing her.

"I'll wear it." Jane shed her robe.

"You're going to love it." She helped Jane pull the garment over her head, and then stood back to admire her. "I knew it would be perfect. I saw it online when I was shopping for a dress for the wedding, and I simply had to buy it." She held up a pair of low strappy heels. "Along with these fabulous shoes."

Jane sat on the bed and slipped them on. It took her a few minutes to figure out all the buckles, but they were actually comfortable, and matched the dress perfectly. It seemed her fairy godmother was her actual mother all along. "Thank you." She turned a slow circle, glancing in the mirror. The dress really did fit like it had been made for her.

"So, is there any particular reason you're obsessing over what to wear to this party tonight?" her mother asked, sitting as though settling in for a chat.

Uh-oh. Jane hadn't breathed a word about the time she and Toby had spent together to her mother, or to anyone else for that matter. But her mother had always been weirdly intuitive.

"It wouldn't have anything to do with Toby Garrett, would it?" her mother pressed.

"No." Damn her tendency to blush. It always gave her away. "Sheesh. I just wanted to dress up a little. This is my best friend's wedding shower and the whole town will be there." If only she had a fan, she could use it to cool off her cheeks.

Her mother gazed into her eyes as though searching for the hidden truth. "Well you look lovely, Jane." Seeming to give up, she stood. "I know it hasn't been easy for you being back here, but I'm glad you came home for longer than a few days this time. I've missed you so much."

"I've missed you too." Being here never failed to spark memories of her father, which sometimes made her feel like she was experiencing the loss all over again. Coming home this time though felt different. She'd started to find her rhythm with writing again. She'd gotten to spend some time with her brother, and she was starting to find a connection with her mom she'd never had. And sharing this time with Beth before her wedding had reminded Jane how much she needed a friend.

"I should've spent more time here the last few years." It had been easier for her to build a new life somewhere else. Somewhere she didn't have to confront the loss of her father everywhere she looked. "I should've helped you with the ranch more."

"I'm thinking of selling," her mother said abruptly.

"Selling?" Jane stopped, blocking her mother's path to the door. "I thought you loved it here."

"After your dad died, taking care of the ranch saved me." The words were almost apologetic. "All these years it's been my whole focus, and I've realized I'm missing out on my life. I'm almost sixty, Jane," she said as though she couldn't believe it. "I want to travel. I want to be there for my kids, and someday my grandkids. I want to sleep in and have my summer weekends free."

"Of course." Jane couldn't quite name the emotion building in her chest. She understood. As hard as it had been for Jane to lose her father, she couldn't quite imagine the fear and pain her mother had faced. She deserved to move on, to build a life she dreamed about. "When do you think you'll sell?"

Her mother moved past her and walked to the door.

They both walked down the hall and slipped out into the cool evening. "I'm going to try to make it through this season. But hopefully it will be my last."

Jane looked around as they walked down the steps and followed the path toward the old barn. The surface of the lake glistened in the setting sun. Her dad had taught her to swim here. Though she hadn't dipped a toe in the water since his kayaking accident. They'd canoed on the lake and had built sandcastles on the beach. He'd called this their little slice of heaven on earth...

"You're being awfully quiet," her mother murmured.

"I guess I'm surprised." Jane paused near the water's edge. She shouldn't be. Of course, her mother wouldn't want to stay here forever, working every day from late spring all the way through the fall. But Jane couldn't shake the feeling that they were going to let go of her father's legacy. She wasn't sure she was prepared to let go.

"I can't keep it, honey." Her mother stopped. "It's too much. Wes only comes home once in a while and I hardly ever see August."

Jane rarely saw her eldest brother either, though he lived in Napa. They talked once in a while but managing one of the high-end wineries out there kept him pretty busy. "I understand." She let her eyes wander to the lodge farther down the shoreline. Her father had built it shortly after he'd bought the property.

"I know it'll be hard to say goodbye to it all." Her mother put her arm around Jane and led her forward. "But none of you kids want it either and I won't burden you with the responsibility. I think it's best to sell soon, while the market is still strong, and then we can divide up the money."

Jane didn't want any of the money. She could definitely

use it, but she didn't want it. She'd rather find a way to keep her father's memory alive.

"Maybe you should hire a manager." Jane knew what her mother was saying made sense, but she couldn't imagine the ranch not being in their family.

"Even if I hired a manager, I'd still have to be involved. I'd still be thinking about it and sticking my nose into the business. After all this time I wouldn't know how not to." Her mother sighed. "I just need to let it go. It's time."

They walked along the lake, the water lapping gently at the sandy shore and then followed the path worn into the grass all the way to the barn.

More arguments flooded Jane's thoughts, but she kept them to herself. Her mother had obviously been thinking about selling for a while, and she had every right to make that decision.

Why should it matter to her what her mother did with the ranch anyway? Jane planned to go back to California right after Beth's wedding, and she'd hole up in her condo until she decided to look for another teaching job.

The sounds of music and laughter greeted them as they neared the old barn.

"Sounds like a fun party."

Her mother looked so relaxed, while nerves blitzed through Jane. Social scenes like this had never been her thing. In high school, she used to barricade herself in her room with a book anytime there was a big party or dance. On the night of her winter formal, she'd binge read the entire Chronicles of Narnia series.

"I still can't believe Toby wanted to have Beth's elegant wedding shower here." Her mom frowned at the structure's ragged exterior.

"Neither could the bats." The memory of Toby running

around with a trash bag full of bats made her laugh. Inevitably, though, thinking of the bats made her think of the kiss they'd shared and suddenly the low evening sun seemed ten times hotter.

Jane opened the barn door for her mother and followed her inside. "Wow. He really pulled everything together." She hadn't expected to be impressed—especially given the state of the barn earlier that morning, but it looked amazing.

"Toby did this?" Her mother's eyes opened as wide as Jane imagined hers were.

He'd set up the space to look like a mountain fairyland. There were white lights strung from all the rafters giving the dim room a festive glow. On one side, he'd set up round tables, which were covered in white table linens and rustic accents. Each table had its own twinkling mason jar chandelier hanging overhead. Across from where they stood, Toby had created a makeshift bar out of old wine barrels and pallets. There was also a dance floor, the catered food tables she'd ordered, and yes, there was the mechanical bull. She had to admit, it wasn't quite as obnoxious as she'd thought it would be.

"It looks beautiful in here," her mother marveled, wandering away.

There was no way Toby had done this all on his own. It would've been too much, even for both him and Wes. Though the barn was packed with people, it still felt plenty roomy. Everyone had spread out and was enjoying the food, drinks, and the country music blaring from the speakers.

Nudging her way through the crowd, Jane gawked in disbelief at the transformation.

"Oops! Sorry." A woman bumped into Jane from behind.

She turned. "It's okay—" Her eyes met Aubrey Munson's and once again she was falling back through the years and landing with a horrible thud into her tattered high school memories. Beth had invited Aubrey Munson to her wedding shower?

Jane pushed her glasses up on her nose, but it didn't change anything. Aubrey hadn't seemed to age since their senior year. Apparently being a blond bombshell never went out of style.

"*Jane?*" The woman's jaw dropped. "Jane Harding? It *is* you! I knew you were coming, but I didn't realize you'd already made it back."

Why would she realize it? They'd never been friends. Aubrey had been everything Jane wasn't—popular, pretty, athletic, especially when it came to cheerleading and dance, and oh, yeah. There was that other thing. She'd dated Toby.

"Hi Aubrey. So nice to see you again." She tried to smile. She really tried, but it was hard to forget the mean-girl comments Aubrey and her friends always uttered when they thought she wasn't listening. Back then, they'd been really into rhyming: "plain Jane" had always been a favorite of course. Her parents had set her up for that. But there'd also been "stained Jane," "weight-gain Jane," "insane Jane," "shame Jane." She could go on...

"Oh my God," Aubrey bubbled. "What's it been? Like ten years or something?"

Math had never been the woman's forte. "Roughly." She tried to keep a hold on her smile, but it had started to give. "What're you doing back here?" She'd heard from her mother that Aubrey had gone to University of Denver and was currently working her way up to be an anchor at a local news station. Mara had always loved Aubrey. She used to try to force Jane to invite Aubrey to her house after school. But Jane had never been good at pretending to like people.

"What am I doing here?" the woman repeated with a giggle. "Well I guess it's no surprise that Toby and I have been hanging out some since he's spent so much time in Denver recently." Her expression turned pouty. Or maybe that was simply the work she'd had done on her lips. "The poor man. I try to meet up with him every time he comes down for a doctor appointment."

She was here for Toby? *With* Toby? Jane blinked at the woman, her throat constricting. "Right. Of course." Well, wasn't that interesting? "So, you're here as Toby's date?" Jane had to get this straight, because only a few hours ago he'd been lying in the grass kissing her like he was single.

"Not officially." Aubrey leaned in. "But I think we're moving in that direction, if you know what I mean."

Jane didn't know. She couldn't possibly know because about six hours ago, Toby had told her she was beautiful. And yet…like she'd told the man himself, he said that to all the girls. Jane gave herself a good mental shake. He was a good-time cowboy. Even when he'd kissed Jane, she'd known that. It wasn't like things between them would ever go anywhere. Not with him traveling the circuit. She'd already told him her philosophy on love anyway. He knew where she stood, so he probably figured there was no risk in kissing her. Still, it was a pretty crappy thing to do if Aubrey thought the two of them were in a relationship.

"You look so…*different*." A catty smile wrinkled Aubrey's nose.

"I would hope we're all different, considering we're not in high school anymore," Jane said, scanning the crowd for Beth. Maybe her friend would come and rescue her. Beth had known how terrible Aubrey had been to her in high school.

Jane took deep, even breaths to ease the sudden burning dead center in her chest. She'd told Aubrey she hoped they were all different as adults, but clearly that wasn't true.

"I really need to go find Beth." She was here for her friend, not to be forced back into the past by someone who'd never liked her. "Excuse me," she said to Aubrey. "Great to see you."

"Maybe we can catch up some time," the woman called behind her.

Jane didn't even turn around to acknowledge the invitation. Instead, she kept her gaze focused straight ahead, hunting for her best friend. There she was! Over by the mechanical bull with Ethan. And Toby. The sight of him brought on a minor explosion where her heart had once sat. Yep, definitely the good-time cowboy. He was currently climbing onto the mechanical bull, waving to the crowd that had gathered, showing off that cocky grin.

"To-by! To-by!" The deafening chant reminded her of high school football games.

Trying to stay in the shadows, Jane edged her way around the crowd. She needed to block out everything else and make sure Beth had a great time at her shower.

The mechanical bull started up and everyone cheered louder. Toby ate up the attention, raising his arm in the air and whooping to get the crowd even more riled.

Almost there. Jane tried not to watch him while she made her way to Beth's side, but she couldn't help herself. He was so good—moving with the bull, all that upper body strength keeping his form sturdy. And right before she grabbed her friend's hand, Toby's eyes seemed to meet hers. Then the bull spun, flinging him off onto the sawdust covered floor.

Everyone seemed to gasp and hold their breath.

"That wasn't even eight seconds!" someone yelled.

"Oh my God! Toby!" Aubrey rushed to his side and knelt next to him. "Are you okay?"

"Sorry. I forgot to warn you Aubrey was coming," Beth whispered into Jane's ear.

"Yeah about that." She turned to her friend. "What the hell is she doing here?"

Beth shrugged. "She said Toby invited her."

Of course he did. Toby had started to stagger to his feet, noticeably wincing while he tried to shrug off Aubrey. "I'm fine," he called out. But that wasn't his real smile. Or maybe he'd only been giving Jane his fake smile. She had no way of knowing, did she?

The crowd started clapping and then chanting for him to get back up on the bull.

"I'm gonna take five," he said, walking away. "Let someone else have a turn." He moved stiffly with Aubrey following behind him.

Jane watched the two of them. Toby said something to the woman, and she scurried away while he slipped out the door.

"Jane!" Beth elbowed her. "Go with him. Make sure he's okay."

Oh, no. No. Way. "Babysitting the best man isn't the maid of honor's job," she informed her friend. She'd already saved him once today. If she would've known about Aubrey a little while ago, she would've let the bats swarm him.

"Please." Beth did that puppy-dog begging thing with her eyes. "Otherwise Ethan is going to go after him and who knows how long that'll take. I want to enjoy the shower with him."

"Of course you do." Beth and Ethan had both been working so hard. They deserved to enjoy the evening without any worries. "You two go dance. I'll go check on Toby." She put on her best bridesmaid smile and headed for the door.

Chapter Thirteen

Toby headed for the lake, trying to walk off the pain in his shoulder. When he'd hit the ground, he'd heard—and felt—a distinct pop.

He couldn't take another setback—especially not one delivered by a damn mechanical bull. He'd been on plenty of mechanical bulls in country-western bars all over the good ol' US of A, and he'd never fallen off. But then again, Jane Harding had never walked past him mid-ride and turned his head like that either.

She was wearing a formfitting dress with a neckline that showed off graceful shoulders and more skin than usual. He'd done more than a double take…he'd rubbernecked so hard it had thrown off his equilibrium.

Pausing at the water's edge, he raised his hand to his opposite shoulder. The joint was on fire. He shrugged to make sure it still worked. Burning pain aside, at least he could move it.

"Are you hurt?"

Toby turned around to find Jane standing a few yards behind him. Her tone was as stiff as her posture. It had gotten dark, but the nearly full moon gave off enough light to see the wariness in her eyes. But there was something else in them too; something he couldn't name.

The sight brought him back to the last time he'd seen that look in Jane's eyes at the New Year's party eight years ago. He hadn't been looking for Jane particularly, but when he'd found her, curled up in her father's study, he'd been drawn to her. The kiss they'd shared had been spontaneous, something he didn't even know he wanted until it was over. And by then she was walking away. It had been easier to let her go than to try and understand why. But now, looking at her standing in the moonlight, he found all he wanted to know was what she was thinking. Although he was probably better off not knowing.

"I think I'm fine." He raised his right arm, grinding his teeth against the wince.

"You don't look fine." Jane kept her distance. "You look like you're in pain."

"I'll be fine." He'd better be fine. "But I really appreciate you coming to check on me." He smiled to show her everything was A-okay.

Jane didn't smile back. Her stare was cold. "Beth asked me to. I'm not sure why. It would probably make more sense for Aubrey to be out here."

"Aubrey tried to come out here with me and I sent her away." He and Aubrey had hooked up a year ago, but they'd agreed that neither of them was looking for a relationship. And yet somehow, she seemed to know every time he had an appointment in Denver. He strongly suspected his mother had been feeding Aubrey information. Aubrey had called him up a couple of times, inviting him to dinner, which he'd agreed to assuming she'd understood they were just friends.

Jane had crossed her arms as though the night air chilled her skin. "I'm not sure why you would send her away when you invited her to come to the shower in the first place," she said stiffly.

Despite the throbbing in his shoulder, Toby managed to laugh. He slipped off the flannel he had on over his T-shirt and draped it over her bare shoulders. "Is that what she told you? I definitely didn't invite her. Last time I was in Denver I mentioned the wedding and from what I hear, she informed Beth that she was my plus-one. I hadn't counted on her being my date." He'd been as surprised as anyone else to see Aubrey walk in tonight.

"You might want to tell her that." The truth didn't seem to loosen Jane up any. She still stood at a distance, feet planted on the grass instead of the sand. He studied the rigidness in her shoulders, the gloss of detachment in her eyes. It didn't look like anger. It looked more like...fear. That's when it hit him. Her father had drowned in the river outside of town. Kayaking accident. He looked at the reflection of the moon shimmering on the water. Beautiful, but Jane likely didn't think so.

"How long did you and Aubrey date in high school?" The question drew his attention back to her.

"I don't know. It was on and off for a few years, I guess." He walked up to where Jane stood, trying to keep his shoulder from moving. "It feels like a lifetime ago though." He didn't want to talk about Aubrey. The only thing on his mind right now was Jane, even though he knew it made no sense for him to pursue her. She wasn't someone who did casual, and that was his only speed in relationships. But she'd kissed him earlier today—that had to mean something, didn't it? He went to reach for her, but his shoulder seized up and he couldn't stop the hiss of pain that escaped his lips.

"Oh, God." Her hand came to rest on his arm. "You really hurt yourself, didn't you?"

"Nah," he lied. It looked like he'd be making another trip to Denver tomorrow. "I have some ice packs back at my place." He cradled his arm against his chest. "I'll pop some anti-inflammatories, ice it for twenty minutes, and then I'll come back to the shower." He started to walk away before she could see how much pain he was really in.

"I'll come with you." After a few steps, Jane caught up with him.

"You don't have to." If she came home with him, he'd only want to kiss her again. He'd only want to do more than kiss her again, and as much as the idea appealed to him, Jane didn't seem to be feeling the same way she'd felt when he'd kissed her earlier.

"I'm coming."

Toby knew better than to argue again.

They crossed the meadow and approached the edge of the forest where his cabin sat. When he'd started working at the ranch, Mara had given him his pick of cabins. This one was tucked back into the trees, but he still had a view of the lake and the mountains beyond.

"This was my dad's man cave." Jane said the words so quietly it took him a few seconds to translate them. "He used to come here with his fishing buddies, even though it's so close to the house." She walked up the steps seeming to inspect the old stair rail as though remembering her father's hand running along it. "He called it his vacation home at home."

"You almost don't need a vacation when you live in a place like this." Toby opened the door with his good arm and gestured for Jane to go inside. He hadn't known the history of the cabin, or that her father had used it that way, but he could see why. "I bet you see his fingerprints all over the ranch, huh?" He went to the freezer and pulled out the ice pack. When he turned around, he was shocked to see tears in Jane's eyes.

"My mom wants to sell."

He'd wondered. Mara had hinted on and off about getting the place ready for the market. Still, he was surprised to see so much emotion from Jane. As far as he'd heard she hadn't exactly spent much time at home during the last eight years. "You don't look like you're happy with the news," he said, sitting down at the kitchen table with the ice pack balanced on his shoulder. The cold didn't seem to reach through his shirt.

"I want to be happy for her." She came to sit across from him, staring down at the table.

"But," he prompted. She wasn't happy. That much was obvious.

"But it made me think about all the memories we'll lose. Of him. Of our life with him." A tear slipped down her cheek. "Like you said, my dad's fingerprints are all over this place."

"Is that why you never stay very long when you visit?" Toby asked, repositioning the ice.

"You should put it under your shirt." Jane pointed at the ice pack. "It's not going to do you much good unless it's against your skin."

She was as good at avoiding questions as he had been during their talk at the library. Toby tried to shove the ice pack inside his shirt, but there wasn't enough room.

"Just take off your shirt," Jane said, coming to his side of the table.

"Are you sure you can handle it?" Teasing Jane had always been one of his favorite pastimes. She took it a lot better these days than she had back in high school, simply rolling her eyes. "Your muscles don't impress me, Toby Garrett. I'm not Aubrey Munson."

"Thank God for that." He raised his shirt with a wince, and Jane helped him slide it off his shoulders. She gently molded the ice pack to his shoulder, her fingertips grazing his skin, bringing on a whole new kind of ache.

"There." The woman peered down at him, her gaze more empathetic than it had been before. "Now where's your ibuprofen?"

"In the cabinet by the sink." He started to stand, but her hand guided his good shoulder back to his seat.

"I'll get it. You focus on keeping that ice in place."

Toby watched Jane walk to the sink, the dress swishing around her thighs. The sight made him forget about his pain and think instead about sliding his hand up one of those legs. "I'm still waiting for you to answer my question, by the way." He wasn't going to let her off the hook that easily. "Why haven't you come home much?"

"I'm not exactly sure." She came back to the table and set the pills in front of him along with a glass of water. "I told myself it was because I didn't love it here growing up. Especially after my dad passed away." She took her seat across from him again, gazing over the table with a thoughtful look. "But being here, I'm finding that's not exactly true. There's a lot I love." Jane pushed the pills closer to Toby's hand as though reminding him to take them. "I think I stayed away because I never felt like I fit in here. Like no one...except for Beth and my dad knew the real me. Though I know a lot of that was my fault. In a lot of ways, I'm the one who didn't let anyone get to know me." She looked up at him abruptly, like she worried she'd said too much. "Even if it was my own fault, it's a terrible feeling not to be known."

Forget the pills, he held his whole focus on her. "I'd like to know you." It might have been the most honest thing he'd ever said, but even to him it sounded…tentative. They were only here for a short time and God willing he'd be back on the road again by fall. He didn't have much to offer her.

Doubt filled her eyes. "I've spent eight years moving on, building a new life. But then I came back here and seeing the ranch…reconnecting with Beth…it makes me realize how empty my life was back in California. A little lonely." Looking down, she picked at one of her nails. "When my dad died, I lost my champion. He understood me in a way no one else ever seemed to. When I lost him, I felt like I lost everything that mattered, and I never want to feel that way again." She peeked up at him. "I guess that's part of the reason I left. But I didn't really leave behind the fear or the pain."

"Yeah, those tend to stick with you." No matter what he'd done to stave it off, the fear and pain still followed him around too. "It's easy to look past them when you're away though. It's easy to pretend the fear and pain isn't there." He blew out a sigh. "And then you come home and you find it's still there waiting for you."

Surprise parted Jane's lips. "How do you know?"

The question edged him closer to the cliff he'd been dancing around since he'd gotten home. Every time he came back it got harder to pretend. Maybe because he'd grown up and he didn't want to pretend anymore.

"You need to take the medicine." Jane reached across the table, picked up the pills, and spilled them into his hand.

Before she could pull away, he clasped his fingers around hers. "I want to know you." He'd screwed up when he was a stupid kid. He should've considered how her loss had made her want to hide. He knew the comfort hiding could bring, at least temporarily, but in order for him to know her he needed to let her know him too. "You said I've never had to deal with anything hard, but that's not true."

Jane didn't look away from him. She simply waited for him to continue.

Toby gazed at her, at the tears still glistening in her eyes, at the concern furrowing her brow. He'd never told anyone. He'd never felt the freedom to tell anyone, not when his own parents never discussed Tanner, and then so much time had passed it seemed too late. How could he tell anyone when he'd ignored his brother's memory for so long?

But Jane would understand, and he knew she'd never breathe a word of it to anyone else if he didn't want her to. "I lost my brother." That was the first time he'd spoken those words out loud, and even though they brought a rise of pain, they also opened up something inside of him.

"Your brother?" Jane's voice had dropped to a whisper. "I thought you only had younger sisters..."

"That's what everyone thinks." He adjusted the ice pack, even though he hardly felt it against his skin. "But we lost him before we moved here. Tanner was my twin, he died when we were seven." Emotion gripped him by the throat and for once he didn't try to fend it off.

"Toby," Jane uttered through a gasp. "Oh, no. That's... unimaginable."

"As unimaginable as losing your dad as a teenager," he murmured gently.

Jane nodded, her eyes brimming with tears again. "I'm so sorry." She let out a sad laugh. "I used to hate it when people said that to me. What good does it do?"

"Coming from you it does a lot of good." An ache raced through him, settling in his fingertips. He wanted to touch her, wanted to pull her to him and let the feel of her in his arms dull the pain. "Everything was fine until the year we turned two and then my parents started to notice something wasn't right with him." Toby didn't remember that part. He didn't remember Tanner always tripping and falling while Toby was able to run as fast and as far he wanted. He didn't remember his brother's struggles with speech and motor skills.

"The doctors diagnosed him with Duchenne muscular dystrophy when we were three. I don't remember him before that. I don't remember him ever being healthy." His brother had already been in a wheelchair full-time by the time they turned four. "He was my best friend though. I pushed him around in his wheelchair. I helped him eat. I played catch with him. And I read to him. He loved that. He loved cowboy books."

Jane pressed her hand to her mouth, and brushed away her tears, but she said nothing. She simply waited for him to continue.

Talking about Tanner made a burn rise in his gut. But he had to tell her. He *needed* to. Like Jane had said, it was a terrible thing not to be known. Tanner deserved to be known. "When we'd go out, everyone would stare at him, but he was just my brother." Toby hadn't thought of him any different. "He couldn't do the physical things I could do, but he was smarter than me, and he was funny too. He always had a joke to tell." He smiled, remembering, and Jane smiled too. "I never thought…I didn't realize he could die. But one night his heart just stopped." He couldn't say more. Not without losing it, and he couldn't lose it. He'd never been allowed to lose it.

Jane rested her hand over his, not even trying to hide her tears now. A few tears may have slipped down his cheeks too. He couldn't be sure.

"I think I was in shock. Because I hadn't considered he would die, but my parents…I think they'd been preparing for it all along." They must've because they'd so quickly and efficiently planned his funeral and packed up the medical equipment. In just days, it was like Tanner had never existed at all. "They were sad and they were different. Almost angry all the time." They'd seemed short with him and impatient. Now he understood that was just their grief but at the time…"I felt like I had to make them happy. Like it was all up to me. I did everything I could to make them smile and to be okay so I could keep them from getting upset."

"That's too much," Jane said, touching her hand to his cheek. "That's too much for a child to carry."

It had been too much. Too heavy. "A few weeks after Tanner's funeral, my parents told me we were moving. That we were starting over. Moving on."

"But you never really move on." Jane scooted to the edge of the chair so that her knees touched his.

"No. You never really move on." He set the ice pack on the table and stretched out his shoulder. "My parents still won't talk about him. We don't have any pictures in the house. And yet I still see him everywhere."

"Because he was an important part of your life," Jane

said. "Which means he's a part of you." A light went on in her eyes. "That plaque. The one on the outside of the library. It says 'In Memory of Tanner.'"

He didn't bother to look away. She knew. Jane was not only smart, she'd always been intuitive. "He loved books. It was one way I could think to honor him."

"It's the perfect way." Leaning forward, she wrapped her arms around his bare shoulders and held on.

* * *

With her arms wrapped around Toby, Jane couldn't stop picturing him as a grief-stricken seven-year-old unsure of how to mourn his brother's death.

Her heart broke for him, for that little boy who never got to be a cowboy. Her heart broke for his family, for their desperation to move on and simply get past it. In all the pain she and her mom and Wes and August had gone through, never once did her mother try to shy away from their dad's memory. She kept all of their family pictures exactly where they'd been. Her mom kept her father's memory alive for all of them, and she'd never expected them to be okay. They'd talked about her dad, they'd all acknowledged what they'd lost. But Toby hadn't been allowed to do any of that.

She wasn't sure how long they sat that way, Toby's forehead resting on her shoulder, her cheek brushing his hair. He was quiet and she stayed quiet. She already knew words didn't matter. In the unspeakable aftermath of loss, it was the being there that mattered. After her dad's funeral, Beth would sometimes come over and simply sit in the chair that had been in the corner of Jane's room doing her homework. A lot of times they wouldn't speak at all, but Jane knew her friend was there and that had mattered more than anything.

"I've never told anyone." Toby's voice was muffled by her shoulder. "I didn't even know how to talk about it, where to start." He slowly raised his head. "But I knew you would understand." His eyes found hers. They were red around the rims, but any tears he'd shed seemed to have already dried.

Her eyes, however, filled again. "I do." The crack in her heart deepened. How had he kept that a secret all these years? How had he carried it all alone? "It helps to talk about it, actually. It hurts too." She could see the pain in him. "But it helps."

"Yeah. It does." His face had centered on hers, those eyes of his so magnetic and full of energy. The intensity of his gaze quickened her pulse. She remembered seeing that look a few other times. The night of the party back in high school. Last night at the brewery when he'd caught her in his arms. And then earlier when he'd kissed her in the soft grass.

"I probably shouldn't kiss you," he half whispered.

"Probably not," she agreed. When he'd kissed her earlier she'd gotten caught up in the moment, but he'd still been Toby the good-time cowboy. He'd still been the man who didn't take anything too seriously. Now, though, she'd seen so much deeper into him, and she wanted to be there for him, but she couldn't let her emotions overpower her.

She'd meant what she'd said about love. For someone like her, someone who felt so completely and deeply, it only ever seemed to end in heartache. And, despite what he'd told her, Toby still lived his life on the edge. He lived for risk, *thrived* on it, and she knew herself too well; she couldn't stand another loss. She wouldn't survive it.

"We should get back to the shower," she said before she gave in to the desire to kiss away his pain. Before one of them started something that would be impossible to stop. Sitting with Toby had opened her emotions, bringing her to the same raw, vulnerable place he was in right now, and this wouldn't end well for either one of them.

He closed his eyes and nodded as though trying to convince himself. She couldn't seem to move either. Something in her wanted to wrap her arms around him again, to lose herself, to let him lose himself, but crossing that line would bring too many complications for them both. "I think you should talk to your parents," she murmured instead of touching him. "They should know how you felt, Toby. How you *still* feel." She knew how important that was, how much healing it could provide.

"I'm not sure I can. But I'll try." With a sad smile he stood and pulled his T-shirt back over his head like he couldn't stand to sit there anymore without touching her.

It was only then she realized she was still wearing his flannel shirt over her dress. He'd slipped it onto her shoulders outside so casually and effortlessly, that she hadn't even realized he was doing it until she was wrapped in his woodsy scent. At the time she'd still been annoyed with the Aubrey situation, so she hadn't even acknowledged it for the thoughtful gesture it was. Two weeks ago, if someone had told her Toby Garrett had a thoughtful sincerity hiding deep down, she would've laughed, but now she'd seen it for herself.

Forcing herself to her feet, Jane slipped the shirt off

her shoulders and handed it back to him. He wasn't just the charming sweet-talker she'd always thought he was...maybe he never had been. Maybe he'd always had a depth he'd hidden from the world. But now that she'd seen it, now that she knew, she had to be careful not to lose her heart to him.

Chapter Fourteen

Anxiety locked up Toby's chest the second he walked into the medical building adjacent to the hospital. He'd become too familiar with this place over the last three months, spending a whole lot more time than he would've liked to with his orthopedic surgeon. He stepped into the elevator, his knees buckling under the weight of the what-ifs. What if he ended up back in the operating room? What if he had to give up everything he'd worked for?

The doors rolled open to the sterile hallway he'd walked so many times before. The doc hadn't given him good news from the start, but throughout his recovery, their visits had grown more optimistic. If the pain in his shoulder was any indication, he was about to have a major setback.

Damn. Toby paused outside the office, taking a minute to get it together. All that work he'd put in, all that pain he'd gone through to get where he was now, and he might have to hang it up for good. A sudden anger fisted his hands. He should've never climbed onto the mechanical bull. He shouldn't have been showing off, trying to entertain the crowd.

A door across the hall opened, and Toby turned to walk into the office, fighting for a smile to greet the receptionist.

"How's the day going, Gloria?" he asked the middle-aged woman who was always so polite to him.

"Can't complain." She typed on a computer while she answered. Her ability to multitask and still hear everything he said amazed him. "Saturdays are always good. Much quieter around here." Her fingers paused on the keyboard and she smiled up at him. "The doc will be with you in a few."

"Thanks." He wandered to a straight-backed chair against the wall dragging the weight of failure behind him. It wasn't only the mechanical bull idiocy that had gotten to him. It was what had happened after.

Emotions surged through him the way they had four nights ago when Jane had wrapped her arms around him—grief and pain but also what felt like a fragile hope. She hadn't thought he was a terrible person for keeping Tanner a secret. She hadn't asked why he'd never said a word about his brother. Instead she'd pulled him in and had offered a reassurance that had somehow made his grief easier to carry. The empathy, the physical contact had roused that craving in him again. But the fear in her eyes when he'd raised his face to hers had told him everything he needed to know. She didn't want him to kiss her. She deserved more than someone who'd come and go in her life.

"The doc just buzzed me," Gloria said, still typing away. "He asked me to apologize. He's running a few minutes late."

Big surprise there. "Thanks." A weight seemed to press into his shoulders. Trying to ignore it, Toby opened the book he'd checked out from the library, ready to lose himself in the story again. That was better than losing himself in thoughts about Jane.

Flipping through the pages, Toby found his place. He'd made it about halfway through and he still couldn't see why Jane had gotten so weird about him checking out the book. The story was well written. Intelligent. But it also had these witty undertones. The characters seemed familiar to him somehow. Maybe it was because the main dude was a cowboy, but Toby couldn't shake the feeling that the guy seemed like someone he knew.

"I loved that book," Gloria called. "There's supposed to be another one coming out next year. I tried to find the author online, but it's like they don't exist."

Toby studied the book cover again. "Yeah, sounds like whoever it is writes under a pseudonym." Which made no sense to him at all. If you're that successful and that talented, why hide it? Unless...

"Whoever it is must be real shy." Gloria's fingers clacked the keyboard. "More of a behind-the-scenes person than someone who likes the spotlight."

"Exactly. It has to be someone who doesn't like attention," Toby added. Someone a lot like Jane...

"I can't imagine not liking attention," Gloria half muttered. "If I wrote a book like that, I'd enjoy the accolades."

Toby thought about Jane's reaction when he'd picked up the book. Her face had gone white. And she'd tried to talk him out of reading it. *It's not your kind of book.* She'd seemed pretty damn sure when she'd said it.

"Toby." Dr. Petrie appeared in a doorway on the other side of the waiting room. "Why don't you come on back?"

Tabling the thoughts about Jane and the book, he trudged to the door to face his fate.

"Good to see you." The doctor greeted him with a handshake. "Although I wish the circumstances were different."

"You and me both." He'd been so careful since the surgery, still working hard, but favoring his right side. And all it had taken was the chant of a crowd to make him stupid. He never could say no to accolades himself, but he'd better learn how.

The doctor led him down a short hallway to an open exam room. "Have a seat." He gestured to the chair instead of the exam table and closed the door.

Toby did as he was told, prepping for another lecture. Not like the other ten had done him any good, but this time he'd do his best to make it stick.

"So, you want to tell me what happened?"

"I was at a wedding shower and there happened to be a mechanical bull there." Enough said. There was no way to make that sound good.

To his credit, Dr. Petrie didn't laugh. "So, you tweaked your shoulder?"

"I fell on it," Toby corrected. "Felt a small pop. Nothing crazy, but afterward I experienced pain and swelling." He'd been experiencing pain and swelling ever since.

"I'd imagine you did." The doctor walked over. "Why don't we take a look?"

Toby eased his shirt up and gingerly pulled it over his head. He'd iced it and had taken his anti-inflammatories earlier that morning, but the pain still sliced through him.

The doctor examined him, pushing and prodding. "Raise your right arm for me."

Toby did his best, but he couldn't pull it up past chin level without a throbbing in the joint. "What about opening out to the side?" He did it, but he had to fight a grimace the whole way.

"There seems to be a lot of inflammation and bruising." The doctor backed up and sat on a stool in front of the small desk where a computer sat. "I'll put an order in for an MRI to check things out and make sure you didn't damage the repair." The man sounded doubtful.

"How soon can they get me in for the MRI?" How long would he have to wonder whether he'd be headed for another surgery?

"I'd guess you could come back down on Monday." The doctor typed something into the computer and turned back to him. "But I don't have to tell you, this is a serious injury you've been dealing with. Some people never fully recover."

Here we go again. He'd heard this speech before. "I've come a long way since the surgery. I've done all my rehab and regained a lot of strength." He wasn't even thirty yet. He couldn't be washed up already.

"You've recovered faster than most of my patients," the doctor acknowledged. "But many people with that kind of injury are never the same. I'm only telling you this because I want you to be prepared. You know I wouldn't say this to anyone else, but you're like family." The doctor waited until Toby looked at him. "Maybe it's time for you to consider what your future holds. Even if you didn't tear it again, you're not going to be able to do this to yourself forever."

"I've still got a few years in me." He pulled his shirt

back on, ignoring the ache. He'd managed to ignore all kinds of pain since he'd started riding, he could do it a few years longer. He had to.

Tanner was always out there in the arena with him. That was where their bond came back to life. He couldn't give that up.

"I understand how you feel," the doctor said sternly. "But there's a chance you won't regain full strength and range of motion. Especially if this turns out to be a major setback after a minor fall. Think of what a fall from a real bull could do."

"I never think about it." He only focused on the next competition. That's what he had to do now. He had to focus. He had to force his body to do what he needed it to do. "It won't be a major setback." He refused to even consider this a minor setback. He'd be fine. He'd work extra hard on the range-of-motion exercises his PT had given him. He'd get back to full strength, and he'd get back on a bull.

"Go get the MRI and make another appointment with me in a week or so." Dr. Petrie seemed to have given up on talking sense into him. "Then we can reevaluate based on the images. Depending on what I see, I may have to send you back to physical therapy. Hopefully we won't end up in the operating room again."

"We won't." He'd do everything he could to avoid that scenario. He stood and walked out of the room. "Thanks, doc. I'll see you soon."

"In the meantime, don't get on any more mechanical bulls," the man called behind him.

Dr. Petrie wouldn't have to worry about that. Showing off for the crowd hadn't exactly given him the thrill it once did. When Jane had walked past the mechanical bull, she'd seemed upset, and he'd realized then he didn't care what everyone else thought nearly as much as he cared what she thought.

* * *

Jane made a mad dash into the library, doing her best to smooth down her hair and straighten the clothes she'd thrown on before she left the lodge. She'd spent the last three days locked in her room writing and had forgotten all about her meeting with Bernadette.

"There you are!" Beth came running from a table near the romance section to meet her. "Oh, thank God. I thought you weren't going to show, and I've been looking forward to this for two days."

Jane laughed. "Looking forward to me babysitting your grandmother?"

"Yes." Her friend's eyes widened. "I've had to bring her to the café and all she does is search for grease and grime and messes in the kitchen. Well, either that, or she goes around the dining room calling out customers on their bad manners."

"Hopefully she spent some time reading too." That had been the point of their little two-person book club. If she hadn't read anything they could discuss, Jane had no idea what they were going to do.

"She's a very fast reader," Beth said sadly. "I think this time you're going to have to load her up with a whole series or something."

"I have a few that I can recommend." Jane peered past Beth to the table where her grandmother sat impatiently waiting. "You go and don't worry about us at all. We'll have a fabulous time." Even with the woman's uppity attitude, Jane liked her. There was something almost endearing lurking beneath all those stuffy layers.

"Thank you!" Beth threw her arms around Jane's neck. "Feel free to keep her as long as you want. You can drop her off at the house later."

"Will do. Maybe after we finish up here, I'll drive her back to the ranch and we can have lunch with Louise." She could keep her out of Beth's hair all day if that was what her friend needed.

"Yes, keep her for lunch. That would be great!" Her friend slipped on a pair of bedazzled cat-eye sunglasses. "Thanks again! See you soon!" She practically skipped out the door.

Still flustered from her mad rush to the library, Jane made her way to the table. Bernadette had chosen a seat by the window. Sunlight poured in, warming Jane the second she sat down. "Sorry I'm late. I've been working on a project and I totally lost track of time." A sense of relief allowed her to relax. She was over halfway done with the book, and all the emotions Toby had stirred up in her seemed to work themselves right onto the page.

It had been so hard for her to walk out of his cabin the night he'd told her about his brother, but she'd managed to distract herself with writing ever since, which was just as well. She wasn't sure she could trust herself alone with Toby now.

"What kind of project are you working on over the summer?" the older woman demanded. "Don't professors get summers off too?"

"For the most part." She reached into her purse and pulled out the book they were going to discuss: Sandra Brown's *Hello, Darkness*. "But you still plan and research and work on curriculum." She didn't feel like explaining she wouldn't have a contract come fall, and she couldn't tell her about her predicament with the book she'd turned in either. She didn't want to think about the fuss Bernadette would make if she knew Jane wrote those "inappropriate" books. "So, what did you think about the book?"

"It was…interesting." The woman's chin tipped up slightly and her gaze darted around like she wanted to make sure no one was listening in on their conversation.

"Interesting in a good way?" Jane loved every one of Sandra Brown's books—the mystery, the suspense, the intrigue, the sexy romance.

"It was a bit racy," Beth's grandmother whispered. Like they'd get in trouble for discussing a sexy book at the library.

"That's one of the best things about it," Jane replied, not caring who heard. "It's not a bad thing to get swept away by a compelling love story. Right?" There was something so hopeful about it. She supposed that's why she read romance. She may have given up on love, but she still wanted to believe it was possible.

"It's been a long time since I've gotten swept away in a love story, missy." Bernadette leaned into the table. "But I will admit, the book did give me certain…*feelings*." Her voice reduced to a whisper again. "I haven't had any feelings for quite a while. Not since my Henry passed twenty years ago."

"I'm sorry." Maybe loneliness drove Bernadette to nitpicking and overstepping. Jane could certainly understand that. "That's one of the reasons I love to read. Even when things aren't going so well in your life, even when you're lonely or missing someone you love, you can surround yourself with characters you come to know and love and root for."

When she'd written her first novel, she'd given herself a place to belong. Maybe it wasn't healthy to spend so much time with her made-up friends, but it had gotten her through a lot of lonely years. Last week, she likely wouldn't have even called those years lonely, but now she realized that's exactly how her life in California felt. Lonely. Safe but also empty...

"I haven't thought of reading like that. Like surrounding yourself with friends." Bernadette ran her hand over the book's cover. "It has been awfully lonely since I buried my husband. We were married for over thirty years, and I'm not sure where my place in the world is without him."

"Your place will always be with the people you love. The people who love you. Although fictional characters can be much easier to spend time with than real people." She tried for lightness, but she could feel her smile wobble. Real people took so much energy. Real people could die or leave you or simply decide they didn't love you anymore.

"Isn't that the truth." The woman harrumphed. "Real people leave you eventually. You can't be with them forever. But I suppose it's worth it. Loving someone. Even in the loneliness afterward." She caught Jane in a perceptive gaze. "I noticed you left the shower with a certain gentleman the other night."

Bernadette didn't even have to say Toby's name for Jane's stomach to get that light fluttery feeling.

"He seems like a nice young man." Coming from Bernadette, that was a colossal compliment. "A bit showy, maybe. But what cowboy isn't?"

Jane picked up her book. That's what they were supposed to be discussing. Not Toby. She spent enough time thinking about him. About the depth she'd never given him credit for as well as the reckless, impulsive side of him. "Let's talk about the romance between Paris and Dean."

A rare, slow smile replaced Bernadette's frown. "You like him. Toby Garrett. Don't you?"

"I've known Toby for a long time." Jane squirmed. "But we're not a good match." She could kiss him all she wanted, but it didn't change the fact that their lives were headed in opposite directions. It didn't change the fact that he charmed women but had never had a serious relationship. Although if Aubrey had anything to say about it, that would change soon.

"He likes you as well," Beth's grandmother told her as though it was a fact. "I can tell. When I mentioned to him earlier that we were meeting here today, his eyes lit right up. He said he had a book to return so he might see me at the library."

Jane's shoulders got heavier. She started to look around, but she didn't have to look far. There was Toby settled into an easy chair near the reference desk. The cover of a very familiar book hid his face.

"That's him, isn't it?" Bernadette clapped her hands. "I told you he liked you." A knowing expression pursed her lips. "Maybe it's time for you to stop spending your days with fictional characters and let a real man sweep you away."

"We're not here to talk about me," Jane gently scolded. Clearly, she was a bad influence on Beth's grandma. Girlish smiles had replaced the woman's disapproving glares. Begrudgingly though, Jane had to admit "swept away" would be a good way to describe her heart at the moment. And she'd only caught a glimpse of Toby.

"*What?*" The older woman seemed to pout. "It might

be too late for me, darlin' but it's definitely not for you. Go talk to him! At least say hello."

Well, she had to now, if only to show Bernadette—and herself—they could simply be friends without any awkwardness between them. "Sure. Toby and I are *friends.* I can go say hello. Be right back." Jane stood and casually wandered over to where Toby sat. No big deal. She'd say hello, ask how his doctor appointment went, and then they could quickly discuss the upcoming welcome events for Beth's family, all while ignoring the fact that he was reading her book. "Hi there," she said a little too brightly as she sat down next to him.

"Hey." He lowered the book and turned up her internal thermostat with one of his signature smiles. "How's it going?"

"Good." She tried to relax her shoulders, but her heart had decided to go rogue on her and skip a couple beats. "How's the book?" she asked, keeping her expression even.

"It's good. I'm surprised you didn't like it." His eyes lingered on her face.

"Oh. Well. I liked it. Sure, I liked it," she sputtered. "I mean, it was really good." If she did say so herself. "What'd the doctor say about your shoulder?" If that wasn't an obvious change of subject, she didn't know what was.

"No news yet." Toby's eyes seemed to dull. "I'm having an MRI next week. We'll know more after that." He didn't smile or joke around or make light of the situation like he normally would have. In fact, his jaw tightened with what looked a lot like worry.

Jane reached for him without thinking, grazing her fingers over his arm. "I'm sorry. Waiting is hard." It seemed to be torturing him.

He studied her for a few silent seconds, his eyes drawing out another rise of emotion in her.

"Thanks," he finally said. "I know you're hanging out with Grandma B, but maybe we should talk about the welcome events with Beth's family. Sorry I haven't had much time to help."

"Right. No. That's okay." Jane blinked hard, trying to order her thoughts. What she really wanted to do was pull him into her arms and ease his worry the way she'd comforted him the other night, but instead she jumped into the details. "It'll be pretty simple. I figured we could start with a huge cowboy welcome breakfast before their mountain trail ride. Maybe have a picnic at the Lookout."

The tension that had been engrained in his expression softened. "Lookout?"

Oh, right. Not many people knew about the special spot her father had always taken her to. "Yeah, I used to go up there with my dad. There's a trail on the west side of the lake. It leads up to a ridge with a gorgeous view of the valley."

"Sounds amazing." He said it with a gentleness that prompted the threat of tears. Jane blinked them away. "Then we can ride back to the lodge and have full use of the beach and lake until dinner. I mean, that's what I was thinking, but if you have other ideas, we can discuss them." It was just that Beth had been talking nonstop about the wedding shower and how much fun she'd had. Jane felt compelled to make the next event even more memorable for her.

"That all sounds fine to me." He studied her for a long minute. "I'm assuming you remember how to get up to the Lookout then?"

"Oh." She would never forget that route, but… "I wasn't

planning to go on the ride." She hadn't been on a horse in years. Not since her dad had taken her. She looked away from Toby. "I can tell you how to get up there. And Pete should know." The wrangler had been happy to lead the ride when she'd asked him.

Toby sat up straighter. "Really? You're not coming?" He seemed to hesitate, but then continued. "You sure you don't want to? Sounds like the Lookout is a pretty special place."

"It is." The prospect of going to a place she'd shared with her father felt like too much. "I'm not sure I can do that."

He nodded as though he understood. "If you decide you want to, I'll be there. You won't have to face anything alone."

She wasn't sure that offered much consolation. Something happened when Toby looked at her. Her heart melted and her joints softened, and the practical logic that had always served her so well seemed almost out of reach. "I'll think about it," she managed.

Chapter Fifteen

Toby pulled up in front of Aubrey's parents' house, grateful that only her BMW SUV sat in the driveway. He parked along the curb and climbed out of the truck. This conversation would be much better without an audience.

Based on what had happened at the shower, it was pretty clear Aubrey had misread his intentions when he'd met with her those few times in Denver. There'd been a time he might've been okay with that, but that time had passed. He didn't intend to start up a relationship with the woman and she needed to know that.

Toby walked up the front porch steps and heard a dog barking somewhere inside. He rang the bell, ready to get this over with even though he wasn't sure exactly what to say.

Aubrey peeked out the window before she opened the door with a happy smile. "Toby! What a great surprise. I was just thinking about you."

He didn't know how to respond to that, so he simply said, "Hey, do you think we could talk for a minute?"

"Sure." She stepped aside as though she wanted him to come in. "Your timing couldn't be better. My parents are both at work."

He stayed where he was. Somehow it didn't feel right going in the house. "We should talk out here."

"Okay." Her smile fell away. "How's your shoulder?" she asked, leading him to a bench in front of the window.

"It's better." Thankfully. "The doc should call with the MRI results anytime." And he was torn between wanting to know where he stood and wanting the radiologist to take as much time as she wanted to read the results in case they weren't in their favor. But he hadn't come to talk about his shoulder. "Listen, Aubrey." He sat next to her. "I feel like maybe I gave you the wrong impression when we met for dinner after my surgery."

She turned to face him, moving closer. "What'd you mean?"

Toby moved to the end of the bench and made himself look at her. "I mean, I didn't intend to give you the idea I was looking for a relationship." But he could see how she would've misunderstood. He liked to be friendly. Sometimes he came across as too friendly. "The thing is, I don't think of you like that. You're a great friend, but I'm not looking for anything more than that."

The words sounded so trite, but they were genuine. He hadn't meant to lead her on, even though that's obviously what had happened.

He braced himself but Aubrey looked more confused than angry. "I don't understand."

He tried again. "When I told you about the wedding, I wasn't inviting you to go with me."

"Sure, you were." Aubrey laughed.

Toby couldn't even crack a smile. "No. I never asked

you to go with me. We were talking about our old friends from high school and I mentioned Ethan and Beth were getting married." He thought back through the conversation. They'd started reminiscing and there had definitely been flirting on both their parts. "I should've been clear about what I meant. I'm sorry."

"Are you saying you don't want me to be your date?" She took his hand in hers. "Because I've already made plans. Reconnecting with you has been amazing."

Whoa. He was so bad at this. He carefully withdrew his hand and pulled it back to his side. "It's great to see you again too, but I'm interested in someone else." That was the plain truth of it. Even if he wasn't sure she felt the same, even if he couldn't quite imagine what the future might look like. "I'm sorry I gave you the wrong impression."

Aubrey's mouth fell open with a look of disbelief. "So, you're dating someone else?"

"Not exactly. But I'm definitely interested in someone else." He might not be free to pursue Jane, but he wasn't going to lie to Aubrey. "We're both only home for the wedding though, so—"

"It's Jane?" The woman gasped. "You're not interested in Jane, are you? You can't be!"

Toby stood. "Why not?"

"Plain Jane?" Aubrey raised her voice. "She's totally not your type."

First of all, he got to decide who his type was, and second, had she really called Jane "plain"? "Listen, I'm sorry I've upset you, but it's really none of your business who I'm interested in." And anyway, his feelings for Jane weren't something he could dwell on. Once the doctor gave him his clearance that would be his sole focus again—getting back out on the circuit in time to qualify for the finals. "This isn't about Jane. It's about me." He'd made a mistake and he had to own up to it. "I meant what I said. I'm not looking for a relationship with anyone right now."

Aubrey stood too. "And there's nothing I can do to change your mind?" she asked with a teasing pout of her lips.

"I'm afraid not." There was only one woman he wanted, but he didn't know the first thing about being the kind of man she needed.

* * *

"This is the best breakfast I've ever had!" Beth looked up from the plate in front of her. Jane had to admit the authentic cowboy skillet she'd made had turned out even better than she'd hoped. All of Beth and Ethan's family members and the friends they'd invited to join them for the day were on at least a second helping.

The ambience didn't hurt either. Louise had directed her small kitchen staff to serve the breakfast in the ranch's outdoor pavilion on the south side of the lake. It provided the perfect vantage point to see the sun hovering over the eastern peaks beyond the water. Speaking of the lake, the water was glass this morning—completely still and glowing turquoise. Hints of steam rose off the surface, evaporating in the cool morning air.

"Everything really is delicious." Beth's mom wandered over. "I couldn't think of a more perfect place for Beth to get married." She hugged Jane. "All the memories you two have here make it even more special."

"I couldn't agree more." Beth sighed happily. "Janie,

do you remember when we snuck out with our sleeping bags and spent the night here?"

Jane laughed. "We hardly slept at all. Every time we heard a noise we were sure a bear was coming to eat us."

"You girls." Beth's mom shook her head with a smile. "So many stories. Many I'm sure I don't know about."

Jane shared a secretive smile with Beth. There were definitely stories neither of their moms had ever heard. Like the time they'd smoked a cigarette behind the boat shed. They'd both coughed until they'd thrown up. A nostalgic sigh slipped out. So many memories. So many stories. Would she lose them all when her mom sold the ranch?

"Anne!" Beth's dad waved her mom over. "There's an eagle over there." He pointed to the other side of the lake.

"Oh perfect! I've got my camera." Her mom hurried off with most of the other guests to ogle the majestic bird as it soared above them.

Fighting off sadness, Jane walked down the table refilling glasses of orange juice.

"Is Toby coming?" Beth glanced around.

"He's part of the wedding party, so I assume he'll be here." Jane kept her tone light. She hadn't seen Toby since they'd briefly spoken at the library almost a week ago and she'd told him she would consider going on the ride today. Her palms had been sweating ever since. There'd been a time when she wouldn't have thought twice about climbing on the back of a horse, but now riding would only bring up every memory she had with her father out on that trail.

"My grandmother mentioned he happened to be at the library when you two met the other day." Her friend's eyes sparkled with mischief, as if she'd already read into the news.

"We saw him." Jane cleared an empty plate from the table and dumped it into the trash can. She didn't mention her conversation with Toby. She hadn't mentioned their conversation after the wedding shower either. When it came to Toby, Jane didn't need any encouragement. Instead, she needed someone to remind her why it wouldn't be a good idea to spend more time with him. Only she couldn't think of anyone who would tell her that.

"My grandmother seems to think he likes you." Beth took another bite of the eggs, which had been combined with crunchy hash browns, pieces of thick-cut bacon, cheese, and local green chilis. "And I seem to remember you having a thing for him once upon a time. I warned Toby before you got home that he'd better behave himself, but he seems different around you. Less...," she paused as though searching for the right words, "...showy."

"Toby will always be showy." Being a performer was part of what made him such a good bull rider. Though knowing what she knew about him now, she understood what he was hiding behind that showmanship and the thought made her heart hurt. She shook her head. She couldn't allow her emotions to carry her away. "We would drive each other crazy. Don't you remember how we always argued back in high school? How we were always trying to outdo each other?"

"Well you know what they say about rivals." Her friend sipped the hot cowboy coffee that had been simmering over the fire. "They also make the best lovers."

"Only in romance novels." There were plenty of tropes to prove it—opposites attract, enemies to lovers. Jane's stomach did that annoying flip again, and she'd never liked gymnastics. "Besides, we're not rivals anymore." Time to change the subject. "We're just two people trying to give our dearest friends the best celebration we can."

Beth's eyes teared up. "Thank you again, Jane. I know this is a ton of work for you." Her friend pulled her into a half hug. "I appreciate it more than I can say. With the café, there's no way I could've figured out how to entertain everyone before the wedding." Beth rolled her eyes. "You get married in Colorado and everyone expects to be able to make it into this big vacation."

"Well, it's been really fun." That part had surprised her. Truthfully, she'd been so caught up in her feelings about being home she hadn't let herself think much about the wedding beyond making it as stress-free as possible for Beth. "Now I'd better go check on the horses. I have to make sure Pete is getting them all saddled up." And she may have to ask the wrangler for a quick refresher course on riding. It had been too long.

"Okay, we'll see you over at the stables in fifteen minutes," Beth said excitedly. "I might have just one more plate of this cowboy skillet first."

"Have as much as you'd like." If her friend thought the breakfast was good, wait until she tasted the smoked barbecue brisket sandwiches they were packing in for the picnic lunch on the trail.

Jane hurried from the pavilion, following the path along the lake to the stables. Eight horses were already tethered to the fence, all saddled up and ready to go.

Toby came walking out of the small building, leading a ninth horse by the halter. The sight of him brought on more internal acrobatics that set her off balance. She'd never realized her heart could spin like that.

"Morning," Toby said cheerfully, moseying on past

her to tie the horse to the fence. "Perfect day for a ride, huh?"

It had been. It had felt so cool out here ten minutes ago. Now, though, she almost felt warm enough to take off her sweatshirt. It was those damn jeans of his. Or maybe not so much the jeans as the way he filled them out.

Jane leaned into the fence to steady herself. "So, um, where's Pete?"

"Pete called and asked if I could lead the ride." Toby disappeared into the stable briefly before walking out with another saddle. "Sounds like he's not feeling so hot this morning."

Likely because he was out partying last night. She should've asked one of the older wranglers to help out today. Rookie mistake.

"I'm happy to help though." Toby hoisted the saddle onto the stallion's back and strapped it in place. "What do you think? Are you going to join us?"

She'd been ready to tell them no, that she had a lot of other details to attend to. But talking with Beth's mom made her realize she might not have this chance much longer. The chance to visit the places she used to love going with her dad. She might not get to relive memories that might be painful but were also such a big part of who she was. "I think so?"

Toby smiled, seeming to accept her hesitation. "Well you have a few more minutes to make up your mind. I still have to load the food." He gestured to some saddlebags lying on the ground nearby.

"There're only nine horses." Jane walked down the line to be sure she hadn't miscounted.

"Yeah." Toby started to cart over the saddlebags. "That's all we've got at the ranch these days."

Only nine? They used to have at least fifteen horses. Panic started to edge in. "What happened to the others?" Her father always boarded horses in exchange for letting the ranch use them for trail rides.

"It was too much work for your mom to keep caring for the horses, so she asked people to find other places to board." He went down the line attaching the lunch bags to the saddles.

"What're we going to do? We've got twelve guests, including us." She never neglected details like this. Now some of the guests would have to sit out of the ride, and that was one of the best parts of the day…

"It'll be fine." Toby walked over and messed with one of the horse's saddles. "Some of us will have to double up, that's all. I figure Ethan and Beth won't mind being in close quarters." He seemed extremely focused on that saddle. "And I guess you and I should pair up too. Since we're not paying customers and all."

"Or I can stay here." Yes, that would be better. She could work on confronting her issues another day. Emotion already sat thick in her throat. She didn't need to cry all over Toby.

"It's a beautiful day for a ride." Toby worked on one of the horse's bridles. "I bet the view at the Lookout will be perfect."

"It will be." She could almost picture it, with the lake glistening below. She watched him tend to the horses with those sure hands. There was no way she could do this alone but maybe she could do it with Toby…

Just then Beth and Ethan came walking up to the stables with the crowd of chattering family and friends trailing behind.

"This is going to be so great!" Her friend started to pet

one of the horses. "It feels like forever since we've been out on a ride." She turned to Ethan, her whole face shining with a smile. "Remember when we went on that romantic picnic last summer?"

"I'll never forget it." He put his arm around his fiancée, gazing at her with a steady sureness. Jane had to turn away. No one had ever looked at her like that. Or maybe she simply hadn't let anyone get close enough to look at her like that.

Toby joined them near the fence. "Jane's not sure she's going to go with us, but I can handle leading the group so no worries."

"You have to go!" Beth grabbed Jane's hand. "Please. It won't be the same without you." She sidled up to Jane and lowered her voice. "Besides, my grandmother is coming. I *need* you there to be my buffer. She loves you. You're all she talks about these days, and that means she's not complaining or telling me what to do."

Jane's eyes followed the path and found Bernadette stopped by the lake taking a picture on her phone.

"All right, all right, I'm coming." Jane dug around for some resolve. She would go, and she might cry, but at least she wouldn't keep hiding from the memories.

"What a lovely day." Bernadette traipsed up the path to where they stood. The genuine smile on her face made her look years younger.

Jane greeted the older woman with a hug. "I didn't know you were coming on the trail ride." But she was glad. At first Bernadette had seemed like a sourpuss, but Jane had enjoyed getting to know her.

"I didn't know I was coming on the ride either," Bernadette said. "But I guess there's no time like the present to start living." The woman winked at Jane. "Am I right, girl?"

"I suppose." That was exactly the kind of philosophy she needed to adopt right about now.

"We're out of horses," Toby said apologetically.

"She can ride with my grandpa." Ethan pointed out a distinguished-looking older gentleman who'd already made friends with one of the horses.

"Hey, Pops. You won't mind if Beth's grandma rides with you, right?" he called.

"Not a bit." The man sauntered over in true cowboy fashion and gave Bernadette a kind smile along with a nod. "I'm William. It's nice to meet you, ma'am."

Jane could've been wrong, but she swore the older woman blushed. "And I'm Bernadette. You'll have to go easy on me, I'm afraid. I haven't been on a horse in years."

"Well, it seems like a good day to get back in the saddle." William held out his arm to her. "Come on. I'll introduce you to our horse."

Aw... Jane couldn't help but smile watching the two of them walk away.

"You look like you're thinking up a plot for a romance between two people in their golden years."

She swung her head to look at Toby. He knew. Or at least he suspected she'd written *Mountain Destiny*. His grin made it clear he was fishing, and she had to make sure he didn't catch anything.

"I'm not plotting. The woman looks happy, that's all. When I first met her, she seemed to have a permanent frown in place."

"She likes you."

Funny. That's exactly what Bernadette had said to her about Toby. *He likes you.* Maybe. Or did he simply like a challenge?

Toby almost looked like he wanted to say more, but instead he turned to the horse next to them. "I guess we should get this party started, huh?"

"I guess." Jane kept her distance from the horse. He was beautiful with a black shiny coat, but also so tall and powerful. Her dad had taught her that horses were unpredictable. Even the sweetest of them could spook without warning...

"Are you ready for this?" Toby asked, messing with the stirrups.

"It's been a long time." And her father had always been there when she'd ridden, keeping her safe. He'd had a way with animals. He'd had a way with her. A curtain of tears fell over her eyes. She quickly looked down in an attempt to hide them. The floodgates were about to open, and she didn't need Beth and Ethan's family and friends to witness an emotional breakdown.

"He's not gone." Toby drew her in closer. "You know that right? You said so yourself, he's everywhere here."

Jane bit her lip, nodding.

"We'll look for him while we ride." Toby lifted her face to his. "You point him out to me when you see him. Okay?"

Sniffling back those burning hot tears, she nodded again.

"I'll give you a boost." Toby nudged her toward the horse. Everyone else had already mounted and the animals were getting restless. She couldn't procrastinate any longer.

Toby laced his fingers together so she could step into his hand. "One, two, three." He boosted her up and she swung her leg over the horse's wide girth. Being up so high almost left her breathless. She shifted and wiggled her way to the front of the saddle so Toby could get on behind her.

He effortlessly pulled himself up and sat *right* behind her, his muscular chest cradling her back. Strong arms came around her as he took ahold of the reins, and she could feel the warmth of his breath against her neck.

"Ready?" The deep murmur put the entire left side of her body on high alert.

"I'm ready." She tried holding on to the saddle horn, but when the horse started off with a lurch, she rocked sideways, so instead she steadied her hands on Toby's thighs.

"Everyone can fall in behind me," he called to the group. Her touch didn't seem to affect him nearly as much as his affected her.

"Your mom told me that your father built this trail." Toby steered the horse into the trees where the narrow, rocky path started.

"He did." She'd been a little girl back then. "He told me he was building the trail for me. So I would always have a path to follow and I wouldn't get lost. I did get lost though." She had gotten lost after he died. She'd lost the ability to build connections. She'd lost the ability to see herself through her father's eyes and had instead started to believe what everyone else said about her. Plain Jane…

"Maybe this trail will lead you back to him," Toby murmured against her hair. He took the reins in one hand and slid his other arm around her waist, steadying her with a strength that settled the ache building in her heart.

Chapter Sixteen

I guess we should clean up and get ready to head back." Toby leaned back on his elbows on the blanket he'd ended up sharing with Jane, but he didn't move to get up.

Currently, she was lying on her back staring up at the white clouds billowing in the sky above. All around them, the group was in various stages of finishing their lunch. A few people were exploring the small pond nestled into the mountainside, but most were sitting on the comfortable blankets enjoying the view. He hadn't known about this spot, but Jane had remembered the way to the place her dad used to take her, so that's where they'd come.

While everyone else ate lunch and wandered, he and Jane had spent the hour talking on the blanket. He knew they were being watched. Mainly by Ethan and Beth, as well as Bernadette. They all had to see what he saw—the chemistry he felt with Jane, the way he couldn't stop watching her, the way he seemed to forget about everyone else even though he was supposed to be the trip leader.

He'd been so distracted he'd lost sight of the trail a few times.

"I guess we should get ready to go soon." Jane didn't get up. Instead she turned onto her stomach, propping her chin on her fist, looking carefree and sexy. "Thank you for encouraging me to come. I needed this."

"I'm glad you came." Toby inched closer to her. God, it was impossible for him to stay away from her. When he'd seen her sadness earlier, all he'd wanted to do was take it away, to make this easier for her. He knew he might not be the best choice for her. He knew their paths didn't necessarily travel in the same direction, but he couldn't deny his feelings for her. "I know how hard it is to confront those memories." But she seemed happy too. Sure, she'd cried, but she'd also smiled a lot while she told him about her father. And now, lying here, she looked serene.

"I know you understand," Jane murmured, watching him carefully. "And as difficult as it is to remember, it helps. In some ways this has brought me back to him." She rested her hand over his. "What about you? Have you talked to your parents about Tanner yet?"

"Oh. No." He'd thought about it, but what was he supposed to do? Bring it up out of the blue all these years later? They'd already built a life without his brother. None of their friends knew. He couldn't change things now.

Jane sat up and hugged her knees into her chest. "I thought you wanted to try."

"I do. Eventually." But he was tired of obsessing over what he would say to them. The truth was, he didn't know. "Let's talk about that another time. This day is too perfect." Toby tucked her long dark hair behind her ear. "You're perfect," he said, trying to lure out her smile again. He could live to make this woman smile.

But Jane simply shook her head and ducked her chin to her chest, staring at the ground.

"What?" Toby sat up too. After a morning of talking and taking in the scenery together, Jane had opened up to him. Now she was shutting down again.

"You don't have to pretend for me, Toby." She picked a blade of grass and rolled it between her fingers. "In fact, I don't want some big performance. I want to see the real you."

"You've seen more than most—"

"We're going to head back."

Toby turned around to find Ethan and Beth standing behind them.

Right. He and Jane were supposed to be leading the ride. He started to stand. "If everyone's ready, we can all pack up—"

"Actually, would you two mind staying back to clean up?" Beth asked sweetly…and a little suspiciously. "I really have to pee. Ethan and I can lead the way down. You two can catch up in a little while."

Jane narrowed her eyes. "You can't wait ten minutes for us to pack up so we can all head down together?" She wasn't buying the act. Toby wasn't either. Their friends obviously wanted to give them some alone time.

"Nope. I definitely can't wait." Beth dragged Ethan away. "Come on people! Mount up! We're heading back. Follow Ethan and me."

Shaking her head with a small smile, Jane watched the group pack up, but she sat still while the group got their things together and headed off down the trail. As soon as the last horse disappeared, she lay on her back and stared up at the sky again. "That was real subtle."

Toby laughed. "Beth is never subtle." He lay down on his side next to her and guided her face to his. "I'm not trying to put on some big performance you know." He realized sometimes it just happened. "I won't say anything I don't mean. Not to you."

Her eyes shied away as though she didn't know what to do with that. He didn't either, but he'd also gotten tired of fighting that pull between them. Why did he have to figure it out now? Maybe he should quit worrying about the future and live now.

"I'm not sure what to say to my parents," he admitted.

The admission drew Jane's eyes back to his.

"I know you had a great relationship with your dad. You were close to him." He propped himself up on his elbow so he could stare steadily into her eyes. "But I don't have that kind of relationship with my parents. I never have. My parents and I have never discussed how I felt about anything. Ever." So, he wasn't good at this. Talking about real stuff. Figuring out how to fix the underlying issues. He was much better at distracting himself.

"Maybe that could change," Jane suggested. "Maybe talking to them will turn that around."

"Maybe." He didn't let his doubts show. Instead he shot Jane a grin. "Would it have changed things between us in high school?"

"What'd you mean?" she asked warily.

Toby inched closer. "I mean would it have made a difference if I'd told you how I really felt about you after I kissed you?"

"How did you feel about me?" she half whispered.

She didn't know. She'd never known. "It caught me off guard. That kiss...it was different." The chemistry between them had taken him by surprise. "I liked you. I wanted you." Maybe he always had, he didn't know. Maybe that's why he'd always teased her and challenged her.

Jane stared past him at the mountains. "I liked you too."

"But you said—"

"That kiss terrified me. And I was so embarrassed when everyone saw us kissing." Jane turned her face back to his. "I didn't want to like you. I'm not sure I want to like you now. It's not safe." An honest doubt lingered in Jane's eyes. He could see it there holding her back.

"I understand. But my feelings for you are real." That's all he knew. His feelings for Jane ran deeper than his doubts. Toby brought his hand to her jaw and guided her lips to his. Jane's chest rose with a sharp intake of breath, and he knew she felt it too—the same desire pouring through him. He savored the taste of her lips, the heat of her mouth, the quiet whimpers that came from her throat.

Jane swung her leg over his hips, and he shifted to his back, guiding her to lie over his body. Their lips found a rhythm, moving together, opening so he could explore the wet heat of her mouth with his tongue.

Jane raised her head for a second, her eyes closed, her breathing ragged, and Toby took the chance to kiss his way down her neck, lingering just below her ear.

"I definitely want to like you now," she gasped.

Toby pulled his lips away from her skin. "Thank God. Because I sure as hell like you." He pushed up to a sitting position and Jane repositioned herself so she was straddling his lap. "Back in high school you always looked at me like I annoyed you." She'd roll her eyes at him or discount the answers he gave in class.

"Well you did annoy me." A smirk plumped her swollen lips. "But you were hot. And pretty nice most of the time. Obnoxious as hell, but also pretty nice."

"I'm even nicer now." Toby leaned in and brushed his lips across her neck.

"You're hotter too," Jane murmured. "But we need to pack up and meet Ethan and Beth to finish the party." She scooted off his lap.

The party? What party? Toby eased onto his knees and distracted her with another long, sultry kiss. "When can we finish *this*?" he asked.

Jane wrapped her arms around his neck. "I guess we'll wait and see."

* * *

Toby had so many stories. She liked listening to him talk about riding—the traveling, the people he'd met. He'd entertained her the whole way down the mountain. But she hadn't forgotten how he avoided talking about his parents back at the picnic, or that when she'd brought up the subject, he'd simply turned it into a walk down memory lane, revealing he'd liked her back in high school. And she'd fallen for it, of course. Willingly.

When Toby touched her, when his eyes pulled her in, she didn't want to think about anything else. She only wanted to feel something. But it didn't take long for her thoughts to catch up with her. For that nagging reminder to kick in. He'd be headed back out to the circuit as soon as he was able and if she wasn't careful, he'd take her heart with him.

"Maybe we should skip the lake activity and take a detour to my place." Toby rested his chin on her shoulder.

"I think we've been spotted." Beth waved at them from across the lake where she and Ethan were kayaking.

"Damn." Toby steered the horse in the direction of the stable and behind a grove of aspen trees. "Guess we'll have to hold that thought then." He said the words as if they caused him physical pain. He stopped the horse and dismounted, grinning up at her. "At least a dip in the cold lake will help."

She wouldn't be going for a dip. No way. She didn't even want to get near that water. In fact, she needed a little space. The thoughts, the fears, the doubts were growing louder. "I have some things to check on." She swung her leg over the horse and slid off, landing in Toby's arms.

"Maybe they're things I could help you check on?" he asked, locking his arms around her waist.

Desire rolled through her, drowning out everything else. She wanted him to hold her. She wanted him to kiss her. She wanted more. But she had to be practical. "People will wonder why we both disappeared." Though after what they'd pulled at the picnic, it seemed their friends were trying to throw them together. "I'll come down to the beach as soon as I make sure dinner is all set," she promised.

"I'll get the horses situated so I can meet you over there." He kissed her lips and Jane started to sink against him again, letting him pull her away from everything else. She let herself stay there, let herself kiss him back, feeling that pull between them intensify. God, she wanted to surrender to it, but instead she clung to her doubts and eased out of his embrace. "I'll see you soon."

Toby's expression fell into disappointment, but he nodded and started to tend to the horses.

Avoiding the beach area, Jane hurried up the path to the main lodge and found Louise in the kitchen. "I'm here to help," she announced looking for an apron in the pantry.

"I don't need help." The woman finished wrapping a pan with cellophane. "You know my staff is more than capable. We got all the prep done and I'll just throw it all in the ovens to warm it up later."

"Oh." Jane hung the apron back up. "Well there must be something I can do."

"There is." Louise stuck her hands on her hips. "Go on out there and have fun with your friends." The woman peered out the window in the direction of the beach. "The day's too pretty to be stuck inside."

"I don't mind being stuck inside." It would be better than watching everyone enjoy themselves while she sat a safe distance away from the water. Jane scanned the counters, which were unfortunately clear. "What about dessert? I can help with that."

Tsking at her, Louise shook her head. She wasn't having it. "Already in the refrigerator." She gave Jane's shoulder a gentle nudge in the direction of the door. "Don't let them have all the fun out there, dear girl. You can put your suit on and lay out in the sun. You don't have to go near the water."

"Yeah, maybe." Or maybe she'd head back to her cabin and work on her book. She could get in an hour or so before anyone missed her. "I am helping with cleanup tonight, though," she called on her way out the door so she couldn't hear Louise's reply. The woman would likely tell her she didn't need help cleaning up either, but her "very capable" staff consisted of two college-aged assistants, and they could all likely use an extra set of hands.

After slipping out the door, Jane moved stealthily down the path back toward her cabin, trying to stay in the shadows of the trees so she wouldn't be spotted. From the sound of things, everyone was having so much fun they wouldn't notice her anyway.

Once she was safely inside, Jane sat at the small writer's desk where she'd spent hours reworking her story. The desk was right in front of a large picture window that had a perfect view of the lake. It had provided plenty of inspiration before, but now she stared out at the beach and found herself searching for Toby.

Her heart did a leap. He and Ethan were doing handstands on the paddleboards, the show-offs. Everyone else seemed to be lounging on the beach cheering for those two, only encouraging their reckless—

Hold on. Jane leaned closer to the window. Was that Aubrey? She quickly scurried over to the binoculars that sat on the living room windowsill and brought the group into focus. Yes, that was definitely Aubrey. Wearing a revealing red bikini. No surprise there. She was clapping her hands together, obviously quite impressed with Toby's theatrics. It looked like some of their other high school acquaintances had shown up to join the party. A few of Ethan and Toby's old football buddies. Some of Aubrey's friends.

Well, good. Jane was glad she hadn't gone down there then. They'd never been her friends anyway. She'd just hide out in here for a while and get another chapter written.

For some reason though, she couldn't seem to put down the binoculars. Toby did a side flip, splashing into the water. A gasp caught in her throat, but within seconds, his head bobbed on the surface, his wet face shining with a grin.

"Knock, knock." The cabin door opened, and her mom poked her head in. "There you are! I've been looking everywhere for you."

"Oh." Jane quickly tried to hide the binoculars behind her back. "Did you need something?"

Her mother walked fully inside the cabin. "I noticed you weren't out there with the other kids. I wanted to check and make sure everything was okay."

"Everything's fine." She didn't mention they weren't kids anymore. Some of the boys out there still acted like they were. Jane couldn't stop her gaze from drifting back to the beach where they'd started a volleyball game. Aubrey was on Toby's side of the net of course.

"Are you sure?" Her mom walked over, obviously suspicious. "It doesn't seem like everything's fine. Why are you hiding out in here? And what're you holding behind your back?"

Oh Lord, why did it feel like she was back in high school again? When Jane didn't say anything, her mother walked past her and spotted the binoculars.

"Bird-watching?" she asked with a smile.

Jane thought about lying, but it wouldn't do any good. "I was just making sure everyone was staying safe down there."

Her mom held out her hand and wiggled her fingers in a silent hand-them-over gesture. Jane gave her the binoculars with a huff. This was definitely a little too reminiscent of high school. Her mother checking on her, concerned because she wasn't out "having fun."

"I see Aubrey stopped by," her mother commented, peering through the binoculars. "I'm not sure that's the best attire for playing beach volleyball."

"Depends on your goals." Jane shouldn't sound so snarky. The truth was, in some ways she envied Aubrey. She'd always been outgoing and confident and fun, and yes persistent, but that seemed to be working out for her. Jane, on the other hand, had always felt more like she did right now—standing on the outside looking in.

"Sweetie..." Her mom set the binoculars back on the windowsill. "Why aren't you out there too? Beth and Ethan are your good friends. And Toby...I think he likes you."

"Toby likes everyone." And everyone liked him. People were drawn to him the same way people were drawn to Aubrey. Maybe those two belonged together. And she belonged behind her computer. "Besides, I have a lot to do." She brought her laptop out of sleep mode, hoping her mom would take the hint.

"Are you sure that's what it is?" Her mom dragged over a chair from the kitchen table and sat next to her. She'd never let Jane off the hook that easily. But instead of annoying her like it used to when her mother would pester her, Jane was grateful for the chance to talk.

"I've never been good at it." Jane let her shoulders slump. "Being in a big crowd, fitting in." She generally didn't mind being reserved and introverted, but watching Aubrey out there made her wish she could be more outgoing, more laid-back, always ready to have fun. Instead she tended to be serious and cautious, maybe too cautious. But that's who she was. And she wasn't going to pretend to be someone she wasn't. Not even for Toby.

"I love that you don't fit in," her mom said.

"I'm sorry, what?" Jane didn't hide the shock. Was this the same mother who'd tried to buy her all the cool clothes? Who'd bugged her about inviting Aubrey over and becoming friends with her? "I always thought you wanted me to fit in."

"I worried about you, Jane." Sadness echoed in her tone. "Especially after your dad died...I desperately wanted to reach you, to help you, but I felt like I was constantly failing. You two were so close..."

"That's because we both loved books. We loved to debate. We loved to read *National Geographic* together." They were alike in so many ways, but Jane definitely hadn't inherited her father's adventure gene.

"He understood you." Her mom dabbed at her eyes. "I watched you change after he passed. You were so closed off. You hid from everything. In my own way I tried to help you, but I couldn't seem to reach you. Not the way he had."

Jane reached for the tissues, handing one to her mom and keeping one for herself. She couldn't remember the last time she'd cried this much. Back in California she'd had no reason to cry. No reason to feel anything. It was actually nice to feel the tears flowing down her cheeks. "You didn't fail me. I knew you loved me. But after he died, it was hard for me to let myself be loved." It was still hard. Love felt temporary. "And I didn't think I could stand losing it again. I still don't think I could stand it." It wasn't only the grief and the sadness. Those, she'd expected. Even the fear made sense. But there was something else hiding in her heart too. A stronger emotion that almost felt like...anger. She could never say it, but sometimes she was still so mad at her dad for going on that trip.

"You did survive, Janie. You're so strong." Her mother pressed her palm against Jane's cheek. "To me, you've always been this beautiful old soul. Too good for most of the kids your own age. Too good for almost anyone now." Her mom stared up at the ceiling for a second before looking at her again. "But I suppose, perhaps, maybe Toby could someday convince me he deserves you."

That made Jane smile through her tears. Maybe, perhaps. "You are right about one thing though." Her gaze drifted back to the window. Outside, the volleyball game was still in full swing. "I hid from everything." From relationships, from anything she perceived as risky. "I still hide."

Her mother nodded. "I do too."

"Really?" Her mother had been so brave, so stoic.

She'd taken the ranch and made it hers. She'd supported her family. Not once had she acted scared.

"I hid behind this place, behind work." Her mom looked around the cabin. "It gave me an excuse to stay here, to stay busy, to ignore the things I really crave—some adventure, maybe the chance to love again." She looked at Jane with a sad smile. "Those desires are easier to ignore when you cover them up with other things."

Jane understood that. She'd trained herself to ignore those cravings, to hide behind things like studying and work, and yes, even writing.

"It's scary stepping out from behind the things you use to guard yourself," her mother said. "But we both have to step out, honey. There's a whole life waiting for us on the other side of our fears."

Chapter Seventeen

There you are."

The sound of Toby's voice was all it took to warm Jane in the chilled evening. True to her word to Louise, Jane had been cleaning up the pavilion after the bonfire and s'mores. She'd collected two bags of trash and had wiped down the tables while Toby had driven some of their friends home.

All evening they hadn't had a moment alone, but now Jane turned to see him walking toward her. He'd put on a flannel over his T-shirt, and his hair was tousled from the long day of swimming. Even though it was a dark evening with no moon, the dim lights from the pavilion seemed to brighten his eyes.

"You look cold." He ran his hands up and down her arms in a caress.

"Do I?" She couldn't hold back a smile. She definitely wasn't cold. Her heart beat fast and a fiery heat stirred low in her stomach. After her conversation with her mother earlier that afternoon, anticipation had been simmering. Toby made her feel things, and while that was what scared her the most about him, it was also freeing somehow.

She couldn't deny she had feelings for him. They were still fragile, still tentative, but they'd already put down roots in her heart and even though her knees were shaky at the thought, she wanted to let those roots grow.

"Want to take a walk?" Toby's voice sounded lower.

"Sure." She slipped away from him and came back carrying the trash bags. "We can bring these to the dumpsters."

"Romantic," Toby said with a laugh. But he hoisted both the bags in one hand as though they were weightless.

"What can I say? I'm practical." Jane led the way out of the pavilion to the path that skirted the lake. The night was calm enough that the lake's still surface reflected the stars shining overhead. Jane pulled her phone out of her pocket to light the trail in front of them.

"You are practical," Toby agreed. "But I also think you're a romantic too."

Even with the light shining on the path, Jane nearly stumbled. "What makes you say that?"

Toby kept quiet, simply continuing down the path to the dumpsters they kept behind the boatshed. Jane quickly caught up with him, holding her breath.

The man seemed content to keep her in suspense. After he'd stowed the trash and latched the bear-proof containers, he took her hand and led her closer to the water. "I have a question for you. It might sound crazy."

Jane snuck a peek at his face. He knew. He had to know…

"Did you write that book I checked out from the library?"

Jane opened her mouth to tell him no. That was crazy. Of course, she hadn't written the book. But something stopped her.

Toby turned to her fully as though he wanted to gauge her expression. "Because it's an incredible book. And there were times when I was reading it that I swear I heard your voice. I felt like I recognized the characters. And I especially liked Beau." A grin hiked up one corner of his mouth while his eyes searched hers. "Maybe it's a coincidence. And maybe it's not."

Jane stared back at him, holding perfectly still, so tempted to protect her secret, to keep her guard up.

"You don't have to tell me—"

"Yes," she blurted out before she lost the nerve.

"Yes?" Toby's mouth fell open. He obviously hadn't expected her to confirm his suspicions.

Jane swallowed hard, grasping at courage. He'd told her his secret. She could trust him with this. "I wrote it. *Mountain Destiny*. That's my book."

"I knew it." He half laughed. "At first I thought I was crazy, but the more I read the more I thought you had to be the author." He shook his head, something that resembled pride beaming from his eyes. "I couldn't put it down. You're so talented, Jane."

"Really?" Tears pricked at the corners of her eyes. She'd poured her heart and soul into that book never thinking it would amount to anything…

"Really." He took both of her hands in his, warming her skin. "Why don't you want anyone to know you're the author? That's a huge accomplishment."

"It's scary to put yourself out there like that." Not for him maybe with that larger than life personality, but it terrified her. "I'm glad you know though. Because I have a confession to make." Jane eased closer to him and rested her hands on his chest. "In order to write a cowboy, I had to sort of dig into my past and remember what I'd learned about them."

"Oh yeah?" He didn't look at all surprised by the revelation. "What had you learned about them?"

"Well, I only knew one, really." She moved her hands up to his shoulders. "And he was sexy..."

"Was?" Toby's grin dipped into a frown.

"*Is*," she corrected. "And he's fun and funny. Strong. Confident. Sometimes cocky, but only when he has a right to be." She brushed her lips against his in a fleeting kiss. "And he's also thoughtful and noble." Her hand drifted back to the left side his chest. "He has a huge heart."

"He's flawed too," he told her. "But he tries hard."

"We're all flawed." Jane held his face in line with hers. "That's what makes us real."

Toby lowered his lips to hers, stroking her cheek with his thumb. The kiss started off slow and searching, a heat building between them. "Let's go inside," she whispered against his lips.

Murmuring an agreement, he slipped his hand in hers and they hurried off along the path together. Jane found it hard to hold her cell phone light steady. "Your cabin is closer," she murmured, watching the ground so she wouldn't stumble.

Toby grinned over at her, moving faster. He led her up the porch steps and hurriedly opened the front door, gesturing for her to go in first.

It still amazed her that the place looked nothing like it had when her father had made it his own. Not long after he'd died, her mother had the cabin completely renovated when she decided she wanted to focus on weddings. The interior still had rustic undertones with aged, wide-plank oak floors and the original stone fireplace, but the kitchen had been redone with sleek modern touches—stained concrete countertops, gray cabinets and stainless appliances. It was simple but nice—an open living room, kitchen, and dining room, and she knew there were two bedrooms down the hall…

"Want something to drink?" Toby guided her into the kitchen.

She moved her gaze back to his lips. "No." All she wanted was for him to kiss her again, to help her step out from behind her walls. But she didn't know what to say…how to put words to what she felt, how to tell him what she wanted him to make her feel. So instead of talking, she pulled her sweatshirt up and over her head and dropped it on the ground next to her.

Toby's gaze held hers before lowering down the front of her. He seemed to take his time studying the details of her body. Jane's heart pounded as she unbuttoned her jeans and slid them down her hips so she could step out of them and kick them aside.

Goose bumps prickled her skin, but she didn't feel cold anymore. Toby's heated, smoldering gaze started a pulsing burn inside of her.

"I love looking at your body." His eyes wandered back to hers.

"I don't think I've ever let anyone look." In every romantic encounter she'd ever had she'd made sure to move through the undressing part and getting into bed part as quickly as possible. But Toby seemed to like taking it slower. She was liking it too. It made her heart pound so hard it felt like it could burst through her chest.

"I want to see everything. All of you." His arms stayed

down at his sides, giving her the freedom to show him, to take control.

"I want to see all of you too." Leaving her bra and underwear on, she unbuttoned his shirt and pushed it off his shoulders, then brought her hands to his bare chest before moving slowly down, dragging her fingertips over his skin. Toby had started to breathe harder, deeper, his shoulders rising and falling.

Jane slipped her fingers under the elastic band on his boxer briefs and started to inch them down over his chiseled hips.

He took over, quickly shoving them down to his ankles like he couldn't wait to get rid of them.

Now Jane took her time looking at him—the way muscles rippled all down his body. His obvious desire for her stoked that inner fire, and she reached around to unclasp her bra, slowly sliding it down her shoulders while Toby fixed his gaze to her body. Next, she shimmied her underwear down her hips and bent to pull it off.

"You are the sexiest woman alive," Toby said with a low seductive growl.

He definitely made her feel like she was the sexiest woman alive. Jane took his hand and pulled him to her. His other hand skimmed her hip, the touch sparking an aching desire for more.

Right there in the kitchen underneath the dim recessed lighting, Toby smoothed his large callused hands up her sides drawing her in against his body. Jane clasped his wrists and guided his hands to her breasts, holding them there. Toby lowered his mouth to hers, sealing her lips in a wet, arousing kiss. She opened her mouth to him and found his tongue with hers, taking the kiss deeper. Toby caressed her breasts, his fingers drawing circles around her nipples.

Jane had to pull away from his mouth to gasp in a breath. She swore her lungs were on fire. Toby tilted her head back and kissed her chin, then ran his tongue down her neck. She threaded her hands into his hair, urging him to move lower.

His mouth was even hotter than the fire burning inside of her. He kissed a path between her breasts and then glided his tongue to her right nipple, which he took into his mouth.

So, this is how it felt. All those scenes she'd written in her book…she'd never felt all the things she wanted her characters to feel. The deep stirring of passion and pleasure. The desperate longing for release.

"Toby," she whispered. "Please. Oh, God please." No man had ever reduced her to such a desperate plea.

"Tell me what you want, sweetness," he murmured against her skin.

She had moved way past want. "I need you to make love to me. Right now." So she could break apart in his arms and he could hold her together.

Toby moved away from her and found a condom in his wallet. After he'd put it on, he secured one arm around her and pulled her right leg up, edging her against the wall. Securing her leg around his waist, she opened her knee out to the side and tugged on his hips until he was against her, pressing into her.

She gasped as he pushed deeper. God, he went so deep. His hand held her backside, coaxing her to move with him. Her body trembled so much she could hardly stand, but he was strong enough for both of them. Toby gazed down into her eyes, moving inside of her, thrusting his hips, building that tantalizing pressure until she couldn't hold it together anymore. The orgasm shattered her control, quaking through her, forcing a cry from her lips. Relief crashed over her as Toby thrust once more, holding her tighter while he came into her.

Jane leaned against him, resting her head on his shoulder. He kissed the top of her head, and then guided her leg down so she had both feet on the floor. Not that she could stand up straight.

"I'm a little wobbly," she confessed, still holding on to him.

"Then let me help." He swept her up into his arms and started off down the hall.

She laced her arms around his neck. "Where are we going?"

"To the bedroom," he said, veering to the left. His bedroom smelled like him, like fresh laundry and aftershave. Toby set her on the bed. "Do you need anything?" he asked.

Shaking her head, she pulled him to the bed with her. "Only you."

Chapter Eighteen

When Jane opened her eyes, two things occurred to her. One, she was in Toby's bed with him sound asleep next to her. And two, she had to be late. "Oh my God!" She was supposed to meet Beth at the café so they could have coffee and then walk over to the beauty parlor for manis and pedis! "Shoot." She scrambled to find her way out of the tangle of sheets and blankets while trying not to reinjure Toby in the process.

Eyes still closed, he groaned and captured her in his arms, pulling her in against his naked body.

Jane instantly went still, luxuriating in the feel of his skin against hers, his breath warm and even on her neck. Contentment seemed to weight her to the mattress. She really could stay here all day.

Toby's breathing deepened as though he'd fallen back asleep. She could too, but instead her gaze drifted to the window, to the bright sunshine outside. No, no, no. She really could not stay here all day. It had to be at least nine o'clock.

"What time is it?" she asked, shaking Toby's arm.

"Don't care." His hand slid down her hip, hitching her body even closer to his.

His sleepy tone prompted a smile. She could relate. They hadn't exactly gotten much sleep last night...not that she was complaining.

"Toby, I have to go." She shifted onto her side to face him fully, which turned out to be a mistake. His eyes fluttered, and then his lips came for hers, pulling her back into oblivion with another kiss. A buzzing sound coming from the floor interrupted.

"That's my phone!" She squirmed free and nearly fell all the way off the bed reaching for her discarded jeans so she could pull her phone out of her pocket. "It's ten after nine!" She sat straight up. "And I have four missed calls from Beth."

"So?" Toby crawled over to her. "Call her back and tell her you're staying in bed all day." He snuck a hand up her thigh, but she swatted it away with a laugh. "I can't stay in bed all day. I'm the maid of honor and I take my duties very seriously." She quickly hit the call button and brought the phone to her ear.

"Are you alive?" Beth asked before Jane could apologize. "Because you're exactly forty minutes late, and you're never late."

"I'm so sorry!" Jane pushed off the bed, searching for her other clothes. "I overslept. But I'll be there as soon as I can."

"She needs to stay in bed all day," Toby called.

Jane covered the speaker with her hand and shot him a look. "Give me twenty minutes," she said, then cut off the call before Toby blew their cover. Holding her jeans against her chest, Jane darted out to the kitchen where her other clothes lay in a pile. She'd only brought her jeans in last night so her phone would be close by and thank God she had. Poor Beth would've been calling all morning.

"Want me to make you some breakfast?" Toby strutted out of the bedroom in a pair of black boxer briefs and it was a darn good thing she'd already put on her underwear and bra. She'd had no idea a cowboy could look his sexiest in the morning.

"I make a mean buttermilk pancake." He came over and slid his arms around her, gazing down into her eyes.

"I wish I could stay." She really really really wished, but… "I promised Beth we'd get our nails done. And I'm the maid of honor."

"I get it." Toby kissed her and then let her go.

"What're you doing today?" She pulled on her sweatshirt and wobbled while she put on her jeans.

"I have to head to Denver later this afternoon for a doctor's appointment."

"Oh. Right." He'd mentioned something about that, about finally discussing the results of his latest MRI with the surgeon. "I hope it goes well." She wanted those words to be sincere, but there was a part of her that also hoped the doctor would tell him he wasn't ready, that he couldn't go back out on the circuit. Not yet. God, she was a terrible person. But if his shoulder had fully healed, it would change things. Right now, with him sidelined, she could pretend this was the way it would be, them waking up together in the morning, maybe sharing breakfast together before they went about their days. But once the doctor released him, she wouldn't be able to pretend anymore. She'd have to let him go.

"When can I see you again?" Toby held her hands in his, weaving their fingers together.

Her heart pounded with anticipation and ached with dread at the same time. “Not sure.” She wasn’t sure about a lot of things. All it took was one doctor appointment for that uncertainty to creep back up.

“How about tonight? I’ll take you out. We can go on a real date.”

“Sure.” She covered up her doubts with a smile. “I’m free tonight. Just call me after your appointment.” Before he could see her hesitation, she brushed a kiss across his lips and hurried out the door.

Exactly eight minutes and one blown red light later, Jane slid into the booth across from Beth, noting her friend had already finished her coffee. “I’m soooo sorry.”

Beth wasted no time accepting her apology or making small talk. Instead she seemed to give Jane a critical assessment. “Aren’t those the clothes you had on yesterday?”

Jane glanced down at her wrinkled sweatshirt. *Crap.* If Beth found out she’d slept with Toby, her friend would get all excited and have so many expectations. She really should’ve thought up a good excuse for the rumpled clothes on the way over. “Um, yeah I did wear these yesterday…” *Think, damn it.* She wrote fiction for crying out loud! “I haven’t had time lately to do much laundry.”

“Mmm-hmm.” Beth propped her head on her fist. “I find it very curious that Toby wasn’t answering his phone all morning either.”

“That *is* curious.” She cleared the squeak of guilt out of her throat. “He must’ve been busy.”

“Oh, I’m pretty sure he was busy all right.” Beth leaned back and crossed her arms eyeing the messy bun on top of Jane’s head with a knowing smile. “It looks like you were awfully busy as well. Too busy to do your hair.

Hmmm. What could you be that busy with so early in the morning?"

Jane let a sigh sag her shoulders. She couldn't spin a story fast enough to get her out of this. "Okay fine. I spent the night with Toby," she whispered, glancing around to make sure no one seated around them was taking notes.

"I knew it." Her friend squealed. "Oh Mylanta! This is amazing. My best friend and Ethan's best friend! We can go on trips together!" She gasped. "We can raise our babies together!"

Jane shushed her before the whole town of Silverado Lake heard she and Toby were having babies together. "It's not like that."

Her friend's hands dropped into her lap. "Then what's it like?"

"Toby's injured right now, but he'll go back out on the circuit eventually." Jane stopped there and simply let Beth read the rest in her eyes. Her friend still knew her better than just about anyone else. After walking through the aftermath of her father's accident with her, Beth knew she couldn't do it.

"Maybe he won't go back out on the circuit," Beth said hopefully. "He could find another job. He could do something else. He's smart. And I know he finished his business degree while he was on the road—"

"No." She said it firmly to solidify it in her own heart. "He won't give up riding. He can't." His job held a much deeper significance to him because of Tanner. "I wouldn't want him to."

Her friend chewed on her lower lip as though searching for an answer. "He's not going to be a bull rider forever, Jane." Beth slid the coffee mug to the end of the table. "Most of them don't last beyond thirty."

"But it will always be something else." Like her father, Toby had an adventurous spirit. He liked to push himself, he liked to push the limits. "I like him. I like spending time with him." He made her feel things she'd never felt with anyone else. "But that's all." When it came to Toby, she could give him her body, she could even give him a small piece of her heart, but she couldn't risk giving him more.

* * *

Nothing like waiting for a doctor to tell you your fate. Toby sat in the reception area—well, "sat" wasn't totally accurate. He'd sat for a few minutes, then he'd paced the waiting room, then he'd gotten up to get a drink of water. He was running out of things to do. He might actually have to resort to reading a *People* magazine to pass the time and settle his nerves.

"It'll only be a few more minutes," Gloria called over from the reception desk. "He's running behind today."

"It's fine. I'm good." He wasn't good. Anxiety had held him by the throat the whole drive down from Denver. He had no idea what he'd do if the doctor told him he was done riding.

"How are your parents?" Gloria was good at making small talk when the doctor was running late, but today Toby didn't feel like chatting.

"They're fine." He still hadn't taken Jane's advice and talked to them. Things were okay right now. He had Jane and hopefully he'd get his spurs back at this visit. He had enough going on. Talking to his parents would blow up everything, and he didn't even know what good would come from it.

The door opened and Dr. Petrie waved him into the hallway.

Damn, his heart was racing. If the doc told him he needed surgery again, he'd lose it. That would set him back another three months and then the season would be over.

"Right in here." Dr. Petrie ducked into an exam room and waited for Toby to come in and sit down before he closed the door and sat across from him on the stool. "How's the shoulder been feeling?"

Toby wasn't sure how to answer that. "It's not as sore. It's tighter." He'd done the stretches his physical therapist had recommended, but he couldn't tell if they had helped. He'd kept up his routine, lifting weights every day, doing push-ups and planks—everything he could to keep his upper body strong. Had it all been for nothing?

"Well, I looked over the MRI results." How did doctors always manage to keep such deadpan expressions?

"How bad is it?" he choked out.

"It's not bad at all." The doctor opened a folder and glanced over the chart. "In fact, you've healed remarkably well. I didn't see any damage to the repairs or additional tears."

It took a second for him to process the words, for him to let out the breath he'd been holding. "Really?"

"Really." Dr. Petrie set the folder aside, his expression still grim. "I almost wish I could tell you there was a small tear so you'd sit out longer and take more time off, but it's simply not there."

Shock still bolted Toby's mouth closed. He was done. He was cleared. He should've been doing backflips, but a realization tempered the news. Going back meant leaving Silverado Lake. It meant walking away from Jane…

"Based on the pictures, I would say you could go back to riding any time," Dr. Petrie went on. "But I'll give you the same speech I've given you from the beginning. Just because there's no tear and the repair is holding doesn't mean you're going to be as strong as you were before. And in your profession that can be a serious liability."

"You mean it could affect my ability to hold on." He remembered that feeling when his shoulder tore, the ripping sensation inside his arm, the immediate lack of strength and range of motion.

"It *will* affect your ability to hold on," the doctor corrected. "There's no question. It's not the same shoulder joint it was before the injury. It never will be."

That wasn't a surprise. "So, you don't think I should get back on a bull."

"I didn't say that." Dr. Petrie raised his hands defensively. He even smiled a little. "Your parents would probably say that, but I'm your doctor." A doctor who acted like a parent sometimes, but Toby let it go.

"I would recommend strengthening the muscles surrounding the joint as much as you can before you go back. And you might have to adapt, to change how you ride."

He'd already been thinking through that. If he could strengthen his core, it would help his stability. And he could step up the leg work too. But none of that could ensure he wouldn't be right back in here again someday. "Do you see a lot of repeat customers with this injury?"

"I do."

That was what he'd guessed. So now the question became whether it was worth it. Was it worth it to risk another tear? Another surgery?

"But you're in good shape, Toby. There's no denying that." Dr. Petrie stood. He likely had a lot more patients to see. "You're strong. And you're young. And from what I can tell, you take care of yourself. You've got all that going for you."

Toby stood too, rolling his shoulder back. Still tight, but not painful. "You're telling me I could compete again tomorrow if I wanted to." He hoped the doctor would tell him no. Three weeks ago, this kind of news would've sent him running out of town to get back to some real training, but now...maybe he could delay going back a little longer.

"I don't know about tomorrow." The doc opened the door. "I'd take my time with the training if I were you. Maybe give it another month and ease back into it. You've been working out, but it's not the same as getting tossed around by a bull."

"Yeah there's no way to mimic that." You just had to get back on and ride again. He'd have to travel out to the training ranch he'd used in Texas over the years. It'd probably take him a good month of practice rides to prep him for competition. Once again, he thought about Jane. She was a writer...she could work anywhere. Maybe she'd come with him. Or at least visit. They could figure out the long-distance thing.

"Thanks, doc." He shook the man's hand. "Don't take this the wrong way, but I hope I won't be seeing you again soon."

Dr. Petrie laughed. "Well not in here anyway. Your parents invited me to come up for a weekend if I can ever find the space in my schedule."

He wouldn't. His father had been extending the invitation for years.

"Call me if something doesn't feel right." Dr. Petrie rested a fatherly hand on his shoulder. "And be careful out there, kid. You were luckier than most of those riders who go down."

"I know." He didn't take that for granted either. "Appreciate everything you've done for me." Toby grinned. "I'll tell all my friends."

The doctor shook his head and laughed his way down the hall. Toby went the opposite direction, stepping back out into the reception area.

"Good news?" Gloria asked, her fingers pausing over the keyboard.

"Yes." And he couldn't wait to share it with Jane. After being with her last night, he had to believe they could work this out.

Chapter Nineteen

"You look lovely, honey." Mara clasped a delicate pendant around Jane's neck. "Your dad gave this to me when we first bought the ranch."

Jane gazed in the mirror, touching the white gold charm shaped like mountains. A small blue stone sat atop the tallest one.

"He told me I'd always be his jewel in the mountains." Her mother's smile beamed at the memory.

"Thank you for letting me wear it." Jane turned to the side to make sure her bra wasn't showing. "Thanks for the dress too." After Toby had texted her and told her to dress up for their date, she'd decided to ask her mom for a loaner dress so there wouldn't be another dressing crisis. The blue one she'd worn to the wedding shower had fit her perfectly.

"It looks much better on you than it ever would've on me." Her mother fluffed the hem. "You're absolutely gorgeous. Toby is going to keel right over the second he sees you."

Jane tried to grasp at the same excitement her mom had for her date with Toby, but she couldn't quite hold on to it. He had good news. She could tell from his text, and she knew she had to celebrate with him, but part of her had already started to retreat. She could feel it happening, and she couldn't seem to stop it.

A knock echoed on the door. She'd asked him to pick her up at her mother's house so Mara could help her get ready, and so she could chat with her mom to distract her from her own thoughts.

"I'll answer it! Oh, this is so exciting. I feel like you're going to prom or something." Her mother rushed out of the master bedroom, leaving Jane to give herself one more appraisal.

She'd never considered herself beautiful. Not since she was a little girl and her daddy told her she was. Since then too many other voices had crowded out his. She really hadn't gone on any dates in high school. She hadn't dressed up or tried to draw any attention to herself. And now she had this man, this wonderful man coming to pick her up, a man who'd told her she was beautiful, a man who made her feel special, and she couldn't fully embrace him.

Jane touched the mountain pendant against her collarbone, remembering that day her father had left her for the last time. She'd followed him out to his truck, asking him again why he had to go.

"I need this, Janie. This is part of me," her dad had said. "Someday you'll understand." But she didn't. She didn't understand then and she still couldn't understand now. What had made him choose to go? Why would he risk his life for something that seemed so trivial?

Inhaling deeply, she smoothed down her dress. She couldn't think about this now. Toby was waiting, and she couldn't ruin his night. Raising her shoulders, Jane grabbed her purse and walked out of the bedroom to where Toby and her mom were chatting in the kitchen.

He went silent when he laid eyes on her.

"Would you two kill me if I took a picture?" her mother asked, already looking for her phone.

"Yes." Jane smiled as she said it, but a hollowness spread through her. She couldn't let them see her doubts. She couldn't let herself feel them. One foot in front of the other. She would give Toby this night.

"A picture would be fun." Toby strode over to her. The closer he got, the more her knees seemed to melt. He had on dark jeans and a distressed jean shirt, open a few buttons at the collar. He'd left his cowboy hat at home, and dear Lord she loved his hair. One moment at a time. She had to take this one moment at a time and stop thinking about what would happen later.

He slid his arm around her, drawing her to his side. Jane inhaled the masculine spicy scent on him, letting the physical touch, the feel of him at her side, quiet her uncertainty.

"Smile," he said, posing for her mom's cell phone camera.

Jane found her smile come more easily. Right as her mom took the picture, Toby grabbed her butt.

"Hey." She peered up at him and he leaned down to kiss her. "Just making sure you were smiling."

"Oh, she was smiling all right." Jane's mom studied the picture on her phone. "You two make such a sweet couple."

Jane's ribs seemed to tighten together, making it difficult for her to draw in a full breath.

"I'll have her home before midnight," Toby joked.

"Just go and enjoy." Her mother walked them to the door.

A second after they stepped out onto the porch and the door he closed, he turned to her and pulled her into his arms. "Seeing you in a dress does things to me." He worked his gaze down her body. "Maybe we should skip what I have planned and go straight to my place."

"I wish we could." She wished they could sneak away and have one more night together—hidden from the future and simply living in the moment.

"Sadly, we have reservations." Toby led her down the porch steps to his truck. "But we can make it an early night." He opened the passenger door.

Jane climbed in without responding and smoothed out her dress, her heart sinking again. How could she do this? How could she celebrate good news with him and also be honest about where it left them?

Toby walked around and got into the driver's seat. He started the engine and drove the truck down the ranch's winding driveway.

"So where are we going?" Jane asked, trying to make conversation.

"Someplace nicer." At the end of the driveway, Toby turned left, heading in the opposite direction of town.

There wasn't much up this way... "You're taking me to Valentino Bellas?"

He exaggerated a frown. "I should've blindfolded you."

"I still would've figured it out." She couldn't help herself whenever there was a mystery or puzzle to solve. "I haven't been there in years." She'd only eaten at the winery once on her parents' anniversary years ago. The memory warmed her even as it stung. Her parents had been so happy that night. And the restaurant had been beautiful; she remembered feeling like she was eating in a castle overlooking the entire valley. Excitement slipped past her earlier worries. There would be plenty of distractions in a restaurant like that. They could have a nice dinner, sip some wine, and maybe it would feel like a normal date as long as she didn't worry about where the future would take them. "I can't wait to see if it still looks the same."

"Good. I'm glad you're looking forward to it." Toby rested his hand on her thigh as he turned the truck off onto the paved road that switchbacked up and eventually went beneath a wrought-iron gate.

Jane waited, but he didn't offer any information about what the doctor had told him earlier. Maybe she'd been wrong. Maybe the doctor hadn't given him good news after all. She hated the hope that raced through her heart. Even if he hadn't gotten the clearance to go back now, he would someday. Toby wouldn't give up. She knew him well enough to know that.

"You okay?" Toby asked as he turned into the parking lot. "You're pretty quiet."

"Sure," Jane said quickly. "Just a little tired."

"I'm tired too." Toby's grin reminded her of last night. "But like I said, we can head back to my place early. After we have some champagne to celebrate." He quickly got out of the truck and hurried over to open her door for her.

"You got good news from the doctor?" She said it quietly so her voice wouldn't shake.

"I'll tell you all about it once we get to our table." He folded her arm under his and escorted her across the parking lot to the winery's grand stone entrance.

"Table for Garrett," Toby said to the hostess once they'd moved through the heavy wooden doors.

"Of course." The young woman grabbed two leather-bound menus and led them into a dimly lit dining room.

When they were seated, Toby ordered a bottle of their best champagne and Jane braced herself for what he was about to tell her.

"I'm cleared." A laugh slipped out as he said it. "The doc said everything looks great. The shoulder's all healed up and he can't tell me to sit out anymore."

"That's amazing." Jane found it easy to smile because she cared for him, she wanted this for him too. But tears still burned behind her eyes. She would keep them hidden though. She wouldn't let them out tonight.

"I didn't think it was gonna happen." He looked so relieved, so over-the-moon happy.

"I knew it would happen." She brushed her hand across his. "You've worked hard for this. You deserve it. You deserve to get back out there." Based on his emotion, she could see how much it meant to him. "When do you think—"

"Yo! Toby," some guy called from the bar.

Jane looked over her shoulder. There were quite a few men at the bar...and a few familiar women too.

"Is that Andrew Vincent?" Toby squinted.

"I think so." Jane looked down the line. It seemed half the old high school football team starters and their cheerleaders were seated at the bar. Aubrey included. Those weren't exactly the distractions Jane had been hoping for.

"Hey, man!" Andrew called. "Come on over here. It's been forever."

Toby hesitated, but Jane waved him away. "You'd better go. He won't quiet down until you at least say hi."

"Well then you're coming with me." Toby stood and took her hand, leading her to the bar.

"Andy..." Toby reached out and shook the man's hand. "How's it going?"

"Can't complain." The man seemed to notice Jane standing behind Toby. "Hey. I'm Andy. And you are?"

"Jane." She shook his hand politely and stepped out of view again.

"You remember Jane Harding, don't you?" Toby put his arm around her and nudged her forward.

"Can't say that I do." Andy gave her a good long look. "Wait. Were you a couple years behind us?"

"No, silly," Aubrey called from a few seats down. "Jane was in our class. She always did have a thing for Toby." She and a friend shared a secretive look. "Don't you remember the New Year's party?"

"That was you?" Andy laughed. "Hell yeah, I remember that. You're the one who made out with Toby?"

Thankfully, a server with a tray of full wineglasses approached. "I brought the reds out."

"One of those is mine." Andy moved off his stool and sidled up to Toby. "You should hang with us for a while. We can catch up. I gotta hear all about the rodeos. You're really making a name for yourself out there."

"Trying." Toby leaned an elbow into the bar. "I've been sidelined with an injury, but I just got clearance from the doc today." He went on to tell the guys what happened. They all crowded around him hanging on every word, while Jane hoovered nearby listening.

"Man, you lucky son of a bitch." Andy shook his head. "I saw the whole thing on YouTube. I thought you were a goner."

"Nah." Toby shrugged it off. "But I'll tell you what…if I would've been five inches to the left, that bull would've stepped dead center on my chest, and then it definitely would've been over."

Jane's stomach lurched. Five inches? He'd come within

five inches of dying and he was standing there bragging about it?

"Damn, what a rush," one of Toby's friends said. She couldn't tell who. Her vision had dimmed too much. All those faces blurred together.

"Which bull were you riding?" someone else asked.

"Devastation. And he's not even the meanest one." Toby started talking about the various bulls he'd ridden while Jane edged her way out of the circle. How could she even pretend to be happy for him when she didn't understand? Her blood ran hot and fast. He risked his life for an adrenaline rush? Why couldn't he just ride a damn roller coaster like everyone else?

"Another time I got thrown into a fence." Toby laughed. He actually laughed. "Turned out to just be a bad bruise, but it could've been a hell of a lot worse."

That was it. She didn't want to hear more. Jane crept along the bar. She had to get away. This was a mistake. Letting herself care about him had been a huge mistake.

Chapter Twenty

As soon as you get back on that bull, I'm gonna come cheer you on." Andy slapped Toby on the back. Once they'd gotten him started talking about the circuit, he couldn't seem to stop. He missed it more than he would let on and it felt good to relive some of his glory days while he was forced to take a time-out.

"We'll all show up." Patrick, another one of his high school football comrades brought over another bottle of wine.

Toby moved his glass out of the way. "I think I'm done here, fellas." He'd already finished a glass and he had a date to get back to with Jane. He turned around to look for her, but she wasn't there.

"Where's Jane?" She'd been standing right there with them only a few minutes ago.

"Who's Jane?" Andy asked, refilling his glass.

"Jane. The woman I introduced you to five minutes ago." He turned a full circle searching for her.

"Oh right." His old high school buddy laughed. "Maybe she ran out on you again."

Toby ignored him and walked down the bar. Aubrey stepped up to him. "She went that way." The woman pointed to the doors. "About five minutes ago."

She left? Jane had walked out? "Did she seem okay?"

"Not really." Aubrey shrugged. "It's Jane though. This totally isn't her scene. It never has been."

But they were on a date. They were supposed to celebrate his good news. Why would she walk out on him? Toby rushed outside and scanned the parking lot. Jane was seated on a bench near the road.

"Hey." He ran over to her. "Are you okay?" Something wasn't right. Something hadn't been right since he'd picked her up, but he hadn't wanted to push.

Jane looked at him, her eyes red and watery.

"What's wrong?" He reached for her, but she scooted away.

"I'm sorry." She dried her cheeks with the backs of her hands. "I'm really sorry. I called Wes to come pick me up."

"Are you sick? I can take you home if you want." He settled his hand on her shoulder, and this time she didn't move, but she tensed under his fingertips.

"No." She stood and turned away from him. "I'm not sick. I wanted to be happy for you. I wanted to be happy that you get to go back to doing what you love. But then I heard you talking in there about how you almost died, and I can't do this." She turned to face him. "I can't."

"Do what?" He stood too, trying to get a good look at her face. He hadn't asked her for anything yet. They could take it slow. He didn't want to scare her away. He'd do whatever she needed.

"I can't love you." There was a force behind the words, almost an anger. "And I can't keep spending time with you because it makes me want to love you." The tears fell faster now, and there was nothing he could do to stop them.

"This has to be over," she whispered. "Right now. I have to walk away, or I will lose myself."

He stared at her, not knowing what to say, what to do. He finally went with the truth. "I don't want you to walk away." But he also didn't know how to keep her there. Not when it obviously caused her so much pain.

"You know what I've been through." A horrible sob followed the words. "You know why I can't do this."

He knew. He understood. Nothing he could say would change her mind, but he couldn't simply stand there and watch her hurt. He walked over to her, pulled her into his arms, and held her while she cried against his chest.

Wes's truck pulled into the parking lot and her brother hopped out. "What the hell is going on?"

Toby didn't want to open his arms and let her go, but Jane pushed him away. "I just want to go home. I need to go home."

She ran to the truck and climbed in while Wes stomped over to Toby.

"What did you do to her?" He looked angry enough to throw a punch, and Toby wouldn't care if he did. He was so numb he probably wouldn't feel it anyway.

"I scared her," he said, looking for Jane through the truck's window. Her face was in her hands. "I was talking about my accident, about what a close call it had been, and I scared her." He hadn't meant to. That was the last thing he would ever want to do…

"She'll be okay." Wes's scowl loosened into a look of understanding. "Just give her a little space. It'll be fine."

Toby shook his head, still reeling from the anger, the despair, and the defeat he'd seen in her eyes, that he'd heard in her voice. "I don't think it will." What could he possibly say to change her mind? "I think I've already lost her."

* * *

"Ten more reps." Toby pulled his chin up over the bar he'd mounted in one of the outbuildings near his cabin.

"You're crazy." Ethan dropped off the bar next to him and collapsed into the broken lawn chair in the corner. "I'm done, man. I got nothin' left."

"Suit yourself." Toby continued on with his pull-ups, sweat rolling off him. His biceps burned but he pushed himself to keep pulling, to keep straining. This had to be a new record for him, even pre-shoulder injury.

"You're gonna kill yourself," Ethan muttered, watching him from the chair. "You're pushing too hard. For the last week, all you've done is work out."

"I got into a competition in Wyoming in two weeks." He'd managed to get in at the last minute, so he had to work out nonstop or he'd make a fool out of himself in that arena.

"Sure, that's all it is." His friend rolled his eyes. "It's all about the competition. None of this is about distracting yourself from what happened with Jane."

That got him down off the bar. "What do you know about it?" He hadn't said a damn word about Jane to Ethan. To anyone actually. Talking about it wouldn't change the fact that she'd walked away from him and had been avoiding him ever since.

"My fiancée is her best friend," Ethan said, stretching

his arms over his head with a wince. "And Beth tells me everything."

"Then you know there's nothing to talk about." Toby picked up a kettlebell and started to do some swings. He had to keep moving, to keep his mind off everything except getting back into that arena. It had become his obsession over the last week. It had gotten him through. If he could keep getting his body stronger he could keep focusing on the future. He could move on...

"Beth thinks Jane is in love with you," Ethan said abruptly. "That's something to talk about."

"If she loved me, my job wouldn't matter." That was selfish as hell. He knew it. That's why he hadn't pushed things with her. That's why he hadn't forced her to talk to him since that night.

"Do you love her?" Ethan eyed him the way he always did when they played poker—watching for a bluff.

"I could. Real easily. Why do you think I'm killing myself here?" He'd been trying to keep his mind off Jane, trying to keep himself from storming into her cabin to show her he could make her happy. He could love her like crazy, even being a bull rider. If she'd let him.

"But you're letting her go?" Ethan demanded. "You're going to run off again, disappear on the circuit and forget all about her?"

He wouldn't forget all about Jane. He couldn't. Toby held the kettlebell against his chest and started some squats. "What choice do I have?" His muscles screamed and pinched, but it only drove him to move faster.

Ethan watched him, shaking his head. "You're my best friend, but I gotta tell you, man...you've never fought for a damn thing that mattered."

Toby stopped and stood up straight. "What the hell are

you talking about? I work hard." He'd fought for a place on the circuit. It had taken everything in him to work his way up, to compete, to win.

"I'm not talking about work." His friend stood up and took the kettlebell out of his hands, tossing it aside. It hit the ground with a hard thud. "I'm talking about people." He got in Toby's face. "Instead of running, instead of distracting yourself with all this shit, you have to fight for relationships that matter. You have to fight for the person you care about most. That's what Beth and I have done, and I can tell you, man, that's the only reason it's worked out for us. You don't stay and fight, you'll never have anything that lasts."

Toby stared him down, pulling his hands into fists, but his anger only proved Ethan was right. He hadn't fought for anything that mattered. He hadn't fought for his brother's memory. He hadn't fought for his parents' understanding. And he was running from Jane. "I can't ask her to be okay with me competing." Not with the fear he'd seen in her at the winery. He didn't want to be the source of that pain.

"Do you have to keep competing?" He could always count on Ethan to ask the tough questions.

Toby collapsed into a nearby chair. Did he have to keep competing? For the last week, he'd ignored the pain in his body, along with every raw emotion, but now it all hit him at once. He didn't have to keep competing. He could give it up. He could walk away from that, and it might be easier than watching Jane walk away from him. "If I quit the circuit, I'll be letting him down. It's all my brother ever dreamed of."

"Your brother?" His friend looked at him like he'd gotten hit in the head with a kettlebell. "What brother?"

"Tanner." He stared at nothing, seeing his brother's face. "My twin brother. He died right before we moved here."

"Shit, are you serious?" Ethan found a bucket and turned it over, sitting across from Toby. "I had no idea."

"No one knows." Except for Jane. And that was his fault. He could've been the one to talk about Tanner. He could've been the one to tell his brother's stories. But he hadn't. He'd failed him. "He wanted to be a cowboy, but he had muscular dystrophy. It didn't stop him from loving life though." He told Ethan how they'd taken Tanner horseback riding shortly before his death. How he'd laughed and whooped, how he'd hugged the horse and named him Tonto. He had so many stories like that about his brother. Talking about Tanner made him real, brought his memory back to life.

"He sounds like a pretty cool kid." Ethan grinned. "Even cooler than you."

"He was." And he may have been the only one Toby had ever felt a soul connection with. He loved his parents, and he knew they loved him, but he and Tanner had this bond that couldn't be described. It had felt like they were a part of each other.

Toby had never come close to feeling that with anyone else. Not until he'd told Jane his secret and she'd been so careful with his pain. Maybe that's why he wanted to run. She'd left her fingerprint on the deepest part of him much like his brother had and then she'd turned him away. For the first time in his life, Toby didn't want to be let loose. "How do I fight for her?" He looked up, hoping like hell his friend had an answer.

The abrupt change of subject didn't seem to throw Ethan off. It was almost like he knew they'd go down this path eventually. "You decide what's most important to you. And then you build your life around that."

Chapter Twenty-One

In the short time Jane had known Bernadette, a startling transformation had taken place. Jane watched the woman as she made her way across the library to their usual table. Was it possible that Bernadette looked younger? She'd pulled her soft white hair up on her head, letting strands cascade down to frame her face. Somehow the woman's eyes seemed brighter and her cheeks pinker. She even carried herself differently as she walked, shoulders not so weighed down and an unmistakable bounce in her step.

"I'm so sorry I'm late," she sang, approaching the table. "I completely lost track of time again." Laying her notebook on the table between them, she collapsed into the chair with a happy sigh. Joy seemed to bubble right out of her. She was definitely not the same woman Jane had met a few weeks ago.

"So obviously you've been keeping busy." Jane raised her eyebrows to politely ask for more information. Beth had told her this morning that Bernadette hadn't come home a few nights over the last week.

"Oh, have I ever." Roses bloomed on her cheeks. "I'm telling you, Ethan's grandpa sure has a lot of energy."

"He seems like a nice man," Jane said to elude any additional details on that front. She was happy for her and everything, but Jane still couldn't shake the sadness that had overtaken her. For the last week she'd done nothing but write. It seemed that pain and heartache had a way of inspiring the kind of real, raw emotive writing Jane had once found so difficult to compose. Not having anywhere else to channel it, she'd finished the book, pouring her heart and soul into the story, experiencing every emotion right along with the characters.

"That man is so nice. He's passionate. He's romantic..."

Jane's head snapped up. She could've been talking about Toby, but of course she wasn't. She was talking about Ethan's grandpa again. Jane was the one thinking of Toby.

"He's asked me to go on a cross-country RV trip with him this fall." Bernadette clasped her hands in front of her chest. "Isn't that wonderful?"

Jane didn't want to be a fuddy-duddy—that used to be Bernadette's job—but she said, "Isn't that a little fast? You just met him."

"That's the best part about it." Beth's grandma sat up straight, her face animated with excitement. "We'll have months on the road to get to know each other, to learn who we are, to discover things about each other and about ourselves."

"Don't you know who you are?" Jane couldn't help but ask. She'd figured by Bernadette's age things would be clearer, more comfortable. Surely she'd have her life figured out by then.

"I *thought* I knew. In those years after I lost my husband, I became a different person—stuffy and miserable, but coming here has woken me up to this whole side of myself I'd forgotten about." She reached into the bag and pulled out a stack of books. "Thanks to your book recommendations, and thanks to William, of course, I've opened up to the more sensual side of life."

"I'm glad I could help." If only she could help herself. Jane looked through the pile of books Bernadette had set between them. "*Mountain Destiny.*" She pulled her book out of the pile.

"Oh, yes." The woman stole it out of her hands. "I loved this one! I picked it up on my way out the last time I was here." Bernadette leaned in closer. "Talk about sensual. It's brilliant."

The compliment reached in and squeezed her heart.

"Have you read it?" Bernadette asked.

She almost said no and moved on to discuss another book, but she stopped herself. "I've read it." Her voice seemed to shrink. She'd never wanted anyone to know. It would be like they could see too much of her, too much of her heart, too much of who she was. But when she'd told Toby it hadn't been nearly as scary as she'd thought it would be. "I wrote it actually."

Bernadette laughed. "And I wrote *Pride and Prejudice*."

"I'm serious." Jane took the book away from her. "Didn't the hero remind you of anyone you know?" Surely Bernadette had noticed where she'd gotten her inspiration.

"Well, I thought of Toby, of course. He's the only cowboy I know." Her eyes narrowed and she snatched the book away from Jane with a gasp, flipping through the pages. She stopped near the beginning and started to read.

"'Celeste had always thought cowboys were tall, dark, and handsome, like in the books her mama read. Beau wasn't tall or dark, but he somehow managed to be sinfully handsome.'"

Jane jumped in to recite the words with her. "'When he took off his Stetson the sun highlighted dusty blond hair long enough to run her fingers through. But it was Beau's eyes that posed the biggest threat to the manners she'd learned in finishing school. Those eyes burned blue. Never had she seen a blue so vibrant, so fierce, so alive.'"

"Oh my stars." Bernadette snatched the book shut. "You wrote this! You wrote *Mountain Destiny*!"

Jane nodded, tears crowding her eyes. She didn't even care if everyone heard. "I finished a second book this week."

"And Toby was your inspiration?" Bernadette carefully set down the book. "Well, I'll be. I had a feeling about you two from the very beginning. Your history together makes it all the sweeter."

Jane let a few tears spill over before fishing a tissue out of her purse. "He would make the perfect Beau." And the perfect Amos. He had the same attributes as her heroes, the same humor, the same swagger, and the same rugged, brave, tender heart. "I fell for him when I came home." A rock lodged itself in her throat. "But I had to walk away from him." She tearfully told Bernadette about the night at the winery, about the panic and the anger that had torn her apart. "I don't want to love him."

"But it seems you might anyway," the woman said gently.

Jane didn't deny it. Over the last few weeks he'd touched her heart. Yes, he was a show-off sometimes. Yes, he had wounds that made him cover up a deeper part of his heart. But he was also fun and thoughtful and romantic. And he cared about her. He'd shown her that. "There's this deep part of him I don't understand, that I'm not sure I can support." Even simply hearing him talk about riding had nearly broken her. "I don't know that I could love that part of him." Would she be angry every time he left? Would her stomach lurch every time he talked about getting thrown?

"I understand, dear girl." Tears gathered in Bernadette's eyes too. "Believe me, I do. But I can tell you from experience, loneliness will kill you much faster than worry."

Jane closed her eyes, letting the truth of those words sink in. Before she'd come home she hadn't necessarily felt lonely, but now she couldn't fathom going back to California, back to her empty, quiet condo. She couldn't imagine never experiencing the kind of tenderness and happiness she'd felt when she was with Toby.

"Can I ask you a question?"

Jane nodded but braced herself too. It must be a tough one if Bernadette was requesting permission.

"Why do you write so much adventure and danger and risk into your novels?"

"Because that's what people want to read about." That's what she wanted to read about. "People read for the experience, the escape." That was why she'd lived behind books after her dad died. They took her away while also letting her process her pain.

The woman smiled as though she was hoping that's what Jane would say. "You claimed you don't understand that part of Toby. The part of him that wants to have those kinds of experiences, but you crave adventure too, my dear." She picked up *Mountain Destiny* and handed it back to Jane. "It's all in here. You want something more, even if you're denying yourself. I think you might relate to him more than you realize."

* * *

Toby parked his truck on the road in front of his parents' house and let it idle. He was half tempted to text his mom and tell her there'd been a change of plans and he wouldn't be able to join her and his father for dinner. But, in some ways, he'd been putting off this conversation for over twenty years. Too long.

He cut the engine and climbed out of the truck, taking his time as he made his way to the front door. Everything about their house had always looked perfect. It was a rambling ranch-style structure, built with timber and stone based on his father's specifications. They'd moved in when Toby had turned eight, about a year after they'd arrived in Silverado Lake. Being the meticulous man that he was, their father kept up with everything—updates, repainting every couple of years. If he wasn't working at the hospital in Denver, it seemed Dad was busy with a project. Toby's mom had always called it puttering, but now Toby couldn't help but wonder if it had all been in avoidance of other issues.

He walked up the steps with nerves zinging through him. The front porch seemed to have a fresh coat of stain and his mother had already put out her American flag collection for the upcoming Independence Day holiday.

The front door stood open, so Toby slipped through the screen door and wandered down the hall to the kitchen. Lasagna. He could smell it—the garlic, the tang of the tomato sauce. His mother stood at the counter buttering slices of thick-cut French bread.

"There you are." Her smile seemed to be a little too big. "Just in time! Why don't you go ahead and toss the salad?" She nodded to a large bowl sitting next to her on the counter.

"Sure." Toby grabbed the tongs sitting next to the bowl and stirred up the lettuce, tomatoes, cucumbers, and generous helping of feta cheese.

"So, how's everything? How's the ranch?" His mother slid the tray of sliced bread into the oven and then wiped her hands on her apron.

"It's good. I like being there." These were the same kinds of conversations he'd had with his parents his whole life. The small talk, the catching up on the details of his day. But knowing what he wanted to say to them now made it feel phony.

"It's amazing what Mara has done with that place," his mom chatted, washing a dish in the sink. "Making it into such a profitable business after everything she went through. I admire that woman."

"Yeah. She's pretty great." Her daughter was pretty great too. Toby couldn't seem to have a conversation without Jane popping up in his thoughts. But his threshold for small talk was coming to an end. Now that he was here, he couldn't imagine why they'd never talked about what really mattered. He couldn't imagine how she looked at him every day and didn't see Tanner. He walked to the table and set down the salad bowl.

"Hey, son." His father appeared in the doorway, fresh home from work it seemed. He loosened his tie and pulled it off over his head, tossing it onto the back of a chair. "How's the shoulder?"

"I'm cleared." He smiled as he said it, but the news came with a gut-sinking reminder that it had driven Jane away from him. His chest tightened.

"I knew it." His dad squeezed Toby's other shoulder. "Dr. Petrie may be lousy at golf but he's a miracle worker in the operating room."

"We have to celebrate!" His mom brought a bottle of wine over to the table and Toby helped out by carting over the French bread that had warmed in the oven for a few minutes and then the lasagna.

"When are you headed back out on the circuit?" his father asked serving Toby's mom salad and lasagna.

"I assume you'll take a little more time off." His mother opened the wine and poured Toby a glass. "There's no sense in rushing things after what you've been through."

"I'm not sure when I'll go back." Toby dished up his own food but didn't lift his fork. He wasn't hungry. "There's something I've actually been wanting to talk to you about for a while."

"Oh?" His father helped himself to a piece of bread and his mother poured dressing on her salad. They weren't anticipating what was coming.

"I want to talk about Tanner."

Both of his parents stopped what they were doing. They looked at each other and then at him.

"What about Tanner?" His mother's customary smile faded.

There were so many things he wanted to say, to ask, but it all seemed to jumble in his brain. "Why don't we have any pictures of him?" He pointed to the dining room wall, to all those family pictures of him and his sisters and his parents. "We don't have any with Tanner." Unchecked emotion lurched his voice. "He's not in any of the pictures. It's like he never even existed."

Staring at him with wide, disbelieving eyes, his mother slowly set down her fork. Next to her, his father's jaw had tightened, but Toby had to keep going. That emotion boiled inside of him. It had to come out. "We never talk about him. Once we moved, it was like you forgot. Or you wanted to forget. I don't know. But I didn't. I never have forgotten. I can't."

"You think we forgot about him?" His mother's voice shook. "How could you think we'd forget about our *child*?"

His father took Toby's mom's hand. "Where is this coming from?" he asked gruffly. "Why are you attacking us?"

Toby inhaled deeply. "I'm sorry. I didn't mean to say it like that." He didn't know how to say it, not after all this time. Emotions were fast and he didn't know how to wrangle them. "I just want to understand." He brought his voice back under control. "I want to understand why we had to move, why we had to leave his memory behind and start over without him."

"That's not what we were doing." His mother's tone edged toward a shout. "We weren't leaving him behind. We were trying to survive." She choked out a sob. "You have no idea what that was like for us."

"No, I don't," he admitted. But he would've liked to. He would've like to have known he wasn't alone. "You never told me. You never talked about it."

"I didn't know how." The words dissolved into more tears. His mom balled up her napkin and pressed it against her mouth, quietly sobbing.

"I'm sorry." Seeing her grief made him look away. This had been a bad idea. He shouldn't have brought it up. "I didn't mean to hurt you. I just miss him. Still. Even all these years later. I miss him."

"So do we." His father slipped his arm around Toby's mom. "And you have every right to bring him up." Toby had never seen his dad cry, but tears glistened in his eyes. "Losing your brother..." He blew out a sigh and shook his head. "It almost broke us. We were used to caring for him, to devoting so much energy to making him happy and comfortable. And then when he died..."

"We were lost," his mom finished. "Oh, my God, Toby, we were so lost."

He looked across the table at his mom, seeing the real her for maybe the first time in his life. Now he knew why she worked so hard to make everything perfect. Why the house always seemed flawless, why she worked herself half to death to make meals and do laundry and create perfect holiday memories. She would forever be trying to get back what she'd lost, what they'd all lost.

"That was the only way I could get through it," she murmured. "To find another focus, to keep putting one foot in front of the other, to go somewhere I didn't have to explain it over and over, reliving it every single time."

"I know it was hard on you." His dad's shoulders slumped with what looked like defeat. "And I'm sorry if you thought we were trying to leave Tanner behind. We were doing our best. It wasn't good enough, but it was all we could manage."

And that was all Toby could ask of them. To do their best. It didn't mean they'd never failed, but now, hearing them talk about it, he could understand why they'd made those decisions.

"I wanted to die with him." His mom had stopped crying and now her eyes pleaded with him to understand.

"But I knew I couldn't. I knew I had to force myself to live without him so I could still be a mom."

"You're a great mom," Toby told her. Like his father had said, they'd done their best with what they'd been given. He hadn't seen their perspective back then. He couldn't. He'd only been seven years old and all he'd known was that his brother was gone and no one else seemed as sad about it as he was.

"He loved you much." His mom took Toby's hand, squeezing it in hers. "You were his favorite person in the whole world."

"I loved him too." He loved him even more now that he'd lost him. "And I've been trying to keep his memory alive." He'd done his best, but he couldn't do it alone anymore. He couldn't orient his whole life around trying to bring his brother back.

"The library," his mother murmured. "'In memory of Tanner.'"

"You saw it." He'd wondered if they'd ever noticed. In some ways, even though he'd kept it a secret, he'd hoped they had. "I never wanted to upset you, but when I heard they wanted to upgrade, I knew what I had to do."

"We're not upset." His father shared a sad smile with Toby's mom. "It's hard for us to talk about. That's all. Even now. It's hard to remember."

"We can do better." His mother jumped up suddenly. "I have a whole box of pictures upstairs. I'll bring them down." She disappeared into the hallway leaving Toby alone with his dad.

"I'm proud of you, son." His dad had said that a handful of times. Mainly after a competition or out on the football field in high school. But he'd never said it with tears in his eyes. "I know it couldn't have been easy to bring that up. But I'm glad you found the courage to do it. It was something we needed to hear."

"I had to." Ethan was right. He had to stand up and fight for the relationships he wanted. He had to learn to walk through the tough stuff. With his brother's memory. With his parents. And most of all with Jane.

Chapter Twenty-Two

"It's been too long since I've used power tools." Ethan flicked down his safety glasses and turned on the saw, slicing the two-by-four in half while Toby stood back and watched, primed and ready to jump in if needed. As far as he knew Ethan wasn't exactly into woodworking, but his friend had gotten the brilliant idea—two days before the wedding—to build his wife an arbor for the ceremony that they could put in their garden afterward. More accurately, Ethan had gotten the brilliant idea that Toby should make the arch and let him do the cutting, even though angles weren't his friend's forte.

He tried not to tense up watching his friend wield the saw, but Ethan's cut wasn't exactly straight. He'd made it halfway through the board in a zigzag line that Toby would have to fix later. Suddenly the saw shut off and the lights in the garage went out.

"Damn." Ethan tried to pull out the saw, but it was wedged in there.

"Power must've gone out." Toby checked his watch. That wasn't good. The rehearsal dinner was supposed to start in just over two hours. "Guess we'll have to sit tight. I'd better go check on Louise in the kitchen. She's probably ready to blow a gasket." Last time this happened, they realized the generator didn't work. He'd ordered another one, but it wouldn't be delivered for another few weeks.

"Guess we'll have to finish the project tomorrow." Ethan pulled off his gloves and tossed them onto Toby's workbench. "Oh, speaking of tomorrow, a bunch of our family wants to go on a white-water rafting trip before they head home after the wedding. Beth found a company that can take us. You in?"

"Uh..." Toby walked out into the sunlight and automatically thought about Jane again. She likely wouldn't be going, and he'd been hoping to find some time to talk to her.

"Come on." His friend followed him out of the garage. "I could use you there. Beth and I would love to have at least one more experienced paddler."

"Okay." Why not?

"Great. We'll add you to the reservation."

"Sounds good." Toby said goodbye to his friend and jogged all the way to the lodge, heading straight for the kitchen to check on how Louise was handling the power outage. Sure enough, the woman was rushing around with the phone attached to her ear.

"I don't care if there's a widespread outage. I have eighty people coming here for dinner in two hours. What am I supposed to feed them?" she demanded.

He winced. He'd hate to be on the other side of that phone call.

"I want to talk to your supervisor." Louise slammed

down the pot she was holding. "Then I want to talk to your supervisor's supervisor."

There was a pause.

"Don't give me that—" she started but then she pulled the phone away from her ear. "He hung up on me. Can you believe that?"

"Kind of." Toby scanned the mess on the countertops. It looked like she'd been in the middle of prepping the food when the power went out.

"They said it's going to be at least six hours before the power comes back." Louise's hands flew to her head. "Six hours! I thought this would be an easy one, so I already let my kitchen staff go for the day. What am I going to do?"

"We are going to figure it out." Toby walked the length of the stainless-steel prep island taking stock of what they had. He was about to make a recommendation when Jane crashed through the door dressed in her bathrobe and a lopsided hairdo. Looked like she'd made it through curling only one side of her hair, but man she was beautiful. He hadn't seen her since she'd gotten so upset at the winery. He wanted to apologize again, but she spoke before he could.

"Why is the power off?" She caught sight of Toby in the corner and immediately halted.

"They gave me some song and dance about the wind last night," Louise grumbled. "Something is busted somewhere and it's going to take six hours to fix!"

Jane hadn't looked away from Toby. He didn't look away from her either.

"I was just starting to cut up the vegetables and pull out ingredients for my sauce," the older woman lamented. "Now we're going to have to order pizza for Beth's rehearsal."

"No pizza." Toby finally found his legs. He smiled at Jane. "We can figure this out together. The three of us."

"Right." Jane's hand clamped the top of her robe closed even though she had it belted at the waist. "We'll figure it out, Louise. After I get dressed."

Did she have to? Toby let his eyes linger on her smooth, toned legs as she walked out the door. He was so tempted to follow her, to ask her to hear him out, but now wasn't the time.

"Well?" Louise brought him back with an elbow to his ribs. "What's the plan then?"

Toby turned his attention back to the counters. It looked as though she'd been preparing to serve steak and chicken along with potatoes, zucchini, and onions. "Kabobs. We can make them over the fire." They had plenty of grill grates for campfire roasts. "We'll move the dinner out of the dining room and into the pavilion. It'll be lighter outside. We can decorate and light the space with candles after the sun goes down."

"Kabobs." Louise seemed to mull it over. "What about sides?"

"We can use some of the big pots Mara uses for canning and set them over the fire to boil up some risotto." He didn't know much about risotto, but if you dumped in enough broth and parmesan it always tasted pretty good.

"I do have a lot of rice." It appeared Louise was coming around to the idea. "Here." She walked over and handed him a knife. "You start cutting up the meat. I'll work on the veggies."

"Perfect." They could get her all prepped and set up and then head to the ceremony spot to run through the wedding before dinner.

The door flew open again. This time, Jane was dressed

in jeans and a T-shirt, which she somehow made look as sexy as the bathrobe. Her hair seemed to be in a state of chaos, but Toby liked that too. It reminded him of how she'd looked when she'd woken up in his bed.

"What happened to your hair?" Louise handed her a knife. "Go on over there and help Toby cut the meat."

Jane did what she was told. "My curling iron quit working." She joined Toby at the island and glanced down at the cubes of meat he'd cut. "I thought we were having chicken and steak."

"Toby suggested kabobs. We can cook them over the grills and do some risotto in pots over the fire." Louise sliced through a zucchini. "He's a smart one. Good in a crisis too."

"He's definitely good in a crisis," Jane murmured, but Toby couldn't tell what she was thinking. She cut the meat like it took all her concentration.

"Goodness girl, slow down," Louise scolded. "You're going to take off your finger moving so fast."

"Right." Jane inhaled and seemed to hold her breath, her hands settling into a more normal rhythm.

"I like your hair," Toby offered.

"Right," she grumbled, but a smile peeked through.

"Nothing a little updo won't fix," Louise clucked from the other side of the island. "I'll help you with that later. Right now, we need a little more chopping and a lot less talking."

* * *

"That boy cares for you." Louise hovered over Jane, pinning strands of her hair into a creation that Jane hoped would be better than what she'd walked in with. Judging from the pins stabbing her head and the way Louise muttered occasionally, she wasn't sure they'd ever get there.

Jane shifted on the stool that they'd set up next to a credenza in the great room. "What makes you say that?" She flinched as another pin went straight into her temple.

"It's all in the way a man looks at a woman," Louise insisted. "He gets those starry eyes when he sees you, just like my Craig still does for me."

"I know he cares about me." She didn't doubt his feelings, but she'd started to doubt her own. Bernadette was right. Jane did crave more. But still something held her back. Something she wasn't even sure she had the strength to acknowledge.

"Do you care for him?" Louise never beat around the bush.

"Of course I do." She swallowed the tears that proved that statement true. "But I got so mad at him last week." She'd totally lost control at the winery, and she was so ashamed to admit why.

Louise stopped working on her hair. "Mad? Whatever for?"

Jane closed her eyes, feeling that anger rise up in her again. "He was talking about riding, about his injury. He was making light of the fact that he almost died..."

"Ah." Louise picked up another pin. "Well, it's understandable that upset you."

Jane couldn't let herself off the hook so easily. It might've been understandable, but it certainly wasn't rational. "I'm still angry at my father." She couldn't manage more than a whisper. It sounded awful to say that out loud. "I'm still mad, Louise. I'm still mad he went on that trip when he didn't have to," It was ridiculous. In her heart, she knew he didn't want to die. She knew he never would've chosen to leave her for good, but she'd held on to that anger, and it had all come out with Toby.

The revelation didn't seem to horrify Louise though. Instead of a shocked gasp, the woman simply nodded. "Oh, I was angry at your father too."

Jane turned to look at her. "You were?" Or was she only trying to make Jane feel better?

"I was." Louise spritzed some hairspray over Jane's bangs. "I couldn't believe he'd take a risk like that when he had everything."

Pressure built in Jane's chest, relief bubbling to the surface. Was it possible someone understood what she felt, what she'd been so afraid of? Everyone understood the sadness, the grief, but the anger…it had been so undeserved. That's why she'd stuffed it away. She couldn't talk about it. Not even with her mother. Her father had been the most amazing person. He'd loved her. She had no right to feel that way.

"But then," Louise continued, "maybe a month later, I was standing in the kitchen kneading bread dough. The sun was coming in through that window above the sink." She sighed as though she could see it now. "The colors on that mountain were so vibrant they were alive. And this sense of purpose and fulfillment washed over me, and I realized that was how your dad must've felt when he was climbing a mountain or boating on that crazy river."

Jane held her breath. "You think being out there gave him a sense of purpose."

Louise leaned down bringing her face in line with Jane's, her green eyes brimming with tears. "I think doing all of those things made him feel more alive. The same way I feel when I'm baking or cooking for people. The way you probably feel when you're teaching."

Not teaching. Writing. That sense of purpose and fulfillment washed over her whenever she discovered something new about her characters, or when she found exactly the right words to describe a mountain sunset.

"We all need that feeling, Janie," the woman murmured, patting her cheek. "And we all find it in different ways."

Those words set her tears free. She'd never thought about it like that before. But she couldn't imagine giving up writing. Even if she was never able to publish another book, she would still want to write. "In a way he was chasing his dreams then." She'd always assumed he was being reckless, living for the adrenaline rush. She'd thought the same thing about Toby. But it went deeper.

"Yes, sweetie." Louise carefully pressed one more bobby pin into her hair. "And your father would want you to chase your dreams too. Whatever they look like."

Jane nodded, catching the tears with the tips of her fingers in an attempt to preserve her makeup.

"Hold on. One more pin." Louise tilted Jane's head to the left and worked another bobby pin in—that had to be at least fifty—and then handed her the mirror Jane had brought. "Ta-da! You look lovely."

"Especially with bleary eyes." She laughed a little. She could always count on Louise to understand, to offer what she needed to hear. That had been the missing piece. She'd allowed herself to feel the sadness, to feel the pain. But she'd been too afraid to acknowledge the anger.

"Come on now." Louise helped her off the stool.

Jane stood, feeling lighter inside. She peeked into the mirror again. "You're a miracle worker." Louise had fashioned a twisty updo that looked neither too refined nor too messy. She'd taken a frizzy head of hair and made it into a masterpiece.

"Sometimes your mom and I have to help fix the bridal party's hair." The woman put the leftover bobby pins into a small bag. "I suppose she's told you she's thinking about selling the place."

"Yes." Jane didn't know if anyone else was aware, so she hadn't talked to anyone about the plan. Well, except for Toby. "I think she should. She should be free to follow her dreams too." Jane had no doubt her father would want that for all of them. "How do you feel about it?"

"It's impossible to know if whoever buys it would keep me on." Louise led the way back into the kitchen where they started to load the bags of marinating kabobs into a box. "I'd sure miss this place, but I'm getting close to retirement. It's time for me to spend more time with my grandkids. And Mara needs to do what's best for her too."

"Yes, she does." Jane abandoned the stool. "Whoever buys it would be crazy not to keep you on." She went to hug the woman. "What kind of kitchen manager can also do hair while offering free therapy sessions?"

Louise laughed. "Only one that I know of. I'm sure gonna miss you when you go back to California."

"I'll miss you too." She would miss all this more than she'd ever dreamed, but she had to make herself stop crying now or she'd never get through Beth's rehearsal.

"We'd better get the meat down to the pavilion." Louise handed Jane one of the food boxes they needed to carry. Toby had gotten most of them, but they'd wanted to keep the meat refrigerated. "After you, my dear." Louise fell in step behind Jane and locked the door on their way out.

"At least the weather cooperated." Jane meandered along, feeling a sense of calm. The power might've gone out, but the late afternoon sun shone bright and cheerful, scattering sparkles across the lake's tranquil surface. "It might actually be more fun out here." The rehearsal dinner was supposed to be a little fancier—Jane had even bought a new dress for it at the boutique in town yesterday, but they were still in the mountains, and the pavilion would give the evening a rustic elegance.

"I have to admit, I was worried," Louise said. "But these things always have a way of working themselves out." She winked at Jane. "Love has a way of working itself out too."

"Can I take the box?"

Jane had been so focused on her footing as they walked down the path that she hadn't noticed Toby waiting for them in the pavilion.

Her heart latched on to Louise's comment about love. "Sure. You can take the box." She handed Toby the food.

He took the box from her but stood and admired her instead of setting it down. "New dress?" he asked, his eyes telling her how much he appreciated it.

"Yes." Had she thought of him when she'd bought it? Maybe.

"You look stunning," he said simply before he carted the box to a table.

Louise raised her eyebrows in a silent *See?*

She did see. She saw how Toby looked at her, she saw how his eyes intensified every time they met hers. And it made her float.

After he set down the box, Toby came back to where they were standing. "We'll head up to the hillside for the rehearsal and then I'll help you cook the kabobs," he promised Louise.

"I can get started, but I'd appreciate the assistance."

She unpacked the boxes. "I hired extra serving help too. Just for the night."

"Great." Toby turned to Jane. "Ready?"

"Sure." She wasn't sure she could find her footing, but she could try to walk up that hill with him. At least he'd be there to catch her if she didn't make it.

They started off taking on the trail behind the pavilion and followed the steps her father had built into the incline. There were so many things Jane wanted to say to Toby, but she wasn't sure where to begin. He was quiet too, but he smiled at her and squeezed her hand as they neared the top.

When they crested the hill, Jane's mom met them at the start of the aisle. "There you are. Did you help Louise get everything together?"

"It's all taken care of," Jane said. "Thanks to Toby."

The compliment seemed to startle him. "We make a great team."

"We do," she agreed, letting her gaze linger on his.

"Everyone's taking their places." Mara cut off the moment and all but shoved Toby down the aisle. "You'll stand on the steps of the gazebo with the other groomsmen to start the ceremony. And Jane"—she steered her in the opposite direction—"you'll be walking down the aisle right before Beth."

"Got it." She almost teased her mother about her militant attitude, but that wasn't a good idea when Mara was in wedding coordinator mode. "We can talk later?" she asked Toby almost shyly. His smile perked up. "Of course," he murmured before walking away.

Beth traipsed over to where Jane stood. Jane smiled, but her gaze kept drifting over to Toby. He'd taken his post on the top step of the gazebo and was talking with Ethan.

"Everyone take your places!" Jane's mom yelled like the director on a movie set.

Looking a little startled, the pastor joined Ethan at the center of the gazebo.

"I can't believe I'm doing this for real in two days," Beth squealed. "This is so much more fun than I ever dreamed it would be."

Jane hugged her friend tight. "I'm so glad."

The violinist started to play, giving the flower girls their cue. Beth's nieces twirled and skipped down the aisle, making everyone's hearts melt. Jane took her spot in line right before her best friend. It wasn't even the real ceremony, and already tears were stinging the corners of her eyes.

"You forgot your bouquet." Her mother shoved a bundle of wildflowers into her hands.

"Of course." She had to practice holding flowers while pretending to fluff the train on Beth's wedding dress. That would be a trick.

Her eyes wandered to Toby again and she wasn't surprised to realize he was looking at her too. The air charged between them, even across so much distance. She smiled at him, tears still threatening to fall.

"You're supposed to go," her mother hissed from the sidelines.

Right. She had to walk. She had to move. She couldn't stand still anymore. Not here and not in her life.

She'd made it all of two steps when Toby suddenly strode to the middle of the aisle to meet her.

"Hey! What're you doing?" Jane's mother hurried toward them, but Toby held up a hand to stop her.

"Give me a minute," the cowboy said, addressing everyone. "Please. I need one minute with Jane."

Everyone seemed to quiet instantly. Even Jane's mom backed off to give the two of them space.

Jane stared into Toby's eyes, her heart threatening to leap out of her chest. But it wasn't because everyone was staring at them. At her. For once in her life she didn't care about being the center of attention. For once she didn't want to run away and hide. Let them stare. Never in her life had she seen a man look at her the way Toby looked at her now.

"I don't want to go back to riding nearly as much as I want to stay with you," he said.

"Oh my God," Jane heard Beth say behind her. She turned around to shush her friend and quickly faced Toby again, her knees wobbling violently.

"I'll give it all up." He eased a step closer to her. "My whole career. I'd rather give it all up than walk away from you. I love you. Maybe I've always loved you and I was too afraid to realize it."

The mountain air seemed to thin even more. Jane couldn't draw in a deep enough breath to speak.

Toby grinned at her a little, and then he stepped back into his place by Ethan. "I just wanted you to know that. I couldn't wait one more minute to tell you." He glanced around sheepishly. "Sorry for the interruption everyone. We can get back to the rehearsal now."

Jane wanted to tell him no, they needed one more minute. Something in her heart had shifted. She wanted to tell him everything—that she couldn't let him give up riding and she couldn't walk away from him either. But her mother rushed over and prodded her toward the gazebo. "Okay everyone," she called. "Let's keep this moving. We still have a lot to cover!" Jane knew she was trying to protect her. From the attention, from being put on the spot. But strangely, Jane didn't want to be protected.

Everything around her moved again—the pastor, Beth and her father walking slowly down the aisle.

Jane's mother moved her into position. She'd missed her moment to respond. She'd missed her moment to tell Toby what she knew in her heart. She was finally free to love him too.

Chapter Twenty-Three

Wake up! Wake up! Wake up!" Beth jumped onto Jane's bed and shook her. "I'm getting married tomorrow! And we're going white-water rafting today!"

Groaning, Jane pushed her hair out of her face. Truthfully, she'd been awake since about four o'clock in the morning sorting through the worst-case scenarios for what could happen on a white-water rafting trip. Last night, at the rehearsal dinner, she'd decided to jump and agreed to go along on the trip, and now she was trying to claw her way back up the cliff.

"My throat hurts," she croaked, forcing herself to a sitting position.

"Oh, no, no, no." Beth waggled her finger back and forth. "Nuh-uh, lady. You are not turning back now. You told me last night not to let you bail, and, as your best friend, I take those requests very seriously."

"But—"

"Stop." Rising to her knees on the mattress, Beth

posted her hands on her hips. "What did you tell me last night?"

"That I had to go white-water rafting to prove to myself I could conquer any fear," Jane recited dully.

Her friend raised her eyebrows. "And?"

Jane huffed out a breath. "And this would be my first step in embracing a new adventure."

"A new adventure with who?" Beth prompted.

"With Toby." Oh, she wanted him. She wanted this, and yet she was going to have to battle against herself every step of the way. Last night he'd been so busy helping Louise with the cooking that she hadn't had much of a chance to talk to him. Then he'd gotten roped into giving rides to people who'd had too much to drink, and Beth had wanted to spend the night with Jane. Probably to make sure she showed up for the rafting excursion. Beth knew her well.

"This is going to be great." Her friend popped off the king-sized bed they'd shared last night and started to pull on clothes. "I know you're worried, but this is exactly what you need to do. Toby offered to walk away from everything for you. Can you even imagine his face when you show up today?" Beth flopped back onto the mattress and cast a dreamy gaze at the ceiling. "It will be the perfect way for you to tell him you're all in."

"Maybe I could start with dipping a toe in first." Her baby toe. "Getting into a boat in raging rapids isn't very practical..." And yet that was supposed to be the point. This was her grand gesture. Her way of saying screw you to all her fears so she could ride off into the sunset with the man she loved. She smiled a little. It felt good to let herself admit she loved him.

"Jane..." Beth collected her hands and squeezed them

as if trying to infuse her with a more adventurous spirit. "Only for today, please for the love of God, tell your brain to go to hell and listen to your heart."

Her heart. That spot inside of her that pulsed with warmth when Toby looked at her, when he held her hand, when he kissed her like he'd only ever wanted her. Jane rested her hand there on the left side of her chest, feeling it pound with life. Follow your heart, follow your heart, follow your heart. She silently repeated the mantra, trying to find a handhold.

"It's so perfect that you didn't tell Toby you were coming." Once again Beth rolled off the bed. "He's going to be shocked to see you. He'll know how you feel about him the second he sees you coming."

Jane could do this. Right now, in this moment, all she had to do was get out of bed. She swung one leg over the side of the mattress and found the floor, then the other. That wasn't so hard.

"Here." Beth dug through the dresser drawers for her. "Swimsuit, shorts..." She knelt and crawled around in the closet. "Sandals!" she called triumphantly.

It took Jane twice as long to get dressed thanks to her jittery hands, but finally she pulled a sweatshirt over her head. On the way out of the lodge, they stopped in the kitchen and swiped a muffin from Louise. Thankfully, Beth volunteered to drive—again, most likely so Jane didn't attempt any detours that would result in missing their river meet time.

"This is going to be thrilling." Her friend pulled the SUV into a dirt parking lot next to a shack that said RAFTING.

Jane eyed the weathered sign. "Did Ethan vet this company? Check online reviews? Make sure no one has died in one of their boats recently?"

"I know this is scary, Jane. Just breathe." Beth's voice was teasing, but she could see the compassion in her friend's eyes. Beth understood how scared she was. She understood why. "You'll be fine. We'll all be fine," her friend continued, climbing out of the car.

"Right." Follow your heart, follow your heart, follow your heart.

Most of Beth's family and friends who'd opted into the madness were already gathered down on the riverbank. The sight of the swirling water churned her stomach and she tossed her half-eaten muffin into a nearby trash can.

"There's Toby and Ethan!" Beth dragged her by the arm down the small embankment to the river's edge where four blue rubber rafts sat.

She couldn't swallow.

"Look who's here!" Her friend made the announcement in a singsongy tone.

Everyone went silent, but Jane kept her focus on Toby, on that warm pulsing dead center in her chest. She could do this. With him. She could do anything with him.

"What're you doing here?" He seemed to forget about everyone else. Or at least that was how his gaze made her feel. Like she was the only one standing there. He'd been so thoughtful to call and see if she wanted him to sit out the trip. Of course she'd told him no. She didn't want him to sit out on anything for her. She didn't want to sit out either.

"I'm going on an adventure," she said, nearly breathless. "With you."

He reached for her hands pulling he closer. "You don't have to prove—"

"All righty folks, circle up!" A college-aged mountain man came bounding down the hill. Their guide, presumably. With his tanned weathered skin and long blond hair, he looked like he lived outside. "I'm Brody and I'll be the head river guide today."

Toby continued to stare at Jane, but they didn't have time to talk now. She would tell him everything later. Inching closer to him, Jane threaded her fingers through his, and he held on to her.

"My colleague here is going to hand out life jackets. Make sure you get 'em on nice and tight," Brody said, climbing onto a rock in the center of the group.

Someone shoved a bright orange life vest into Jane's hands. She quickly put it on and secured the buckles.

"We have to go over some of the safety regulations we touched on in the waivers you signed."

Jane frantically looked at Beth. What waivers? She'd never read a waiver…

"Don't worry. I signed it for you," her friend whispered. Before Jane could ask what the waiver had covered, Brody held up a miniature toy raft. "If we flip the boat, everyone's gonna be dumped in the water." Brody tipped over the boat he held in his hands. "And, dude, let me tell ya, it'll be cold." He narrowed his eyes and seemed to fix his gaze on each person before continuing.

"It'll be chaos, but you can't lose your head, man. Just get your feet downstream so you can steer clear of the rocks—"

Heads bobbed in expectant nods all around her, but visions of bouncing off boulders in a violent current edged Jane closer to a panic attack.

"By the way, it's critical that you don't *ever* stand up in the river, gang. Even if it's shallow." Brody pushed wisps of blond fluff away from his eyes. "If your foot gets stuck between the rocks, the current's so strong that it'll push you right under."

Under?

"We call that scenario a 'foot entrapment.'"

The gripping pain in her chest intensified. She hadn't even considered that situation on her list of worst-case scenarios. Jane cleared her throat so she could breathe.

Toby's blue eyes found hers, flickering with concern. "Are sure you're okay with this?" he whispered.

"No." Her face had to be pale. "But holding your hand helps."

He smiled and squeezed her hand tighter.

"Now, if we happen to hit a boulder sideways, we could have a wrapped boat situation on our hands." Brody knocked on the tiny boat's inflated tube.

"This is serious, folks. The current presses against the boat until it grips the rock like Saran Wrap." He held up a fist and cupped his other hand around it as if they really needed a visual demonstration. "If the boat wraps, you gotta bail and self-rescue to the nearest riverbank."

Self-rescue. Umm... Jane raised her hand.

"Yeah?" Brody pointed at her.

"Aren't you guys supposed to rescue us if we happen to fall in?" She tried to make it sound like a joke.

A few people chuckled, Brody included. "That depends. If we're all in the water, it's every man for himself. But if I'm still in the boat, I'll get you back in too. Don't worry."

Don't worry. Brody obviously didn't have her number. Toby did though. He moved even closer and slipped his arm around her.

"Okay, moving on." Brody held up the toy boat again. "If I think we're about to flip, I'll yell, 'High side.' That means everyone's gotta jump to the side of the boat that's tipping up in the air." Once again, he demonstrated with the toy raft. "If we all get there in time, we can save it and everything will be fine. I think that's about it. Make sure you listen to your guide for your paddle commands." Brody looked down at Jane again. "Any other questions?"

She had a million, but she kept them to herself.

"All righty then." Brody hopped off the rock. "Let's all get loaded up and we'll ship off."

"This is going to be so great!" Beth walked around high-fiving people, but when she got to Jane she opted for a hug. "You can do this," her friend whispered in her ear. "Be brave."

Jane could only nod. Adrenaline spiked through her and she hadn't even dipped a toe in the water yet.

"You guys are with Ethan and I," Beth instructed, climbing into Brody's boat. Jane started to move but Toby held her back. "Are you sure you want to do this?" He took her shoulders in his hands. "Because if you don't, I'll drive you back to the ranch right now. We don't have to go."

Looking into his eyes raised her up. "I want to do this with you. I—"

"Hop in, dudes!" Brody waved them into the boat. "We gotta push off so we can stay on schedule."

Of course. She seemed to get interrupted every time she tried to tell Toby something important. He took Jane's hand, helping her climb over the boat's rim. "You sit here." He pointed to a seat in the middle. "And I'll be right behind you."

"Okay." Her knees gave out and she thumped down to the inflated tube.

Brody handed out paddles. Jane found it hard to grip hers, thanks to her shaking hands.

Across from her, Beth shot Jane a giddy smile. She really tried to smile back but it likely resembled more of a grimace. Follow your heart, follow your heart, follow your heart...

"Here we go, peeps." Brody shoved them off and hopped into the boat, taking the side on the back right tube. "Paddles at the ready, everyone."

Jane tightened her grip, easing in a breath and forcing herself to hold it so she wouldn't hyperventilate. The boat bounced as the river took it downstream, the waves gently lapping the sides.

Jane peered over her shoulder. "This isn't so bad," she said to Toby. He leaned forward and kissed her lips.

"I like to call this the calm before the storm." Brody went on chatting about the section of river they were on and the rapids they had coming up, but Jane closed her eyes and let the sun warm her face. It really was beautiful out here, seeing the mountains from a different perspective. Sitting with Toby behind her and Beth beside her. A cautious joy bubbled up. Maybe her life really could look different.

A distant rumble thumped in Jane's eardrums. She opened her eyes and looked downriver. The water ahead looked nothing like the section they were on now. It churned and thrashed. Jane sat straighter, stretching her neck to see.

White water, like the mouth of a foamy monster, ready to slurp and swallow.

Surges of adrenaline sputtered from a fountain somewhere inside of her, burning her veins, dropping the bottom out of her stomach.

Breathe. Swallow. Things that had always come naturally suddenly stopped. The sound of rushing water rang in her ears.

Brody crouched low, adjusted his visor, tightened the strap. "Okay, guys. This is it. Our first rapid. It's a class four."

Class four? What did that mean again? Heat continued to dance through her body, forcing her knees to pump, her shoulders to shudder.

"I'm gonna need all you got here. Remember all the commands we went over."

That must've been when Jane wasn't paying attention. "When I say paddle, you'd better paddle hard." Brody clamped his gaze onto the river and dipped his paddle into the water.

The motion rocked her. The noise absorbed her. Somehow the straps on her lifejacket tightened, the bulky padding started to shrink, to squeeze the life out of her.

What were those commands again?

Shallow breaths edged in and out of her open mouth. Left turn—did that mean she had to paddle forward? Or was it backward?

The boat jerked, stretching and snapping her body like a rubber band, sending her sprawling forward. Her kneecaps thudded into the inflated floor. Freezing water oozed over the sides of the boat, splashing her cheeks, scraping her legs. She clawed the rim, pulled and tugged, slipped and fell back to the floor.

Toby reached for her hands, but Brody started to yell. "Paddle! Now! Forward! I need everyone!" The rest of the group paddled in a frenzied synchronization. They reached forward, pulled, leaned back.

All she could do was stare. At them. At the water.

A trail of fire coiled around her sternum. She had to focus and grab her—

A collision thrust the boat sideways and all Jane could see was a huge rock coming straight for them.

"Paddle!" Brody yelled over and over. The tone of his voice edged into panic.

The boat spun into the rock and lurched one side of the tube up. Higher. They were going over.

"High side!" The thundering water smothered the guide's command. Jane tried to climb up to the tube, but she kept slipping. Everyone was slipping.

The river seemed to slurp the boat, and in an instant, they were all in the water.

The cold shocked her. "Toby!" She tried to scream, but a wave slapped her in the face, stinging her nose, clogging her burning throat.

The overturned boat bobbed so far away. She couldn't get there. The water was dragging her down.

Be strong. Be brave. She thought of Toby, tried to scan the water for him, but only white froth filled her vision.

Feet downstream. That's what Body had said. Jane flailed her arms to assume the right position. As long as she paddled her arms, the lifejacket buoyed her mouth and nose above the surface.

You're so much braver than you think you are. That was her father's voice in her head—telling her to be brave, to be strong. *I love you, Janie. You can do this. You can rescue yourself.* That warm pulsing in her chest started again, replenishing her strength. She was brave, damn it. She wouldn't go down.

Chapter Twenty-Four

Where was she? Damn it, he had to get out of the water. Toby fought the current's drag, turning on his stomach to swim. This wasn't the first time he'd gotten dunked on a white-water rafting trip, but Jane hadn't been with him then. Water sprayed him in the face, blinding him. Hell, he couldn't even see the riverbank. Shouts seemed to ring out in all directions, but he couldn't see anyone.

The struggle taxed his lungs, so he turned over onto his back again, pointed his feet downstream.

Panic raced through him so hot he couldn't even feel the cold. He should've grabbed on to Jane's hand before they went over. He'd been so sure he could right the boat. He'd flung himself onto the tube, and then she was gone. That's when he'd bailed too, jumping into the water after her.

The current was too fast though. By the time he'd hit the water Jane had disappeared.

Grunting in frustration he flipped back to his stomach. He had to get out of the water so he could see. Toby pulled against the waves, kicking his legs until they burned. There! The bank. He propelled himself forward, gasping and gagging with the water and exertion.

Brody had made it out. Beth and Ethan too. The other boats had pulled over behind them. "Where's Jane?" Beth screamed.

"I don't know." He pushed himself out of the water, crawling until he could get to his feet.

"One unaccounted for," Brody was saying into a radio.

Unaccounted for. No. "No!" Toby stumbled down the riverbank, sloshing through the water, his eyes trained on the waves. There were only whitecaps and rocks everywhere he looked.

"Oh my God, we have to find her!" Beth had started to cry.

"We'll find her," Toby growled. He would find her.

About thirty yards ahead, the river disappeared around a bend. "She must've gotten swept farther down." The water was so high this time of year—still swollen with snowmelt. Toby tried to sprint, but the uneven ground and sand turned his run into a clumsy jog. The other day Louise had said he was good in a crisis, but panic was seeping into every cell. If he let himself, he could throw up right now. This was Jane. Beautiful sassy Jane. The love of his whole life. And he couldn't find her.

"Jane!" He tried to yell above the rapids, but they sounded like a freight train thundering in his ears. Blood rushed hot and fast, pounding through his temples. Toby had to wade deeper to avoid a rocky embankment at the side of the river. He edged around the outcropping, feeling his way with his hands. As soon as he came around the corner, he saw the empty overturned boat caught on a rock near the river's edge. Jane wasn't there.

Oh Jesus, was she trapped underneath? Fueled by adrenaline, he sprinted the rest of the way and flipped the boat, searching underneath. Where was she? "Jane!" The roar of the rapids crashing around him swallowed his shout.

"Toby!"

He spun, the world blurring around him. There. On the other side of the river about a hundred yards down. "I found her!" he yelled. But it was doubtful anyone had heard him, and he wasn't going to wait for anyone else. Toby shoved his shoulder against the boat and pushed it into the water, jumping in as the current took it.

Jane was standing. Waving. She looked fine. Wet and cold but as far as he could tell from so far away fine.

He dug a paddle into the water, steering the boat across the river, letting the current pull him right to Jane. There had always been a current pulling them together—even when they were kids. It had grown stronger over the years, and when she showed up that morning, he'd known she felt it too.

"Are you okay?" he yelled. The current wasn't getting him there fast enough. He paddled harder, his shoulder locking up.

"I'm okay!" She'd started to move up the riverbank toward him, slowly, maybe limping a little. *Screw this.* Toby jumped out of the boat and into the water again, swimming with the current this time instead of against it. He made land and started running, catching Jane in his arms, sweeping her feet off the ground. Holding her had never felt so good. "I might not let go," he warned her.

"You don't have to." Jane wrapped her legs around his waist and held Toby's face in her hands, gazing at him with tears spilling down her cheeks. "I did it. I made it out."

"You did so good, sweetness." He set her feet on the

ground but continued to hold her. He couldn't seem to loosen his grip. They were both sopping wet, muddy, and shivering, and he may have just set himself back with the shoulder injury, but everything in his world was right. He pulled back to examine her, to be sure.

Blood trickled down her leg from a wound on her knee. "You're hurt." Toby knelt to inspect the cut, but Jane pulled him back up to her. "It's a little bit of blood," she said dismissively. "It doesn't mean you can't kiss me."

Toby didn't waste one more second. He brought his lips to hers, letting the whole world around them pause while he showed her how worried he'd been. Jane's arms wrapped around him and that whimper in her throat made him smile against her mouth. "I love that sound," he murmured, tasting the heat of her mouth. He kissed her until that aching need threatened to overpower him. Then he pulled back and rested his forehead against hers. "You scared me, Jane. I've never been so scared."

"I wasn't about to give up," she said with a playful roll of her eyes. "Not when I still have some things to say to you."

"What?" He wanted to hear everything.

"I love you too, Toby. That's why I was so mad at you at the winery. Because I love you and I never want anything to happen to you."

"I know." He smoothed his hand over her hair. "I won't ride anymore. I don't have to—"

"Yes, you do." Jane interrupted him. "You have to ride. You have to ride for Tanner, and you have to ride for yourself. And you have to ride for me. I'm not afraid anymore." She half laughed, half cried. "Look at me! This was the most terrifying thing I've ever done, and I made it."

"I'm sorry." He brushed her wet, sticky hair off her

forehead. "I know you're afraid of the water, and I'm sorry I couldn't protect you." From the fear she must've felt, from the thoughts about her father dying that way...

"It's okay." She looked at the river flowing next to them. "I realized it wasn't the water I feared. It was the letting go. The knowledge that I couldn't control what happened." She clasped her hands together behind his neck. "But I want to let go." A smile brightened her eyes. "I want an adventure."

Toby brushed his lips against hers. He went in for a real kiss, a kiss that would give her a prelude to the things they would experience out in the world together.

A scraping sound broke them apart. The other boats had made their way down, along with Beth and Ethan and Brody.

"Jane!" Beth half laughed, half sobbed. "Oh God, I was so worried. If you died it would've been all my fault!" Beth crowded out Toby trying to hug Jane. He'd let her, but only for a minute.

"Don't be silly." Jane looked at him over Beth's shoulder and smiled. "I'm *fine*. I've never been better actually."

"You sure?" Brody moved in, looking official and concerned. "I should check you out."

"I already checked her out," Toby said, still feeling their kiss on his lips.

"He did," Jane agreed. "Very thoroughly."

Well, he would do a more thorough job later.

The guide seemed to accept his assessment. "Well if everyone's fine, then we can get back on the river."

Toby took Jane's hand and led her away from everyone else. "No one would blame you if you didn't want to get back in that boat. We could hike back to the cars. It's not that far."

"Thank you." Jane rested her hands on his hips and urged him closer. "I want to get back into the boat though."

"You're not afraid?" Hell, he was still reeling from thinking something terrible had happened to her. He wouldn't mind not getting back into the boat. He wouldn't mind taking her home right now.

"I'm terrified," Jane said with a laugh. "But I won't let it stop me anymore." She hooked her thumbs under the waistband of his board shorts. "I won't let anything stop me from building the life I want."

* * *

It wasn't difficult for Jane to find her bridesmaid dress in the closet of her room at the lodge. The bright orange garment stuck out in the midst of her sensible, neutral clothes. When she'd first opened the package back in California, she'd let out an audible groan. The tag attached to the gown read MARMALADE for the color. Marmalade!

That hadn't been the only strike against it either. It was also strapless, made out of chiffon, and belted at the empire waist with a braided ribbon. Oh, and she wasn't a fan of high-low hems either. They had always messed with her sense of order. Jane hadn't been able to look at herself in the mirror while she was having the alterations done but looking at it now on the hanger brought a wide, toothy smile.

She'd been smiling a lot today, and it wasn't even her wedding. Though she had a feeling she'd be going home with the best man tonight. After the rafting trip, Toby had been wary to let her out of his sight, but Jane wanted to spend Beth's last night as a single woman with her. They'd watched chick flicks, ate ice cream from the cartons, and had smeared on hideous face masks while they'd giggled and talked about their boys.

Jane hadn't giggled in years.

This morning they'd woken up and Louise made them a huge brunch, then helped her do her hair and makeup. All she had left to do now was put on her dress and meet everyone downstairs so the golf carts could take them up to the ceremony.

Jane slipped off her clothes and wrestled her way into the first strapless bra she'd ever owned, cursing the entire time. After putting on more deodorant, she pulled on the dress and managed to zip the back roughly all the way up. Bracing herself, she turned to the mirror.

The color was so vibrant it shocked her. In a good way. This was different than anything she'd ever worn before, but it seemed to fit the day. It seemed to fit the occasion. It seemed to fit her.

Jane leaned closer to the mirror and applied a fresh coat of the subtle lipstick she'd chosen at the store last night when they'd picked up the ice cream. It was cherry flavored, in case she and Toby had a chance to sneak away and kiss.

Grabbing her bouquet, Jane hurried out of her room, grateful that Beth had let her choose their own shoes. Jane had chosen a pair of ballet flats that almost matched the dress. There was no way she could navigate the outdoor aisle in heels.

Chaos and noise floated up the stairs as she made her way down.

"Beth," Jane gasped when she saw her friend. "You look so beautiful." Beth's mom had wanted to help her daughter get dressed alone, so Jane hadn't seen the wedding dress before. She could hardly see it now through her tears. The gown fit her friend perfectly. It was an A-line princess cut with off-the-shoulder capped sleeves. The bodice had been stitched with embroidered flowers while the chiffon skirt flowed elegantly to the floor. A short sweeping train trailed behind, the delicate material resembling a rose petal. "It's the loveliest dress I've ever seen." Jane dabbed at her eyes with her fingertips trying to keep her mascara intact.

"Thank you!" Her friend positively glowed.

"All right, everyone." Jane's mother herded them outside. "The golf carts are ready. They'll take you up the hill and drop you off, so you don't mess up those beautiful dresses or your shoes."

Her mother really impressed her. Back when her father ran the dude ranch, they were hardly breaking even some months. But after he'd passed away, her mother had researched and labored and figured out how to provide for their needs—and had tripled her income in the process.

"Are you coming, Jane?" her mother called, glancing at her watch yet again.

"Yes." She paused on the porch. "It's amazing what you've done here, Mom." She'd never told her, never complimented her on her hard work and her resilience. "You've created a beautiful haven. The perfect place to celebrate love." The perfect place for Jane to find love.

"You really think so?" Shock rippled through her mother's tone.

"Yes." Jane hadn't appreciated any of it in high school. There had been so much change. Too many transitions. She'd simply tried to shield herself from all of it. "I'd like to keep it." The words surprised her, but they'd been building for a while.

"Keep what?" Her mother glanced between her and the golf carts.

They were running out of time, but Jane needed to tell her now. "The ranch. I want to keep it. To run it." Just like that, she'd let go of her life in California. After the last few weeks she couldn't imagine writing anywhere but here. She would travel with Toby as often as she could, but this would be their haven.

"Are you sure?" Her mother's hand reached for hers. "Really, Jane? You want to stay here?"

"Only if you'll let me buy it." Her mom deserved to go find that life she'd been talking about. She deserved to travel and live comfortably.

"You don't have to buy it." Her mother's eyes filled with tears. "Really. Just keeping it in the family would be the best gift. It could be a gathering place for all of us when we need a respite from our adventures."

"It will be," Jane agreed. "But I will pay for it. I have enough for a down payment set aside." And when she sold her condo in California, she'd get another good chunk to put toward the mortgage.

"Mara, we're running late!" Louise barked.

"We should go." Jane took her mom's arm and they made their way to the empty seats in the second golf cart. "We can talk about the details later."

Her mother nodded as though she was unable to speak.

All the way to the ceremony site, Jane asked questions about the honeymoon. They weren't supposed to have one, but Beth had opted to surprise Ethan by planning a trip to Banff in Canada. "It's his dream vacation," she explained as they climbed out of the cart and moved out of sight into the trees to hide from the guests who'd already started filling in the seats. "Apparently the mountains in Banff are even better than the ones we have here," her friend said.

Looking around her, Jane found that hard to believe. “Well, I can’t wait to hear all about it.” She fussed with her friend’s veil and dress.

“We have about ten minutes before we’ll start the processional,” her mom announced. It seemed she’d regained her composure and was all business again.

Ten minutes huh? Jane ventured out of the tree cover a few steps searching for a certain best man. She immediately located him standing near the gazebo, but they hadn’t taken their places yet. Trying to be discreet, Jane edged along the trees. The flash of orange seemed to draw Toby’s attention. He definitely looked at her. Then he said something to Ethan and hurried toward her. As he approached, Jane moved into the shadows of the evergreens.

“You’re wearing orange.” Toby took his time surveying the dress.

“Yes I am.” She twirled for him. “What do you think?”

“I think you look pretty in anything.” His eyes got that wicked tint. “What’re you wearing underneath it?”

“The most complicated strapless bra this side of the Mississippi and an uncomfortable G-string,” she told him, hiking up her dress only a few inches.

A long-suffering breath inflated Toby’s chest. “I’d be happy to help you do away with both as soon as I have the opportunity.”

“That might be a while.” She tried to look apologetic, but she loved teasing him as much as he loved teasing her.

“Not sure how long I can wait.” Toby nudged his lips against hers, making her very impatient as well. “Especially because you had to spend last night with Beth.”

“I can spend tonight with you,” she whispered in his ear. “And the next night. And the next.”

“When are you going back to California?”

He was cute when he pouted. "I'll go back next week like I planned. But only for a few days. Only to pack up my stuff and find a Realtor."

"Really?" His grin took over his whole face. "You're moving here?"

"Really." She clasped his hands in hers. "You could come with me, if you want. To help me pack."

"Yes." He didn't even think about his answer. "I'd go with you anywhere." His expression turned naughty again. "Someone has to be able to help you out of all your complicated undergarments."

Jane laughed. "And you're the perfect man for the job."

"I'm the perfect man for a lot of jobs. Just let me—"

"How about you be the perfect best man and get your ass over here?" Ethan said as he approached them. "Mara is about to have a heart attack," he informed them. "I told her not to worry. Her daughter and her best employee were probably only sneaking around the woods."

"Gotta go." Toby held Jane's jaw tenderly in his hand and drew her face to his. "I'll see you out there."

"See you out there." Jane pulled away and started to jog in the opposite direction. She nearly ran straight into her mother. "Sorry," she blurted out before Mara could say a word. "I had to talk to Toby." And she hadn't even been able to tell him all the things she'd wanted to say.

"Toby, huh?" Her mother linked their arms together and led her to her place. "What did you have to say to Toby?"

"Um." Well, most of what they'd said, her mother probably shouldn't hear. "I was going to tell him about the ranch and ask him if he wants to be part of it, but I didn't get the chance."

Mara stopped walking and faced Jane. "Your father

would be so incredibly happy to know you're coming home. He'd be thrilled about Toby too. He always liked that boy."

The music started, but Jane leaned closer to her mother. "I've always liked him too."

Chapter Twenty-Five

This day is taking for. Ev. Er," Toby whispered to Jane. They were on their five thousandth picture with the wedding party, and every minute until he could get Jane alone seemed to stretch longer and longer. Forget posing and smiling, strapless bras and G-strings were all he could think about.

"We need another one," the photographer informed the group, aiming a glare at Toby. "This time no whispering."

Damn he'd been caught. Now they'd have to stand here even longer.

Everyone except for Jane groaned. She laughed.

"If you behave, we'll get through this much faster," she told him primly.

"I don't want to behave." He and Jane had been behaving all day and they hadn't even started the reception yet.

"Okay, everyone looking at the camera, please." The photographer seemed to mainly be addressing Toby. If it would move this along, he'd give the man his best smile.

"Perfect. Everyone hold it right there." The man snapped

what had to be a thousand pictures, and Toby smiled for every single one of them.

"That's it. I think we're done with the wedding party." The photographer lowered his camera. "We'll take a few more family shots, then you can head to the reception."

Thank. God. Toby turned to Jane, but she was busy helping Beth straighten her veil. Two more hours. They only had to be here for two more hours. They could leave the reception early, right?

Jane finally finished touching up Beth and wandered over to him, a smile shining in her eyes. "This has been the best day. Wasn't that ceremony beautiful?"

"It was pretty spectacular." Emotion may have even tightened his throat once or twice seeing Ethan cry with obvious joy when he'd watched Beth walk down the aisle. And don't get him started on the vows they'd written themselves. Toby had pretended to sneeze once to cover up a few tears.

"Did I see you wiping away a tear?" Jane faced him, resting her forearms on his shoulders and clasping her hands behind his neck.

He should've known she'd see through the sneeze. "It's allergy season." He moved in a step closer, placing his hands on the curves of her hips.

"I don't remember you ever having allergies." She closed the space between them, pinning her body against his. "It's okay to cry you know."

"Maybe I was crying because I knew it would be hours until I could get you alone again," he suggested. "Seriously. Why do people insist on doing pictures between the ceremony and the reception?" In his opinion, they could knock those out ahead of time and rush through the reception.

Jane only laughed. "Ethan didn't want to see his bride before she walked down the aisle. I think it's sweet."

"I think you're sweet." Toby couldn't hold back anymore. He lowered his lips to hers, seeking out that connection that sent shock waves through him every time.

"Okay everyone!" Jane's mom came walking down the aisle breaking off their kiss way too soon. "We need to move on to the reception hall. Everyone's waiting."

"I've been waiting," Toby murmured, giving Jane a pout.

"You've been very patient." Jane drew her lips to his ear. "And I promise your patience will pay off," she whispered, nibbling on his earlobe for a quick second before she pulled away.

"Now you're just torturing me." Not that he was complaining.

Smiling, she took his hand and led him to where everyone was piling into the golf carts to head down to the reception hall. They climbed in and sat close as Mara drove them down the hill. Music already blared from the new reception hall. With how long pictures had taken, the party was likely already in full swing.

"Family and the wedding party can go ahead on in," Mara instructed when she'd parked the golf cart. "We'll send Ethan and Beth in after."

Toby slid out of the seat first and then helped Jane stand. "Have I mentioned how much I love that dress?" He admired it again, paying particular attention to the strapless neckline.

"You may have mentioned it." Jane seemed to take her time checking him out too. "I'm definitely a fan of that tux on you." She straightened his bow tie. "Though I prefer your jeans."

"Why is that?" Toby asked. He knew, he just wanted to hear her say it.

Before Jane could answer, Mara ushered them toward

the reception hall doors. "Come on you two. We're running behind schedule. There'll be plenty of time for flirting later," she said wearing a knowing look.

They'd gone way past flirting, but Toby didn't point that out.

"Come on." Jane held on to him as they navigated the path to the reception hall. "Let's go dance."

He'd never liked dancing much, but something told him he'd like it with Jane. He'd like doing just about anything with Jane.

Inside the reception hall, the wedding crowd was milling around enjoying appetizers and drinks while they anxiously awaited the bride and groom's arrival. Toby swiped two glasses of champagne from a passing waiter. He was more of a beer guy, but today felt like a good day to celebrate. "Cheers." He handed Jane a glass and they clinked them together.

"Are you trying to get me tipsy so I'll kiss you again?" she asked after her first sip.

"I'd like to think you'd kiss me regardless."

Jane teased him with a shrug. "I *might*." Her playful expression turned serious. "There's something I've been meaning to talk to you about—"

"There you two are." Wes strode between them. "I thought you'd snuck off into the woods to make out again."

Toby might have to sneak her off into the woods in order to avoid any more interruptions. What had she been about to tell him?

The music stopped suddenly, and the room went silent. "Introducing Mr. and Mrs. Rockford!" the DJ announced. "Stayin' Alive" by the Bee Gees started playing and the whole crowd went crazy while Ethan and Beth disco danced their way into the room and headed straight for the dance floor.

Jane had been about to tell him something important, but now the party had really started, and she seemed to forget all about it. She pulled him and Wes to the edge of the crowd and started to clap along with the music, cheering on their friends while they lit up the dance floor with some impressive disco moves.

Just as Toby was about to lean in and ask her what she wanted to tell him, Beth danced her way over to them.

"Come on!" She pulled them both out into the center of the circle with her.

Toby almost expected Jane to edge her way back to the crowd, but she surprised him by doing the hustle instead. Toby joined her, mimicking her movements since he couldn't dance to save his life.

The crowd really got into it then, and their cheers and whoops seemed to make Jane shine even more. She put it all out there, swinging her hips, shaking her shoulders. The rest of the wedding party joined in, but Jane seemed to steal the show. Toby stopped dancing and simply watched her, utterly amazed. That night at the brewery she hadn't wanted any attention on her, and now she seemed to thrive on it.

The song ended and Jane made her way back to him, her face flushed and her eyes still dancing.

"That was amazing." Toby pulled her against him. "I had no idea you could dance like that." There were so many things he hadn't discovered about her yet. He hoped he had the chance to learn everything.

"I didn't know I could dance like that either," she said, still out of breath. "I can't remember the last time I've had so much fun."

"I love watching you have fun," he told her. "And so did everyone else."

She turned a slow circle looking around her. People still clapped and smiled, staring at Jane in awe.

She turned back to him, cozying up. "I guess they're finally seeing me for who I really am."

"I've always seen you." Toby stared steadily into her bright, happy eyes. "I may not have known what to do with you back then, but I still saw you." A slow country song started, and he cradled Jane in his arms, urging her back to the center of the dance floor.

They swayed to the music and Jane lifted her face to his. "There's something I've been meaning to talk to you about."

Oh, yeah. He'd gotten so wrapped up in watching her dance, he'd forgotten. "You can talk to me about anything."

Jane inhaled deeply. "I—"

"Selfie time!" Beth crashed their two-person party, breaking them apart and snapping a picture of the three of them.

"No. No way." No more interruptions. Toby quickly resumed their slow-dance position and danced Jane into the corner where they had more privacy. "What were you going to say?" He had to know why her face suddenly looked so serious. Nerves buzzed in his stomach.

"I was going to say..." She seemed to think for a minute. "Or rather, I was going to ask, do you want to buy the ranch with me?"

"Yes." He'd buy a shack with her. If it meant he got to spend his life making up for lost time, he'd buy anything. "Tell me when and how and I'll sign the papers. I'd do it today. Right now."

Jane's laugh made him want to kiss her. "Well, I don't think we can move that fast. But I talked to my mom about it, and I want to keep the ranch in the family. I know you'll be traveling a lot—"

"And now I'll have every reason to hurry home." Because Jane would be here. Because this place would be theirs. Together.

"I still want to travel with you too sometimes." She stopped dancing and bit into her lower lip shyly. "I still want to have adventures with you."

"We're gonna have so many adventures." Toby kissed her letting his lips linger over hers while he continued. "I'm going to give you everything."

* * *

"Thank you so much!" Beth threw herself at Jane, holding her tight. "I never would've made it through this without you."

Jane squeezed her back. "And I never would've faced everything I needed to face here if you hadn't gotten married."

"You're going home with Toby tonight, I would hope?" her friend whispered. Like it was some big secret after the way she and Toby had danced and kissed during the entire reception.

"Oh, yes. I'm definitely going home with Toby tonight." Her gaze wandered off to find him. He stood by Ethan near the door. They were shaking hands instead of hugging of course. The rest of the close family and friends who'd lingered to see Ethan and Beth off were clustered around the reception hall doors.

"In fact, the faster you get going, the faster I can go

home with Toby," Jane said, giving her friend a nudge. *Hint, hint.* "Ethan is looking pretty impatient himself."

"I'm going, I'm going." Beth didn't budge. "I want details on you two as soon as I get home. Before you go back to California."

"I'm not going back to California. Well not for long, anyway." With all the craziness, she hadn't had the opportunity to discuss her plans with Beth. "I'm buying the ranch from Mom, staying right here."

"What?" Her friend leapt into another hug, and Jane was pretty sure she saw Ethan's foot start to tap. "Staying forever? Living at the ranch?" Her friend started to cry.

"Yes." Jane started to walk her to the door. "So, we'll have plenty of time to catch up."

"And we can have babies together!" Beth blurted out.

Toby's eyes went wide.

"When you're ready, of course." Her friend patted Toby's shoulder.

"I think that's our cue to make a fast getaway." Ethan took Beth's hand. "Ready?"

"I think so." Beth glanced at Jane over her shoulder. "But we'll talk soon, right?"

"Of course." Jane helped herself to a small container of bubbles sitting in a basket nearby.

"Bye everyone!" Beth couldn't seem to leave the party. She'd never wanted to leave a party early.

"Have the best time on your honeymoon!" Jane called, blowing the bubbles in their direction. Everyone else followed suit and soon they were trailing Beth and Ethan out the door with bubbles floating in the soft moonlight.

The couple climbed into Ethan's Jeep, which the groomsmen had covered with streamers and balloons, and then they drove away, Beth waving frantically out the window.

The crowd started to disperse, with everyone going their separate ways.

"I'm glad your mom hired a cleaning crew." Toby tucked Jane under his arm.

"Me too." The wedding had been so much fun, but she was ready to collapse into Toby's arms and stay there as long as he would let her.

"You want to get out of here?" he asked hopefully.

"I would love to get out of here." She held on to him and they snuck away from the reception hall, following the path by the lake. Moonlight bounced on the water, filling the whole area with a soft glow.

"What a gorgeous night," Jane said, almost afraid to disturb the peace.

"It's perfect," Toby agreed. He led her to the edge of the sand where they both removed their shoes. After a full evening of dancing, the cool grains felt nice against her feet. They walked along the edge of the water in a quiet contentedness. Everything was still and peaceful, Jane almost didn't want to ruin it with words.

Taking her hand, Toby pulled her to a stop. The moon gave off enough light that she could see his face, his captivating blue eyes. He'd lost the bow tie somewhere along the way, and the buttons on the starched white tux shirt had mostly come undone. Jane's heartbeat seemed to resound all through her.

"You're the reason this night is perfect." A note of reverence lowered Toby's voice. "I love you, Jane."

The sincerity of his words engraved them into her heart.

Jane let the stillness descend again so she could savor the moment she gave her whole heart away. She memorized how the lake looked like it was made of glass, how the dark outline of the trees hemmed them in, how intent

Toby's eyes were in telling her what he felt, and when she had catalogued every detail to hold it in her heart forever, she finally said, "I love you too." This time she kissed him with no reservations, with no fears, with no logic to fall back on.

And then Toby swept her up in his arms and carried her all the way home.

Chapter Twenty-Six

You don't have to do this," Toby said, rubbing his hand up and down her arms.

"I want to do this." Jane found his hands and weaved her fingers through his. She understood he wanted to protect her, but it was time for her to step out from behind her walls. And sharing her books with her hometown was a great place to start.

"It's going to be fine," she assured him. "I'm sure people will be surprised, but I want them to know." For the last few weeks, the library had been promoting this mystery author event, touting the fact that attendees would get the chance to meet E. J. Mattingly—who had never made a public appearance—and have their books signed. Tickets had sold out, and they'd raised over three thousand dollars for the library. For Tanner's library.

"This is part of who I am," Jane said, and she'd never been prouder of that. Toby was proud of her too, he'd made it clear. He read everything she wrote, always giving her thoughtful feedback. "It's part of who we are together," she reminded him. "I don't know what I would do without my favorite research partner."

It didn't matter what her cowboy was up to, all she had to ask to get Toby's full attention was, "Do you think it's possible to make love in a—" Regardless of how crazy the place she'd dreamed up was, Toby always did his best to prove it could be done.

"I like the research." He leaned in closer. "In fact, maybe we should do some research tonight."

"We have to. I was thinking about writing a canoe sex scene." Since she and Toby had been spending pretty much every night together, her sensual imagination tended to run a bit wild.

"No problem," he said, wearing her favorite grin. "Leave it to me. I'll figure it out."

She had no doubts.

Someone knocked and the door opened. "Are you ready?" Lucinda, who'd become Jane's favorite librarian, asked. "Everyone is so excited. I don't think they can wait much longer."

"We'll be right out," Toby said, still shielding her in his arms.

"Okay. This is it." Jane checked her mirror one more time.

"You look ravishing." Toby brushed a kiss on her cheek. "And I'm so proud of you, sweetness."

"Thank you." She snuck an extra moment locked safely in his embrace and then took a deep breath, squared her shoulders, and found the signing pen she'd selected. Holding tightly on to Toby's hand, she walked out of the room and followed the path to where they'd set up the line.

A collective gasp sent a hush over the crowd.

Lucinda stood at a small podium they'd set up. "It is my great honor to introduce you all to the incredibly talented E. J. Mattingly, otherwise known as Jane Harding." She swung her arm out in dramatic presentation and a rowdy applause swelled.

"A local!" someone yelled. "A famous author is one of our own!"

"Jane!" Patti, her old friend from the gas station, frantically waved her arms from the middle of the line. "I always knew you were a talented writer! Oh, this is so exciting! I can tell everyone one of my dearest friends is an author!"

Toby gave Jane a look that cracked her up.

"Jane, would you like to say a few words before we start the signing?" Lucinda asked.

"I would love to." She walked as gracefully as she could to the podium given her trembling knees. "Thank you all for coming here, for supporting the library. For supporting me." Her voice sounded strange in the microphone. "As some of you may know, my goal is to write stories about strong heroines who are brave and feisty and independent. That is the kind of woman I've always wanted to be." She paused to stare at the love of her life.

Toby gave her a wink and the grin he reserved especially for their sexy times.

"When I came back to Silverado Lake, someone very special showed me that is who I've always been, even when I felt lost. Thank you, Toby, for helping me find that part of myself. The part I'd protected. The part that needed to be free."

A chorus of *awwws* moved up and down the long line.

Jane had to pause until the emotion cleared from her throat. "I also want my books to be about strong, close-knit communities," she went on, smiling at all those faces staring back at her. "Growing up here, I didn't appreciate this community the way I do now. I didn't feel I belonged. But this summer I've realized it was fear holding me back. After my father died, I closed myself off to feeling much of anything, to embracing relationships." Jane glanced at her mother, who was dabbing her eyes. "Being back here has helped me open up to both of those things. And I'm looking forward to building a life here." She couldn't wait to build a life with her love here. Her eyes met Toby's again.

A month ago, she never would've dreamed her heart could hold so much love, and yet here she was, walking straight into a new life with Toby at her side.

Epilogue

Jane stared at the cursor blinking back at her on the computer screen. *Ugh.* She couldn't seem to get this sentence right. Leaning back in the chair, she tipped her head, gazing up toward the ceiling as if she'd find the answer written there. She didn't, of course. Unfortunately, it never proved to be that easy.

What she needed was a break—a chance to stretch her legs. Jane pushed back from the desk and walked away from the computer, attempting to pace some energy into her imagination. Over the last two months, Toby had provided her with plenty of romantic inspiration, but he'd been gone for almost two weeks with back-to-back events, so she had to finish this book without him.

Hmmm. Pacing didn't seem to be working. Chocolate! She needed chocolate. Jane marched into the kitchen and opened the cabinet where she kept her secret chocolate stash only to find a pile of empty wrappers. *Nooooo.* She'd forgotten she'd finished it off last night when she'd started the final chapter. In the last twenty-four hours, she only managed to eke out twenty-five words onto the page and no amount of chocolate seemed to be helping.

Okay, plan B. She pulled out her cell phone and started flipping through the pictures she and Toby had taken the day before he'd left to return to the circuit. They'd taken a horseback ride up to their spot where they'd had a picnic…and quite the memorable make-out session on a blanket underneath the trees. They'd taken a series of selfies together, and even though she couldn't write to save her life right now, she had to smile flipping through those pictures. Her face glowed in each one, and it wasn't only because of the beautiful sunshine. There was one with Toby kissing her cheek, one of him making a face while she laughed, one of him simply staring at her with that intense loving gaze while she smiled for the camera.

She sighed the happy sigh that seemed to come out of her whenever she laid eyes on the man she loved. Yes, she missed him when he was gone, but it felt wonderful to have someone to miss. It felt wonderful to have someone to call, someone to dream with, someone to share her successes and failures with. She flipped through a few more pictures, but it didn't seem to help her get any writing done so she went back to her computer and forced her butt into that seat.

The cursor winked at her again. Jane did her finger stretches, but that didn't seem to generate any words either. She stood up again. This was getting serious. She'd promised herself she wouldn't leave her cabin until the final chapter had been written, but she could really use an entire box of dark chocolate covered almonds. Maybe she could send Beth an SOS text and beg her to drop off some of her specialty brownies…

The phone rang in her hand—Toby's picture lighting up the screen and her heart. Jane fumbled with it before she finally managed to answer. "Hey." It was something between a breathless plea and a whimper.

"Hey, sweetness." That deep resounding greeting was enough to melt her. "How are ya?" he asked with wind whispering through the speaker. He was probably outside at a rest stop somewhere between Texas and Oklahoma where his next event was supposed to be.

"I'm okay, but I'd be even better if you were here," she said in her sultriest tone. "How are you?"

"I'm good." She could hear him smiling. He must've had a good feeling about his upcoming competition. "How's the book coming along?"

"Weeellll..." She glanced around at the mess on her desk. "I'm out of chocolate." That explained it all.

"Oh no," he said in mock horror. "How can I help?"

"I don't know." She sighed. "Maybe I'm not cut out for this writing stuff." Maybe she didn't have any more books in her. Going down this path was part of her process. "I wish you were here." She simply wanted him to pull her into his arms and kiss away her doubts. Then they could fall into the bed they'd shared most of the summer...

"Go sit down at your computer, sweetness," Toby murmured. "Not only are you going to finish the book, you're going to write the hell out of that last chapter."

How did he know she wasn't sitting at her computer? Jane did as she was told. He'd likely seen her battle enough writer's block that he knew what to expect.

"I don't know what to write." Jane stared at the computer screen. "I've tried so many different angles, but none of them are working."

"Try a different angle," Toby suggested. "Look up."

"Look up?" With a gasp, Jane raised her head to peer out the window. There. Down by the lake. Toby stood at the shoreline in front of a canoe, his jeans rolled up to his knees.

"God, you look gorgeous."

She couldn't say anything. She couldn't find words. He wasn't supposed to be home for another week and a half!

Squealing, she scrambled out of the chair, dropping the phone in the process, and ran for the door, tearing it open so she could jump into his arms. "You're home!" She finally found her voice halfway down to the shoreline.

Toby opened his arms and she stumbled into them. "What're you doing home? What about the competition? What—"

He silenced her with a long, savoring kiss. "That's all I've been thinking about since I left," he uttered when he pulled back.

Jane simply sighed a happy, contented sigh. "Mmm-hmm." She peered up at him. He looked a little tanner than he had when he'd left. "I thought the Oklahoma ride was important." He'd already qualified for the finals in November, but she knew he needed to get as much practice and experience as he could before then.

"Oklahoma's not as important as you are." He locked his arms around her waist. "Three weeks was too long. Hell, two weeks was too long. I can miss one ride if it means I get to be with you."

"Thank God." Jane shot him a smirk. "Now that my muse is back maybe I'll actually be able to finish my book."

"I think I can find some ways to inspire you," Toby whispered in her ear. "But first, I was wondering if you wanted to go out on the lake with me."

"I would love to." Three months ago, she would've said

no. She wouldn't have even been standing this close to the water, but the lake didn't scare her the way it used to. Not much scared her anymore.

Toby helped her climb into the canoe, and then he pushed them off. It was the perfect late summer afternoon—the sun seemed to amplify the blue sky to be a hundred times brighter and the surface of the lake sparkled.

"I still can't believe you're here." Jane couldn't take her eyes off her cowboy, off that mix of passion and tenderness in his eyes when they met hers. "How do you always seem to know when I need you?"

"Probably because those are the same times I need you." He rowed them away from the shore, effortlessly working his arms while Jane sat back and enjoyed the view. "I do, Janie. I need you in my life."

Emotion settled in her chest, swelling her heart. "This is the best surprise I've ever gotten." She never would've asked him to come home, to sit out a competition just to be with her, but she couldn't remember ever being happier.

"Well, I have another surprise that might be even better." Toby let go of the oars and reached into the well behind him, removing a blanket to reveal the most beautiful bouquet of flowers Jane had ever seen.

The canoe wobbled as he lowered to a knee in front of her, holding out the mix of roses and sunflowers and daisies. "I hate being away from you because I belong with you. We belong together. You are smart and strong and so incredibly talented. And you are the most beautiful woman in the world to me."

"Toby…" Jane wiped the tears away. "I love you. And I know I belong with you." On some level she'd known it since that first time he'd kissed her. She'd known there was passion and strength and substance between them even then. It had simply taken them both some time to grow into it.

"Marry me, Jane Harding. Marry me, and I promise that I will always be here for you. To inspire you, to love you, to make you happy." He held out the bouquet toward her, and something very sparkly caught the sun. He'd tied a delicate solitaire engagement ring to the stem of a red rose. "I didn't want to drop it in the lake," he explained with a sheepish grin.

Jane laughed through happy tears. She eased as close as she could to him without tipping the canoe. "I promise I'll always be here for you too. I'll always love you no matter what, Toby Garrett. You're the man I've been waiting for my whole life."

Toby's smile grew. "So that's a yes?"

Unable to keep one inch of distance between them any longer, Jane got on her knees and wrapped her arms around his neck so she could kiss him. "That's definitely a yes."

About the Author

Sara Richardson grew up chasing adventure in Colorado's rugged mountains. She's climbed to the top of a fourteen-thousand-foot peak at midnight, swum through class four rapids, completed her wilderness first-aid certification, and spent seven days at a time tromping through the wilderness with a thirty-pound backpack strapped to her shoulders.

Eventually Sara did the responsible thing and got an education in writing and journalism. After a brief stint in the corporate writing world, she stopped ignoring the voices in her head and started writing fiction. Now she uses her experience as a mountain adventure guide to write stories that incorporate adventure with romance. Sara lives and plays in Colorado, where she still indulges her adventurous spirit, with her saint of a husband and two young sons.

You can learn more at:
SaraRichardson.net
Twitter @SaraR_Books
Facebook.com/SaraRichardsonBooks
Instagram @SaraRichardsonBooks

Sparks fly when daredevil Wes Harding's ex-fiancée shows up for a weeklong vacation at his ranch.

Look for another heartwarming romance in *One Night with a Cowboy*!

Available Early 2021

For a bonus story from another author you'll love, please turn the page to read *Cowboy to the Rescue* by A. J. Pine.

Designer Ivy Serrano is looking for a fresh start but her Meadow Valley homecoming has been one disaster after another. Lucky for her, one very capable—and handsome—fireman is there to save the day. Also new to small-town living, Lieutenant Carter Bowen is determined to prove himself at the fire station, which means no mistakes, no distractions, and *definitely* no Ivy. Yet as the attraction between them heats up, Carter realizes Ivy is the one for him—but can he convince her they have a future worth fighting for?

Chapter One

Ivy Serrano smelled smoke.

Not the *Ooh! Someone must be having a bonfire* kind of smoke or the *Mmm! Someone is grilling up burgers* kind of smoke. She smelled the *Shoot! Something's burning* kind of smoke right here, in her new shop, on the day of her grand opening.

She glanced around the small boutique, brows knitted together. She'd been about to flip the CLOSED sign to OPEN for the very first time when it hit her. Something was burning.

After two years of putting her life on hold due to a family tragedy from which she thought she'd never recover, here she was, back home, starting over. And of all things, she smelled *smoke.*

It didn't take long for the smell to be accompanied by sound, the high-pitched wail of a top-of-the-line smoke detector. Although, if anyone was keeping score, *she'd* noticed first. One point for Ivy, zero for technology.

Except then she remembered that each detector was wired to the next, which meant that in five, four, three, two, one...a chorus of digital, ear-splitting screams filled eight hundred square feet of space.

Her senses were keen enough, though, that it only took a second to register that the first alarm came from the back office.

Her design sketches! And samples! And *Oh no!* It was opening day!

She sprinted through the door that separated the shop from her office and storage. The only appliance she had back there was a mini refrigerator, because every now and then a girl needed a cold beverage and maybe even a healthy snack and *ohmygod* this was *not* happening.

She gasped when she saw the charred cord and the licking flames dancing up the wall from the outlet. Items on her desk were turning to kindling as the fire reached paper. She grabbed the extinguisher from its prominent space on the wall and, amid the incessant shrieking, snuffed out the fire in a matter of seconds. She yanked on the part of the cord that hadn't been completely cooked and unplugged the appliance.

Problem solved.

Except the design drawing on her desk, the one she'd been working on for the past week, was partially burned and now covered in foam.

No big deal. She'd simply start over—on the first piece she'd been brave enough to attempt that reminded her of Charlie. And now she had to muster that courage again after—of all things—a fire.

Or it would be, once she remembered how to turn the alarms off. Did she rip the battery out of the first one and all the rest would follow? Or did she have to somehow reset each and every one? She spun in a circle, panic only now setting in, because she knew what happened once the first alarm triggered the rest.

She ran back to the front of the shop and pushed through the door and out onto First Street. Sure enough, an emergency vehicle had already pulled out of the fire station's lot, siren blazing.

She dropped onto the public bench in front of her store and waited the fifteen seconds it took for the truck to roll down the street.

"It would have been faster if you all had walked," she mumbled.

Four figures hopped out of the truck in full gear. One who she recognized as her best friend Casey's younger sister, Jessie, started to unfurl the hose while another—yep, that was Wyatt O'Brien—went to open the nearby hydrant. The third was Wyatt's younger brother Shane.

Ivy stood and crossed her arms. "Fire's out already."

The last one—the one she hadn't recognized yet—strode toward her, his eyes narrowed as he took her in.

"Sorry, miss. But we still need to go inside and assess the situation, figure out what type of fire it was, and if you're still at any sort of risk."

She shrugged and cleared her throat, trying to force the tremble out of her voice. "It was an electrical fire. Probably caused by faulty wiring in a mini fridge cord because I had this place inspected a dozen times and know it was up to code. Used a class C extinguisher. I have smart detectors, though. Couldn't get the fire out before you guys were automatically called. Sorry to waste your time."

The fire was out. That wasn't the issue. Fire didn't scare her after the fact, especially now that she was so prepared. It was—*them.* She didn't want them here, didn't need them here, and certainly didn't require anyone's assistance. Just seeing their uniforms made it hard for her to breathe, made it impossible not to think of how Charlie wearing the uniform had cost him his life.

The man in front of her took off his firefighter helmet and ran a hand through a mop of overgrown dark auburn hair. If he weren't wearing the uniform, he'd have been quite handsome. She knew it was backward, that most women found men in uniforms sexy. But there was nothing sexy about a man who risked his life for a living. Noble? Absolutely. That didn't mean she had to find him attractive.

There was something familiar about him, though, even though she swore she'd never met him. Ivy knew just about everyone in town, especially those who worked at the fire station. So who the heck was this stranger?

"You still need to let us inside," he said. "We're not permitted to accept civilian confirmation of fire containment."

Ivy scoffed. "Just tell Chief Burnett it was Ivy's place and that I said everything is fine. He knows me well enough, so that should suffice."

The stranger grinned, but Ivy got the feeling it wasn't because he was happy.

"Chief Burnett is also my new boss, and I don't think he'd take kindly to me slacking off on my first call. But, hey, appreciate the heads-up and the unneeded paperwork I'll have to file when I get back to the station."

Definitely not a happy smile. Well, that made two of them. He wasn't happy to be here, and she wasn't happy to have him here.

He pushed past her and through the front entrance of the store—aptly called Ivy's—while two of his crew assessed the outside of the building's facade and the fourth jogged down to the end of the street and disappeared behind the row of stores that included her own.

"I really do have things under control in here," she called over the continued screech of the multiple alarms. When she received no response, she followed into the back office, where Needed-a-Haircut Man was inspecting the charred cord from the mini fridge and the blackened outlet.

"Don't you turn those off or something?" she yelled, barely able to hear her own voice.

The firefighter stood, pulled off his glove, and climbed onto her office chair. He reached for the smoke detector on the ceiling and pulled it out of its holster. Then he pressed a button, and it and all other alarms ceased.

"Thought you had things under control in here," he said with a self-satisfied grin as he hopped down to the floor, his boots hitting the linoleum tile with a thud.

Her mouth hung open for a second before she regained control.

"I did. I mean, I *do*. The detectors are new. This is the first time I've had to use them." *And I grew up in a firefighter household, thank you very much. So who are you to question what I do and do not have under control?* Of course, she kept all that to herself because her family was her business, but still—this guy had a lot of nerve.

He pointed to a button on the device marked with the word RESET.

"All you have to do is press and hold for five seconds, and they all turn off. But, if you accidentally do the same thing with the TEST button, all alarms will sound for half a minute. So I don't recommend doing that during business hours. Might scare customers away."

Ivy rolled her eyes. "I can read, but thanks for the warning."

"My pleasure," he said, smiling. "I'm gonna grab the rest of the crew so we can do a full assessment on the outlet, check your circuit breaker. Glad to see you're not using power strips."

"It was the *fridge*. I'm sure of it." That was the last time she took a hand-me-down appliance even if it was still under warranty. "Look, Mr...."

"*Lieutenant* Bowen," he said.

Her eyes widened. "What happened to Lieutenants Russo and Heinz?"

"Nothing. Lieutenant Heinz runs his team, and I run mine. Russo's wife got a really great job in Seattle. They're moving at the end of the month. I'm taking over his team. You new in town?"

She scoffed and smoothed out her A-line blue sundress, then straightened the shoulder straps made of small embroidered daisies she had painstakingly created on her sewing machine. It was one of the few items in the shop that was an Ivy Serrano original. Part of her wanted him to notice. The other part called her out on even considering flirting with him. Firefighters were not her type, yet today she seemed to need extra reminders.

"*No*," she said, indignant. "I was born and raised in Meadow Valley, California. Been here all my life. Mostly. But I can't believe I didn't know Jason and Angie were leaving town." She'd been in her own little world the past couple of months getting the shop ready to open. Had she really been so wrapped up in her own life that she'd missed everything happening around her?

"I might be a little out of touch," she admitted. "But I know *you're* not from Meadow Valley."

He chuckled. Even though it was a small smile, this one was genuine, going all the way to the crinkle of his blue eyes. *Not* that she was noticing his eyes. Or how his broad shoulders shook when he laughed. "Just got here last week from Houston. You're very perceptive, Ms...."

She could hear his light accent now. "Serrano," she said. "Ivy Serrano."

He raised a brow. "Any relation to Captain Emilio Serrano, who practically ran the Meadow Valley Fire Station up until a few years go?"

Ivy swallowed and her eyes burned. "Guess you did your homework. Captain Serrano is my father."

The playfulness left the lieutenant's eyes, but his gaze didn't falter. "I'm sorry to hear about your brother. From what I've been told, he was a hell of a lieutenant himself."

"Thank you." It had been two years since Charlie died in the line of duty, but it still felt like she'd found out only five minutes ago. She cleared her throat. "You were saying something about inspecting the outlet?" She was 99 percent sure the outlet was fine, but right now she'd let him and his crew tear apart the drywall if it meant this conversation would end.

"Right," he said. He pressed a button on a small radio clipped to his collar and called for the other three firefighters. "We should be out of here in less than an hour."

She nodded. "Can I still open the store? Today was supposed to be my first day."

"That'll depend on what we figure out after a short investigation," he said.

The three firefighters she knew poured into her office from the back door.

"Hey, Wyatt," she said.

Wyatt O'Brien, always the gentleman, tipped his helmet. "Hey there, Ivy." Then he turned to Lieutenant Bowen. "All clear out back, sir."

The lieutenant nodded. "Thanks, O'Brien."

"This was a waste of time," Shane said, storming past them all and back out front. That was pretty accurate. Wyatt's younger brother always had a bitterness about him that clung tight. Looked like not much had changed.

The lieutenant's jaw tightened, but he didn't say anything.

"Hi, Ivy," Jessie said.

Ivy forced a smile. She'd known Jessie all the young woman's life. But all she could hope when she saw her in uniform was that Casey would never have to go through what Ivy and her family did.

"Heard you're working the front desk at the guest ranch on your off days," Ivy said. *It's safer there. Maybe you'll like it and sign on full-time.*

Jessie nodded. "Those school loans aren't going to pay themselves off." She looked nervously at the lieutenant. "I'll go check on Shane." And she hurried after him.

Ivy pressed her lips together and forced a smile. "Thanks, gentlemen," she said to the two remaining men. "I guess I'll just wait up front and let you do your job."

She blew out a shaky breath and headed back into her unopened shop—past the checkout counter and the table of baked goods and refreshments she'd set up for her very first customers.

All she'd wanted was to start fresh and instead she'd started with a damned fire and four firefighters bursting her bubble of safety.

A small crowd had gathered outside the store, which meant the gossip mill was in full effect.

She knew to fight an electrical fire with a type C extinguisher. But the only way to fight small town gossip was to shift the focus. The last thing she needed was every person in Meadow Valley talking about poor Ivy and how fire had brought tragedy into her life again.

She squared her shoulders and fluffed out her brunette waves, then pushed through the door and out onto the street.

"Nothing to see here, folks! Just a quick inspection before Ivy's doors are officially open."

"I heard sirens!" a man shouted, and Ivy recognized Lonny Tate, the owner of Meadow Valley's Everything Store. Most small towns had a general store or a small supermarket, but not Meadow Valley. Lonny Tate prided himself on carrying everything from toilet plungers to the occasional bottle of Coco Chanel. The only problem was that because the place was a quarter of the size of the Target the next town over, you never knew for sure if what you needed was in stock.

"Was there a fire?" a woman cried. It was Mrs. Davis from the bookstore. "Oh, poor Ivy. Not another fire."

"I'm fine, Mrs. Davis," Ivy said. "Promise."

"If you're fine, then you'll call me Trudy like I've been asking you to do for decades," the woman said with mild exasperation. "The only Mr. Davis I know is my father."

Mrs. Davis—*Trudy*—was practically family to Ivy, so she understood the worry and wanted to put the woman's mind at ease. But *Poor Ivy*? The whole town would be calling her that before long if she didn't set the record straight.

She kicked off her wedge sandals and climbed onto the bench. A hush fell over the growing crowd of Meadow Valley residents. The town was still abuzz after the annual Fourth of July festival. Ivy had hoped to open up shop before then to capitalize on the event, which was one of their biggest tourist attractions, but—as her good friend irony would have it—her electrical inspection hadn't yet gone through.

"There's no fire," she lied. "Everything is fine. Just a misunderstanding. The store will be open soon. But in the meantime..." She held a hand to one side of her mouth like she was telling them all a secret. "How about that dude ranch on the outskirts of town? I hear we got ourselves some real live cowboys over there."

"Oh!" Mrs. Davis exclaimed. "And I hear they hired that good-looking new fire lieutenant to give some trail tours. Turns out he's a bit of a cowboy himself!"

Suddenly the mumblings changed from the likes of *Poor Ivy* to things like "I've always had a thing for redheads" and "There's nothing sexier than a man on a horse," along with "You mean a redheaded firefighter on a horse."

Funny. Ivy thought the lieutenant's hair was more of a brown with a hint of red. And maybe there was something *slightly* sexy about a rancher on a horse, but not when fighting fires was in the mix. Fire was dangerous. Fire took lives. For the bulk of hers, her family had always worried about her father. But once he hit fifty and still hadn't let any blaze get the best of him, they'd all been lulled into a false sense of security, one that let Ivy and her family believe that Charlie, her brother, would also be immune.

They'd been wrong.

The throng of locals *Oohed*, snapping her back to the present. They weren't looking at her, though. They were looking past her. So she gazed over her shoulder to find the supposed sexy redhead striding through her shop door and out onto the sidewalk, his three cohorts following close behind. While the other firefighters pushed through the crowd and headed back to the truck, Lieutenant Bowen did no such thing.

When he saw her standing on the bench, he crossed his arms and grinned.

“Are you gonna sing or something?” he asked. “And if so, are you taking requests?”

She rolled her eyes.

He thought he was so charming with those blue eyes and that one dimple that made his smile look a little crooked but at the same time really adorable.

Again, all of the *nopes.* Men who played with fire were far from adorable.

“Am I open?” she asked. *Please say yes and then go away.*

“Open for business, Ms. Serrano. Though I think you’ll need to retire that pesky appliance of yours.”

“You heard the man!” Ivy said. “We are open for business!”

She hopped off the bench, slid back into her shoes, and held open the door, ushering much of the crowd inside.

“So,” she said. “I was right?”

He nodded once. “You were right. But it’s still my job to make sure.”

“And it’s *my* job to sell the stuff in there, so I better head back inside,” she said. “Thank you, by the way. I know what you do is important. I just wish I could have caught the alarm before you all had to gear up and head over here.”

He shrugged. “Beats pulling kittens from trees.”

She laughed. He was funny. If he weren’t wearing all that gear and the uniform underneath…But he was.

“You obviously haven’t met Mrs. Davis yet,” Ivy said. “She fosters kittens when she’s not at the bookshop. And she’s got a big old oak in front of her house. I’m sure you’ll hear from her sooner rather than later.”

"I'll consider myself warned." He glanced up and down the street, then back at her. "So what do people do around here for fun?"

Her brows furrowed. "I hear there's a new firefighter in town who leads trail rides at the guest ranch. Maybe you can look into that."

He chuckled. "Checking up on me already, are you?"

She brushed her hands off on her skirt. "Not sure how much you know about small towns, Lieutenant, but around here we don't need to check up. Information is pretty easy to come by, especially when someone new takes up residence."

"Okay, then. When I'm not riding trails or saving kittens, what do you suggest? What are *you* doing tonight?"

She shook her head. "Oh no. I don't date firefighters."

He leaned in close and whispered in her ear, "I wasn't asking for a date, Serrano. Tonight's my first night off since I got to town. Just figured if you were going out, it might mean you knew a thing or two about where some-one might let off a little steam."

His warm breath tickled her ear, and a chill ran down her spine.

"Midtown Tavern," she said. "It's the only place open after eight o'clock."

She didn't wait for a response. Instead she headed into the safety of her shop and headed straight for the thermostat.

It was getting hot in here.

Chapter Two

Even though he'd technically had a few nights off in his first week in town, as a new lieutenant—who'd beat someone on his team for the job—he wanted to hang around the station, get the lay of the land, and hopefully ingratiate himself to those who saw him as an interloper. Chief Burnett wanted to keep it under wraps who it was that lost the position to Carter. Regardless, things were tense. And it was never easy being the odd man out.

He'd had a good job back home at the Houston Fire Department. It was the *home* part of the equation that made leaving so easy. There was nothing like a father who disapproved of your life choices. Carter's solution? He left when opportunity presented itself.

Now here he was, a stranger in a strange land who didn't even have a place to live, which meant the firehouse bunk room was the closest thing to home for the time being.

He checked his watch. It was six o'clock on a Saturday evening, and aside from a trail ride he was leading at the

Meadow Valley Ranch tomorrow morning, he had the next forty-eight hours off.

"Hey," he said to Wyatt and Shane, the two guys on his team. "What's the best place to go around here to get a burger and a beer?"

"Midtown Tavern," the two said in unison as they stared at the rec room television watching a baseball game that was *not* the Astros, so he didn't care what it was. But it looked like the consensus was in on nightlife in Meadow Valley. He nodded his thanks to the other two men, whose gazes stayed glued to the screen.

He shrugged, assumed the T-shirt and jeans he'd changed into was proper attire, and headed for the station's front door.

The sun shone over First Street like it was still high noon, which made it easy to spot his destination—right in the middle of the main block. He laughed. *Midtown Tavern* was quite literally *mid* town.

He crossed the street and strolled past the inn. Pearl, the owner—and Carter's great-aunt—had offered him a room when he'd first arrived in town, but he'd preferred the station. She was the reason he was here—the reason he'd learned about an opening for a new lieutenant and possibly part of the reason the chief had even considered an outsider, but both Carter and Pearl were doing their best to keep that under wraps until his one-month trial period was over.

"Secrets don't stay buried for too long around here," Pearl had told him. "So make sure they all realize how good you are at doing what you do before they have a chance to claim favoritism."

Carter knew he was good at his job. Damn good. *That* was why the chief had brought him in and why he was in the running—along with the other lieutenant—to be the next captain when the chief retired in a couple of years. This was it. One false move, and he would have to start from square one again at another station. He couldn't go back to his job in Houston. And truth be told, he needed this distance from home. Going back wasn't an option.

So he was bent on proving himself to everyone at the station, which meant no mistakes, no distractions, and no reason for anyone to say he got the job because of who he knew rather than because of his long list of qualifications.

He passed the Everything Store and chuckled at the signs advertising a flash sale on vegetable peelers in one corner of the window and the release of a romance novel in the other corner.

He sure wasn't in Houston anymore.

It might have looked like noon outside, but when he stepped through the doors of Meadow Valley's Midtown Tavern, it was officially Saturday night.

He grinned at the dark wooden tables and booths that framed a square bar in the center of the space. *This* was what he needed. A place to unwind and mix with the residents of what he hoped to be his new hometown.

He grabbed an empty stool at the bar and cleared his throat to get the attention of the woman behind it. Her back was to him as she typed something into a cash register, so all he could see was the dark ponytail that swished across the back of a black T-shirt that said MIDTOWN SLUGGERS in a baseball-style yellow font. The pockets of her jeans were painted with what looked like pink lily flowers. *Not* that he was paying special attention to the pocket area of her clothing. The vibrant art simply drew his eyes.

His eyes widened when she turned to face him, a receipt and a few bills in her hand.

"Serrano," he said. "And here I thought you owned a clothing store."

She smiled, not at him but at the older man on the stool next to him. "Here's your change, Lonny."

The man waved her off. "Keep it, Ivy. Put it toward repairing the damage from the fire." He shook his head. "Such a shame something like that had to happen on opening day."

Ivy leaned over the bar. "*Nothing* happened, Lonny. The shop opened. I sold a bunch of stuff. There's nothing to repair, but I *will* accept your tip because I was an excellent server."

She brushed off her hands and turned her attention to Carter.

"Evening, Lieutenant. Yes, I do own a clothing store. But sometimes I help out around here."

"You got a thing for flowers?" he asked, remembering the dress she was wearing earlier that day, the straps made of daisies. Or maybe it was *she* who stood out in his mind's eye, and the memory of what she wore simply followed.

Another woman sidled up to Ivy before she could answer, nudging her out of the way with her hip so she could get to the beer tap. "This is the new guy?" she said to Ivy while looking straight at Carter.

"Sure is," Ivy said.

"You're right," the other woman said, blowing blue-streaked bangs out of her eyes. "Totally not as sexy as everyone keeps saying."

Ivy backhanded the other woman on the shoulder. "*Casey*!"

Casey laughed. "Thanks for covering for me while I took that call. I'm good here, so you can—you know—punch out or whatever."

"You don't *pay* me," Ivy said, rolling her eyes.

Casey finished pouring the beer and winked. "Yeah, but I let you drink for free. And I'll add a bonus. You can take *Dreamboat's* order." Then she disappeared around the corner to deliver the drink to a patron on the other side of the bar.

Ivy's jaw tightened, and then she smiled what Carter guessed was her patented customer-service smile. "Yes, I like flowers," she said matter-of-factly. "What can I get for you, Lieutenant?"

"I'm off duty," he said. "You can call me Carter."

"Sure," she said. "Now, what can I get you, *Lieutenant*?"

He laughed. She sure was determined *not* to like him, which was fine by him. It didn't matter that he'd been attracted to her the second he'd hopped out of the truck in front of her store. He could have a drink, blow off a little steam, but that was it. No other distractions.

"I'll have whatever's on tap," he said. "How about you choose?"

She grabbed a beer and filled it with a dark wheat beer, then slid it across the bar to him.

"I didn't call you a dreamboat," she said. "Just for the record."

He nodded. "But there was talk of my sexiness, or I guess lack thereof?"

She shook her head and gave him a haughty lift of her chin. "*No*. I mean, I just don't get what all the fuss is about. So you're cute in a uniform and can supposedly hold your own on a horse. It's not like it's newsworthy." She looked around the bar and rolled her eyes. "Although not much happens in Meadow Valley, so I guess around here it is."

She poured another beer, then took a sip before setting it down. She glanced down each side of the bar, pursing her lips at the occupied stools.

Carter cleared his throat. "There's an empty stool right here." He nodded to the vacant seat on his left. They could sit next to each other and have an innocent beer, right?

She blew out a breath. "Yeah, I know, but—"

"But there's an empty stool. You obviously need a place to sit. You don't even have to talk to me." He took another pull of his beer. "I'm perfectly happy to drink alone."

Ivy groaned, set her beer down next to his, then disappeared the same way Casey had gone. A few seconds later she appeared next to him, hopped on the stool, and took a good long swig from her own mug as she stared straight ahead, not sparing him a glance.

"This is good," she said more to herself than anyone else. "Drinking alone, just me and my thoughts." She sighed. "Me and *my*self."

Carter stifled a laugh. "You don't do alone, do you?" he asked.

She finally shifted her gaze to him. "I do alone just fine. Quiet, though. Quiet isn't my thing."

He laughed out loud this time. "You're in a noisy tavern."

She threw up her hands. "I'm a talker, okay? An extrovert. I get energized by being around others, by interacting with them. If I were sitting over there?" She pointed to the side of the bar on Carter's right. "Lonny and his fishing buddies would be telling me all about what they caught today, and I'd tell them how the highlight of my day was *not*, in fact, the fire but the grand opening of my very own store." She directed him to the row of patrons on the side to their left, a group of women who looked to be about the same age as his mom. "If I were hanging with the knitting guild, we could talk design and what kind of pieces I'm thinking of making for the store when the colder months roll in."

"But instead you're stuck next to me," he said matter-of-factly.

"Exactly." She gasped, her hand covering her mouth. "I didn't mean it like *that*."

But she did, didn't she? And he should be relieved she wanted nothing to do with him, but instead he was—disappointed.

"So you think I'm cute in my uniform?" he asked, brow raised. What was he doing? He wasn't sure, but the urge to flirt with her just sort of took over.

"Of course not," she insisted.

"Like, kitten-hanging-from-a-branch-in-Mrs. Davis's-tree cute?" he added.

"No one is *that* cute." She snorted and took another sip of her beer. "By the way, I'm simply enjoying a drink after a long day. I know you weren't asking me out earlier. This doesn't mean anything. You just happen to be sitting next to the only free seat. So let's just forget whatever this is." She motioned between them.

So they were in agreement. There was *something* between them. Something neither of them wanted, but something nonetheless.

He laughed. "Wow. And here I thought your sunny disposition meant you were a people person." He threw back the rest of his drink.

"I *am* sunny…with the right company."

She buried her face in her mug, catching up with him.

"Yeah," he said with a laugh. "About as sunny as a box of kittens."

"You really have a thing for kittens, don't you?" she asked.

"Actually, I'm allergic. You were saying?"

"I wasn't saying *anything*, just that this isn't anything more than two locals drinking a beer at a pub. My opinion of you in your uniform is irrelevant, as is what you think of me. Not that I'm assuming you think anything of me at all or that you're any more or less attracted to me than I am to you. I'm not—by the way—attracted to you." She rolled her eyes, but it seemed more at herself than at him.

"Oh, I'm attracted to *you*, Ivy Serrano," he admitted. "But I don't want to date you."

Her mouth fell open, but she didn't get a chance to respond. A second later, Casey appeared from around the corner carrying a liquor bottle and three shot glasses.

"You know if I comply with your request, I'm enabling you, right?" Casey said.

Ivy nodded. "But a *fire* on grand opening day. Of all things. It destroyed more than my fridge. Got my latest sketches too."

"The ones with the—"

Ivy interrupted Casey's question with another nod. The two women had a language all their own—an immediate understanding between two people who knew each other better than anyone else. He'd had a friend like that once. He also knew loss not unlike Ivy's. How similar they were. If they'd met under any other circumstances...But they hadn't. There was also the issue of her not exactly supporting his career. That was an automatic deal breaker no matter how attractive she was.

Casey blew out a breath, lined up the three shot glasses, and filled them all with a light brown liquid.

Carter lifted his glass and sniffed. "That is *not* whiskey."

Casey shook her head. "No, Lieutenant, it is *not.* It's Ivy's favorite, apple pie liqueur." She groaned, then stared at her friend. "You know it actually pains me to say liqu*eur* instead of liquor, right?"

Ivy smiled. "I know. But it's also how I know you love me." She lifted her glass, her big brown eyes softening as they fixed on Carter's. "You know who my family is, which means you also know I have nothing but respect and admiration for what you and everyone else in that firehouse does. You save kittens and you save lives, and that's a really big thing. But you also risk your own lives, and I've already lost enough for this lifetime."

Casey grimaced at her shot glass. "She, Charlie, and I used to sneak this crap from her parents' liquor cabinet when we were teens. *My* tastes matured. Hers have not."

"To Charlie," Ivy said, and Carter guessed her brother was exactly the reason why she still drank the stuff he couldn't believe he was about to drink. Despite bad timing and the surety that nothing could happen between him and Ivy Serrano, he couldn't ignore the warmth that spread through him at being included in such an intimate act—toasting a loved one who'd been lost in the line of duty.

"To Charlie," he and Casey said together. Then all three of them drank.

The gravity of the moment was quickly lost once his taste buds caught on to what was happening.

"That was *terrible,*" Carter said.

"I know," Casey replied.

"One more!" Ivy exclaimed.

Casey shook her head but poured her friend another. Ivy quickly threw back the shot, narrowed her eyes at the almost-empty bottle, then snatched it from her friend.

"Serrano..." Casey said with brows raised.

Ivy looked at her imploringly, her brown eyes wide and her lips pressed together in an exaggerated frown.

Casey relented, and Ivy poured and drank the remaining shot.

"Something stronger for you?" Casey asked him. "She doesn't usually drink like this," she whisper-shouted with one hand covering her mouth.

"I don't usually drink like this," Ivy parroted, her eyes narrowed at her friend. "But today kinda caught me off guard." She turned her attention to Carter. "Anyway, three is good luck, right?"

He held his hand over the top of his shot glass and shook his head in response to Casey's question. "It's my first full day on the ranch tomorrow. How about a burger," he said. "Hear they're pretty good around here."

Casey shrugged. "Probably because it's the only place to get one around here. You want something a little more gourmet—and I stress the *little*—head on over to Pearl's inn. Otherwise, I got you covered."

He laughed and guessed there was some friendly competition between the two main eateries in town. Because if there was one thing he knew for sure, his great-aunt's recipes were a force to be reckoned with. But he was steering clear of Pearl's during the busy hours, and a burger sure did sound good.

"Then I'll have a burger with everything and fries." He nodded toward Ivy. "She should probably eat something, too." He knew a thing or two about some days catching you off guard. Life was funny that way. It never waited for you to prepare for the worst before the worst got handed to you on a silver platter.

"This isn't a date, by the way," she told her friend as she pointed at Carter and then herself. "He finds me attractive but doesn't want to date me, and *I* don't date firefighters, so we have an accord." She hiccupped.

Casey raised her eyebrows. "An accord? Did you two write a treaty or something when I wasn't looking?"

"I'll have my usual, please," Ivy said, ignoring her friend's ribbing.

Casey winked. "A burger and fries for the gentleman and fried pickles for the lady who are on an *accord* and not a date."

She reached behind the bar and grabbed a tumbler glass, then used the soda gun to fill it with water. "In the meantime, drink this." She set the water down in front of Ivy, who pouted but did as she was told. Then Casey headed out from behind the bar and back toward the kitchen.

"You okay?" he asked.

She nodded, then swayed in her seat.

"Whoa," he said, catching her before she toppled off the side of the stool. "Maybe we should switch to a booth so we don't have another emergency today."

She nodded again, then let him help her down. She wasn't quite steady on her feet either, so he wrapped an arm around her torso and carried her water in his free hand as they made their way to an empty booth. She didn't object but instead responded by wrapping her arm around him.

His palm rested on her hip, and he had the distinct urge to rub his thumb along the curve of her waist. He didn't act on it. But holy hell he wanted to.

Once she was situated in the booth, he slid into the seat across from her. Then he nodded at her half-empty glass.

"Drink more of that." He ran a hand through his hair. He really needed a cut. "You eat anything at all today?"

She drank, both hands wrapped around the glass, and

shook her head. When she'd drained the contents, she set the glass down and swiped her forearm across her water mustache.

Damn she was cute. There was nothing wrong with thinking that or wanting to sober her up so he could keep her sitting across from him for as long as this night went on, was there? It was nothing more than two strangers getting to know each other, and where was the harm in that?

"The day just sort of got away from me," she said. "The fridge fire, the first day of the store being open—I kind of forgot to schedule myself a lunch break. I might need to hire on an assistant or something, but the store has to make some money first."

Carter caught Casey looking for them at the bar and waved her over to their booth.

"Pickles were up first," she said. "Figured you wouldn't want me to wait."

Ivy's brown eyes lit up. "Did I ever tell you you're my bestest friend in the whole wide world?"

Casey nodded. "Once or twice."

Ivy pointed at her friend but looked at Carter. "Isn't she beautiful? She broke *all* the hearts in high school, especially Boone Murphy's. Do you know they almost got married?"

For a second Casey looked stricken, but then she laughed. "And now he's getting married, so everything worked out for the best. Speaking of work, I'm closing, which means I need some backup in the friend department." She glanced at Carter. "Can you make sure she gets home okay? It's a short walk from here, ten minutes tops."

Carter nodded. "I'm on it."

Ivy dipped a fried pickle slice into a small bowl of ranch, took a bite, and sighed.

"See?" she said, chewing. "Now I have my best friend and my new friend. Today wasn't so bad after all."

"Atta girl," Casey said, patting her friend on the top of her head. "Also, nothing other than water for you for the rest of the night. You're supposed to open at noon tomorrow, and you don't want to miss the Sunday out-of-towners who want to go home with an Ivy original."

Ivy gave Casey a salute then went back to her pickles.

"Be back with your burger in a minute," she told Carter. "Want another beer?"

He leaned back in his booth and shook his head. "Just a soda," he said. "Coke or Pepsi. Whatever you got."

A second later it was only the two of them again.

"I don't have much of a tolerance," Ivy said.

Carter laughed. "Yeah. I sort of figured that out."

"Thanks for walking me to the table," she added.

"Mind if I try one of those?" he asked, eyeing her food. "If you're looking for a way to repay me, food always works."

Ivy shook her head. "I guess I can spare one. You did keep me from butt planting or face planting at the bar. Not sure which it would have been."

He snagged a pickle disk, dipped it in the ranch, and popped it in his mouth.

"Mmm," he said. "Those aren't half bad. And it would have been a butt plant, judging from the angle of your sway."

Ivy blew out a breath, and a rogue lock of hair that had fallen out of her ponytail blew with it. "I'm not usually half in the bag before seven o'clock," she said. "Today was just—"

"One of those days," he said, finishing her sentence. "I get it. No need to explain. And the pickles and water seem to be helping you crawl back out of that bag, so no worries."

She smiled, and he was sure in that instant that Casey wasn't the only one breaking hearts when they were teens. He'd bet the last fried pickle that her smile alone had devastated a heart or two along the way.

"Food and water," she said with a shrug. "Who knew they were so much better for you than three shots and a beer?"

Casey took a break for dinner and ate with them. When they finished their food and Casey headed back behind the bar, Ivy insisted they head back as well.

"I don't want to hold up a four-top when there's only two of us," she said.

But he knew the truth. She didn't want to be alone with him because that would have been like a date, even if it wasn't. And though he knew that was the right thing to do—to keep Casey as their buffer—he'd have stayed at that table alone with her if she'd wanted. He'd have stayed until the tavern closed, if only to avoid the inevitable for as long as possible—saying good night to Ivy Serrano and good morning to a reality that didn't include terrible liquor or fried pickles or the woman he hadn't stopped thinking about since walking through her shop door that morning. She was beautiful, yes. But she was also strong-willed and funny. What it boiled down to, though, was that simply being in her presence made him forget the stress of the job, of being a new person in an unfamiliar place he hoped to call his permanent home.

He was in big trouble.

Carter had played with fire plenty in his line of work, but never had he felt more in danger of getting burned.

Chapter Three

The sun had finally dipped below the horizon when they left the tavern two hours later. While country music blared inside the bar, as soon as the door closed behind them, all Ivy could hear was the buzz of the cicadas and the occasional chirp of a cricket.

"Wow," Carter said, looking up and down the street. "This place really does shut down at night, doesn't it?"

"Did you live in Houston proper?" she asked. "I imagine this is a far cry from city life. Spent some time in Boston when Charlie and Allison first had the baby and then again after he..." She cut herself off and shook her head.

Charlie had thought their parents would flip when he told them he was moving to the east coast to be near Allison's family. Instead they'd seen it as an adventure—a reason to travel more—especially with their father nearing retirement. Ivy hadn't expected them to move there permanently, but then no one expected Charlie to die. After that, her parents couldn't leave the place where their son was buried, and Ivy couldn't blame them. "It's like it's happening for the first time every time I think of it. I wonder if it will ever get any easier."

They walked slowly, Carter seemingly careful to keep his hands in his pockets, which she appreciated. If his pinky accidentally brushed hers, she might do something stupid, like hooking her finger around his.

Why had it been so easy to mention Charlie's name with a man who was a stranger before this morning? To share a sacred shot of apple pie liqueur and even her fried pickles? Opening day was a success, but she couldn't get past how it had started, with a fire and the reminder of what she'd lost. And here was this man who was the embodiment of that loss, and he'd somehow made it better.

"Couldn't you have been a jerk instead of a perfect gentleman?" she mumbled.

"Did you say something?" he asked.

She turned her head toward him, her eyes wide. "What? *No.* Cicadas," she said, protesting a bit too much.

"Cicadas," he mused. "Sure thing, Serrano."

She shifted her gaze back to the sidewalk and tried to ignore the charming lilt of his accent. They ambled along the sidewalk to where it looked like the street hit a dead end at the trees, but she kept on to the right and led him to a small residential area where most of the Meadow Valley locals lived if they weren't farmers or ranchers.

"It'll always hurt," he said as they slowed around the curve. "But after a while the hurt has a harder time clawing its way to the surface. It gets covered up by the good memories of the person you lost and eventually by new joy you let into your life—when you're ready, of course."

She stopped, shoved her hands in the back pockets of her own jeans, and turned to face him.

She stared at him for several long seconds. They were the only two people outside at the moment, but the way he looked at her made it feel like the quiet street was their own little world. If he were anyone else—if he *did* anything else for a living other than risking his life—she would...What would she do? The only relationship Ivy'd had for the past two years was with her own grief. She still wrapped it around herself like a blanket—a reminder to protect her heart from ever having to go through that again.

"You ever lose someone close to you?" she finally asked.

He nodded once but hesitated before saying more.

"It's okay," she said, breaking the silence. "You don't have to tell me. It helps enough simply knowing when people understand."

He cleared his throat. "We already shared my first emergency since coming to town, my first taste of fried pickles, and my first and *last* shot of apple pie liqueur. Why not share personal loss as well?"

His attempt at humor would have sounded callous if she couldn't tell it was a defense mechanism. She was an expert there.

"I'm all ears," she said.

He shrugged. "I was an idiot kid who got in the car after a party with a buddy who shouldn't have been driving. But because I'd been drinking, too, I believed him when he said he was okay to drive. Made it all the way to my street before he lost control and wrapped the car around a light post. Front end caught fire. I got out—and he didn't."

He said the words so quickly and matter-of-factly, like it was the only way he could get them out. It didn't stop her heart from aching, or the tears from pooling in her eyes. He more than understood what she'd been through yet hadn't said a word all night while she'd cocooned herself in her grief blanket tighter than she had in months.

She reached for him but pulled her hand away before making contact. This was too much. Their connection kept getting harder to ignore. She had to make a concerted effort to keep him at arm's length.

"I'm so sorry, Carter. I—you—this whole night you were so nice to me, and I had no idea that—"

There were no right words for wanting to wrap him in her arms while also wanting to run as far from him as possible.

"Hey there," he said, resting a palm on her cheek and wiping away a tear with his thumb.

She shook her head and stepped back, hating herself for doing it. But all she had left was self-preservation, and Lieutenant Carter Bowen was the biggest threat to it.

He cleared his throat, taking a step back himself. "It was more than a decade ago. And I meant what I said. It does get easier. I can talk about Mason now—remember how he was the best at making people laugh, even our teachers. He kicked the winning field goal at our homecoming game junior year. And he had a real future planned, you know? Football was going to take him to college, but he wanted to be a doctor. A pediatrician, actually." Carter laughed. "*He* was the one on the straight and narrow path while I cut class more often than I went."

Her eyes widened. "I don't believe that for a second."

He forced a smile.

"It's true. I never cut for the sake of cutting. It was always for work. My brothers and I knew from the time we were young that our future was already mapped out. After graduation, my two older brothers went to work at my old man's auto body shop. I was supposed to do the same. It wasn't like there was money for college for three kids, least of all the youngest." He shrugged. "I accepted my fate like my brothers had—until Mason died."

Ivy crossed her arms tight over her chest, the urge to touch him—to comfort him—almost more than she could bear. "You changed direction after the accident," she said. It wasn't a question. She knew.

He nodded. "Much to my father's dissatisfaction, but I was done letting others make decisions for me, especially when I know better than anyone else what's right for me."

"What about your mom?" she asked, tentatively.

"She was sort of caught in the middle. She understood us both but wasn't about to take sides. So I got my grades up senior year. Did two years at community college, got my EMT certification, then took out a loan so I could finish my bachelor's in fire science."

"So fighting fires is your penance for surviving when Mason didn't?"

He shook his head. "Maybe it started that way, but the more I learned, the more I realized I could help people in all sorts of capacities. Even did some presentations at local schools about my firsthand experience being in the car with someone under the influence. I hope to set up a similar program in Meadow Valley and neighboring areas."

She let out a shaky breath. "You're a good man, Carter. Your father should be proud of you. I hope he comes around someday." Ivy dropped her hands to her sides. "I'm only a few more minutes this way. You can head back if you want."

He glanced up at the star-studded sky, then back at her.

"Don't really have anywhere to be. Plus, I promised Casey, and I don't want to get on the bad side of the person who runs the one nighttime establishment around here."

She shrugged. "Suit yourself."

But she smiled softly as she turned away from him and strode toward the bend in the road. The safest thing she could do was put as much distance between herself and Carter Bowen as possible, but a few more minutes with him by her side wouldn't hurt anyone.

He didn't say anything for the rest of walk, letting her silently lead him to her porch, where she stopped short of the front door and pivoted to face him once again.

"Can I ask you something?" he finally said.

"Okay," she answered.

He scratched the back of his neck, avoiding her eyes for a moment, then squared his shoulders and set his blue-eyed gaze right at her.

"I've dated plenty. Some relationships got more serious than others, but I've never told a woman about Mason until tonight, and it hasn't even been twelve hours since I met you, Ivy Serrano. Why do you suppose that is?"

Because, Lieutenant, there's an undeniable connection between us.

Because, Lieutenant, if I believed in such a thing, I'd say we were kindred spirits.

Because, Lieutenant, it feels like it's been more than twelve hours. If it didn't sound so crazy, I'd say I felt like I've known you all my life.

But it wouldn't help either of them to say any of that. So she swallowed the knot in her throat. "Because, Lieutenant, I'm simply a good listener. It's my blessing—and maybe my curse. People like to tell me things they wouldn't tell anyone else. I guess I just have one of those faces." She shrugged, hoping it would sell the lie. "I wouldn't read any more into it than that."

Except that I'm a liar, and I want to kiss you, and you scare me, Lieutenant.

She finally gave in and skimmed her fingers along the hair at his temples and where it curled up above his ear. She couldn't let the night end without any sort of contact, hoping he understood this was the most she could allow herself to give.

"You need a trim," she said. "I could do it. Casey went to cosmetology school right after high school. She used to practice on Charlie, even taught me how to do a simple cut."

He laughed. "And here I thought you were going to break your own rules and do something crazy."

"Like what?" she asked, but she knew. She wouldn't be the one to say it, though. *She* wouldn't break the rules.

"Like kiss me," he said. And even though he was teasing her, hearing the words out loud made her realize how much she wanted them to be true.

Her cheeks flushed. "I don't date firefighters, Lieutenant. And you made it very clear that you don't want to date me."

"Good. Then we're both on the same page. I can't let anything get in the way of work right now. My future rides on everything that happens in the next month. Plus, I've already dated a woman or two who either couldn't handle the hours I worked or the risks I took. I won't change who I am, not for my father and not for any woman, even if it means missing out on something great. On *someone* great. No matter how much you bat those big brown eyes at me."

"I do *not* bat my lashes," she insisted. "Wait, what did you just say?"

She stood there, eyes wide, for a long moment as everything he said registered. Then she held out her right hand.

"Friends, then?" she said, the word leaving a bitter taste in her mouth. But it was all she could offer and all that it seemed he'd be willing to take.

He wrapped his hand around hers, his calloused palm sending a shock of electricity up her arm as he shook.

"Friends it is."

"Well then," she said. "I'm around after five tomorrow if you want that haircut. No charge, of course. Just a favor from one friend to another."

He nodded once, then let her hand go. "Appreciate the offer. I'll get back to you on that. Good night, Ms. Serrano."

"Good night, Lieutenant."

He flashed her a grin, spun on his heel, and then headed off the way he had come.

Ivy leaned against her door and let out a long, shaky breath.

"Friends," she said to herself. "*Friends*."

If she said it enough, she *might* even it believe it was true.

Chapter Four

Ivy went through the store, checking all outlets. even though she hadn't used any up front. You never could be too careful. Then she went to the back office, where she checked on her new battery-powered mini fridge and powered down and unplugged her laptop. She went to her design table, where she'd been trying out a new pattern, hated it, and went at it with the seam ripper, then unplugged the sewing machine as well. Then she scanned the small space twice, made sure the circuit breaker looked up to snuff, and locked the back door. Once over the threshold and into the store, she doubled back one more time to make extra sure she hadn't left an unknown fire hazard behind.

It was a quarter past five. She remembered her offer to Carter the night before. It had been in the back of her mind the entire day. One minute she hoped she'd make it home to find him waiting on her doorstep while the next minute she prayed he'd forgotten the whole thing.

Why had she even put the offer out there? A haircut, one-on-one? It was almost as intimate as kissing. It wasn't like she could blame it on the alcohol. By the time he'd walked her home, she was as sober as could be. But the things she'd confided in him about losing Charlie—and what he'd told her about Mason? She'd connected with him in a way she hadn't anticipated.

Shake it off and move on, she said to herself as she turned off all the lights in the shop. *You get close to someone like that and you'll never find peace.* It was why she'd established her rule. And it wasn't just firefighters but police officers, too. She had the utmost admiration for those who put their lives before others, but she couldn't fall for someone like that. No way. No how.

When she'd finally satisfied herself that the shop was safe to leave for the night, she hoisted her bag over her shoulder and slipped out the front door and locked it behind her. After spinning toward the sidewalk to walk home, she gasped to find Carter Bowen leaning against a dusty, beat-up red Ford F-250.

"Evening, Ivy," he said. "Didn't mean to scare you."

She shook her head, half hoping she simply needed to clear her vision and it would be Shane or Wyatt or any other guy she didn't think about kissing the second she saw them. But nope, it was Carter Bowen all right. *Lieutenant* Carter Bowen. And tonight he was wearing a blue-and-white-plaid shirt rolled to the elbows, jeans that looked about as old as his truck, and dirt-caked work boots.

Shoot. He looked as good in clothes that should probably be marched straight to the washer as he did in his uniform. He'd have to take said dirty clothes off, and she'd bet he also looked pretty darn good—

Stop it, Ivy. You aren't doing yourself any favors letting your mind go there.

"Ivy?" Carter said, and she realized she had not offered him any sort of verbal response yet.

"Lieutenant. Hi. What are you doing here?"

He crossed his arms. "First, when I'm not in uniform, Carter will do just fine. Second, are we going to do that thing where we act like you didn't invite me around last night for something as innocent as a haircut?" He ran a hand across the stubble on his jaw. "Could probably use a shave, too. Don't suppose that's included with the cut?"

She swallowed, her throat suddenly dry. "I'm not pretending anything," she said. "Guess I was expecting you at my house, though, rather than outside my shop. My trimmer and barber shears are back at home."

He shrugged. "It's early yet. Sun won't go down for another few hours. Figured we could take a ride first, show you the trail I rode with some ranch guests earlier today. It's real pretty, and there's a great view when you get to the hill. Though I have to admit the view's pretty good right where I am now."

She rolled her eyes and fidgeted with the messy bun on top of her head. Today she wore a chambray linen tunic that had wrinkled the second she'd put it on, but she loved it anyway. It was so comfortable and looked great with her floral leggings and black moto boots. Comfort all around. Maybe she'd been sober when she'd gotten home last night, but that didn't mean waking up this morning was easy after putting away four drinks the evening before. She hadn't had it in her to wear wedges today.

"With corny pickup lines like that, it's a wonder

you're still single. Wait, you are single, right? Not that it matters. I mean it might matter to *other* women, but not to *me*."

She winced. She was about as smooth as sandpaper.

Carter grinned. "I'm single. Not that it *matters*, since we are just friends. Is that a yes to the ride, then?"

She opened her mouth, then closed it.

"Everything okay?" he asked. "You said you were free after five. It's after five. It's not too hot, now that the sun is headed west…"

Not too hot. Ha. He was funny. Carter Bowen was an actual riot. Had he looked in a mirror? He was hot on a stick dipped in hot sauce. That was part of the problem. His overall charm didn't help either.

She rolled her eyes again and groaned.

"Okay now I feel like I missed a whole conversation," he said.

She laughed. "Only what's going on in my head. And trust me, you do not want access to what's in there."

He pushed off the side of the truck and took a step toward her. "May I?" he asked, lifting her bag off her shoulder.

"Um, sure," she said.

Now that he had her stuff, she guessed she had no choice but to go with him. Her house keys were in that bag, which meant she was practically stranded. That was sound logic, wasn't it?

He opened the passenger door and held out a hand to help her climb in. She plopped down onto a black leather seat with a stitched-up tear down the middle. The interior was clean as could be, but the dashboard looked like something out of an old movie. There was no USB port and a very minimal digital display for the radio.

When Carter climbed into the driver's seat and pulled his door shut, she gasped.

"Is that a tape deck?" she asked.

He nodded. "Works, too."

"Wait a minute," she said, brushing a hand over the dashboard. "Does this thing even have airbags? Because I'm not sure if you remember my safety setup in the shop, but I don't do risk."

He laughed. "The truck's old, but it's not ancient. Twenty years never looked so good on another vehicle."

She put one hand on the door handle, threatening to get out. "You didn't answer my question, Lieutenant."

He cocked a brow. "I'm not in uniform, Ivy. See how easily I bypassed the Ms. Serrano? I bet you can do it, too."

She sighed. "I can call you by your name." Except that meant they were dispensing with formalities, which also meant they were—what? They'd agreed on friends, but this little after-work activity already felt like something more.

"That's funny," he said. "Because I didn't hear you say it."

"Please, *Carter*, can you confirm that this vehicle is safe by today's standards?" She smirked.

He laughed. "*Yes*. There are airbags. It has four-wheel drive if we ever get stuck in the mud or—highly unlikely for this time of year—snow. Hell, it even has working seat belts. You forget I'm the son of a mechanic. I know a thing or two about maintaining a vehicle."

She pulled her seat belt over her shoulder and clicked it into place, then crossed her arms over her chest. "Tease me all you want, but there's no reason to ride in a death trap when I can walk almost anywhere I need to go around here. Plus, it's enough that you do what you do for a living. The least I can do is make sure you're cruising around town in something safe."

He laughed harder this time. "*Cruising*? Darlin', you don't cruise in a machine like this. You ride, drive, and sometimes even tow, but wherever you're going, it's always with a purpose. Cruising is aimless, and I am anything but."

Damn he was sure of himself. In any other man, that quality would be sexy as all get-out. But she didn't want Carter Bowen to be sexy as anything.

He put the key in the ignition and shifted the truck into drive. She expected the tailpipe to backfire or the vehicle to lurch forward, but the engine purred quietly as Carter maneuvered smoothly onto the street.

"It's been a few years since I've been on a horse," she said, her heart rate increasing. It wasn't because she was afraid of riding, though. It was being next to him, the thrum of anticipation, but of what she couldn't say. If he'd have kept to the plan and come over for a haircut, she'd have been in control. But Carter Bowen was literally at the wheel, and Ivy had no idea what came next. "Used to ride every summer at sleepaway camp," she continued. With her big brother, Charlie. There he was again, creeping into her thoughts and reminding her of what unbearable loss felt like. Her throat grew tight, and she hoped Carter would fill the silence while she pushed the hurt back into its hiding space.

"Well," he said with a grin. "This is your lucky day. Because in addition to this morning, I've been riding my whole life. My father may be all about cars, but my mother is a rancher's daughter. We spent a lot of time on my grandad's ranch growing up, and our mama made sure we could all handle ourselves on the back of a horse."

This made her smile, the thought of a young Carter and his big brothers, ribbing each other like brothers do, riding around a ranch.

"Sounds like you and your family were really close growing up," she said.

He nodded. "My father always preferred four wheels to four legs, but he managed." His jaw tightened, and his smile faded.

"I feel like there's another *but* in there somewhere," she said.

He blew out a long breath. "He makes a good enough living doing what he does. My brothers do, too. And for a long time I was fine with following along." He shrugged. "Meant I didn't have to take school too seriously and it meant my parents weren't breathing down my neck about grades and stuff like that as long as I was serious about the auto shop. And I was."

She laid a hand on his forearm and gave him a gentle squeeze. "But it wasn't important to you."

He shook his head. "I'd trade everything to have Mason back, even if it meant fixing cars the rest of my life. But I know now that something would have always felt like it was missing if that was the path I took. I wish I'd figured out what I was meant to do in a different way, you know? But I'm happy where I am now. What I do means something to me, just like I'm sure what you do means something to you."

Her hand slid off his arm and back into her lap. "I have a degree in fashion design," she said. "The stuff I sell in the shop comes from a lot of local designers. But—some of it's mine, too." Her cheeks heated. She was proud of the few pieces she had in the shop and would be even prouder when she sold them. But after growing up with a firefighter for a father and watching her brother follow in his footsteps, it was still scary to share her creative side, to run the risk of someone not liking a design or thinking her work wasn't as important, even when it was to her. "It's not saving lives," she blurted. "But it means something to me."

He rounded a corner and came to a halt at a four-way stop sign on a rural road outside the main part of town. She could see the sign up ahead welcoming her to Meadow Valley Ranch, but Carter put the truck in park.

"What are you doing?" she asked.

He turned to face her, one arm resting on top of the steering wheel.

"I'm making sure you can see the truth in my eyes when I say what I'm gonna say so you don't think I'm blowing smoke."

"Okaaay," she said, drawing out the word with a nervous laugh.

"Is making clothes your passion, the one thing in your life you can't live without? Filling your bucket and whatever other mumbo jumbo means you've found your calling?"

She nodded slowly, his ocean blue eyes holding her prisoner so that even if she wanted to look away, she couldn't.

"Then don't ever sound apologetic about it," he said, his face serious. "Because you're never going to change the minds of the naysayers, if there are any. And worrying about what other people think of what you do? All it does is rob you of some of the joy you're due."

He stared at her long and hard until she nodded her understanding, though she knew he was likely trying to convince himself even more than convince her. Still, the power of those words and the intensity in his gaze? No one had ever looked at her like that.

Once he got his response from her, he turned back to the wheel, put the car in drive, and drove them the final thirty seconds to the ranch.

After that speech and the way his eyes had bored into hers, she'd held her breath, thinking he might do something crazy like lean across the center console and kiss her right there. Only when they rolled to a stop in front of a stable and riding arena did she realize she hadn't yet exhaled. Or how much she wished he *had* planted one on her right at the four-way stop.

"You ready?" he asked.

To ride a horse? To find herself even more attracted to him by the day's end? To wonder if he *did* want to kiss her and what she'd do if it happened? Or how in the heck she was going to get this little crush out of her system once and for all? Because Carter Bowen could and *would* break her heart eventually. So no, she wasn't ready for any of it. Not one little bit.

"As I'll ever be," she said instead, and Carter flashed her a smile that knocked the wind straight out of her lungs.

Honey, you are in trouble, she said to herself as he rounded the back of the truck and opened her door.

"Did you say something?" he asked, offering her a hand to help her down. He had a pack over his shoulder he must have grabbed from the bed of the truck.

"Just how much I'm looking forward to an evening ride," she said.

Lies, lies, lies. Her words were nothing but lies. Only the flutter in her belly when her palm touched his spoke the truth. So she pushed it down deep, hiding it where she'd tried to hide her grief for two long years.

“Me, too,” he said. Then he laced his fingers with hers and led her toward the stable doors.

And just like that, butterflies clawed their way to the surface without any warning at all.

Trouble with a capital *T*.

Chapter Five

Carter held the door for Ivy as they entered the stable. Sam Callahan—one of the ranch owners and also a recent transplant to Meadow Valley—greeted them inside.

"Ivy Serrano, this is Sam Callahan. Not sure if you've met him or his brother Ben yet. Or Colt, the third owner of the ranch."

Ivy shook her head and also shook the other man's hand. "I've seen you about town but don't believe I've officially made your acquaintance, Mr. Callahan. It's nice to meet you."

"It's just Sam," he said. "I'm not big on formalities, Ms.—*Ivy*," he said, grinning and catching his own error.

Sam, Ben, and Colt were young transplants to Meadow Valley, just like Carter. When it felt like he didn't yet fit in, which was most days, he at least had them as allies—and a horse to ride if he needed a quick escape.

"Ranch is officially open for business?" Ivy asked Sam.

"Sure is. It's a slow start, but we hope to get things off

and rolling in the next several months. First year in a new business is the most important. Keep your fingers crossed we start drawing more folks into the area."

She smiled. "I'll cross all my fingers and toes that you have a great first year. Business for you means more business for the town, so it sounds like a win-win to me."

Sam shook Carter's hand as well. "Glad to have you back. You did a heck of a job this morning, even if we only have ten total guests at the moment."

Carter laughed. "Yeah, but those ten will tell ten more about it, and then *those* ten will tell ten more. You see where I'm going here?"

Sam shook his head ruefully, then waved his index finger at Carter. "I sure hope so. Building a new business in a new town isn't as easy as I'd hoped."

Carter shrugged. "If your mare treats Ivy well enough, she may just be the person to start spreading the news in town. Heck, when that happens and you're booking my riding services on the regular, I'll lower my commission from fifteen percent to ten."

Sam clapped Carter on the shoulder. "I sure met you at the right time. Someday I may really be able to pay you."

"As long as you let me ride the trails, consider me paid," Carter said.

Sam grabbed a straw cowboy hat off a bale of hay and tossed it on his head. "Have a nice ride, you two. Ace and Barbara Ann are all ready to go. You're welcome to stop by the dining hall when you get back, but I'm guessing by the saddle pack that you might have things under control."

Carter nodded. "Thanks for the offer all the same."

Sam turned back to Ivy. "It was nice to officially meet

you. I'm sure we'll run into each other again sooner or later." And with that he strode out of the stable.

Ivy stared after him as he left. And then she stared some more. If Carter were the jealous type, he'd be—well—jealous. But how could he envy a man who caught her attention when she was nothing more than a friend? Pretty easily, it turned out.

Carter cleared his throat. "Not that it matters, but if I *were* trying to properly court you, would I have just introduced you to my competition?"

She spun to face him, cheeks aflame. "What? No. I mean—competition for what?"

He laughed. "I'm just wondering—and this is only a hypothetical, because this is in no way a courting situation—if I'd have shot myself in the foot by introducing you to someone who not only doesn't fight fires for a living but also must be pretty easy on the eyes for someone such as yourself."

Her throat bobbed as she swallowed, and her blush deepened.

"I'll admit that if anyone ever needed a visual display of what tall, dark, and handsome was supposed to be, it's the cowboy who just strode out those stable doors. And he has a brother? My oh my," she said, fanning herself.

He'd been teasing her initially, but now his confidence began to waiver.

"*But,*" she added, "there's one big problem with all of that."

Her tone encouraged him, so he took a step closer, even had the audacity to skim his fingers across her temple. "What's the problem, darlin'?"

She blew out a breath. "It's this other cowboy. One who, after barely knowing me, helped sober me up after a bad day and even made sure I got home safely. He also *donates* his free time to lead trail rides at a new ranch in town. And truth be told, I prefer something closer to a redhead than a brunette. In fact, if this particular cowboy didn't risk his life for a living, I might very well be developing a little crush on him, which *would* make this a courting situation. But it's not, correct?"

It wasn't, as much as he wanted it to be. He'd thought about her the whole walk home last night, about what it would have been like to kiss her if she could only see him differently. Maybe that was what he hoped to accomplish by taking her out on the trail. All he knew was that sharing the view with ranch patrons earlier that day had been fun, but sharing it with Ivy would be something else. He hoped by the time they made it to the trail's end he'd figure out what that something else was.

He dipped his head, his lips a breath away from her ear. She smelled like the lavender fields from the farm that bordered his granddaddy's ranch, and he breathed her in, this intoxicating scent of home.

"No," he whispered. "It's not." Because a new job in a new town was tough enough. He was being tested by the chief, his captain, and everyone in his company. If he lost focus and slipped up, then where would he go? But the real issue was her. If he lost focus while falling for someone who, in the end, couldn't handle what he did for a living, then he wasn't simply putting his career on the line but his heart, too. He understood that Ivy's fear was based in reality, that she'd experienced a heartbreaking loss. And while he'd never push her into something she didn't want, it was impossible to deny this thing between them.

"Courting you, Ivy, would eventually mean kissing you. And I'm not sure you could handle my kissin'."

"Why's that?" she asked, her voice cracking.

"Because," he said softly, "I'd leave your lips swollen and your brain so foggy you won't remember your own name." Yet he wouldn't push her too far too fast. She had to choose him. Because despite bad timing and he being the type of guy she swore she'd avoid, a part of him had already chosen her.

She sucked in a breath, and it took every ounce of his resolve to straighten and take a step back when all he wanted to do was exactly what he'd said.

"Then I guess we're on the same page," she said, but he could hear the slight tremble in her voice. It matched his quickened pulse and the irregular beat of his heart.

He nodded. "I'll just throw my pack on Ace's saddle, and we'll be good to go." He glanced down at her boots. They weren't riding boots, but they looked sturdy enough for a motorcycle, which meant they were sturdy enough for a horse.

His gaze trailed up her toned legs. He could see every curve of muscle, her round and perfect backside, in those form-fitting pants.

"See something you like?" she teased, having regained her composure.

Good lord did he ever.

How the heck was he supposed to read that? He wanted something other than friendship from her but only under the right circumstances. But after all her protesting—was Ivy flirting back?

"Just making sure you had proper boots for riding. Those will do," he said coolly, doing his best to maintain control.

He got Ace ready to go, then introduced Ivy to Barbara Ann and helped her into the saddle. At least, he *tried* to help her, offering to give her a boost, but she stuck one foot in the mare's stirrup and hoisted herself into the saddle like she'd done it every day of her life.

She shrugged and stroked the horse's mane. "Guess it's like riding a bike. You never really forget." She pulled her sunglasses from the collar of her shirt, batted her big brown eyes at him, and then covered them up. "I'm just waiting on you, cowboy."

He crossed his arms and stared up at her. "You want to take her for a lap or two in the arena before we hit the trail to make sure you've got the hang of it?"

"Sure," she said. "Meet you out there."

He stepped aside, and Ivy led Barbara Ann out of her stall and into the arena with ease.

He laughed and shook his head. She could make clothes, cut hair, put out her own fires, and hop onto the back of a horse like she grew up on a ranch herself. She also seemed to be able to make him forget that there was no room in his life for romance right now, especially with a woman who couldn't support what he did for a living.

He strode to a shelf right inside the stable's entrance and grabbed the cowboy hat he kept in there for his trail rides, then headed back to Ace's stall and mounted his own trusty steed. When they trotted into the arena, Ivy and Barbara Ann were galloping around the track. Damn she looked good on the back of a horse. Maybe this was their common ground. Back in town she was a woman still grieving an incomparable loss, and he was the man who—by the simple nature of his profession—reminded her of it. Maybe out here on the ranch for one perfect evening they could just be Carter and Ivy.

She rounded a turn and pulled on Barbara Ann's reins so she came to a halt beside him and Ace.

"Color me impressed, Ms. Serrano," he said. "You're a natural."

She beamed. "That. Was. Amazing! I've never felt so—so—"

"Alive?" he asked.

She shook her head. "Free. Free of all the worry swirling around my head, you know? Will the shop do well? Will my own designs sell? And everything else that gets me all twisted up in knots." She blew out a breath. "*Thank* you for bringing me here. I don't know if you knew it was what I needed or not, but wow. This is the perfect end to a stressful opening weekend."

"Now you know why I help Sam and the boys out for free. Ain't nothing like being on top of a horse and leaving the rest of the world behind every now and then." He nodded toward a gate on the other side of the arena and a path that eventually forked into three different directions. "You ready? We're going to do the open trail to the right."

"Ready," she said.

And they hit the trail.

* * *

How was it that Ivy had grown up in this town but had never seen these rolling green hills? It probably had something to do with there not having been a Meadow Valley Ranch or a stable full of horses until now. Maybe, though, the town wasn't the only thing she was looking at from a different perspective.

She tugged gently on Barbara Ann's reins and slowed to a stop a few yards behind where Carter was doing the same thing. When she'd met him yesterday, he was a walking, talking, embodiment of her biggest fear—losing someone she loved. But today he was this cowboy who gave her exactly what she'd needed at the end of a weekend that had started off on a very wrong foot.

He looked back at her over his shoulder and tipped his hat.

Her stomach flipped.

"Just a few paces ahead and we can tie off the horses. I brought snacks," he called.

She nodded and followed him over the hill to where it leveled into a small clearing overlooking the ranch and beyond it the main street of town.

A short length of fence was set up—most likely by Sam Callahan and the other ranch owners—that seemed to be there for the sole purpose of making sure you could relax awhile without your horse running off.

She hopped down into the overgrown grass and walked Barbara Ann to an open spot on the fence. Carter secured his horse while she did the same with hers. He removed the saddle pack and tossed it over his shoulder.

"Sam said the horses like this spot for grazing, and riders like it for gazing down at the town or up at the stars on a clear night, so I said we should call it Gaze 'n' Graze Hill."

She snorted. "That's the corniest thing I ever heard—but at the same time also kind of cute."

He shook his head. "There you go again with that word. *Cute.* Cute in my uniform. Cute the way I name a hill. I've heard the word so much in the past two days that I'm starting to wonder about that vocabulary of yours."

He nodded in the direction away from the fence, then pivoted and headed that way without giving her time to come up with some sort of witty retort.

"I have a very good vocabulary, I'll have you know," she said when she caught up to him, then rolled her eyes at her less-than-formidable response. She'd never had to work to impress when it came to wordplay, but Carter Bowen threw her off her game. He made her tongue-tied and nervous and anxious to lob witty comebacks without a second thought. She had the undeniable urge to show him how much of her there was to like because—*ugh*—she was really starting to like him.

Where would that get her, though? She didn't want to think about that, not when she was up here, able to let go of the fear, even if it was only for a short while.

He laid the pack on the ground and unzipped one of three compartments, pulling out a blue-and-white-checked picnic blanket.

"Here," she said, motioning to take it, since he was kneeling. "I can do that."

He relinquished the blanket, and she shook it out, spreading it over the grass.

Next he opened a plastic container filled with sliced apples and another with what looked like warm, grilled sandwiches.

"Damn," he said. "I didn't think to ask. You don't have a peanut allergy, do you?"

She sat down across from him and shook her head. "Carter Bowen, did you make me peanut butter and jelly?" she asked with a grin.

"No, ma'am. Pearl did. You know Pearl at the Meadow Valley Inn?"

Ivy gasped. "Did you bring me Pearl's grilled PB and J with brie? Because if you did, I just might have to kiss you." Her hand flew over her mouth. "I meant because of how much I *love* that sandwich, not because—" She greedily grabbed one of the sandwich halves from the container and tore off a healthy bite. Anything to keep her from saying more incriminating statements about kissing. "Mmm. Delicious," she said around her mouthful of food.

Carter laughed and dropped back onto his ass—the ass she'd had her eye on for much of the trail ride. It wasn't like she had a choice. He led the way. And if she was searching her *limited* vocabulary for a way to describe the view, it was a long way from *cute.*

He handed her a thermos of Pearl's equally delicious raspberry iced tea, then picked up his own half a sandwich from the container and took a bite. He unscrewed the lid from his own tea and took a couple of long swigs.

"You know," he said, resting his elbows on his knees, "you don't have to be embarrassed about wanting to kiss me. Hell, you don't even have to use my great-aunt's cooking as an excuse for wanting to do it."

Her eyes widened, and she stopped herself in the middle of taking another bite. "*Pearl*? Pearl Sweeney is your great-aunt?"

He held his index finger to his lips.

"She is, though I'd appreciate you keeping that between us for right now. When she heard the chief might be looking to hire from the outside, she passed him my name. That was it. Her only involvement. I got the job on my own merits. I *know* I'm good at what I do. But I'm an uninvited guest right now, so until I prove myself to the company—which I know I will—I don't want to give anyone reason to doubt my abilities."

She lowered her sandwich onto the lid of the container. "But Jessie, Wyatt, and Shane seemed to respect you just fine when you answered my nonemergency alarm."

He laughed, but the smile looked forced. "That's because I'd just written them up for insubordination before we left the station."

"What? Why?" That didn't sound like either of them.

He shrugged. "Because when they saw where the call was coming from, they argued with me about suiting up and taking the truck. 'It's Ivy's place. That girl knows more about fire than we do. By the time we get there, there'll be nothing left to do but paperwork.'"

Ivy winced because they were right about her. But Carter was in the right as their superior. "You did everything by the book like you were supposed to. I get it. No one should take shortcuts in a possible life-or-death situation."

He set his sandwich down and leaned back on his elbows, his long legs stretching out in front of him. His cowboy hat cast a shadow over his eyes. "Anyway," he said. "You can see why I don't want anyone claiming favoritism."

She moved the food out of the way and stretched out next to him on her side. The sun was low enough that she didn't need her sunglasses anymore, so she took them off and tossed them toward her feet. "Why'd you tell me all that, then? Aren't you afraid I'll spill the beans? For all you know, I'm the town gossip."

"Nah," he said. "I know the type, and you're not it. Besides, I needed to tell *someone*. Figured I couldn't do much worse than you."

She scoffed and backhanded him on the shoulder. "I don't know if that's a compliment or an insult. But judging from the sound of your voice, I'm guessing it's the latter."

He rolled onto his side to face her, but the hat was still

obscuring his eyes. So she grabbed it and tossed it the same way she did her sunglasses.

"There," she said. "Now I can see those baby blues."

"Are they *cute*?" he asked.

Something in the pit of her belly tightened, and she shook her head.

"Then what?" he asked, his eyes darkening with the same mischief to match his tone.

"Okay," she said. "Before *then what?* I need to ask you something, Mr. Bowen."

"Go ahead, darlin'."

She blew out a breath. "There's something about being up here with you, away from everything at the bottom of the hill. It's like I can forget what happens down there, you know? Like nothing matters except for what's up here."

"The Gaze 'n' Graze Hill," he said with a wink.

She rolled her eyes but laughed. "There's something between us, right? I mean, you brought me here with Pearl's best sandwich and—and I'm not imagining any of it, am I?"

"No," he said simply. "I can't be with a woman who doesn't support what I do. So I know my wooing is going to waste, even if I keep saying that's not what this is. But I can't seem to help myself. Guess I was hoping I'd be able to change your perspective."

"I support what you do," she said. "But I just can't put my heart out there like that. You have to understand." She paused and took a steadying breath. "Wait. No, this isn't where this was supposed to be going. What I meant to say is that maybe up here, for today, I *can* forget what's down there. We both can." She propped herself up and squinted over the top of the hill.

"If I say yes, that I'd like the same thing," he said, "then I get to hear what else is in that vocabulary of yours?"

She lowered herself so she was facing him again and nodded. "You'd get to hear me say how sexy your butt looks in those jeans."

He laughed. "And here I thought we were talking about my eyes."

"Those are pretty sexy, too." She grinned. "I might even find you a little bit charming."

He trailed his fingers down the bare skin of her arm. "Darlin', I find you to be too many things to list."

She batted her lashes, and he laughed again. "Why don't you try," she said.

"Hmm, I should get comfortable. This'll take a minute or two." He rolled onto his back and clasped his hands behind his head. "Smart. Beautiful. A competent rider—"

"I like where this is headed," she interrupted. "Feel free to continue."

"A passion for what you do. Oh, can't forget terrible taste in liquor."

"Hey," she said. "I thought you were supposed to be complimenting me."

He raised his brows. "I said there was too much to list to *describe* you. Never said it was all complimentary." He scrubbed a hand across his jaw. "*And*...headstrong." He held up his hands like he was waiting for some sort of physical retribution, but she simply sat up, crossed her arms, and glared.

It was easier to find a reason to be indignant than to admit to herself how much she liked hearing what he was saying—complimentary or not. Because even his ribbing meant he'd noticed her. He'd paid attention to her. And he'd thought about her as much as she'd thought about him since their walk last night.

"That one *was* a compliment," he said, sitting up so she couldn't escape the depths of those blue eyes. "You know exactly what you want and what you don't, Ivy. I admire the heck out of that. Even if it means you *not* wanting to get involved with a catch like me."

Her gaze softened. "And you don't want to get involved with a mess like me."

"You're not a mess," he said. "But no. We already know we're not right for each other. And despite what you're offering up here on the hill, I think we both deserve better than that."

He grabbed his hat, stood, and dropped it back on his head.

She clamored back to her feet. "Wait. That's it? What about forgetting what's down there while we're up here?"

He dipped his head and kissed her. She didn't have time to think because her body melted into his like she was molten metal and he was made to mold her into shape. Her stomach contracted, and her back arched. His hands slid around her waist, and hers draped over his shoulders. His kiss was everything he had promised and everything she'd hoped—firm and insistent while at the same time careful and considerate. Whatever he asked for right now, she was more than willing to give. She parted her lips, and his tongue slipped past, tangling with hers. He was heat and fire and passion like she hadn't known existed.

Erase it all, she thought. *My fear, my hesitation—heck, even my name.* She knew it wasn't that easy, that a kiss couldn't take away two years of grief and how scared she was to even consider putting her heart at risk again.

But now that she knew what she'd tried to resist, she wanted all she could take before logic stepped back into the picture.

But before she could catch her breath, he backed away and tipped his hat.

"Are you gonna forget that once we get back to town?" he asked. "Because I sure as hell won't."

Chapter Six

Carter Bowen was on fire. Not literally, of course. In the two weeks he'd been in Meadow Valley, the closest he'd gotten to any sort of real flame was the fire at Ivy's shop—the one she'd put out before he'd probably had his gear on.

No gear today, just a very sweaty Meadow Valley Fire Station T-shirt and a pair of basketball shorts. Lieutenant Heinz's crew took over a few hours early so Carter and his team could spend the last of their twenty-four-hour shift doing a scrub down of the rig.

In a hundred-degree heat, because even in the late afternoon, the day was a scorcher, and they needed daylight to see what they were doing. Carter paused from waxing the front of the truck to take a water break.

"You know this rig never sees any action, right?" Shane O'Brien said. "Other than the occasional emergency room transport—and for that we use the ambulance—I think the last fire Meadow Valley saw was two years ago."

He was on top of the rig, checking the ladder hydraulics and making sure there weren't any leaks.

"Not that I owe you an explanation, probie," Carter said, and Shane scowled at the nickname. "But I know the station's history. I'd expect that, having grown up in Meadow Valley, you'd know that while things have been quiet *here* the past eighteen months, we don't service only our own town. Our company has been called for backup more than a few times for forest fires in neighboring jurisdictions. In a rural area like this, debris from low-hanging trees and falling ash can cause issues over time if the upper level isn't cleared out and rinsed every now and then." He took a long swig from his canteen of water. "Plus a good day of work builds character for someone who might have taken a job because he thought he could sit with his feet up and watch ESPN all day."

He'd actually kill to be inside in the air-conditioning checking the Astros score, but there was no way he was going to bond with his team without working with them, and a clean rig was always the safest rig.

"Thanks for the exaggeration," Shane bit back. "I can count how many times *we've* been called for backup on one hand. And just so we're clear, my probationary period ended months ago. I could put myself in the running for your job if I wanted. We all know about your one-month trial period. You mess up and you're out, Lieutenant *Probie*."

Carter's teeth ground together. He'd been the youngest of three, the button pusher, all his life. But it had all been because he looked up to his brothers. He wanted to be like them. This was different. Shane O'Brien had some sort of vendetta, and Carter was the target.

Jessie popped her head out of the driver-side door.

"Mats and underneath the mats are all clean, Lieutenant!" she called. "Gotta admit, it was pretty nasty in there."

Carter did his best to shake off his interaction with Shane. "Let me take a quick look. If all looks good, you're clear to go."

He rounded the rig and climbed inside. The cab was damn near pristine, like no one had ever used it.

"Excellent work, Morris," he said as he hopped out. "I'll see you in forty-eight hours."

She grinned. "Thanks, Lieutenant." Then she gathered up her portion of the cleaning supplies and headed into the garage.

She and a few others on his team had seemed to come around in the past week, even though he'd been extra surly after the way things had ended with Ivy on Sunday. Maybe it started with his team not wanting to poke the bear, as it was, but now they'd fallen into an easy rhythm that felt good. The way he felt about Ivy Serrano, though? There was nothing easy about that.

It was Thursday now, and he was finishing the second of two twenty-four-hour shifts since he'd seen her. He hadn't been able to shake off how much he'd wanted her that evening and how much he still did even after putting four days between them.

It had meant keeping to the station and avoiding any other stops at the Midtown Tavern. But it seemed the more he avoided his attraction, the more he thought about it and wished he hadn't gone from a father who didn't support his life choices to a woman who drove him all kinds of crazy but also couldn't get behind what he did for a living.

He drained his canteen and then finished the rig's

waxing. After that he went around the truck, inspecting stations and dismissing his firefighters as they completed their jobs. Until the only one left was Shane O'Brien—who'd decided to take an extended water break.

Carter climbed up to the roof of the truck and found him nestled into a corner, his baseball cap pulled low to cover his closed eyes. But Carter could tell by the rhythm of his breathing that the guy was asleep.

What the hell was it with his guy? It was one thing to push his buttons, but this was a complete disregard for Carter's authority.

He looked down at the small bag of twigs and branches Shane had collected—and at the untouched bucket of soapy water meant to wipe down the roof and ladder.

Carter picked up the bucket and tossed half the contents at the sleeping rookie.

"What the hell?" Shane growled, startling awake.

Carter checked his watch. "I'm off the clock. So is the rest of the team. Except you." He nodded toward the spilled water. "Clean that up and wipe down the rest of the roof. I'll let Lieutenant Heinz know you're not stepping foot off this property until you're done. See you in forty-eight hours."

He gritted his teeth and climbed to the ground before Shane had a chance to be any more insubordinate than he'd already been. Carter needed a shower. And a drink. But that meant hitting the tavern. Except he was *avoiding* the tavern. And right now he wanted to avoid the firehouse as well.

He pulled out his cell phone and called his great-aunt.

"I need a room," he said when she answered.

"Got one ready and waiting. Rough day?"

"Yeah. Does that Everything Store sell liquor?"

She laughed. "And steal business from Casey's place? Kitchen's still open over here, and I might have a few longnecks hiding in the fridge."

He blew out a breath. "You're a lifesaver. Be there in a few." Then he ended the call.

He grabbed his few belongings from the bunkhouse, hoisted his duffel over his shoulder, and headed straight for the front door. He pushed through to find Ivy Serrano heading up the front walkway. Her eyes widened when she saw him.

"Can I help you, Ms. Serrano?" he said with as much formality as he could muster.

Her hair was in two low braids on either side of her head, and she wore a black baseball cap that said SLUGGERS across the top in yellow, a white tank top under fitted overalls, and a pair of what he guessed used to be white sneakers on which she'd doodled intricate floral designs in vibrant colored marker.

Damn she looked cute.

She hesitated, her hands fidgeting with the bag slung over her shoulder.

"Softball practice was canceled on account of the heat, and I figured since I was free and it looks like you're still in need of that haircut…"

He ran a hand through his hair. The overgrown ends were slick with sweat.

"Ivy," he said, more serious this time. "What are you doing here?"

She shrugged. "You were right. I haven't been able to forget about that kiss." She noticed his duffel. "Are you going somewhere?"

"Decided to take a room at the inn. I need a shower and a cold-as-hell beer."

She worried her bottom lip between her teeth. "I've got a shower. And a six-pack of Coors."

He sighed. Despite having thought about her all week, he had every reason in the world to say no. There was something between them, for sure. But they couldn't be together, not when his job seemed to be growing more complicated, especially after what he'd just done. Not to mention the woman standing in front of him couldn't handle his job to begin with.

He got it. He understood and wouldn't fault her for her grief. But he couldn't be anyone else for her.

No, Ivy. I can't come with you. I can't get deeper into this thing we never should have started because it'll keep getting harder to walk away.

The only problem? He couldn't actually form the word *no.* Not with those big brown eyes fixed on him, those dark lashes batting their way past his defenses—because yes, she batted. And it worked.

"Those are the magic words," he said at last. A free haircut and a beer. He could handle that. "But nothing out of any sort of fashion magazine. Just a trim."

She finally smiled, and he swore it was brighter than the still-blazing sun.

"Deal," she said, then held out her right hand.

He shook it. "And for the record," he said, "I haven't forgotten that kiss either."

They strode off down the street and around the bend. When they got to her porch he texted his aunt.

Change of plans. I'll still need that room but not until later this evening.

Or maybe, if they both threw logic out the window, not at all.

Carter showered quickly and threw on a clean T-shirt and jeans. He'd gotten so used to communal living the past couple of weeks that the quiet of Ivy's house made him feel odd and out of place. After college he'd moved straight into a one-bedroom apartment with another probie at the station. It was a tight fit, one of them living in the bedroom and the other in the living room, but it had been a necessary inconvenience. After his father decided he was a colossal disappointment, he couldn't live at home anymore. So he worked to pay the rent, picked up any overtime that was offered him, and moved up the ranks as fast as he could.

And then he left.

It had been a long time since he'd been under a roof with quiet, space, and permanence.

He padded barefoot into the kitchen, where she was waiting on a stool at the kitchen island. One frosty longneck sat on the blue-tiled counter while she sipped another.

"Evening, Lieutenant," she said, raising her bottle. Her ball cap hung on the corner of her high-top chair.

"Evening, Ms. Serrano," he said, striding toward the counter to stand opposite her. "But I'm off the clock."

She nodded. "I know. But the title suits you. You've got this air of authority that doesn't seem to go away even when you're off duty."

He blew out a breath and took a healthy swig from his beer. "I guess it's kind of hard to turn it off sometimes." He set his beer down and pressed both palms against the counter, shaking his head. "I lost my cool with one of my rookies this afternoon."

She winced. "Shane?"

"How'd you know?" he asked.

She sighed. "Shane's always had a bit of a chip on his

shoulder. Wyatt was—and I guess still is—the big brother whose shoes have been hard to fill. He was the starting quarterback our sophomore year. Took the team to state twice. He was as good a student as he was an athlete, and now he's a uniformed town hero in the making. Shane got in with the wrong crowd in high school and sorta disappeared for a few years. Rumor has it that when he turned up in the county jail, his father gave him an ultimatum—clean up his act and get a job or he wouldn't post bail."

"Damn," Carter said. "How long ago was that?"

She raised her brows. "About a year ago."

He whistled. "That explains a lot. Shoot, I'm guessing I fanned the flames pretty good, then."

"Uh-oh." She took another sip of her beer. "What did you do?"

He shrugged. "Caught him sleeping on top of the truck when he was supposed to be scrubbing it down, so I dumped half the bucket of soapy water on him and told him he wasn't leaving until he cleaned up the mess." He scratched the back of his neck. "This sounds kind of crazy, but I think he might have been the internal applicant for lieutenant. It doesn't make any damned sense from an experience standpoint, but now that I know more about his history? I'm nothing more than a reminder to him of not measuring up."

"Oh, Carter," she said, resting a hand over his as she stifled a laugh. "You've got your work cut out for you, don't you?"

"The thing is," he said, "he and I aren't that different. I'm the youngest of three. I always looked up to my brothers. My father. But when I decided to go down a different path, it was like I lost any chance of filling the shoes I was expected to fill."

She squeezed his hand. "I think maybe you and Shane will be good for each other. You know what it's like to be in his place. Now you get to sort of be the big brother, to show him that the right path can still be his own path."

He flipped his hand over and laced his fingers with hers. "Does this mean you've changed your mind about getting involved with a firefighter?"

She shook her head, nodded, and then groaned.

"What kind of answer is that?" he asked with a laugh.

She slid off her stool and rounded the corner of the island so she was standing right in front of him.

"It's the kind where my heart and my head can't come to an agreement. I felt something with you that first night, Carter, and again up on the hill. I tried to ignore it. Tried to keep my heart safe by staying away, but here we are."

He nodded. "Here we are."

"Something died in me the day we lost Charlie. Loving and losing isn't just about romantic love, you know. No matter which way you slice it, the losing is hard. Too hard. I couldn't take that kind of hurt again."

"I know," he said. "All I can do is promise that if this thing with us turns to something real, I'll do my best not to hurt you."

She pressed her lips together and nodded. "Maybe while we're seeing where this goes, we pretend you have a really boring office job where you sit in a cubicle and crunch numbers at a computer."

He laughed. "Fine. But if I don't get to talk about my passion, you don't get to talk about yours." He wasn't changing who he was, just buying them time for her to be okay with it. Besides, after today, he needed a friendly face. He needed to be with the woman he hadn't stopped thinking about all week.

She scoffed at him imposing this rule on their game, but fair was fair. "But I just opened the shop. This is my fresh start, my future, my—"

He pressed a finger to her lips. "If I have to work in a cubicle, so do you."

She pouted, but there was a smile in her big brown eyes. "Okay. No shoptalk. For now."

She held out her free hand to shake, but instead he slipped both his hands around her wrists and draped her arms around his neck.

"I can think of a better way to seal that deal."

He dipped his head and kissed her, and it was everything he needed after the day he'd had. Her soft lips parted, and he felt her smile against him as he tasted what was far better than a cold beer at the end of a hard day.

"Evening, Lieutenant," she whispered.

"Evening, Ms. Serrano."

He slid his hands behind her thighs and lifted her up. She wrapped her legs around his waist and kissed him harder.

"Can we postpone that haircut?" she asked, her voice breathy and full of a need that matched his own.

"Yes, ma'am," he said, and carried her back down the hall. There were three open doors, and one he could tell just from glancing in was clearly her office or design space. So he strode through the only other door that wasn't the bathroom and carried her toward the bed.

He set her down on her feet. "Wait," he said.

She shook her head and slid her overalls off her shoulders, lifted her fitted tank top over her head, and undid her bra in seconds flat.

"Wow," he said, staring at her breasts. "While this is already way better than a haircut, why are we rushing,

Ivy?" Even though he wasn't sure how much time he had with her—how long this would last before she decided she couldn't and *wouldn't* be with him—he wanted to take things slow.

She laughed and lifted his T-shirt up and over his shoulders, then wrapped her arms around his torso and stood on her tiptoes to kiss him again. "Why wait?" she asked. "We're two consenting adults who obviously both want the same thing." She paused and took a step back. "You do want me, don't you?" she asked, the sincerity in her voice too much for him to bear.

"God, Ivy, *yes.* So much it hurts." And likely would hurt for a spell until his body caught up with his brain, but he'd survive. "But I don't want to feel like we're rushing only to get each other out of our systems."

He reached for where she'd tossed his T-shirt on the bed and pulled it back on. For a brief second he wondered if she saw the scarred skin on his left side and simply ignored it or if she was too caught up in the moment to notice. There was also the scar on his right shoulder that had nothing to do with the accident, but she seemed to have missed that one, too. Or maybe it was all a part of their game—of pretending he wasn't fully who he was. That was why he was pumping the brakes. Playing make-believe was fine while they figured out what this was, but he wanted their feelings to catch up with their actions. When and if he and Ivy slept together, he wanted the game to be over.

"I'm sorry," she said, crossing her arms over her chest, and he hated that he'd made her feel self-conscious or guilty. "You're right. I just got caught up, and I—"

He wrapped his hands around her wrists and gently pulled her arms back to her sides.

"You play softball, right?" he said, the corner of his mouth turning up.

She nodded, and he dipped his head down to kiss one breast and then the other. She hummed softly, and he breathed in the scent of lavender and silently swore to himself. Ivy Serrano would eventually be his undoing, but tonight maybe they could simply *be.*

He straightened and grinned when he saw the smile spread across her face. "Well maybe no home run tonight, but I could hit a single or double."

She burst out laughing, then grabbed his right hand and placed it on her left breast, his thumb swiping her raised peak. She sucked in a breath before regaining her composure.

"I think you've already made it to second," she teased. "So what's next?"

He sat down on the bed and patted his knee. She climbed into his lap and wrapped her arms around his neck.

He kissed her and lowered her onto her back, his lips traveling to the line of her jaw, her neck, and the soft skin below. He savored each nibble and taste and watching her react to his touch.

"Who knows?" he asked. "If a good pitch comes along, I might hit a triple."

She pressed her palm over the bulge in his jeans and gave him a soft squeeze.

"Only if my team can, too."

He groaned as she squeezed again, then kissed her once more. "Fair is fair."

"But no home runs," she reaffirmed. "At least, not tonight."

"I predict it'll still be a good game."

"Evening, Lieutenant," she said, echoing her earlier

greeting as he slipped a hand beneath the overalls that still hung at her hips. "Thanks for coming over tonight."

He nipped her bottom lip. "Evening, Ms. Serrano. Best night I've had in a long time."

And hopefully the first of many more to come.

Chapter Seven

Ivy pulled her cap over her eyes and stared at the batter, then glanced at Casey, who was pitching. Her friend gave her a subtle nod, which meant she was sending the ball right over the plate, which in turn would mean a line drive to Ivy, who was covering first base. If she caught the ball, it would be the third out and a win for the Midtown Sluggers. If she didn't, the bases would be loaded, and a grand slam would sink them.

No pressure.

Not like this was the big leagues or anything, but the Main Street Loungers from Quincy—aptly named after the pub who sponsored them—were their biggest rival. The Loungers had creamed them the last time they played each other, and tonight the Sluggers were on their home turf.

Ivy breathed in the fresh scent of the ponderosa pines that rose in the distance. Even in the small residential park, you could see the tree-lined hills that gave Meadow Valley its name. It was more than her grief that had swallowed her up in Boston. It was the city itself. Beautiful as it was and steeped in history, Ivy had longed for the comfort of home—for the place where she and Charlie grew up, where she could feel closer to the brother she still missed.

She wasn't expecting a new reason to solidify Meadow Valley as the place she was meant to be. But there was Carter Bowen, climbing into the bleachers. He said he would come as soon as his shift ended—his boring cubicle office job shift—and there he was. They'd been seeing if this thing between them was real for three full weeks now. She counted the week they avoided each other in there because she'd spent each day thinking about him and wishing they *weren't* avoiding each other.

These days they were very much *not* avoiding each other. Whether it was at her house, his room at the inn, or the afternoon she found him waiting in her office after she closed the shop—he'd snuck back there while she was helping one last customer—they'd pretty much *not* avoided each other all over town.

She smiled at the thought. No one had hit any home runs yet, but they'd been enjoying the game nonetheless.

And now he was here, watching her play softball of all things, and all she could think about was how much brighter Meadow Valley seemed with him around. Others would say it had to do with the incessant sun and lack of rain, but not Ivy. She'd smiled more in the last three weeks than she had in the past two years, and the summer sun had nothing to do with it.

Oof! A burst of pain in her shoulder woke her from her stupor.

"Foul!" she heard the referee call.

She saw Carter bolt up from his seat and then sit back

down, like his instinct was to go to her, and despite how much the impact had hurt, her stomach flip-flopped.

"Time out!" Casey called, and she jogged over to first base. "Are you okay?" she asked.

Ivy rolled her shoulder. It would need some ice, but she'd live. "Yeah. I'm fine."

Casey threw her hands in the air, which looked ridiculous, because one was covered by her glove and the other palmed a softball. "Then what the hell was that?" she whisper-shouted. "You could have caught that ball instead of acting as a shield for—I don't know—any stray lightning bugs who might have been in its path."

Ivy groaned. "I know. I'm sorry. I got distracted."

Casey glanced toward the small set of bleachers and then back at Ivy.

"Dreamboat's got you all bent out of shape, doesn't he?" she asked.

"No," Ivy said defensively. "I mean yes. I don't know."

Casey placed her glove on Ivy's shoulder, the one that, thankfully, wasn't throbbing.

"Look, you know there's nothing I want more than to see you smile like you used to. But you know what he does for a living, right? You know where he disappears to every forty-eight hours." Casey cut herself off before saying Charlie's name. Everyone in town pretty much did the same. Unless Ivy got tipsy on apple pie liqueur and toasted her dead brother, everyone played the avoidance game, including herself.

She had lived in the thick of her grief for over a year in Boston with her parents, Charlie's wife, and her niece, Alice. She wanted to leave that grief behind now that she was home and had a soon-to-be-thriving business.

Ivy cleared her throat. "You know how we pretend?

Like you just did by not saying—by not saying his name. That's what Carter and I do. As far as I'm concerned, he has a really boring job where he sits in a cubicle and crunches numbers."

Casey's blue eyes softened. "Oh, Ives. Be careful, okay? I like Carter a lot, but I don't want you setting yourself up for heartbreak if you can't handle what he *really* does."

The ref alerted them that their time was up, and Ivy nodded.

"Let's win this damn game, okay?" Casey asked. "Drinks are on me if we do."

Ivy laughed. "I've never paid for a drink at Midtown in my entire life."

Casey shrugged. "Fine. If we lose, I'm starting your first tab."

Ivy narrowed her eyes at her best friend. "You wouldn't."

"Try me," Casey said. "Or catch the damn ball next time, and you won't have to see whether or not I'm bluffing." She adjusted her baseball cap and pivoted away, her assured strides carrying her back to the pitcher's mound.

"Make me pay for drinks," Ivy mumbled. "Yeah, right." But when the batter readied himself for the next pitch, Ivy squeezed her eyes shut for a brief moment and pushed everything out of her thoughts except one thing—the game.

When she opened her eyes, Casey was already winding up, so Ivy bent her knees, leaned toward the foul line, and held her mitt open and at the ready.

Again, Casey pitched the ball right over the plate, but this time the batter didn't foul. This time it was a line drive inside first. She barely had time to think before she dove over the plate, arm outstretched. The ball hit her hand hard, and she rolled to the ground, tucking it close to her chest. Nervous as hell to look, she sprang to her knees and glanced down. There it was, the softball that was now the game-ending catch.

She jumped to her feet and held the ball high in the air amid cheers from her team.

"Free drinks for life!" she exclaimed, and Casey barreled toward her, embracing her in a victory hug.

Over her friend's shoulders she saw the small gaggle of Midtown Sluggers supporters cheering in the stands, and among them a gorgeous firefighter cowboy who was striding onto the field with fierce determination.

She pulled out of her friend's embrace, and the two of them stared Carter down.

"I think you're about to get kissed," Casey said with a grin.

"Hell yes, I am."

Ivy jogged toward him, giddy, and jumped into his arms, wrapping her legs around his waist.

"Hell of a catch, Serrano," he said, his deep voice only loud enough for her to hear. And then he kissed her.

"I know," she said when they broke apart. "All I needed was to get the distractions out of my head."

He tilted his head back, and she saw his brows draw together.

"Distractions?" he asked.

She felt heat rush to her cheeks. "I know you said you were coming as soon as your shift ended, but it was the bottom of the seventh, and I figured your shift ran late, and—I don't know. I was really excited to see you. Guess I lost my train of thought."

He lowered her to the ground, then planted a kiss on her left shoulder.

She winced. "There's gonna be one hell of a bruise there by the end of the night."

He nodded. "Come home with me tonight, and I can help you ice it."

She grinned and slid her arms around his waist. "I think that can be arranged. Though I want to know when you're going to stop calling Pearl's inn home and find a more permanent residence."

The corner of his mouth turned up. "You afraid I'm going somewhere?"

Every time you're on a twenty-four-hour shift. Because as much as they pretended out loud, she never really forgot what he did. The only safety was in reminding herself that in her quiet little town, nothing much ever happened. The fire in her shop was the most Meadow Valley had seen in years, and she'd taken care of it with ease. So she convinced herself that it'd be at least a couple years more before something else happened, and other than responding to the station's paramedic services, Carter would be safe.

"Are you?" she finally asked. "Going somewhere?"

He shook his head. "Hope not. But the chief wants to make sure he made the right decision. Fire department is a close-knit team, but most of them are warming up to me. Barring any disasters in the next week, I should be ready to start looking for a real place to call home."

She rolled her eyes. "You make Meadow Valley sound so unwelcoming."

He laughed. "I didn't say the town, just the firehouse. When you're working in a life-and-death profession, trust is the most important thing and—"

He stopped short, likely noticing her wide eyes and maybe the fact she was holding her breath.

"Shoot," he said. "Ivy, it's just a figure of speech. You

know every day I've been on duty has truly been about as boring as a cubicle job."

She bit her lip and nodded. Meadow Valley was safe. *He* was safe. But how long could she keep pretending that the potential for danger wasn't there? How long could she pretend that she wasn't afraid?

"Are you breathing?" he asked, brows raised.

She shook her head. Then she let out a breath.

They weren't going to have this conversation now. Not when things were going so well. Not when she couldn't imagine *not* kissing him again tonight or waking up in his arms tomorrow morning.

"Come on," she said, forcing a smile. "Drinks are on Casey."

They didn't last long at the tavern, even when the celebration moved outside to the tavern's back alley, where Casey's dad had set up a good old-fashioned charcoal barbecue and was grilling burgers and dogs. Not when Ivy knew she could be with Carter in his room. Just the two of them. First, though, they made a quick stop at the inn's kitchen, where Pearl was still cleaning up the remnants of the small restaurant's dinner service.

"Well this is a surprise," she said as Ivy and Carter slipped through the door. She opened her arms—and strode straight for Ivy.

"I heard you won the game!" she said.

Carter laughed. "Even with my own flesh and blood I'm still not the favorite around here."

Pearl gave Ivy another squeeze before releasing her. She waved Carter off.

"As soon as I can shout from the rooftop that my grandnephew is the best lieutenant Meadow Valley could ask for, *then* you'll see some favoritism. Until then it goes to your girl, here."

Your girl. Ivy and Carter spending time together was no secret, but that was the first time anyone had verbalized them as a couple. And Ivy liked the sound of it even more than she'd anticipated.

Carter kissed his great-aunt on the cheek.

"In that case, can we get our star first base player a bag of ice? She took a pretty rough foul ball to the shoulder."

Ivy pulled her T-shirt sleeve over her shoulder, and Pearl gasped when she saw the half-moon purple that had already reared its ugly head.

"Oh, honey. Why didn't you say so in the first place?"

She grabbed a box of gallon-size plastic bags from a shelf over the sink and handed one of the bags to Carter. He headed toward the small ice machine that was next to the combination refrigerator-and-freezer and filled the bag.

"He knows better than I do how to ice a shoulder," Pearl told Ivy. "Did you know he was primed to be the starting quarterback his junior year of high school?"

Ivy's eyes widened as Carter finished at the ice machine and turned to look at her.

He smiled and shrugged, but both movements seemed forced. "Shoulder surgery saw to it that *that* never happened." He let out a bitter laugh. "Turns out a summer of football camp trying to prove myself to the coach combined with my dad putting me on tire changing duty at the shop was the perfect combination for a pretty bad tear in the rotator cuff."

He zipped the bag of ice shut and kissed his aunt again. "Need any help finishing up in here?"

She patted him on the cheek. "You kids head on up. I'm

good here. Just need to take out the trash." She nodded toward a door that was propped open into the back alley. "And I'm sorry, sweetheart, if I brought up old wounds."

He shook his head. "You never have to apologize for anything. You're my lifeline, Aunt Pearl. If it weren't for you, I'd have never gotten out of Houston."

"Someday you and your daddy will see eye to eye without expectations or disappointment getting in the way." She sighed. "Now go on before I *do* put you two to work."

She smiled at them both, then busied herself with rolling a trash can toward the kitchen's back door as if they were never there.

Carter turned to Ivy and raised his brows. "Let's go take care of you."

Chapter Eight

Whoops. When he'd left for his shift yesterday evening, he hadn't bothered to make the bed. Or clean up the clothes strewn over the desk chair. Or hide the pile of leadership manuals he'd been poring over, since he'd had another setback with Shane earlier in the week, and of course Ivy gravitated straight to where they were spread out across the top of the desk.

"Sorry for the mess," he said. "But I made Pearl promise no inn employee would waste any time on my room when I get to live here rent free. I'm just not the best at keeping up with it myself."

She didn't respond, undeterred as she strode toward her destination.

"*How to Make Friends and Influence People*? *The Coaching Habit*?" She closed one book that he'd left open to the last page he'd read. Then she covered her mouth but was unable to stifle her laugh. "*The Leadership Secrets of Santa Claus*?"

He grabbed the book and held it protectively to his chest. "Hey. Don't knock it until you try it. Santa leads one of the biggest teams out there. He's gotta have some good secrets."

He tossed the book back down, set the bag of ice on the nightstand, then quickly neatened the bed and propped the pillows up so she'd be comfortable.

"Come here." He patted the bed, then readied the ice pack in his hands.

She glanced down at herself and tried brushing away the infield dirt from the right side of her body. "I'm filthy," she said. "I don't want to get dirt all over your bed. Got a T-shirt I can borrow?"

He moved to the dresser and opened a drawer. Then he tossed her a gray T that had HOUSTON ASTROS emblazoned on the chest in navy blue letters outlined in orange.

She narrowed her eyes. "I can't wear this in public, you know. And neither should you."

He laughed. "Lucky for you, I'm not planning on us leaving this room tonight. Are you?"

She shook her head. "Nope." Then she sauntered with the balled-up shirt into the bathroom. "Just need a few minutes to freshen up, Lieutenant. Maybe you can read some more about Santa's leadership secrets while you wait."

He crossed his arms defiantly. "Maybe I will."

She closed the door behind her.

He heard her turn the sink faucet on, so he collapsed into the desk chair and did exactly as she'd suggested. *Everything* seemed to be falling into place at the station except for Shane. No matter what method he used to try and connect with the guy, Shane always pushed back.

It had only taken seconds for him to get lost in the books,

so he hadn't heard the faucet being turned off or the bathroom door opened. He didn't even know Ivy was behind him until her hands began massaging his shoulders.

"I think *you're* in need of more TLC than me, mister." She kneaded a knot below his shoulder blade, and he blew out a long breath.

"Good lord, that feels good," he said.

"Tell me about the books." She worked on all his knots and kinks, the physical manifestation of the pressure he'd felt at the station these last few weeks.

He shook his head, happy she couldn't see the defeat in his eyes.

"I don't get it," he said. "I've tried every approach with that kid. And before you tell me he's a grown man, he's twenty-two. That's barely legal and a kid in my book."

Ivy laughed. "I'm simply here to listen, Lieutenant. Not judge."

"Sorry," he said, scrubbing a hand over his face. "I'm at the end of my rope with him. He couldn't have been serious about going for lieutenant seconds after finishing his probation. But it feels like he has this grudge."

"Some people need someone else to take the blame for their mistakes or shortcomings—or fears. I'm not saying it's right, but it happens."

He spun his chair around to find Ivy standing there in nothing more than his T-shirt and her underwear.

"Well shoot, darlin'. That massage was something, but if I'd have known you were behind me wearing next to nothing, I'd have turned around a lot sooner."

She climbed into his lap, her legs straddling his torso. He slid his hands under the T-shirt and rested his palms on her hips.

"How's his big brother Wyatt doing?" she asked.

Carter shrugged. "Perfect. Best driver engineer I could ask for—should we ever get a real call."

Ivy's throat bobbed as she swallowed, but she didn't change the subject.

"Do you and the captain praise Wyatt for his good work?"

He nodded. "Hell yeah. Chief even singled him out last week to commend him on the CPR training he did for the local mother and toddler group."

Her forehead fell against his. "And what's Shane done to earn anyone's praise?"

Carter groaned. "I swear I've tried, Ivy. I've *tried* to use positive reinforcement with him, but it's like he's determined to buck authority just enough so that he doesn't get let go from the team."

She huffed out a laugh. "Because I'm guessing that dealing with you is a shade or two more bearable than dealing with his father. I'm not condoning his insubordination, but you're right. He's a kid who's still trying to find his place in a very small town that knows he messed up and that puts his brother on a pedestal every which way he turns. To him, you're simply one other person reminding him that he can't measure up, so why should he try?"

"I know how that feels." Carter had realized he was competing with his brothers for his father's approval. But once he chose his own path, his father made it clear that if anyone was keeping score, Carter had lost. Maybe this would be his in with Shane. Maybe it wouldn't. But somehow Ivy made sense of what Carter should have seen on his own.

She cradled his cheeks in her palms and brushed her lips over his. "You're good at what you do. You don't need to prove yourself to him, Carter."

"To who?" he asked.

She kissed his cheek. "To your father." She kissed the other. "To the chief." She kissed his lips. "To yourself." She lifted his T-shirt over his head. "To me," she added. Then she brushed a kiss over the scar on his shoulder. "Why didn't you tell me about football? About losing your spot on the team because of surgery?"

He slid his hands up her thighs until his thumbs hit the hem of her underwear.

"Because it wouldn't have mattered if I'd been able to play anyway. I'd have gotten kicked off the team because of my attendance eventually."

He let his eyes fall closed as she peppered his chest with kisses. Everything was better with her in his arms, with her warm skin touching his. The pain of the past fell further away each time he kissed her, each morning he woke up next to her, and each day he got closer to calling Meadow Valley his home for good.

"Did your dad know how important it was to you?" she asked.

He shook his head. "There wasn't a point. Either my brothers and I took over the garage or the business would eventually go under when my old man's arthritis wouldn't let him work anymore. He was a very proud, self-made man. And I respect that about him. But he can't get past seeing me as ungrateful for not wanting what he made."

She brushed her fingers through his hair. "It's okay that you chose a different path. What you're doing is something that not many men or women would or could. Be proud of yourself."

He let out a bitter laugh. "For my boring cubicle desk job?"

"No," she said, a slight tremor in her voice. "You risk your life for others. And there's nothing boring about that."

She ran her fingertips over the raised and knotted skin on the left side of his torso.

"I wasn't just talking about Shane when I said people blame others for their own baggage. I've been blaming you, in a way, for my fear of once again losing someone I care about. It's not fair. If you're not ready to be proud of yourself, then know that *I'm* proud of what you've done, of what you continue to do."

He nodded. His throat was tight, and he wasn't sure what it would sound like if he spoke, but he needed to know what this meant. He needed to know where they stood as far as her not being able to deal with his job.

"But can you let go of the fear, Ivy? If you're really proud of me—of how well I do my job—can you accept who I am and what I do, so that this"—he motioned between them—"doesn't have to come to an end?"

A tear slid down her cheek, and she nodded. "I don't want to be afraid," she said. "Because I think I'm falling for you, Carter Bowen."

He grinned and lifted her up. Her legs squeezed tight around his waist, but the vise that seemed to be slowly squeezing his heart for the better part of a decade loosened.

He laid her down gingerly on the bed.

"I'm head over heels and ass over elbow and whatever other phrase you got that says how hard I'm falling for you, darlin'."

He glanced toward the melting bag of ice on the nightstand.

"We forgot about your shoulder."

She tugged him down to her. "Forget about it. I have another one that's in perfectly good condition."

He laughed. Then he lifted the Astros shirt up her torso and over her head. And there she was in nothing other than her underwear—bare and beautiful and falling for him. Everything in his life finally felt like it was clicking into place. She was simply the missing piece he hadn't known he was missing.

"I have a question for you," she added. "Actually, it's more of an observation."

"I'm all ears."

She smiled, and he swore he'd do whatever it took to make her smile the last thing he saw before he went to sleep and the first thing he laid eyes on each morning—for as long as she'd let him.

"I know Midtown won their big game and all, but I think it's *our* turn to hit a home run."

He laughed. "I think that's an excellent observation." Then he brushed a lock of hair out of her eye and stared at her.

"You're so beautiful," he said. "Here..." He kissed each breast. "And *here*." He kissed the skin above her heart. "I didn't plan on you, Ivy Serrano. But I sure am glad your refrigerator cord caught fire—*and* that you were able to put it out so quickly."

He rolled onto his side, and their legs entwined as their lips met, as if this were a choreographed dance they'd learned years ago.

"I sure didn't plan on a cowboy fireman turning my life upside down. I didn't know what it would be like to come home, with my parents in Boston and Charlie gone for good. The past several months have been real hard. And then you showed up."

She kissed him, her breasts warm against his chest. And it was simply right—she and he like this.

"And," she said, "you're wearing too many clothes."

Almost as soon as she had said the words, his jeans and boxer briefs were no more.

He slid her panties to her ankles and over her feet, and she hooked a leg over his.

"I don't want anything between us tonight," she said, wrapping a hand around his hard length.

"But—" He was all for what she was suggesting, but after waiting all this time, he wanted to be careful. Tonight was the start of something bigger than he'd imagined, and he wanted to get everything right.

"I'm on the pill," she said. "Have been for years. And I haven't been— It's only you, Carter. Just *you.*"

He knew what she meant on a literal level but wondered if she felt it, too—how hard he was falling for her, how he couldn't fathom it being anyone other than her ever again.

He buried himself inside her, hoping to fill her with all that he was feeling but couldn't yet say.

She arched against him and gasped. He kissed her hard, and she rolled on top of him. He watched her move in a rhythm that was all their own. And he wondered how so much could change in such a short time.

He always thought he was running from a father who couldn't accept his choices, but maybe he was running to her all along.

He woke the next morning before she did, their bodies still tangled and her back against his chest.

He kissed her neck, and she hummed softly, but it was a dreamy hum, one that assured him she was still asleep. Still, it couldn't hurt to check.

"Ivy," he whispered. "You awake?"

She didn't stir.

He knew this was right—that *she* was right. So why deny it any longer.

"Maybe this is too soon, but I'm a man of certainty, and I'm certain that I'm not falling for you, darlin'. I'm not falling because I already fell." He kissed the softball-shaped bruise on her shoulder. "I love you, Ivy."

He wasn't ready to say it to her face, not when a tiny part of him kept whispering that eventually his job would spook her and this would be over. It was better like this, not knowing what she'd say in return. Because if the other shoe dropped, he wanted to be prepared. He could handle her walking away if he never knew that she loved him, too. But if he knew and she still left, that might downright ruin him.

Maybe he risked his life doing what he did for a living, but he realized now that the one thing scarier than walking into a burning building was risking his heart.

Chapter Nine

Ivy closed the store at four, since business had been slow. Plus, happy hour at Midtown started at five on Thursdays, and most folks went early to claim their preferred seats, especially those who liked to sit closest to the free appetizers.

"Ow!" Casey said when Ivy accidentally poked her with her hemming pin.

"Sorry," Ivy said with her lips pressed tight around the blunt ends of the remaining pins, so it sounded more like *Srry*.

"I get that you're nervous and all about putting this design on display, but if you poke your very human mannequin one more time, she's quitting. She didn't sign up for acupuncture, *and* she has to get her butt behind the bar soon."

Ivy spit the pins into her palm and sighed.

"Sorry. This is—it's more than the design. It's symbolic, you know? If I can look at the dress in the store—on an actual mannequin who doesn't complain—it'll mean I'm okay. It'll mean that I can remember the good things about Charlie, about growing up here, and be happy instead of—" She trailed off before finishing. Because she would be a horrible person if she said what came next.

"I know," Casey said with more understanding in her voice. She held out a hand, and Ivy grabbed it, letting her friend give her a reassuring squeeze. "It's okay to be angry."

Leave it to her best friend to know exactly what Ivy was thinking.

"He should have known better," Ivy said softly, the tears pooling in her eyes. "They train to know when the building is safe to enter and when they need to get out. He should have gotten out. He should have thought about his wife and his baby and his family and..."

Ivy hiccupped and sobbed. She'd never said any of this aloud, not to her parents or Charlie's wife. She'd grieved as best she could, but she'd never admitted the ugly part of it, the irrational blame she placed on the brother she'd lost.

"I'm the worst," she said. "You don't need to tell me because I already know."

Casey sat down carefully in Ivy's office chair and patted the top of the desk, for her friend to sit. Ivy nodded and complied.

"Hey," Casey said, taking both of Ivy's hands now. "You know this is normal, right? The anger part? I know you've accepted that Charlie's gone, but I think you skipped right over this part. I should have stayed longer in Boston after the funeral. You kept it together for your parents and Allison, but you didn't get to fall apart with your best friend like you should have."

Ivy choked out a tearful laugh. "You mean like now?" She grabbed a tissue from the box on her desk and blew her nose. Then she grabbed two more to try to dry her tearstained face. "You had a business to run. I never expected you to stay. I never expected *me* to stay as long as I did, but I couldn't leave until I knew they were all okay..." She paused for a long moment. "Or until I could come back here, knowing home would never be the same." She blew out a long breath. "So, I'm really not the worst?"

Casey smiled sadly and shook her head. "Do you really blame your brother for doing a job not many are cut out to do?"

Ivy shook her head.

"See?" Casey said. "Not the worst. This is actually a really good step, Ives. I think you're finally starting to move past the worst of it."

Ivy worried her bottom lip between her teeth, and Casey's brows furrowed.

Once she said what she was about to say out loud, it would be real. Like *really* real. And real with Carter Bowen still scared her half to death.

"There's something else you're not telling me." Casey narrowed her eyes. "This is about more than Charlie, isn't it? *Spill*," she added. "You have ten more minutes before I turn into a pumpkin and this badass dress changes back to jeans and a T-shirt."

Ivy laughed. Casey always could make her feel better about any situation. Venting her anger was cathartic, as far as taking a productive step past her grief, but it wasn't the only thing she'd been thinking about.

"Did I mention that Carter said he loved me?" she asked softly.

"What?" Casey threw her arms in the air. Then she yelped as a bodice pin scraped along her skin. "Ow!"

"Sorry!" Ivy cried, fumbling to fix the pin.

"Screw the apologies!" Casey said with a grin. "Tell. Me. *Everything*."

Her pulse quickened at having said what *he'd* said out loud. She'd sat on the information all week, not sure what to do with it. Hearing those words from him had been everything—shooting stars, fireworks, and a lifetime supply of fried pickles. She'd wound up exactly where she never wanted to be, except for one minor detail…Ivy loved Carter, too. And the realization solidified how much she had to lose if anything ever happened to him.

Ivy cleared her throat. "I spent the night at the inn with him after the game last week," she started.

"Bow-chica-bow-bow," Casey sang.

She rolled her eyes even though she was grateful for a moment of levity. "Yes. I'm a woman in my mid-twenties who has sex."

Casey waggled her brows. "Yes, but unless you stopped telling your best friend *everything*, you're a woman in her mid-twenties who up until meeting Lieutenant Dreamboat had not had sex in quite some time *and* who was taking things slowly with said Dreamboat."

"Nine months," Ivy admitted. "But who's counting? *Anyway*. If you want your best friend to tell you everything, you're going to need to stop interrupting." She paused, brows raised, and waited. Casey made a motion of zipping her lips, so Ivy went on.

"It was the next morning," she continued. "I was sort of asleep, sort of not. So I'm ninety-nine percent sure I didn't dream it. But he said something along the lines of knowing it was probably too early to say it but that he was a man of certainty and that he was certain he loved me."

Casey stared at her, eyes wide and mouth hanging open.

"You can talk now," Ivy said.

"Phew! Okay, first things first. I think it's reasonable to fall in love with someone in a few weeks. Plus, we're talking you, and you're pretty damn lovable."

"Thank you very much," Ivy said with a grin.

"But the part of the story that's missing is what you said back to him."

Ivy winced.

Casey's eyes narrowed. "Oh my God, Ivy Serrano. Did you pretend you were still sleeping?"

If it was possible for her wince to get bigger, Ivy's did.

"What if I dreamed it?" she asked.

Casey sighed. "You didn't dream it."

"Well, what if he only told me because he thought I was sleeping and didn't *really* want to tell me for *real* for real."

Casey shook her head. "I don't even know what you just said so why don't you tell me this—do you love *him*?"

Ivy sucked in a steadying breath.

"Maybe?"

"*Serrano…*"

"I don't know if I've ever *been* in love before. So how would I know?"

"*Ivy*," Casey said this time, her patience definitely growing thin.

"What if you're wrong and I'm not past the worst of what happened to Charlie? What if I *have* fallen for him and he—?" She couldn't say it. It was one thing for Casey to tell her she was moving past Charlie's death. It was a whole other to be brave enough to risk her heart in an entirely new and terrifying way.

Casey crossed her arms. "You can be scared, Ives. But you have to be able to answer the question. So riddle me this, Batgirl. When you think of your life without him, how do you feel?"

Ivy's eyes burned with the threat of fresh tears.

Casey laughed. "Oh, honey. It's worse than I thought. You fell *hard*, didn't you?"

Ivy nodded as the truth took hold. "I love him, Case. I *love* Carter Bowen."

"Carter Bowen—who is a firefighter." Casey placed a hand on Ivy's leg and gave her a soft squeeze. "Can you handle that?"

Ivy swallowed and placed her hand over her friend's. "I worked it out in my head. We're not a big city like Boston. My dad made it to retirement here without any major injuries. Meadow Valley is safe, which means Carter is safe, even if he's a firefighter."

"And you'll support him if he has to do something you don't deem safe?"

Ivy nodded. She could do this if she held on to her logic—no matter how convoluted—that she couldn't lose Carter like she lost Charlie. Not here.

"I love him," she said again.

"Then you better finish putting this dress together and tell him," Casey said.

"I haven't even seen him all week. I think he's been avoiding me. I went looking for him at Pearl's after his first shift since that night, and she said he'd decided to stay at the station for the week—iron some things out with his unit." It could have been true. He could be working on the situation with Shane. Or he could be taking extra shifts to keep from running into her.

Casey raised a brow. "Honey, the man's in love with

you and has no idea if you feel the same way. Even the bravest of the brave get a little gun-shy when it comes to matters of the heart. Luckily, *you* can fix that."

Ivy grinned. "Okay." Then she grabbed her phone and hammered out a quick text to Carter.

Meet me at Midtown tonight?

The three dots appeared immediately, and she held her breath.

Sure. Off at six.

Great. Can't wait to see you.

She waited several seconds, but there was no response after that. It didn't matter. He was coming, and she was going to tell him what she should have said that morning.

Ivy shrugged. "Looks like I'm spilling my heart out at six o'clock. Wish me luck."

Casey waved her off. "You got this, Ives. Home run. Or is it a slam dunk?"

Ivy snorted. "Let's go with basketball for this one."

She finished the final pinning and stitching in record time, fueled by the adrenaline of what she'd been afraid to admit to herself all week. When she was done, she and Casey headed to the tavern to celebrate with a drink and whatever was left of the appetizers while Ivy waited for Carter.

She tried not to look nervous when the clock hit 6:30 p.m. and he wasn't there, *nor* had she heard from him. At 6:45, she started to worry. And at 7:00 she was near to panicking. Not that she thought anything had happened to him. She'd have heard sirens if there had been any sort of emergency. But the kind of panic that said even without telling him how she felt, she'd somehow spooked him. Or maybe he had realized she'd heard what he said and was furious she hadn't reciprocated.

"Hey," Casey said from the other side of the bar. "You *can* call *him*, you know."

"Mmm-hmm," she said, popping a fried pickle into her mouth. Because a stressed-out girl in love needed some comfort food. "Or I could eat my weight in pickles. I think I'm going with option number two." Because wouldn't that be just her luck—to realize she was in love with the guy exactly when he realized he'd made a *huge* mistake saying he loved her?

Casey snagged the basket of fried goodness before Ivy could grab another bite.

"*Hey!*" Ivy said, trying to swipe her prized possession back. But Casey held it over her head. The only way Ivy was getting it back was if she climbed onto the bar and stole it back.

She shrugged. She wasn't above such a move.

Ivy was midclimb when Casey whisper-shouted, "He's here!"

Ivy rolled her eyes. "I want my damn pickles!"

"Ivy?" she heard from behind her. "What are you doing?"

She winced but not before grabbing her food back. Then she slid not-so-gracefully back onto her stool.

She spun to see Carter still in uniform, brows furrowed.

"Just taking back what was stolen from me." She held up her spoils. "Pickle?"

He shook his head, his jaw tight as his confusion morphed to something graver. She forgot her panic and grabbed his hand. "Hey, are you okay? I thought I'd see you at six and was starting to worry."

He climbed onto the stool next to hers.

"Here," Casey said, sliding a mug of beer his way. "No offense, but you look like you need this."

He shook his head. "None taken." And he took a sip.

"I spent the last hour in the chief's office, trying to figure out how to fix things," he said.

Ivy forgot about her fried pickles. "What's broken?"

Carter blew out a breath. "Morale? My team's faith in me? It turns out there have been several complaints turned in about me this week, all pertaining to me not knowing how the station runs and questioning the chief hiring someone based purely on nepotism."

"Nepo-*what*?" Casey asked. When Ivy opened her mouth to answer, she held up her hand. "I know what the word means. I just don't get how it relates, unless Lieutenant Dreamboat is the captain's or chief's long-lost son."

Ivy's eyes widened. "We're calling him Lieutenant Dreamboat to his face now?"

Casey popped a piece of pickle into her mouth. "We are *now*!"

Ivy turned back to Carter. "Okay, so someone found out about you being Pearl's nephew. I really don't get how that's nepotism. Pearl isn't a high-ranking firefighter or anything like that. She put in a good word, and you got the job."

Carter shook his head.

"Turns out I'm not the only one keeping a low profile as far as my Meadow Valley connections. Aunt Pearl is *dating* the chief."

If Ivy had been sipping her beer, this would have been her first ever spit take, which wasn't the kind of thing a girl wanted to do *before* she and her significant other officially declared those three little words to each other. *Win him over and* then *start embarrassing yourself while eating and drinking.*

"I didn't know Pearl dated. Period," Ivy said.

"Go Pearl," Casey said. "Not only dating but a younger man, too. I want to be her when I grow up."

Carter sighed. "She took it so hard when my uncle passed away. I don't think any of us ever thought of her being with anyone else. Not that she doesn't deserve to be happy. It was just sort of a shock. And of all people…"

"Wait, wait, wait," Ivy said. "Put a pin in the whole nepotism thing for a second. Pearl's husband passed away a decade ago."

Carter nodded.

"Does that mean you were here for the funeral? I mean—I'm retroactively sorry for your loss. But were you here?"

He nodded again, and the set of his jaw loosened as realization set in. "He was my mother's favorite uncle. My brothers and I liked him, too. We drove out with my mom and my grandma for the funeral."

Ivy's eyes widened. "*I* was at that funeral. I mean, the whole town was, because that's small town life for ya, but we were both there."

The corner of his mouth turned up, the first hint of a smile since he walked through the door. Something about it made Ivy's breath catch in her throat.

"You didn't wear black," he said matter-of-factly, and she shook her head. "You had on a blue dress with a sunflower print. And I thought, *What is up with this girl who doesn't know anything about funeral etiquette?*"

She laughed, and her cheeks filled with heat.

"It was the first dress I ever made," she said. And the one that inspired her latest design, the one she hoped to actually finish and display in her shop window. "My mom loved planting flowers, and she taught Charlie and me. Our favorite was the sunflowers. Did you know that when they're young, before they bloom, they actually follow the sun across the sky each day?"

"Heliotropism," Carter said with a self-satisfied grin. "Solar tracking." Her eyes widened, and he shrugged. "I had to take a lab science in college. Botany was the only one that fit my schedule."

He knew about sunflowers. He *saw* her in her first dress.

Her stomach flipped. Every new thing she learned about Carter Bowen made it harder to resist the connection she felt with him.

She nodded. "I thought there was nothing more beautiful, and I wanted to wear something beautiful for Pearl. But it was more than that. I liked the idea of the new buds repositioning themselves each night so they faced east again. I admired their determination—their fierce sense of direction." Direction Ivy wanted so badly now that she was home. She wanted to face the grief and move past it. She wanted to wake up in the morning with the sun shining on her face instead of under the cloud where she'd lived for more than two years. "Pearl loved it, by the way." Ivy cleared her throat. "It's where my *thing* for flowers comes from. Haven't been able to bring myself to plant my own garden, but I add a rose here, a lily there—when it suits the design."

"I have no doubt Aunt Pearl loved it," Carter said. His brows drew together. "But I can't believe that was *you.*"

Casey waved a hand between them. "Hell*oo*. Before you two start talking about nonsense like *meant to be* or *star-crossed lovers* or whatever, can we get back to the *real* story so I can help actual paying customers? What the heck happened with the chief?"

Carter blinked, and the far-off look in his blue eyes that could have swallowed Ivy whole disappeared.

"Someone who knows about Pearl and the chief also knows about me being Pearl's nephew, and there's a petition going around to get me removed as lieutenant. There are quite a few signatures already."

Ivy gasped. "They can't actually *do* that, can they?"

Carter shook his head. "Technically, no. Family members are absolutely allowed to work in the same company."

"Right," Casey said. "Like Wyatt and Shane."

"Oh no," Ivy said. "*Shane*."

"There's no nepotism clause in the handbook," Carter went on. "But in a job like this, morale is everything. If anyone thinks I got the job because of favoritism from the chief, then they might not trust that I'm up to the task. And if my presence is bringing down the morale of the whole company, then me staying on could be more detrimental than it's worth. Chief won't say who started the petition, but I took a job someone on the inside wanted, and that someone doesn't want me around…"

Casey shook her head. "You really think it was Shane? I mean, the guy carries around resentment like no one's business, but that seems a little over the top even for him."

Ivy winced. "I don't know. He and Carter have been butting heads since the day Carter stepped foot in the station. We were just as shocked when Shane ended up in jail. Maybe this isn't out of character at all."

Carter took another long, slow pull of his beer. "At the end of the day, it doesn't matter who it is if I can't win over the trust of my company."

There was a finality in his voice that made the hair on the back of Ivy's neck stand up.

"So, what does this mean?" she asked.

"It means I'm on leave for the weekend. Captain's taking over my crew. And by the end of next week, I may be out of a job. Leaving Houston for Meadow Valley made sense not simply for the job but also because I had family here. I could find another station in a different city or state, but at my age, a résumé that shows me having already left *two* stations? That doesn't give me a very reliable track record. If I haven't burned a bridge, I could ask for my job back in Houston. But if they say no..." He let out a bitter laugh. "There's always my father's auto shop. I bet he'd love me coming home with my tail between my legs, begging for what I told him I didn't want anymore." He finished his beer in one final gulp, then slapped some bills on the bar.

"Oh you don't—" Casey started, but Carter interrupted.

"It's way less than what I owe you since I got here, but I don't want to fuel the notion that I take handouts. Thanks, anyway," he said. He turned to Ivy. "I'm not gonna be good company tonight." Then he kissed her, his lips lingering on hers even after the kiss ended. "But I sure am happy I got to do that," he finally added. "I'm glad you texted."

Then he stood, pivoted toward the door, and left.

Ivy sat there, dumbfounded, staring at the door for several long moments after it closed behind him. She'd been so scared to lose Carter in the worst way possible that she never had considered him having to leave town.

"You okay?" Casey asked, breaking the silence.

"No," she said, turning to face her friend. "Case, what if he leaves?"

Casey nodded. "What if you go out there and tell him how you feel and see if that makes a difference? Maybe if you let him know you're willing to fight for him, he'll fight for a way to stay. All I know is *not* telling him how you feel will make you always wonder what would have happened if you did."

Ivy's eyes widened. "Are we still talking about me and Carter, or does this have something to do with Boone Murphy's recent engagement?" Ivy had been so wrapped up in everything Carter that she'd forgotten Casey's high school sweetheart was marrying someone else.

Casey rolled her eyes. "You're deflecting, Ives. What this is *about* is not regretting a missed opportunity. If you love the guy, *tell* him. It's as simple as that."

She swallowed the lump in her throat. Casey was right. She *loved* Carter, and he loved her. Once they said it aloud for real, everything would be different, wouldn't it? They could figure this job thing out together.

"I said I was going to tell him, which means I have to go tell him."

Casey nudged her shoulder. "Then get off your ass and go do the thing instead of talking about doing the thing."

She glanced down at Carter's cash on the counter, then back at her friend. "You're okay if I don't make a similar monetary gesture, right? I'll cover your next closing shift for free."

Casey raised her brows. "Yeah, you will. Now *go*!"

Ivy hopped off her stool and bounded toward the door just as she started to smell smoke. She pushed the tavern door open to the blaring sound of sirens filling the street. Along with it came the ringing of the firehouse bell, which meant only one thing.

For the first time in years, there was a real fire in Meadow Valley. And even though he was off duty, amid the ensuing chaos she saw Carter Bowen running across the street, straight toward the firehouse.

Chapter Ten

This was bad. He could already smell the smoke, and the air had taken on the type of haze that meant whatever was burning was feeding a fire that was growing.

"Carter!" he heard from behind him, and spun to see Ivy running toward him.

"I have to go, Ivy!" he called back.

She was out of breath when she stopped in front of him. "But you don't," she insisted. "You're—you're off duty. Lieutenant Heinz and his team will take care of whatever's happening."

"Ivy. You don't have to be a firefighter to know that *whatever's happening* probably needs more than one crew. Even when I'm off duty, I'm still on call. And I'm answering the damn call."

She pressed her hands to his chest as the first emergency vehicle pulled out of the station. The engine would be next, which meant he needed to hurry.

"Please," she said, her brown eyes shining. He wasn't

sure if it was the threat of tears or because of the smoke in the air.

"Are you asking me *not* to do my job? Because I thought we were past this. I thought you were okay with what I did." Yet he didn't really trust her, did he? Or he'd have said how he felt to her face rather than when she was still asleep.

"And I thought you were done trying to prove yourself. You just told me you were on leave for the weekend, which means you don't *have* to go. I can't—" She swiped underneath one eye. "When you said you might have to go back to Houston, I knew right then that I'd beg you to stay, that I couldn't lose you. And now?" She pressed her lips together and shook her head. "I can't do it, Carter. I can't watch you run head-on into a life-threatening situation when there are plenty of others who are prepared to do so. It's selfish of me to ask, and I have no right to do so, but I am begging you, Carter—begging you to stay *safe.*"

The chief's voice sounded on his radio. "All available crews report. I repeat, all available crews report."

"I have to go, Ivy," he said firmly. "And you're wrong. I *do* need to prove that I'm what this company needs, that I'm capable of leading my crew into any situation and bringing them all home—safe, myself included. *This* is what I do. We're not tying up horses on the top of a hill and acting like what's down here doesn't exist. I can't pretend for you anymore."

"I love you," she said. It wasn't another plea or a last-ditch effort to get him to stay. He could hear the sincerity in the tremor of her voice. And God, he *knew* what she'd already lost and how she'd never quite be over it. It was the same for him with Mason. But this was who he was.

This was what he did. He couldn't be what she needed if that meant sitting on the sidelines when there were lives at stake.

"I love you, too," he finally said face-to-face, like he should have all along. "And I understand that this is too much for you. But I need you to understand that it's what I'm meant to do."

He kissed her, tasting the salt of her tears on her lips.

"Maybe, after you've had more time, and they haven't shipped me back to Texas..."

She said nothing after his pause, and he wouldn't finish the rest. Because even though he was done pretending for her, maybe he could do it for himself. Maybe he could pretend for tonight that they hadn't said those three words and then followed it up with a kiss that meant good-bye.

He pivoted toward the firehouse and strode up the walkway and inside to where he was met with the type of organized chaos he was meant to control. The chief saw him and nodded, so Carter started barking orders as he jogged into the engine room and suited up just in time to hop on.

All he had to prove was that he was bringing everyone on this crew home safe tonight. Then she'd see.

* * *

The street was filled with people by the time Ivy woke from her daze and turned around.

Patrons spilled out of Midtown Tavern, and she started to cross back that way. But then the engine's siren roared as the truck pulled out of the firehouse, around the corner, and onto First Street, causing her to jump back onto the curb. She stared at Wyatt in the driver's seat, then past him to where a pair of bright blue eyes stared back. Carter sat in the passenger seat, his jaw set and determined.

Her stomach roiled, and she thought she might be sick.

When the engine passed, she saw Casey coming toward her, her face pale.

"It's Mrs. Davis's house," she said. "The whole thing is up in flames."

"Oh my God," Ivy said. "Is she still inside?"

Casey shook her head, and for a second Ivy was relieved. But then Casey said, "I don't know. A neighbor called 911, not her." She sniffled. "Jessie called. She's on paramedic duty and said she'll give us an update as soon as she can. This is really bad, Ives."

Ivy hugged her friend. Mrs. Davis lived up the hill from Ivy's childhood home. She was like a second mother to her and Casey. As far as they knew, the woman had never married. At least she never said she had. But she was always adopting rescues from Dr. Murphy, the vet just outside of town, which meant she was never really alone. Today that would mean three cats, two dogs, and a cockatoo.

"I told him not to go," Ivy said, squeezing her friend tighter. "I told him I loved him and that he didn't have to go."

Casey stepped back, her hands still on Ivy's shoulders. "Charlie was in an office building whose roof collapsed. This isn't the same thing. It's Meadow Valley. Tragedies don't happen *in* Meadow Valley."

"It's a *fire,* Case. A fire brought that roof down and trapped my brother. Houses have roofs, too." She was arguing like a petulant child. She *knew* she was. But Casey didn't get it. *No* one seemed to get it. "He was my best friend, and he left us. Me, my parents, Allison, and the baby. He left us, and for what?"

Casey swiped her thumbs under Ivy's eyes, then crossed her arms. "My sister's on the scene of that very same fire. Am I scared? Hell yes, I'm scared. But there's a reason Jessie's there instead of me. She's *trained* for this, and because of *her* training and Carter's and the whole company's, Mrs. Davis and her home have their best chance."

Ivy swallowed. "I'm sorry. I'm the worst. I know you're worried about Jessie, and—"

"How many people lived that day because Charlie did his job?" Casey interrupted.

Ivy shook her head.

"How many, Ives?"

Ivy squeezed her eyes shut. She'd thought leaving Boston and coming home to start fresh would mean that her grief stayed out east. But it followed her back to Meadow Valley and reared its ugly head without so much as a warning. And it made her forget how good Charlie was at his job—how safe his company was under Charlie's leadership. How even when he lost his own life, he saved so many others.

"Seven," Ivy finally said. "Seven civilians lived because Charlie was an expert firefighter." But even experts can't plan for every contingency. Charlie's company got him out in time so that he didn't have to die alone. His closest buddies rode with him in the ambulance and stayed with him at the hospital until the end. It was the one piece of the story she and her family held on to like a life raft. Charlie wasn't alone.

The sound of sirens clamored in the air once more. This time it was the ambulance coming back from the opposite direction. It whizzed by them at a speed not normally seen on their quiet little street. Then it rounded the corner in the direction of the highway and likely the hospital.

Ivy's stomach sank.

"It's probably Mrs. Davis in there with my sister, but Jessie hasn't sent any updates," Casey said, and for the first time Ivy detected a note of panic in her friend's voice. "There's no way to really get any answers unless..."

"Unless we get as close as we can to Mrs. Davis's house."

Ivy didn't think she had it in her to see the danger into which Carter had walked. But the not knowing felt even worse.

"Let's go," Ivy said.

They headed down the street, following the throng of curious folks who were likely trying to get close enough to marvel at the spectacle. One person who wasn't following the herd, though, was the older woman standing on the front porch of the inn.

Pearl.

She locked eyes with Ivy and gave her a reassuring nod. "I wouldn't have brought my nephew here if I didn't know he was damned good at his job." She stared wistfully down the street, and Ivy suddenly remembered about Pearl and the chief. Pearl had already lost one great love of her life. There was no way the universe would let that happen again or be so cruel as to take her nephew, too. That's what Ivy hoped and what she guessed gave Pearl her stoic strength.

"I'll text you when we get word about any of them," Ivy said.

Pearl nodded again, and Ivy and Casey kept on.

Ivy's heart thudded in time with the rhythm of her feet

pounding the concrete. But all she could think about was what Carter had said about life-and-death situations and needing the trust of your team.

Maybe he was good at his job, but who had his back when there was a list of signatures who wanted to send him packing? And how could she let him go, thinking that he couldn't rely on *her*?

She started walking faster until she was in a slow jog and then close to a sprint.

She had Carter Bowen's back. If no one else did, it had to be her. Because though she was terrified for him, she also loved him. He needed to know he wasn't alone in this. She would be there. No matter what.

It was only minutes before she reached the blockade in front of Mrs. Davis's house, but it felt like hours.

"Hey!" Casey called. And Ivy turned around to see her friend halfway up the hill, her hands on her knees as she struggled to catch her breath. "What the hell was that, Flo Jo?" She lumbered the rest of the way until she made it to Ivy's side. Casey slung her hand over Ivy's shoulders and held up a finger while she tried to get her breathing in check. "Seriously," she finally said. "We run bases, not long-distance uphill."

An earsplitting crack followed by a crash cut their conversation short. Both startled and pivoted toward the sound. Half the town stood in front of them, so they could barely see over everyone's head. But they could *feel* the heat, the evidence that not too far away, Mrs. Davis's house burned.

"Screw it," Ivy said and grabbed Casey's hand, tugging her forward. "Excuse us!" she said as she pushed through the crowd. "Coming through! Sorry!" she cried as she stepped on someone's toes. But she wasn't stopping. Not until she made it to the barricade and got some answers. All the while, she held tight to Casey's hand, and Casey did the same with hers.

"Oh my God," Casey said when they got to the front.

Ivy couldn't speak. Her hand flew over her mouth, but no sound escaped.

Mrs. Davis's bright blue bungalow stood there at the top of her driveway like it always had. The front porch—decorated with potted plants and flowers, looked exactly the same. If you only stared at the porch and didn't look up, it was the same house Ivy had known for almost thirty years.

But they did look up, and out of the white-trimmed attic window poured livid orange flames. The place was burning from the top down.

Two firefighters controlled the front of the hose. Actually, one manned the hose while the other held him or her steady by the shoulders. She realized that she'd never seen her father or brother in action, had never truly understood what it meant to work as a team the way they did.

The chief rounded the back of the engine and spoke into his radio. When he finished his conversation, Ivy waved wildly, hoping to get his attention.

"Chief Burnett! Over here!" she cried. She'd known the chief most of her life. He and her father were rookies together. If anyone could ease her mind about what was going on inside Mrs. Davis's house, it was him.

Casey grabbed her arm and yanked it down. "I know how badly you want some information, but I think he's a little busy, Ives."

The chief looked up, though, and strode toward the barricade.

"Who was in the ambulance?" Ivy blurted. "Is Mrs. Davis okay? Is—are all your firefighters safe?"

He scratched the back of his neck.

"Mrs. Davis is being treated for smoke inhalation and some minor burns. Looks like she was going through some old boxes in her attic and dozed off while a scented candle was lit. We're guessing one of the animals knocked it over, and once the drapes caught—"

"The animals!" Ivy said. "Are they out?"

The chief blew out a breath. "It may not look like it, but we have the blaze contained. It's gonna be a while before it's out, though. Lieutenant Bowen and a small team are inside, trying to round up the animals."

Ivy had joked about Carter having to rescue one of Mrs. Davis's cats from a tree. The irony of this situation, though, was far from amusing. It was as dangerous as anything Meadow Valley had ever been.

She nodded and tried to swallow the knot in her throat. "What—what was that sound? Is the structure stable enough for them to be inside?"

"One of the ceiling beams in the attic was torn free." He glanced back toward the house. "We've got every available man and woman on the job. Got another engine from Quincy running a hose with some of our crew from the back and a second and third ambulance at the ready in front of our truck. We assess the situation as best we can, making predictions on what we know about the fire and how we believe it will behave. But there's always risk."

Casey squeezed Ivy's hand and pointed toward the house. "Look!"

A parade of firefighters exited the front door, one carrying Mrs. Davis's cocker spaniel, Lois. Another had a box of kittens. And the third held Butch Catsidy, the three-legged foster cat she'd had since he was a kitten—and had kept when no one adopted him. The crowd of onlookers applauded, but Ivy knew Mrs. Davis's beagle was still missing. Frederick was old and prone to hiding, and he was no doubt burrowed somewhere he thought was safe.

A voice sounded on the chief's radio, and he turned his back to listen and respond.

Ivy let go of Casey's hand and pulled out her phone and fired off a quick text to Pearl.

With the chief. He's outside. Mrs. Davis at the hospital but will be okay. No word on anyone else yet.

She couldn't bring herself to say Carter's name. The not knowing was making it hard to breathe. She started slipping her phone back into her pocket but then changed her mind. Even though there was no way he'd see it now, she hoped with everything she had he'd see it soon. So she brought up her last text exchange with Carter and typed.

I'm here. If you'll let me, I will always be here for you. I love you.

She pocketed her phone just as the chief turned back around.

"They found Frederick," he said.

Ivy breathed out a sigh of relief. But it was short-lived.

"He's under Mrs. Davis's bed. Two of them are trying to coax him out while another keeps watch on the soundness of the structure." He shook his head. "I wanted everyone off the second floor by now." He pulled his radio out again. "Lieutenant, you have two minutes to get your team out of there, dog or no dog. Do you copy?"

"Copy that, Chief. Two minutes. But we're coming *with* the dog. Over."

Ivy's heart lifted. That was Carter's voice. Carter was okay. The team was still okay.

The firefighters on the ground had now moved to the bucket ladder just outside the fiery attic window.

"Who else is inside?" she asked.

"It's just Lieutenant Bowen, O'Brien, and O'Brien."

Carter. Wyatt. Shane.

"The dog is secured, sir. We're coming out. Over," Carter said over the radio.

Ivy choked back a sob. In seconds he'd be out of the building and she'd be able to breathe again.

But instead she heard another screech followed by a crash and then the unmistakable sound of the PASS device, a firefighter's personal alarm that meant he or she was in distress.

Seconds later, one of the firefighters and Frederick ran out the front door, but whoever was carrying the dog set him down on the lawn and ran back inside.

Casey hooked her arm through Ivy's and pulled her close. "He's gonna come out, Ives, okay? This is Meadow Valley. We don't do tragedy here. Plus, you've already had your fill for one lifetime, so this is only going to end with Carter Bowen walking out of that house."

Ivy nodded, but she couldn't speak. Maybe she'd had her share of tragedy, but had she played a role in setting herself up for more? She shook her head, a silent argument with her thoughts. She could let her fear close her off from risk—and also happiness—or she could be here for Carter, believing in him and in what Casey said: This was going to end with Carter Bowen walking out of that house.

"What if that's not how it ends, Case?" she asked, her voice cracking with the reality of the situation.

Casey looked at her, the tears in her best friend's eyes mirroring her own.

"Then you will fall apart, and I will be here to put you back together again. You're not alone in this, okay? You will *never* be alone."

Ivy nodded and held her breath.

"Lieutenant, what's your status? Over," the chief said, somehow maintaining his calm.

"Sir, this is Shane O'Brien. Part of the attic ceiling came down over the stairs. Lieutenant Bowen and my brother—I was already at the bottom with the dog—got knocked down by a burning beam." He went silent for a few seconds. "They're under the beam and neither of them are moving."

Ivy could see the fiery beam through the window. It stretched halfway down the length of the stairs.

The PASS alert ceased, and the chief's radio crackled.

Carter's voice sounded over the radio. "The rest of the ceiling's gonna go, Chief. Don't send anyone else in. O'Brien's got this. Shane?" Carter sounded pained, and Ivy stopped breathing altogether. "Shane can you hear me?"

"Copy that. I hear you, Lieutenant Bowen," Shane said. "But—I can't do this. I can't—"

"I need you to stay calm but act fast. Your brother's unconscious and my arm is broken, and my hand is pinned under the corner of the beam. All you need to do is unpin me, and I can help you carry your brother out."

"This shit isn't supposed to happen here," Shane said. "*Nothing* happens here."

"You can do this, Shane," Carter said. "But it has to be fast. The rest of the ceiling is starting to buckle."

The radios went silent after that. Ivy swore she could hear her own heartbeat. Her hand was in Casey's again, the two of them squeezing each other tight yet not laying voice to what they were both thinking.

This was Charlie all over again. They got Charlie out but not in time to save him from the internal injuries the paramedics couldn't treat.

The firefighters on the outside still worked tirelessly, and the flames began to retreat. But Ivy knew that did nothing for the internal damage or the safety of the structure. The ceiling was already compromised, and the extra weight of the water would expedite its complete collapse.

A buckling sound came from within the house, and Ivy knew their time was up.

"Come on. Come on. Come on," she chanted.

Then the roof of the house dipped. Less than a second later, it folded in on itself as two figures burst through the front-door opening with a third figure's arms draped over their shoulders.

Shane and Carter ran with the toes of Wyatt's boots scraping across the grass until they were far enough from what once was Mrs. Davis's home and paramedics were able to retrieve Wyatt and get him onto a stretcher. Carter held his right arm against his torso, and when he tore off his hat and mask, she could see an expression wrought with pain as another paramedic escorted him to a third ambulance.

Ivy dropped down to the ground and crawled under the barricade.

"Go get him, Ives!" Casey called after her.

And Ivy ran. She ran past the chief, who called her name, but she didn't stop to listen. She ran past a police car where she recognized Daniela Garcia, who'd graduated high school with Charlie, standing against the bumper. Except she was Deputy Garcia now, and although Ivy didn't think she was breaking any laws by bypassing the barricade, at the moment she didn't care if she had, as long as she made it to Carter.

"You can't be back here, Ivy!" Deputy Garcia yelled. But Ivy still didn't stop.

Not until she was breathless and banging on the already closed back door of the emergency vehicle did she come to a halt.

A paramedic swung the door open, and she climbed inside without being invited. Carter sat on the gurney still in his protective boots and pants, but his jacket had been removed and a ninety-degree splint was affixed to his right arm from shoulder to wrist. A clear tube that led to an IV bag hanging from the ceiling of the vehicle was taped to his left hand.

"Hi," she said, barely holding it together. "All right if I ride along?"

Chapter Eleven

Carter looked at the paramedic who was closing the door, a younger guy from his team named Ty. "You think you could give us some privacy?" he asked.

The other man hesitated. "With all due respect, Lieutenant—and that's a mighty fine thing you did talking O'Brien through that situation—you know I can't leave you alone back here." He had to give it to the kid for following procedure. He wondered, though, if Ty's name was on that petition.

The ambulance lurched forward, and Ivy fell into the seat meant for the paramedic.

"Guess that means you're staying," Carter told her.

"I can sit here," Ty said, taking a spot on the bench to Carter's right. "And the best I can do about privacy is this." He pulled a pair of wireless earbuds out of his pocket and stuck them in his ears. "Just tap my shoulder if you need something!" he said, already too loud over whatever music he was playing, and Carter laughed.

"Looks like it's just you and me," he said. "Which means that now I can ask you what the hell you were doing so close to the fire. Dammit, Ivy. Don't you know how dangerous that was?"

Her eyes widened. "Me? You're *mad* at me when I came here to show you that I support you no matter what? To tell you that I love you and that you're not alone in this?"

She threw her hands in the air, but with such limited space, she had to keep her arms close to her body. The whole gesture made her look like an exasperated T. rex, and Carter had to bite the inside of his cheek to keep from laughing.

"Are you—laughing?" she said. "I just heard you over the chief's radio say that you were trapped under a burning ceiling beam and that your arm was broken, and you're *laughing*?"

Her voice trembled, and a tear slid quickly down her cheek.

He wasn't laughing anymore.

"Jesus, Ivy," he said. "You heard all that? How long were you out there?"

She sucked in a steadying breath and blew it out slowly.

"Long enough to know that you are really good at your job. Long enough to know that even in the worst situation, you were still in control and knew what to do." She shook her head and pressed her lips together. "I will always be scared when you have to leave that firehouse with sirens blaring. But I also know that you're the best shot your team has at coming home safe whenever you do."

He cupped her cheek in his palm. IV or not, he didn't care. He needed to touch her, and he needed her to know the truth—that as good as he was at his job, he was scared, too, scared that he couldn't guarantee he'd always walk away from a situation like today.

"I can't promise you that'll be the case 100 percent of the time. If we hadn't gone back in for that damn dog, no one on my command would have left in an ambulance. I mean, hell, if Shane wasn't there—if he didn't listen to me?" He dropped his hand and let out a bitter laugh. "You were right," he told her. "The whole month I've been here I've been so hell-bent on proving myself. What if that clouded my judgment? What if—"

"No what-ifs," Ivy interrupted. "I heard everything. You listened to the chief's orders. You're alive. Wyatt's alive. And Shane saved you both. I've spent the past four weeks promising myself I wouldn't let you get too close because of what happened to Charlie. Because of *What if?* I never should have told you not to go tonight. And I never will again."

His brows furrowed. "You'll never tell me *not* to go again or you'll never *not* tell me not to go. Either the pain meds are kicking in or there are too many negatives in what you said that I'm not sure if you meant what I think you meant."

This time she was the one to laugh, and the effect of the pain meds paled in comparison to her smile. He could live with being unsure about the future as long as it meant she was in it.

"Just to clarify," he said, "are you saying that if I stay in town, you're not going to turn the other way if you pass me on the street?"

She let out something between a laugh and a sob. "If you weren't all busted up, I'd punch you in the shoulder or something."

"Well then, I guess I'm safe from any further *physical* distress," he said. "But are you gonna break my heart, Ivy Serrano?"

She shook her head, then rested it on his shoulder. "Nah. I love you too much to do that." She tilted her head up, and her brown eyes shimmered in the normally unpleasant fluorescent light.

"That's a relief," he said. "Because I don't think I could walk by you without wanting to do this." His lips swept over hers in a kiss that felt like the start of something new. He couldn't wrap her in his arms, and maybe the bumps in the road made the whole gesture a little clumsy, but she was here. And she was staying. And petition or not, dammit, so was he.

Carter waited outside the chief's office, anxious more about being late for Ivy's fashion show than he was about what would be said behind the office doors. If he was being let go, he was being let go. He was damned good at his job, and he didn't need anyone's approval anymore to know that was true.

Okay, fine, so he needed the chief's approval to *keep* his job but not to know that he did everything he could for this company in the month he was here.

The door swung open, and Chief Burnett popped his head out.

"Come on in, Lieutenant. Sorry to keep you waiting."

Carter stood and brushed nonexistent dust from his uniform pants. His right hand had cramped, so he flexed it, still getting used to the air cast.

He walked inside, expecting to find the chief alone waiting for him, but instead he saw Shane O'Brien standing in front of the chief's desk.

The chief cleared his throat. "Lieutenant Bowen, I hope you don't mind, but I thought it best for Firefighter O'Brien to speak first."

Carter nodded. "O'Brien," he said. "Heard your brother is being discharged today."

"Yes sir, Lieutenant. It was a pretty bad concussion, but thanks to you, he's going to be fine."

Carter's brows drew together. The formality from Shane confused him. Not that he'd expected the guy to mouth off, but this was a complete one-eighty from what Carter had seen from him.

"He's going to be fine, O'Brien, because of *you*," Carter said. "Neither of us would be here right now if you hadn't gotten us out of that house before the roof caved in."

Shane's jaw tightened. "With all due respect, Lieutenant, I never wanted to be here. And I made sure everyone knew it. And then I made your life a living hell because I knew I wasn't good enough, and it was your job to remind me of that." He squared his shoulders. "The signatures on the petition were forged. Every one of them but mine. I am not proud of my behavior and need some time to regroup."

Carter opened his mouth to say something, but Shane cut him off.

"I need to figure things out without everything that's been hanging over my head since I was a kid. I'm leaving town, sir. And the company. Effective immediately."

Shane held out his hand to shake but then realized that was Carter's broken arm and dropped it back to his side.

"O'Brien," Carter said. "You don't have to do this."

"It's already done," the chief said. "I tried to talk him out of it, but I think his mind was made up the second he rode away from the Davis fire with his brother in an ambulance."

Shane nodded once, his eyes dark and expression stoic.

"You're a good firefighter, O'Brien," Carter added. "I'd have been proud to keep you on my team."

"Thank you, Lieutenant," he said. He nodded toward the chief. "You too, Chief."

The chief clapped Shane on the shoulder. "You always have a place here if you ever decide to come back."

Shane pressed his lips together but didn't say anything else. Then he strode through the door, closing it behind him.

Carter blew out a long breath. "You think he's going to get into trouble again?"

The chief shook his head. "If you'd have asked me that a month ago, I'd have said yes. But something changed in him since you've been around. And the way you handled things in the Davis fire? We're damn lucky to have you, Lieutenant."

He was staying in Meadow Valley. This was—home.

"Thank you, sir. I feel damn lucky to be here."

After a long moment, Carter turned to head for the door.

"One more thing, Lieutenant," the chief said, stopping him in his tracks. "Your family was notified of your injury, and your father has called your aunt four times in the past two days to check on you. I thought you should know."

Carter swallowed hard but didn't turn back around. "Appreciate the information," he said. "But he knows my number."

"Give him time," the chief said. "Father-son relationships can be a tricky thing."

Carter thought about Shane, who was leaving town to deal with his own tricky thing, and the weight on his shoulders lifted, if only a fraction of an inch.

"Yes, sir. I suppose they are."

Then he was out the door and down the steps two at a time. When he pushed through the station's front door, Ivy was there on the sidewalk, right where he'd left her on his way in. The sky was overcast, but she was a vision in her bright yellow sundress, brown waves of hair falling over her shoulders.

He only needed one arm to lift her up and press his lips to hers.

"I'm home, darlin'," he said.

"Good," she said through laughter and kisses. "Because I wasn't letting you go without a fight. Now come on. I need to show you something."

She led him down the street to her shop. She bounced on her toes as they slowed in front of the window where a single mannequin stood displaying a dress that could only be described as a field of sunflowers.

"You made that?" he said. "It's like nothing I've ever seen, Ivy. If I didn't know any better, I'd say those were live flowers."

She smiled the biggest, most beautiful smile he'd seen since the fire.

"I made them," she said, and he could hear how proud she was. "It's my version of my and Charlie's garden. I don't think I'd have ever finished it if I hadn't met you, which is why I wanted you to be the first to see it."

She beamed—a ray of sunshine on an otherwise cloudy day.

He stepped closer and wrapped his arm around her waist. "Are you calling me your muse?" he teased, and she laughed.

"I'm calling you my everything, if that's okay," she said, then kissed him.

He smiled against her. "That's about the okayest thing

I've ever been called, darlin'. So yeah, I think I'm good with that. As long as you're good with me spending the rest of my days making good on that title."

She kissed him again, and he took that as a yes.

* * *

Ivy and Carter tied Ace and Barbara Ann to the fence. She stared at the beautiful, stubborn man she loved and shook her head.

"What would the doctor say if he knew you were on a horse three days after breaking your arm?" she asked. She'd tried to stop him, but he'd threatened to ride off without her if she didn't join him.

He opened and closed his right hand. "Arm's broken," he said. "Thanks to Shane O'Brien, the hand's just fine. Besides, who's snitching on me to the doctor?"

She removed the pack from Barbara Ann's saddle and tossed it on the ground. They'd get to that shortly. Then she wrapped her arms around him and kissed him in the place where they'd kissed for the first time. When they finally parted, he spun her so her back was against his torso, his hands resting on her hips.

From the top of the hill above town, Ivy could see the ruins of Mrs. Davis's home. She could also see the inn where Pearl would give her—and her animals—a place to stay for as long as it took for her to rebuild. She could see the bell above the firehouse, the one that would forever remind her of the day she *didn't* lose the man who held her in his arms right now.

"Can you see that?" he whispered in her ear. "I don't mean the town. I mean what's right in front of you."

Her brows furrowed, and she shifted her gaze from the

tapestry of Meadow Valley to a shock of color just a little way down the hill. A sunflower.

She spun to face him. “I don’t understand. How did it—I mean, those don’t sprout up in a matter of days.”

He laughed. “I talked to Sam Callahan, and we thought it might be fun to start a community garden up here between locals and ranch guests. It’s public property, so there are permits involved, but I’m sure you can point me in the right direction of who to talk to.”

“You want to build me a garden?” she asked, her eyes wide.

“I want to build you everything,” he said. “But if the garden’s too painful—if the memories are too much…”

She shook her head.

“It *is* painful,” she admitted. “But it’s also wonderful and thoughtful.” She pressed her palms to his chest. “I don’t want to forget the painful stuff. And I don’t want to wrap myself in a bubble of fire extinguishers and interconnected smoke detectors and—and loneliness to protect myself from getting hurt again. I want to start something new—with this garden and with you. I will always be scared, but I don’t have to be alone. *We’re* not alone.”

“Although fire safety *is* important,” he teased. “So don’t abandon your extinguishers just to make a statement.”

She laughed.

“You know,” he said, looking past her and down at the town, “if you need to when things get tough, we can always come here to forget the rest of the world for a little while, pretend it doesn’t exist.”

She shook her head. “I want to experience it all, the good and the bad. With you.”

She gave him a soft kiss and ran her hands through his hair, smiling against him. “Starting with a hilltop haircut," she said. "Are you ready, Lieutenant? Brought all my tools."

He laughed and stepped away. "At the risk of you miscalculating and lopping off my ear, I need to ask you one quick thing before I potentially lose my hearing."

Ivy crossed her arms. "Cut off your ear? Please, Lieutenant. And here I thought you trusted—"

He dropped down to one knee, and Ivy lost the ability to form words.

"I know there's supposed to be a ring and everything, but I'm kind of doing this out of order. It's as simple as the text you sent me the night of the fire. Everything's been so crazy the past few days I didn't even see it until later the next day. I'm here, Ivy. If you'll let me, I will always be here for you. I love you. Say you'll marry me, plant gardens with me, and build a life with me, and *then* I'll let you cut my hair."

She wasn't sure if she was laughing or crying because the tears were flowing, but she was smiling from ear to ear.

She clasped her hands around his neck and kissed him and kissed him and kissed him some more.

"Yes," she said against him, and she felt his smile mirror hers. "Yes. Yes. Yes."

About the Author

A librarian for teens by day and a *USA Today* bestselling romance writer by night, A. J. Pine can't seem to escape the world of fiction, and she wouldn't have it any other way. When she finds that twenty-fifth hour in the day, she might indulge in a tiny bit of TV to nourish her undying love of vampires, superheroes, and a certain high-functioning sociopath detective. She hails from the far-off galaxy of the Chicago suburbs.

You can learn more at:
AJPine.com
Twitter @AJ_Pine
Facebook.com/AJPineAuthor

Look for More Heartwarming Western Romance by A. J. Pine!

MEADOW VALLEY SERIES

Available Summer 2020

CROSSROADS RANCH SERIES

Looking for more hot cowboys?
Forever has you covered!

COWBOY STRONG
by Carolyn Brown

Alana Carey can out-rope and out-ride the toughest Texas cowboys. But she does have one soft spot—Paxton Callahan. So when her father falls ill, Alana presents Pax with a crazy proposal: to pretend to be her fiancé so her father can die in peace. But as the faux-wedding day draws near, Alana and Paxton must decide whether to come clean about their charade or finally admit their love is the real deal. Includes the bonus story *Sunrise Ranch*!

COWBOY COURAGE
by Carolyn Brown

Heading back to Texas to hold down the fort at her aunt's bed-and-breakfast will give Rose O'Malley just the break she needs from the military. But while she may speak seven languages, she can't repair a leaky sink to save her life. When Hudson Baker strides in like a hero and effortlessly figures out the fix, Rose can't help wondering if the boy she once crushed on as a kid could now be her saving grace. Includes the bonus story *Wildflower Ranch*!

Find more great reads on Instagram with @ReadForeverPub

MY KIND OF COWBOY
by R.C. Ryan

Avery Grant hates to admit it, but super-sexy rancher Brand Merrick is testing her patience… and her professionalism. She's a born-and-bred city girl, yet she finds herself drawn to the rugged wilderness of Montana and the equally rugged cowboy she's here to help. But when a threat from her past comes calling, can she put her trust in Brand and the growing feelings in her heart? Includes the bonus novel *Cowboy Rebel* by Carolyn Brown!

Discover bonus content and more on read-forever.com.

Connect with us at Facebook.com/ ReadForeverPub

COWBOY COME HOME
by Carly Bloom

As far as Claire Kowalski is concerned, Big Verde, Texas, is perfect, except for one thing: the lack of eligible men. Some days it feels like she's dated every single one. It's too bad that the only man who ever tickled her fancy is the wandering, restless cowboy who took her heart with him when he left her father's ranch years ago. Just when she's resigned herself to never seeing him again, Ford Jarvis knocks on the door. Includes a bonus story by Sara Richardson!

FIRST KISS WITH A COWBOY
by Sara Richardson

With her carefully ordered life crumbling apart, shy and sensible Jane Harding welcomes the distraction of helping plan her best friend's wedding. When she discovers that the boy who once tempted her is now the best man, however, her distraction risks becoming a disaster. Toby Garrett may be the rodeo circuit's sexiest bull rider, but his kiss with Jane has never stopped fueling his fantasies. Can this sweet-talking cowboy prove that the passion still burning between them is worth braving the odds? Includes the bonus story *Cowboy to the Rescue* by A.J. Pine!

Follow @ReadForeverPub on Twitter and join the conversation using #ReadForever.

A COWBOY FOR KEEPS
by Laura Drake

Not much rattles a cowboy like Reese St. James—until his twin brother dies in a car accident, leaving behind a six-month-old daughter. Reese immediately heads to Unforgiven, New Mexico, to bring his niece home—but the girl's guardian, Lorelei West, refuses to let a hotshot cowboy like Reese take away her sister's baby. Only the more time they spend together, the harder it is to deny the attraction between them. Opening their hearts to a child is one thing—can they also open their hearts to a chance at happily-ever-after?

MY ONE AND ONLY COWBOY
by A.J. Pine

Sam Callahan is too busy trying to keep his new guest ranch afloat to spend any time on serious relationships—at least that's what he tells himself. But when a gorgeous blonde shows up insisting she owns half his property, Sam quickly realizes he's got bigger problems than Delaney's claim on the land: She could also claim his heart. Includes a bonus novel by Carolyn Brown!